Jonathan Buckley lives in Brighto: *The*
Biography of Thomas Lang (199 *,*
MacIndoe (2001), and *Invisible* (2004).

From the reviews of *So He Takes the Dog*:

'Buckley is expert at stringing together the tiny dramas of individual lives to make a narrative necklace' *Daily Mail*

'Affecting, carefully crafted, quietly tumultuous. The elusiveness of our emotionally stunted sleuth is its greatest achievement' *TLS*

'This melancholy, upside-down tale is so beautifully written . . . a hugely satisfying read' *Daily Express*

JONATHAN BUCKLEY

So He Takes the Dog

HARPER PERENNIAL

London, New York, Toronto and Sydney

Harper Perennial
An imprint of HarperCollins*Publishers*
77–85 Fulham Palace Road
Hammersmith
London w6 8jb

www.harperperennial.co.uk
Visit our blog: www.fifthestate.co.uk

This edition published by Harper Perennial 2007

I

First published in Great Britain by Fourth Estate in 2006

Copyright © Jonathan Buckley 2006

PS Section copyright © Louise Tucker 2007

PS™ is a trademark of HarperCollins*Publishers* Ltd

Jonathan Buckley asserts the moral right to
be identified as the author of this work

A catalogue record for this book
is available from the British Library

ISBN-13 978-0-00-722829-4
ISBN-10 0-00-722829-5

Set in Postscript Linotype Sabon by
Palimpsest Book Production Limited, Grangemouth, Stirlingshire

Printed and bound in Great Britain by Clays Ltd, St Ives plc for Susanne Hillen and Bruno

1

This happened ten years ago, more or less. It's mid-morning on the second day of January, in the modest but immaculate little bungalow that is home to Benjamin and Christine Kemp. Having clambered over the stile of New Year's Day, the Kemps are now setting out on their trek across the bleak moorland of yet another year of conjoined medium-level misery. Christine is in the kitchen. A row of brass ornaments is laid out on a tea towel on the breakfast table and she is polishing her way down the line. Her husband is there as well, reading the paper. They have recently retired, both of them. For more than forty years, from the year before he married Christine, Benjamin worked for the local council, in the rates department; Christine typed and filed medical records at the hospital for a couple of decades, after raising their daughter, Elisabeth, who at the age of nineteen married a French shop-keeper she'd met on holiday six months previously. Elisabeth then went to live in a village near Limoges, and might as well be living in a village in Tibet for all her parents see of her nowadays.

Benjamin is trying to recall who gave them that horrible brass horse with the spindly legs and massive head when Christine opens a cupboard and the door squeaks. She sighs into the cupboard, and it's like the chill breeze that heralds the storm. 'Are you ever going to fix this?' she asks.

1

'Yes, dear,' replies Benjamin.

'And when would that be?'

'Soon.'

'How soon?'

'This afternoon.'

'That would be nice. Please do it.'

'Yes, dear.'

She closes the cupboard and opens another one. There's a sharp hiccup of irritation and she turns round, showing him the small round handle that's just come off in her hand. She presents it to him, Exhibit 3227 in the never-ending case of Kemp versus Kemp. 'Why does it always take you so long to do the tiniest little job?'

'And why is the tiniest little job always my job?'

'You said you'd do it. It's not as if you're rushed off your feet, is it?'

'No, dearest. It's not as if I'm rushed off my feet. You're quite right.'

'So?'

'So what?'

'When are you going to fix it?'

'This afternoon, dear. After I've fixed the squeak that I alone can fix.' And so on. They have each other now, all day long. Just each other, all day, every day. It's too much; it's not enough.

The niggling becomes a raised-voice row, and as usual it's Benjamin who retreats. What can he say? That he hasn't fixed the bloody cupboard door because he's bored out of his head, today as every day, the same as she is? What would be the point? He puts down the paper and leaves the room. 'That's right,' Christine calls after him, 'you just walk away.' She hears him picking the keys off the table in the hall. 'Where are you going?'

'Out.'

'Out where?' He doesn't answer. 'What about that blasted dog?' she yells. So he takes the dog, a decision which is really going to knock a divot out of his day.

Milo, that's the dog's name. Milo is a sullen and overfed

mongrel, part labrador, part something very much less handsome. They get into the car, Milo beside his driver, and they drive down to the seafront, where Benjamin – seeing that the tide is out – turns eastwards, towards the headland, and parks in the very last bay, where the road comes to an end against the cliffs. They walk on the beach all the way to Straight Point, and there Benjamin takes a rest. He sits on a rock, feeds a handful of biscuits to the dog, stares at the sea. The scene could not be more appropriate to his mood: the sky is a filthy old sponge, the air is thick and cold and damp, the sea is an infinite pavement of grey sludge. It's not truly raining, but there's so much water in the air that he's getting soaked as he sits. He watches Milo moping around the pools, picking a path through the dull green slime that coats the rocks. When you're feeling despondent, gazing into a mirror can make you feel worse, and this is the same: the longer he stays here, the gloomier Benjamin is becoming. He whistles for the dog, and they set off back towards town.

It was a rough night, the night before, and the sea has dumped piles of bladderwrack and rubbish in a thick continuous scum at the foot of the cliffs. Nose lowered, Milo is following the line of seaweed and flotsam, pausing now and again to root about in whatever's been washed up. Short of breath, Benjamin stops again, and the dog disappears into a corral of stone blocks that fell off the rockface in the autumn. When Benjamin reaches the stones, Milo has moved on: his tail is visible, about fifty yards off, wagging above a hummock of sand, between two car-sized slabs. Benjamin whistles, but Milo doesn't come to him. Having been ignored three or four times, he walks a few steps closer and sees that the dog is standing in a long wide groove that the tide has scoured in the sand, and has shoved his muzzle into a well-stuffed black bin liner. Benjamin waits. The dog's pulling something out of the bag, a thick cable or a length of stout rope, and he's having a good chew at it. There's no hurry. Benjamin waits, eyes closed, dozing on his feet.

Milo is still busy with the oversized rope when Benjamin opens his eyes again. The dog's head is snapping from one side to the other, as if playing tug-of-war, and he's making a low snarling noise, of a sort Benjamin has never heard from him before. 'Here, boy,' calls Benjamin, but there is no response. He's covered about half the distance to the bin liner when he notices there's something peculiar about the rope, about the rigidness of it, and the sharp angle at which it's bending. A moment later he stops – or is stopped, because he's reacting before he knows exactly what it is he's reacting to. Then he sees that the thing that Milo's gnawing isn't a rope or a cable: it's an arm, and the bin liner is a body in a waterlogged coat, partly covered by sand. The legs, in sodden grey tracksuit bottoms, are twisted as if they've no bones in them, and there's a gash in one shin, with a mush of dark green stuff coming out, where something, possibly Milo, has taken a few bites out of it. Eyeless, teeth agape, a purple-black face lies wrapped in a veil of wet hair. Beside it a naked arm emerges from the sand at a low angle, the rotted palm directed skywards, as if to make a catch. Scraps of skin dangle from the fingertips, like a shredded glove of black muslin. Worm-like things, white and slick as lard, are squirming in the earhole.

Benjamin is in shock, as who wouldn't be? He's a gentle old man who has reached the age of sixty-seven without ever seeing anything very nasty, and this is very nasty indeed. It's so nasty it's not real. Traumatised, he's looking at the mouldering head and the empty eyes, and it's like a display from a chamber of horrors, a dummy of a man who's been ripped to bits. He stares and stares, as if the body might go back to being a bin liner if he stares long enough, but soon he is seeing the corpse for what it is, a dead man, a real person destroyed. And while Benjamin is being transfixed by the dead man, Milo is continuing his wrestle with the cadaver's right arm, a struggle that ends with a gristly tearing sound and the dog flying backwards, bringing away a hand and a length of forearm, with ribbons of muscle trailing off it.

The dog goes cantering off down the beach, with the limb in

his jaws. 'Come here,' calls Benjamin. 'Here. Here,' he yells. Several repetitions later, Milo at last obeys, bringing the half-arm with him. 'Drop, boy,' Benjamin orders. 'Drop. Drop. Drop.' Milo cocks his head, inviting Benjamin to wrestle the thing from him. 'Drop. For Christ's sake, drop.' The beast is not trained in any way. This is another of Benjamin's multitudinous domestic crimes: he brings this flatulent mutt into the house and can't be bothered teaching it the basics of civilised canine behaviour. A stick is needed, something he can chuck to make the dog lay down his plaything. From the ridge of tidal debris he takes a length of wood and flings it over Milo's head. Milo watches it fly and fall to earth. A second stick is similarly spurned. 'Drop. Good boy. Drop. Drop.' As a rule Benjamin doesn't swear. Benjamin swears once or twice a year, when things with Christine get out of control, but he's almost hysterical now. 'Drop the bloody thing. Please, please, please drop. Put it down. Down. Put the bloody thing down. Now. Drop it. Drop.' Milo deposits the limb on the ground, gives it a shove with his snout, and grabs it the instant Benjamin makes a move.

All Benjamin can think to do is walk towards the town and hope that Milo, losing interest, will relinquish his burden en route. As fast as he can, which isn't fast, he strides across the sand, attended by his faithful hound. Every now and then Milo deposits his portion of corpse on the ground, turns it with his nose, and takes it up again. 'Leave it, for Christ's sake,' shouts Benjamin, looking the other way. The road isn't much further. 'Stay. Stay there,' yells Benjamin. 'Sit. Stay. For God's sake, stay.' Milo sits, and the moment Benjamin turns his back, the dog gets up again to follow in his master's wake. They are about a quarter of a mile from the beach-grave when, out of the corner of his eye, Benjamin glimpses Milo running alongside, his head held up, with nothing waggling out of it. The half-arm has gone. Disinclined to search for it, Benjamin scans the environs quickly, then hurries towards the car.

And that's how we found the body, in two instalments: most

of it lying close to its burial place, ravaged by seagulls and platoons of crawling wildlife, in addition to the routine self-destruction of the dead; and the right forearm and hand, a few hundred yards away, lying on a cushion of seaweed and chewed to buggery.

2

You couldn't have called it a face: stripped of most of its edibles, it was a bonehead with a partial cladding of jellied flesh, plus the semi-attached remnants of a beard. Putting a name to the wreckage, however, was easy. Ian, for one, needed no time to make the identification: seeing the beard and the rotten trainers and the ripped-up coat, he said straight away: 'This will be Henry.' Under the coat there was a rag of a T-shirt and under the rag of a T-shirt there was another rag of a T-shirt, and another one under that, half a dozen of them, all of them torn and the colour of butcher's aprons that haven't been washed for a year. 'One of them will have *SeaShed* printed on it, I'll bet you,' said Ian. 'It's Henry.' And when they got him on the slab and started unpeeling the wrappings, the last layer before the skin had *SeaShed* on it.

Some seaside towns have a dolphin that swims with the fishing boats, some have an inquisitive seal that's famous for a summer, or a monster seagull that snatches burgers from holidaymakers' hands. This place had Henry, the hobo of the beach. A lot of people knew Henry, by sight if nothing else. If you went down to the beach at the start of the day and waited, sooner or later you'd see Henry, guaranteed. Any day, whatever the weather, you'd see him. Rip van Winkle, he was known as, or Captain Birdseye, or Robinson Crusoe, or Howard, as in Howard Hughes.

He was slightly taller than average, about six foot, and broad in the shoulders, but skinny. He looked like a once-hefty man who'd been whittled down by years of living in the open air. When he walked his T-shirts used to flap on his body like towels on the back of a chair, and the legs of his jeans were mostly empty air. In his first summer here that's what Henry wore, every day: a pair of jeans that ended up the colour of salt and frayed halfway up to his knees, and a T-shirt advertising some long-gone medical conference in Acapulco. When the weather cooled, Henry added another T-shirt, and he kept on adding layers until, deep into his first winter on the beach, someone gave him a second-hand overcoat, the one the corpse was wearing.

He was already old-looking when he arrived, but nobody knew how many years Henry had clocked up. Look at the face and you'd think he wasn't far short of seventy, but living rough can easily add a decade to the appearance, so all you could say was that he was somewhere between his late fifties and late sixties, probably. Watch him walking, though, and you'd be confused, because Henry used to move across the beach at the speed of a man in his prime, a fit man at that. Like a mechanical scarecrow in overdrive he'd appear by the cliffs, and within five minutes he'd have covered half a mile of sand, as though there were somewhere he had to be, an urgent appointment at the other end of the beach. Head down, as if striding into a gale, he'd follow a line close to the water's edge, with not a glance to right or left, even when the beach was packed, and he'd keep on going, slaloming through the children, all the way to the harbour and all the way back to Straight Point. No heatwave could slow him down and no downpour could put him off: alone on the beach there was Henry, his T-shirt plastered to his ribs, the tramp in a hurry, battering his head through the deluge. You could watch him until he was out of sight, fleeing into the rain and spray, and if you waited long enough you'd see him return, most likely, charging out of the mist, his beard like a hank of sea-soaked cloth.

Ian first came across Henry only a week after starting at the station. It was late on a Sunday afternoon in August and Ian was on the beach with that month's girlfriend. Some kids were playing volleyball and Henry – coming from the direction of the harbour – was heading right for them, full throttle, eyes fixed on the ground. He was going to plough right into the net, thought Ian, and then, ten yards short, Henry suddenly came to a stop, an absolute standstill, as if there were a glass wall running across the beach and he'd just crashed into it. The kids had noticed him now, and they were looking at him, wondering what was up, waiting for him to move, but Henry was in a world of his own. He was like a man-sized puppet dangling from invisible strings: his mouth was hanging open, his arms dangling by his sides, and his eyes were staring over to his right, towards the town. Of course, there would have been plenty to stare at on a day like this, lots of of nicely filled swimwear, but Henry didn't seem to be seeing any of the girls. Ian and his girlfriend were quite near, near enough to notice that Henry was wearing an Adidas trainer on one foot and a Reebok on the other, and from where they were sitting it seemed that Henry wasn't looking at anything in particular: the eyes were wide open and aimed towards the road, but they were blank, like puppet eyes. And then he did this shudder or jump, as though someone had just clapped their hands by his ears, and he was off again, swerving round the volleyball game. Off around the headland he went, oblivious of everyone.

A few weeks later Ian encountered him again, in town this time, gazing into a shop window. Ian was having a moment with a local nuisance out on the street, about a car that'd been separated from its rightful owner, and on the other side of the road there stood Henry, reading a small ad in the window. It was only a postcard with a photo of a dinghy stuck to it, but all the time Ian and this lad were talking – a good ten minutes – Henry was studying the card. When he was done, Ian crossed over and took up a position a couple of shopfronts away. Something about this dinghy was really troubling Henry. His nose was on the glass and he was frowning as if the advert simply did not make any sense.

For a couple of minutes Ian kept an eye on him. Henry didn't budge: his face was locked in this expression of bewilderment. Finally Ian went up to him. 'Everything all right, sir?' he asked.

Henry turned, smiled graciously, said nothing.

'Are you OK, sir?'

'Yes. Thank you,' Henry responded, nodding slowly, drawling the words as if, after deep thought, he was deciding that he was indeed, on balance, OK. 'And you?' Henry enquired. 'Is everything all right with you?'

'Yes, thank you, sir.'

'Yes,' Henry mused, giving Ian a benign, mild, examining kind of look that made Ian feel somewhat uncomfortable. 'Good,' he said. 'Good.' It was a fresh day, a two-T-shirt day, and Henry was wearing a white buttoned-collar shirt over them, open like a jacket. Wavy lines of salt were all over his jeans, but the ensemble was remarkably clean, Ian observed. What's more, Henry had whiter teeth than Ian, though his beard looked like something you'd find hanging off the walls of a cave and his hair was a mess, an inch-thick carpet of grey matting. You could lob a dart on to the top of his head and it wouldn't reach the scalp. 'Well,' said Henry, pushing a shirt button through the wrong button-hole, 'I should be going. Thank you, officer.'

'Just thought I'd check, sir.'

'Yes,' said Henry. 'Thank you,' he added, with a sincerity that wasn't altogether convincing.

'Hope you didn't mind me asking.'

'No,' replied Henry vaguely, examining askance the photo of the dinghy. 'No. Not at all.' His fingers fastened the buttons of his cuffs, then worked them free again. 'Well, goodbye,' he said, and he sauntered away, gazing at the sky, in imitation of a carefree stroll, or that's how it seemed.

This was the first occasion on which Ian spoke to Henry. Not long after, in January, the acquaintance was renewed, after a call from Mrs Darrow. Dear Mrs Darrow was a serial complainant. If a party started up within a mile of her house, Mrs Darrow would be on the phone within the half-hour to protest about the noise. If a camper van were to be left in a nearby car park overnight, Mrs D would be on the blower, reporting an invasion of tinkers. Now Mrs Darrow had called in to say that there was a naked man wading in the water. She could see him clearly from her window, cavorting in the sea, making a display of himself. Would we please do something about it right away? Ian was sent down to the beach to have a word with Henry.

It was a couple of degrees above freezing and an aggressive wind was slicing in off the sea. The water was chopping up heavily, but Henry was out there, frisking around in the buff while Ian stood on the shore, beckoning this nutcase to come out. Henry noticed Ian. He waved back at him and dived under, as if he thought Ian might be waving for the fun of it. Ian took a couple of steps into the water; he started yelling. Eventually Henry got the point and staggered out, starkers and shrivelled and turning blue.

'Good morning,' Ian called.

'Good morning,' Henry replied.

'We meet again,' said Ian, and Henry smiled, having no idea what Ian was talking about. 'We've had a complaint, sir,' Ian went on.

Long pause. 'I see.'

'From a lady.'

Longer pause. 'I see.'

'About your attire. Lack of.'

Even longer pause. 'Yes.'

'I'm afraid I'll have to ask you to cover yourself up.'

Very long pause. 'Someone has complained?'

'Yes, sir. A lady.'

Henry looked around. There was no one in sight except Ian.

'I take your point, sir,' said Ian. 'But the lady has seen you and has lodged a complaint.'

Once more Henry considered the vast frigid vacancy of the beach. 'Got a telescope, has she?'

'I think we must assume that she has.'

'And I'm blocking the view?'

'So it would appear.'

Henry's skin had by now turned the colour of a dead mackerel and his private parts looked like three tiny acorns in a nest of singed grass. He was on the brink of hypothermia but he was talking to Ian as if they had just happened to bump into each other on a street corner. 'Can't she look the other way?'

'It would appear not. Where are your clothes, sir?' asked Ian, by now alarmed at Henry's hue.

Henry pointed inland, but Ian could not make out what he was pointing at. Together they walked across the sand, Ian and this shaggy nude lunatic, chatting about the weather. On a low mound of sand there lay a small pile of clothes and a towel that would have done fine for lightly rubbing down a chihuahua after its bath. Ian handed him the tiny towel and Henry took it. He held it in one hand, by his side. They regarded Henry's meagre wardrobe and the big red nylon bag lying nearby – a laundry sack, which Henry used to sleep in, until someone gave him a proper sleeping bag.

'Do you have any swimming trunks, sir?'

'No, I do not,' Henry regretfully admitted.

The next day Ian bought him a pair of swimming trunks, but before long Mrs D was back on the line, offended again by the exposure of Henry's genitals. Ian returned to the beach. The wind was Siberian and the waves were going twenty different directions at once. Henry was frolicking in groin-high water, slamming his head in the foam. Summoned, he trudged out of the sea. 'Henry, you're underdressed,' Ian observed. 'You're not wearing them.'

At a loss, Henry frowned. 'What?'

'Your nice new trunks,' Ian explained. 'The trunks I got for you.'

'Yes?' Henry responded, still baffled.

'The trunks I got you last week?'

'Yes,' said Henry, the light dawning.

'You're not wearing them.'

'No, I'm not.'

'She's complained again.'

A blank pause. 'Who has?'

'The woman.'

'The woman?'

'The lady with the telescope. The one who complained last week. Before we acquired the trunks.'

Long pause. 'I see.'

'What's the problem? Don't you like them? I thought you liked them.'

'Oh no. I like them.'

'So where are they? Over there?' asked Ian, pointing towards a dash of red on the rocks.

'Yes,' Henry confirmed.

'Why not there?' asked Ian, pointing to Henry's nether regions.

'They're not dry.'

'Come again?'

'It's a horrible feeling, putting on wet clothes.'

Ian sympathised, but insisted that Henry must make himself decent. This was not to be their last conversation about Henry's swimwear.

For almost three years Henry was here, but he was in residence intermittently, which is why nobody was worried when he'd been missing for a while. He'd left the town before, for weeks at a time, months at a stretch, so no one thought anything of it. But it was odd that he'd gone missing in winter, because previously it was always in summer that he went away.

3

The post-mortem established that Henry was not as old as had been thought, probably nearer fifty than sixty, and that he'd been under the sand for a couple of weeks or thereabouts, before the sea scooped him out to lie in the open air, where he'd remained for a day or so before the arrival of Milo. It was also discovered that he had died because someone had inserted a knife into his chest cavity. Examination of his clothing revealed two small slits in the outer T-shirt; in the layer underneath there were two matching slits, and so on, all the way through to the flesh. Decomposition and wildlife activity had made a mess of the flesh itself, but not enough to eradicate wholly the two wounds, which had been inflicted by a thin-bladed weapon held in the attacker's right hand. One blow had pierced the heart; the other struck a rib, chipping the bone. No signs of defence injuries were discovered on the remnants of his hands, so the attack seemed to have been sudden and brief.

Henry slept on the beach near Straight Point, or in the grass above the cliffs, but most often under the bushes of The Maer, so that's where we searched for his belongings, though nobody could be sure what belongings there were to find, other than the sleeping bag: the superfluous swimming trunks might have been discarded long ago and it was possible that every item of Henry's clothing was on his back when he was found. For a whole day a squad combed The Maer in the quest for Henry's estate, while another squad worked out from the crime scene, looking for a weapon. The next day we began to trawl the whole beach. Come nightfall we'd gathered a few dozen bottles and cans, a couple of camping gas cylinders, three paperbacks, half a deckchair, a syringe, enough driftwood to build a replica of the *Golden Hind*, and a backpack containing one lady's hairbrush, one condom (unused), twenty-four pence in loose change and a substantial quantity of sand. And no weapon.

At this stage of a homicide enquiry we should have been talking to the victim's family, talking to his friends, establishing the patterns of his behaviour, his habits and routines and so on. In this case, however, we were a few hundred yards behind the starting line, because we didn't yet know the man's full name. No identification was found on the body, so we had no route to the next of kin, and there were no known friends to interview. We knew something of the pattern of his days – sleep, go for a walk, sleep – but that was the lot. So George Whittam decides to call in the press.

Within the hour Ronnie Houghton arrives at the incident room. For the past couple of years, after a decade in telesales and advertising freesheets, Ronnie has been reporting on the misdemeanours of our district's druggies, shoplifters, joyriders and after-hours brawlers. He's thirty or thereabouts but as eager as a twenty-year-old, and just as naïve. One day, he knows, he's going to get the story that will bring him the big-money transfer to London and a national byline. Eyes twitching at the thought that this might be the big one, Ronnie absorbs the facts, or the selection of facts that George has judged it useful to broadcast at this point. When the battery of his tape recorder goes flat, one minute into the briefing, Ronnie switches to shorthand, scribbling as though he's taking dictation from God Almighty. A minute later it's over. Half a page of notes and that's it. 'OK. OK,' says Ronnie, trying not to show his disappointment, perusing his scrawl. 'OK. I've got all that. Got a picture?' he asks, but of course we haven't got a picture – that's one reason he's here. SHOCK DEATH OF LOCAL CHARACTER is Ronnie's headline. 'We're appealing to the public for information. If anyone out there has a recent picture of Henry, we'd like them to pass it on to us,' says Detective Chief Inspector Whittan (*sic*).

That's on the Saturday, and the next day the Reverend Beal makes his contribution. Gas heaters beside the altar supply a dash of warm colour but no heat that's perceptible to the congregation. The windows are trickling and the air has a taste like fog. Today, therefore, only the hardcore are in attendance, packed for warmth into the front four pews, except for young Michael Trethowen, also known as Mystic Mike, who's occupying his traditional berth nearer the back, swaddled in the customary brown duffel coat. Beal moves things along as briskly as is decent, but he takes his time with the sermon. There must be a heater up in the pulpit. It's a head-numbingly tedious recital on the theme of the new year, the hopes thereof, the challenges thereof, the responsibilities thereof, et cetera, et cetera. Towards the end of his oration he mentions the dreadful event. His voice drops to a hush of compassion, his face is the face of a man bruised by the sufferings of the world. He urges us to take to heart the lessons of Henry's lonely life and lonely death, to think about what his death tells us about our society, to keep the poor man and his family (wherever they may be) in our thoughts, to pray that the killer be apprehended soon. All nod solemnly, thinking: 'Amen to the last bit anyway.' Alice, however, doesn't nod when told to think of Henry, even though she's had Henry in her thoughts for longer than any of them. She simply closes her eyes and meshes her fingers on her lap, and it's as if she's no longer listening to Beal but instead is in touch with the soul of Henry, or calling for him silently. Her face has no expression that you could describe. It's perfectly still and beautiful, and distant, and almost frightening. It's like looking at the face of a praying woman on a tomb from centuries ago.

Business concluded, the Reverend Beal takes up his station outside the door for the leave-taking. Shuffling his feet on the gravel, he shakes hands with them all, has a few words for everyone, and they in turn have a few words for him.

'Lovely sermon.'

'Thank you.'

'And how is your daughter?'

'Fine, thank you.' A halo of breath hangs around his head. 'Keep moving,' he's thinking. 'Thank you and keep moving.' It's like prize-giving day without the prizes. But he singles out Alice for a lingering clasp and meaningful eyes, as if she has an understanding that the rest of them lack, or perhaps it's just because she's the wife of a man who, he suspects, hasn't yet found a lodging for Christ in his heart. 'A ghastly business. Ghastly,' he says, with a three-second look of pity. Alice bows her head and says nothing.

4

Benjamin Kemp had nothing substantial to add to his original statement. With wide and watery eyes he stared aghast at Milo and the rug on which he was slumbering, as if the dog had brought Henry's remains into the house and spread them out around him. 'I saw him a few times, walking on the beach,' said Benjamin, shaking his head disbelievingly. He kept scratching the back of his head and there was a tremble round his mouth when he wasn't talking. Christine sat on the chair opposite, watching her husband's quivering mouth, and there was no discernible affection in her eyes, none at all. She seemed embarrassed by his lack of backbone and annoyed by the trouble he was putting her to. Looking out of the window, she frowned at the falling rain, vexed by what the day was up to. 'And what about you, Mrs Kemp?' asked Ian, pretending not to have noticed the discordancy of the household. 'Is there anything you can tell us about Henry?' She blinked, frozenly amazed by the question. Why on earth should she know anything about the disreputable old codger?

Five minutes later she was showing us out. 'I'm sure someone will be able to give you more help,' she said at the door, in apology for her useless spouse.

We begin the house-to-house slog, to assemble the victim profile. One of the first calls is at the home of Mr and Mrs

Fazakerly, whose home overlooks The Maer. Kevin Fazakerly is an independent financial adviser; Sophie, his wife, arranges big parties, conferences, weddings, business events and so on. Lucrative lines of work, evidently. The driveway is fancy brick, scrubbed clean as the day it was laid, and the front of the house – a sort of neo-Georgian mansion, but with extra-wide windows – is likewise immaculate. No salt damage to the paintwork and it appears that no seagull has emptied its bowels anywhere on this patch of real estate. Inside, as expected, it's a show home: you're tempted to touch the walls to check if they're still wet. Instantly you know there are no kids. Sophie ushers us into the kitchen, which is not a lot bigger than a squash court. We sit around the breakfast bar, a little pier of top-grade Scandinavian timber. You could perform open-heart surgery in this room, with no risk of infection.

Kevin and Sophie are both in their mid forties. Sophie is wearing tight pale jeans and white socks and narrow little white trainers with very white laces, and up top there's an odd bright-blue zippered cardigan thing, with the zip pulled right up to the neck. She's as tightly done up as a parachute in a backpack, so you get the feeling she might inflate to three times her size when she gets undressed. When you look at Kevin you think of some fourth-division American golfer, runner-up in the North Dakota Invitational, 1986. His hair has a retro ruler-straight parting and sticks out at the front in a little horizontal quiff, and over his shirt he has this horrible salmon-pink floppy cashmere jumper. The jeans are a bit baggier than Sophie's, but precisely the same shade. We receive the impression that they've got things to say on the issue of Henry. Tea is made, biscuits arranged on a plate that perhaps has been designed solely for this function: the Jan-Arne Simonsen Biscuit Plate, £100, plus postage and packing. It is suggested we carry our cups through to the living room. We troop across the acres of laminated floor. The living room is a little longer than the driveway and under-furnished with angular scarlet chairs and a pair of low-backed sofas, all of the same design.

Side by side on one of the sofas sit Kevin and Sophie, facing the two policemen. 'Isn't it terrible?' says Sophie, stroking a thumbnail rapidly with the thumb of her other hand. 'How could it happen?' she wants to know. Kevin pats her knee consolingly and concurs about the terribleness of what has happened, its incomprehensibility. 'It's awful,' says Sophie. 'Just awful.' Sophie examines Kevin's hand – his fingernails are pathologically well-maintained, the sort of hands you see in adverts for very expensive watches. 'To think it happened on our doorstep.' It's another boisterous evening. The rain is ticking quickly on the windows and the trees in the front garden are in spasm. Sophie touches Kevin's hand and he pats her knee; she touches his hand, he pats her knee. They can't get through a minute without touching each other. When a gust rattles something metallic up the drive, Sophie grabs at a cushion. It's as if the monster's out there in the gloom, making an assessment of the security arrangements, and we're their last protection.

'His name was Henry,' Kevin tells us, but he doesn't know his surname. 'He used to pitch camp out on The Maer,' he adds, looking to his wife for verification, and Sophie agrees that Henry used to sleep on The Maer. At night, she adds, they would sometimes see him settling down for the night, in the shelter of the trees. Once or twice he waved to her, when she was at the bedroom window, and she waved back, but they never spoke. 'Kept himself to himself,' observes Kevin.

'Nobody knew much about him,' Sophie contributes. Kevin tries to recall the last time he saw Henry, but cannot; Sophie also tries, and sadly draws a blank. Twenty minutes we're there, learning nothing, reassuring the Fazakerlys that they are not going to be murdered in their beds, but to lock up at night anyway. Of course they'll lock up at night. They always do, always have done. Kevin as a kid used to lock his toy cupboard at night, you just know he did. They're more likely to piss on their twelve-foot hand-woven organically dyed Turkish rug than leave a window open after bedtime.

We might as well have been interviewing ourselves, but Ian loves these house calls, even if he doesn't take a liking to the residents, which is the case in about fifty per cent of our visits. He gets a buzz from checking out where people live, because Ian is convinced that a very large proportion of our fellow citizens are less than entirely sane, and it's only when you get inside their houses that you see what lies behind the day-to-day normalness. Sometimes you have to look hard, but there's inevitably something, a crack in the mask. And as far as Ian is concerned, our fruitless session with Mr and Mrs Fazakerly has proved his case. 'Weird as Mormons,' he murmurs, the moment Sophie has closed the door. 'Did you see the framed menus? In the hall?'

'I did.'

'Signed by the chef, for fuck's sake.'

'And his handshake? Get more grip from an empty glove.'

'Creepy creepy creepy. But', Ian goes on, raising a finger for the point that would settle the issue, 'did you clock the microwave?'

'Everyone's got a microwave.'

'Yeah. But on top of it? Obvious as a bus.'

'What?'

'You didn't notice?'

He taps a fingertip beside an eye, dipping an eyebrow to signify shrewdness. 'Nothing wasted on this boy. Chief Inspector Mowbray, the early years. You were there.'

'Yes, OK. What was it?'

'An item from Peggy's purple shelf. *Debbie Does Dallas*.'

'Who's Peggy?'

In the drive, under a sort of extended porch, there is a new Mazda MX5, gold. 'This'll be hers,' Ian instantly concludes. 'The master vehicle is in the garage, bet you. Kev's more a Mercedes kind of guy. This dinky wee machine is the lady wife's.'

'Who's Peggy?'

Ian gives the Mazda a once-over. He peers through the windscreen at something on the front seat, putting the finishing touches

21

to his profile of the Fazakerlys. 'Granny Thistle,' he answers. 'She's on the list for tomorrow morning,' and then he explains.

The first thing you need to know about Peggy Thurlow, says Ian, is that she regards it as a point of honour never to be nice to tourists, no matter how servile they may be. She's never been known to smile at anyone who is clearly Not From Around Here, and has a reputation for being less than overwhelmingly warm to most non-outsiders too. Peggy's views on citizenship are hardline: you don't really belong to this town unless you have roots that go back three generations or more. Peggy's roots reach back to the nineteenth century and the family of her husband – the late Mr Thurlow, a cheery old fellow by all accounts, whose love of Peggy was for many people one of life's great mysteries – have been here since the Jurassic era. Pure-bred indigenous customers are generally on firmer ground with Peggy, but she's prone to sudden reversals. Just because you're in her good books on a Tuesday, there's no guarantee that you'll still be in favour come Friday, because Peggy is a gossip magnet and as changeable as a baby. Peggy has something on everyone and you're guilty until proven innocent in her private judicial system. She's either for you or against you, with very little in the way of middle ground. Someone passes on a rumour that you've been hitting the bottle and yelling at the kids – you're cast out into the darkness, pending evidence to the contrary. The warmth of human kindness is buried pretty deep within the heart of Peggy, but if you're one of the happy band that has earned her approval, she couldn't be nicer. You want a box of grade-A Cuban cigars for your recently promoted husband? Peggy will get them for you. You need an obscure magazine, Peggy will supply it for you: *Japanese Malt Whisky Review*, *The Kite-Flyer*, *Canoes and Canoeists* – no problem. She also has a sideline in personal finance, for those of the favoured few whose pay packets occasionally fail to meet outgoings. Rumour has it she once loaned a client a couple of grand, at very advantageous rates, to subsidise the acquisition of an E-Type Jag. Then again, woe betide anyone who doesn't repay on the stipulated date. Some hapless sod once settled up a couple of days past the deadline and Peggy burned his ears off with a lecture on the virtue of thrift.

When we walk into Peggy's shop the next morning, her reaction seems to suggest that she thinks she might recognise Ian, but she holds back the half-smile until he flips the badge. Ask a little kid to describe a lovely old granny and Peggy is more or less what you'd get: about five-one, approximately oval in silhouette, purple-grey candy-floss hair, soft fat face, tweedy skirt and chunky cable-knit cardigan with big leather buttons. 'And what can I do for you gentlemen?' she asks, and her eyes have the look that you see in people's eyes when they learn that some unexpected money is coming to them. She's standing behind the counter and right behind her head, at eye level, is Peggy's purple shelf. There's a tray of batteries and a selection of key rings and cigarette lighters, and alongside them there are Peggy's adult videos. The slipcases have been removed and masking tape stuck on to the spines, and Peggy has written non-offensive versions of the titles on to the masking tape – or rather, that seems to be the idea, but the lettering is in thick inch-high capitals, purple, and even a ten-year-old slow-wit could work them out: *S ME, F ME*; *EBONY GANG-B*; *SURFER F-FEST*. It's hard to imagine how it goes. What do the grubby punters say to her? 'Box of matches, packet of extra-strong mints, *Exchange & Mart*. Oh, and *Butt-F Bonanza* up there, next to *Keep on F-ing*. Any good? Really? OK, I'll take that as well, while you're at it.' Perhaps the cuddly little old porn peddler assigns you to the ranks of the damned if you ask.

Sure enough, Peggy has something on Henry – not much, but more than anyone else so far. Every twenty days, 'regular as clockwork', Henry would come into the shop to buy a packet of twenty cigarettes. Surprisingly, given Henry's rootless status, Peggy seems to have been well disposed towards him: he was her only customer for unfiltered cigarettes, she says, and she always made sure she had a packet in stock, just for Henry. His name was Henry Yarrow

23

and he used to be an engineer, but what kind of engineer, and where he was an engineer, and when, she couldn't say. He was from Minehead, she knew that much. Earlier that morning we'd been talking to a neighbour of the Fazakerlys and she'd said that she'd heard from someone that Henry's name was McBain, or McCain, or McSwain, or something like that. Beginning with Mc and ending with -ain, anyway. Had Peggy heard that his name was Yarrow or had he told her himself? 'He told me that was his name,' Peggy replies, the implication being that she is not the sort of person to pass off mere hearsay as fact.

'Definitely Yarrow?' asks Ian, making a note.

Peggy bristles at this, as if she'd been accused of lying. Offended, she locks her arms across her chest, a picture of indignant rectitude, with her library of red-hot muck behind her. But Ian soon wins her round, thanking her for her valuable information, nodding at the name he's written on his pad, as if it's a word in code and any minute now the letters will rearrange themselves and give us a vital clue. Gratitude accepted, Peggy gives us her personal impressions of Mr Yarrow: very polite, always cheerful, didn't smell at all, except sometimes in summer, but we're all a bit ripe then, aren't we? Then she starts on the questioning. Where exactly was he found? When? Who found him? What did we think had happened? Any leads? Ian fends her off, with heavy use of boyish charm. In the end she settles for knowing that Henry wasn't freshly dead when the unfortunate member of the public stumbled across him. 'Poor man,' Peggy laments. 'Poor poor man.' And her head does this slow sad shake as if her good angel is whispering in her ear: 'Shake head sadly now.' More than anything, you know she's irked at not having winkled more information from us.

We resumed the house-to-house trudge and Ian soon had another case for his gallery of the weird. Within sight of the Fazakerlys' palace there was the home of the hearty Miss Ryle, who had turned her residence into something out of *Heidi*. On the outside all was normal: an ordinary pebble-dashed semi, with a neat little garden out front. Inside, it was all wooden walls, wooden ceilings, damned great cowbells hanging in the hall and on the landings, photos and terrible paintings of snow and ice and rocks in every room, and all the way up the stairs. In the kitchen there were dozens of bits of cloth in frames, stitched with rustic sayings and proverbs in German and French, with borders of tiny flowers. Most of an entire wall was taken up by a huge aerial photo of some mountain-top hut, with glaciers left, right and centre, and above the fireplace in the front room there was an enormous curved horn, a monster trumpet, as long as an oar. 'Makes your head swim when you blow it,' grinned Miss Ryle, as if confessing to a penchant for cocaine. Miss Ryle knows nothing about Henry. She was in Switzerland for much of December, she told us. 'I'm always in Switzerland,' she admitted cheerily, waving a stout arm in the direction of the mighty trumpet.

And down the road, three minutes' walk from the *Heidi* house, there lived Miss Leith, similarly nearing fifty, similarly single, but with a liking for inappropriately vivid make-up and fuchsia-coloured shoes. Miss Leith also had a prodigious fondness for those disgusting little porcelain figurines of cheeky shepherds wooing busty peasant lasses, and cute old hobos offering roses to winsome young lovelies on park benches, and rosy-cheeked moppets with baskets of kittens. It was like sitting in a souvenir shop, surrounded by display cases full of heart-tugging tat. From Miss Leith, however, we learned that Henry's name was Henry Ellis, or so she'd heard from someone. She can't recall who that someone might have been.

Not far from Miss Leith and Miss Ryle lived Mr Jonathan Imber – early fifties, also unmarried, and quite understandably so. Mr Imber, a bearded gentleman, had turned his house into a shrine to Old Spice, the famous fragrance for men. He had assembled what he believed to be (and who are we to argue?) the country's (possibly Europe's, but not – sadly – the world's) most comprehensive collection of Old Spice receptacles (not merely aftershave – talcum powder, too, and deodorants), dating back to the year of the brand's creation. Misinterpreting a facial twitch as a glimmer of interest from Ian, he began to talk us through the Old Spice story. For Mr Imber the changing shape of his after-shave flasks is a story as engrossing as the evolution of *Homo sapiens*. 'My little pastime,' he called it, and suddenly 'pastime' became the most miserable word in the English language, a word for people who have not enough in their lives for their allotted time, for whom time is something that has to be got through. Mr Imber knew Henry by sight, but knew nothing about him; he didn't even know he was dead.

A check was run, and there was no Yarrow family in the Minehead area that was missing a senior member who was once an engineer, or missing a senior member who was anything, come to that. 'Interesting,' Ian remarked after morning prayers, after we'd been told the Minehead search had drawn a blank. 'Why would he lie about his name?'

'You tell me.'

'Covering his tracks.'

'Possible. Or he's just saying, "Fuck off and leave me alone." Could be that.'

'Why the different names? Why not stick to one?'

'Prevent himself getting bored. I don't know.'

We had no idea. A dozen people were working on Henry and nothing but Henry. By day four we had seven different surnames, and we were getting nowhere.

Then, late one afternoon at the end of the first week, a woman came into the North Street station, laden with carrier bags. 'I don't know if this will be any use,' she sighed, dumping the shopping. She pushed an envelope across the counter. Inside there was a photograph of the woman and two small girls stamping on the ruins of a sandcastle. Sweet-looking kids, her daughters presumably, deduced the lad on duty, not getting it. 'There,' said the woman, putting a fingernail on the picture. 'I think that's him, the dead man. The tramp.' In the background, obscured by sea mist and out of focus for good measure, stood someone who

26

might well have been Henry, perhaps watching the girls. The face wasn't much more than a beard and two dots for eyes, but the boys in the darkroom blew it up, cropped it, did a bit of magic on it to make the features crisper, and what you had in the end still wasn't a terrific portrait but it was a lot better than nothing, and it was all we had, so it was printed and made into a flyer, and up it went on a hundred lamp-posts.

5

Of all his war stories the one that George Whittam liked to retell most frequently was the story of Billy Renfrew, his first big case after the move from London. Billy Renfrew was seventy-two years old and lived alone in a semi-ruined cottage in the South Hams, as picturesque and uneventful a zone as you could wish to find. One morning in late summer the postman – making his first call at Billy's house for more than a fortnight – rode up to Billy's door and saw that it was open. He knocked, got no answer, pushed at the door and stepped inside. Then he saw Billy sitting on the floor of the hallway and a lump of Billy's brain stuck on the wall beside him.

A labourer all his life, Billy was by nobody's standards a prosperous man, but like many people of his age he had accumulated a few items worth stealing. There was a carriage clock on the mantelpiece, a silver cup in the kitchen, a pair of mother-of-pearl cufflinks by the bed. But none of these had been taken. On the kitchen table was his wallet, with £20 still in it. All the signs were that Billy's visitor had whacked him when he opened the door and then run off. There were no prints on the door except Billy's, no clues except a few yards of indistinct bicycle tyre tracks from the gate to the door, which might or might not have had anything to do with it. Enquiries soon established that Billy had few friends and no known enemies, so George and his colleagues set about interviewing everyone who lived within a mile of the cottage, then everyone within two miles, three miles, till they'd spoken to every adult and juvenile inside a five-mile radius. And from all these interviews not a scrap of illuminating information was garnered. For the best part of half a year after the killing of Billy there was no suspect. So they went back and interviewed almost everyone again, beginning with the village nearest the cottage, working outwards, and in the end, sure enough, the stress fracture occurred.

This individual was a builder-cum-plumber but business must have been bad because he was at home, fixing his van outside his garage, when George happened to drop by in the middle of the afternoon. 'How's it going?' said George and he reintroduced himself, though straight away it was clear that he'd been remembered. The handyman delved around in the engine for a minute, wiped his hands on a rag, dropped the rag into the toolbox on the kerb. 'Water pump,' he explained, and in his eyes there was a hint that he was wondering why he'd been singled out for a repeat visit. They talked for a while about this and that: water-pumps, vans, motors. Within a minute the nervousness, never more than the slightest suggestion of unease, had gone entirely. And then, as the lad picked a spanner out of the toolbox, George looked down at the heap of pliers and drill bits and screwdrivers. The tools were all well used, smeared with oil, pitted with rust. But what attracted his attention was the hammer: the hammer was brand new. Not in itself incriminating, but George felt the dawning of suspicion, the rising of a truth moment, and the dawning grew stronger when he looked into the garage. Partly hidden behind lengths of skirting board and pipes, there was a bicycle. 'Nice bike,' George remarked, though it was battered and spattered and very far from nice. He established the make, pretended he was thinking of buying the very same model for his nephew. 'Mind if I take a look?' It was a blatant pretext, but what could be said except: 'Help yourself'? Telling the cop to bugger off wouldn't have made a good impression, would it? 'Had it long?' asked George, giving the bike a slow close scrutiny.

The interviewee was busying himself under the bonnet, acting unconcerned. 'Didn't hear you,' he shouted, so George asked it again. Our man claimed he'd bought the bike a couple of months ago, second-hand. This turned out to be true, but George didn't believe him. Half the garages in England have a bike in them, but this one, for some reason, was suddenly emitting an aura of evidence.

George took his time. He wasn't looking for anything: he was just letting the man stew for a while, and when he was saying goodbye, a perfectly casual goodbye, he saw a shrinking in his eye and knew that this was the one. Another eight or nine hours of face work it took, but in the end our friend contradicted himself one time too often, and he owned up. From somewhere this numb-skull had got hold of the idea that Billy Renfrew was some sort of miser, with thousands of pounds stashed in socks and jam jars all over the house. He'd meant to help himself to a bit of cash, that's all, but Billy must have heard him gouging away at the lock because suddenly the door opened and there he was, effing and blinding, and there was no option but to dab him on the head with a hammer, was there?

Be patient. That, in a nutshell, is the lesson to be learned from the case of Billy Renfrew. 'Be patient. Let nothing be wasted on you,' George Whittam would say to us. And: 'Every piece of infor-mation adds something to the picture, even if you can't see it at first.' It gave George great pleasure to sound wise, and he was good at it. 'Elimination is progress,' he would tell us. 'You're always getting nearer if you don't stay still. Nothing is a waste of time.' This isn't true. Sometimes, work that feels like a complete waste of time really is a complete waste of time. But it doesn't matter that it's not true. From the story of Billy Renfrew one could conclude that when it comes to solving a tricky homi-cide you can't beat having a sixth sense. Should a sixth sense not feature in your armoury, you need a damned great stroke of luck.

These pronouncements would be truer, but less useful for the maintenance of morale among the juniors.

It was necessary to stoke morale at regular intervals. At the end of another long morning we had no useful information. We had heard about an incident at which Henry was present, that's all. Around Christmas three years ago, in Topsham, there had been a fire. An empty house went up in smoke with such speed that by the time the fire brigade arrived on the scene the roof had gone and the top-floor windows were falling out. Something highly inflammable was in there – presumably to help the blaze – and every few minutes an explosion sent flames shooting out. A seagull got cremated, standing on a lamp-post. It was a hell of a show and it drew a good crowd. Henry was among the spectators, we were told. He stayed until the last flames were extinguished, which would have been around three or four in the morning. It was odds-on that the fire was started deliberately and of course there were people prepared to believe that the disreputable-looking old geezer who hung around till the final curtain might have been in some way involved. But Henry wasn't involved. Within two days it was known that it had nothing to do with Henry. Three schoolkids did it. Having no TV to watch at home, Henry had stayed to watch the fire. Probably warmed himself up a bit into the bargain. End of meaningless episode. We have an anecdote, when what we need is a story.

In the afternoon, as in the morning, we meet people who can't bring themselves to say it but obviously had never thought that Henry was much of an adornment to the locality. Equally obviously, none of them had ever wished him dead. They confirm that Henry was prone to going missing for a week or two, every now and again. No one has a clue where he went. Everyone is sorry he's gone.

No, that's not right: Mr Latimer wasn't sorry. Formerly an airline pilot, today a gin-pickled old fascist, Mr Latimer would have had Henry clapped in irons and set to work in a chain gang if he'd had any say in the matter. 'The Wandering Jew,' he called him, giving us a look to gauge if we are men enough to take his strong straight talking. Between sentences his jaws made fierce little champing movements, as if chewing on tiny cubes of hard rubber. Occasionally, he reported, he saw Henry in the town, 'watching people'. There was something not right in the way he followed people with his eyes. It wasn't just rude: 'You felt he was up to something,' said Mr Latimer, but he declined to specify to what manner of thing Henry might have been up. And once he came across him on the top of the cliffs. 'Ogling a young woman,' he said, with a sneer, then paused for us to work out what he meant. 'Messing with himself,' he elucidated, displeased at our failure to participate in his disgust. We shouldn't pity such people, Mr Latimer insisted, affronted by the permissiveness he'd discerned in us. This isn't the eighteenth century, after all. Our society makes provision for the unfortunate, and anyone who lives like that man lived is doing so through his own choice and for no other reason.

And in the same afternoon we encountered Ferrari man, a taxi driver who lived in a flat with Ferrari-red carpets and Ferrari-red curtains and model Ferraris all over the place, on the windowsills, on chairs, under chairs. It was like a plague of scarlet metal mice. Magnetic Ferraris were stuck on the fridge. The phone was in the shape of a Ferrari. It was news to him that Henry's name was Henry. It hadn't registered with him that Henry was missing until he saw the posters. Another futile conversation, but mercifully brief, and for Ian this character was the highlight of the day, of course.

An hour after the visit to the Ferrari man we're in the pub, where Mary – Ian's new girlfriend – is waiting, with her friend Rachelle. It's one minute past six and they are the only people in the place. This is the first time we've met, so Ian undertakes the introductions. 'Mary Usher, John Donohue. John my colleague, Mary my girl. Rachelle, John. John my colleague, Rachelle my girl's best friend.'

'Nicely done,' says Mary, giving him a smack on the arm.

'He won't be staying long. Has to get home to his wife,' Ian whispers loudly to Rachelle, getting another whack from Mary, then he's off to the bar.

'Hello,' says Mary. For some reason her boyfriend has omitted to mention that Mary is startling to look at, with white-blonde hair and a wide frank face and grey-blue eyes that are as clear as a child. We shake hands.

'Pleased to meet you,' says Rachelle, reaching over the table. A year or two younger than Mary, she's dark and small and sinewy, like a marathon runner. She and Mary have known each other since they were at infants' school together, she explains timidly, as if she feels herself to be under an obligation to establish at once her right to be here. She works in a café up the top of the hill, she says, and she seems almost grateful that the name of the place is recognised. We talk for a minute, then Ian is back from the bar and straight away he's gabbing on about Mr Ferrari.

'Incredible,' he tells them. 'Like a boy's bedroom, but he's what, fifty?'

'Thereabouts.'

'Fifty, and he's got these little cars everywhere. Ferrari lamps, Ferrari mugs. Everything screaming red. Would give you a migraine after five minutes.'

'So what do you think?' asks Mary quietly. 'About –'

'Henry?' says Ian, though the question wasn't addressed to him. 'Can't give too much away,' he explains, with a wink for Rachelle. 'But I think it's safe to say that we're looking for a man. Ninety per cent of murderers are male. The women are domestics, one way or another, nearly all of them. They take a hammer to the husband, or the father who's been molesting them for years.'

'Or stick a knife in the boyfriend,' adds Mary.

'Rarely, but it happens. But Henry was nobody's boyfriend. OK, another interesting thing,' continues Ian, overexcited by his first murder, determined to impress Rachelle as much as Mary, 'is that victim and killer are usually of similar age and similar

33

economic status. Once in a while a millionaire gets wiped out by one of the lower orders, but as a rule it's yob kicks yob to death, dodgy businessman wipes out his partner, husband kills wife. So all we've got to do is find us another middle-aged down-and-out male and we're home and dry.'

Leaning forward, pressing her hands between her knees, Rachelle laughs on cue. Encouraged, Ian gives his audience a welter of facts and figures – it's his homework rehashed, some of it misremembered. 'The crucial periods are the last twenty-four hours of the victim's life and the first twenty four hours after the discovery of the body. Forty per cent of detections occur within two days of the murder being reported,' he tells wide-eyed Rachelle. 'Now we're past that point, and the odds get longer as time passes. But, on the bright side, sixty per cent aren't solved in the first forty-eight hours, and it's early days.'

Another thing about Ian, it turns out, is that he's as jealous as a cat, and when the barman, a good-looking boy with mighty forearms and a complicated haircut, comes over to collect the empties, the smile that Mary gives the intruder wrecks Ian's concentration in mid-sentence, as intended. You can almost see his brain clenching.

'Heard what you were talking about,' says the barman. 'So what do you think?'

'You just said you heard,' Ian reminds him, reddening faintly.

'Yeah. But,' the lad replies, apparently deaf to Ian's tone. His hand is lingering on Mary's glass, his bare arm an inch or two from her face.

'But what?'

'But do we know him?' he goes on, narrowing his eyes in a way that's meant to suggest mystery.

'Do we know him? Who?'

'Who did it.'

'What's your name?' asks Ian.

'Josh.'

'Josh, what the fuck are you talking about?'

Amiably, as if his ears have edited out the expletive, Josh continues: 'I mean we know the person who did it, but the police don't know him yet. It's someone who lives here, isn't it? Got to be. Must be someone who went out there to do him, who knew where he were, otherwise what you looking at? Some bloke is stretching his legs on the beach, comes across your man, doesn't like the look on his face, cuts him up. I mean, I don't think so.' He steps back, eyebrows raised, greatly pleased with his reasoning.

Ian drains his glass and passes it over. 'Thank you, Josh,' he says, giving him a thin wide smile. 'Something to think about.'

'Stands to reason, don't it?'

'It does. You're wasted in this job. The police need men like you.'

Nicked at last by the edge of Ian's voice, Josh hesitates on the point of responding.

'We do,' says Ian. 'Believe me.'

At the realisation of what we are, Josh blinks as though at onion fumes. 'You police?' he asks.

'We police,' Ian confirms.

'Wow. That's –' He smiles to himself, as if until this moment we'd been wearing a disguise that he should have seen through. 'Bugger me.'

'Indeed,' says Ian. 'Your round, John.'

With a shrug and a grin for Mary, this time unreciprocated, Josh withdraws.

'Sherlock the barman,' Ian mutters.

Mary gives him a reproving smile. 'But he has a point, doesn't he?' she says. 'It made sense to me.'

'What you reckon, John?' Ian enquires, feigning deep self-doubt. 'Reckon he's got a point?'

'I reckon he just wants to feel involved.'

'I tend to agree, John.'

'But we don't know that Henry was nobody's boyfriend.'

'You what?'

'We don't know that Henry was nobody's boyfriend.'

35

'No, we don't absolutely know it. But unlikely.'

'Not impossible.'

'Very very very unlikely.'

'Quite unlikely, but you never know. Even Hitler had a girl-friend.'

'Hitler had a nice house and decent clothes and a big black car.'

'Some women don't care about nice houses.'

'No woman's going to go for a man with woodlice in his hair. Isn't that right, ladies?' says Ian, a proposition at which they both nod. From the way Mary puts a hand on his leg, from the way she curls his hand into hers, you can tell that she worries about him, imagining that one night he's going to corner a drug-crazed thug in an alleyway and end up with a blade through his liver. 'We'll get him. Sooner or later,' says Ian, giving the promise of a man whose word is his bond. Leaning back, his arms flat along the top of the banquette, he looks like a character on TV, the overconfident young cop. But he does truly believe that we'll get him, and the next morning, as if in vindication of his baseless faith, the very first visit turns out to be our first promising one, the first to give us anything you might call a lead.

Mr Gaskin is a pensioner, eighty-ish. He opens his front door cautiously, as people of his age tend to do, and opens it just wide enough to make a gap he can stand in. We often get a brief look of dread when we say who we are, but with Mr Gaskin all anxiety vanishes from his face when we identify ourselves and explain why we're here. Solemnly courteous, gratified to be have been called upon to do his duty as a citizen, he invites us in. 'I'm not sure I can be of much help,' he apologises, and in his bearing and his voice there's a sadness that seems long-standing. He's a diminutive chap and extremely unsturdy. The skin on the back of his hands is like greaseproof paper with thin blue wires running under it, and the bones of his face are as sharp as a carving in wood. He is wearing a crisp white shirt and iridescent blue tie, though it's soon revealed that he hasn't been anywhere today and isn't going anywhere after we've gone. In the front room a big leather armchair is aligned four-square with the TV. Beside the chair stands a table laden with books and a standard lamp with fat tassels. Obviously this chair is the only one in regular use, and on the mantelpiece there's a big framed picture of a bride and groom, in the middle of a flock of smaller pictures. You know without looking closely that the bride is Mrs Gaskin and that Mrs Gaskin is deceased. There are photographs all over the place, on every wall and shelf, and the face of Mrs Gaskin seems to be in most of them.

We sit around a table, Mr Gaskin facing us, the blue-wired hands locked lightly on the table top. From the window by which we're sitting Mr Gaskin can see the upper reaches of the path that zigzags down to the end of the beach road, and the start of the path that cuts through the trees, across the High Land of Orcombe. Many times he saw Henry heading over the High Land, or made out his figure down on the sand, sometimes making up a bed for himself against the sea wall, but as he recalls there was only one occasion on which he talked to him. Speaking gravely and with precision, as though from a witness box, he tells us about the evening in the autumn of the year before last, when he came across Henry. About six o'clock, it was, and he'd decided to take a stroll because there was a particularly beautiful sunset. The tide was low, so he went down on to the beach, and no sooner had he turned the corner of the headland, into the next bay, than he heard a loud crack and there was Henry, twenty or thirty yards away, with his back to him, close to the cliff. At Henry's feet there was a pile of four or five wooden crates that must have been washed ashore and he was striking the pile with a long metal spike, the sort that's used for raising a barrier around a hole in the road. 'He was striking the crates with great force. Remarkable violence,' says Mr Gaskin, and he pauses, unnerved anew at the sight of Henry and the crates. 'As if slaughtering an animal. He was in a frenzy, I'd say. Yes. That's not too strong. A frenzy.'

Then Henry turned and saw him, whereupon he lowered the

37

spike and bowed, a deep and extravagant bow, like a swordsman's bow to a rival in a duel. Henry wished him good evening and they talked for a minute or two. They talked about the fire that Henry was going to build. The rest of their conversation has been forgotten now, but Mr Gaskin does remember with some clarity three things about their meeting. The first of these is the peculiarity of Henry's speech, the slowness of it, and the silences. 'He had this air of being baffled, and I couldn't decide if he was a thoughtful chap or a little lacking in grey matter. He seemed perplexed by me or by himself, but it wasn't clear which,' muses Mr Gaskin, and Ian writes it down, nodding in recognition. Every minute or so, as well, Henry would yawn, very widely, without covering his mouth, yet he did not appear tired. 'It was a tic, I suppose, but most unnerving,' he tells us. 'And I think he had a Midlands accent. That's the last thing.'

'By "think" –?' Ian asks.

'I detected a flatness in the voice. In some of the vowels.'

'You're sure of that?'

'I'm sure of what I heard, yes. I'm not wholly sure about the accent. Where it was from, I mean.'

'But something like a Midlands accent?'

'That's how it sounded to me.'

'Interesting,' Ian comments. 'I didn't pick that up.'

'You talked to him?' asks Mr Gaskin, and the next minute Ian's chatting to him about the swimming incident and the unnamed snoop with the telescope, which makes Mr Gaskin smile, with a wistful fondness, as though at the wackiness of a shared acquaintance. 'One other thing occurs to me,' he says, apparently prompted by something in Ian's story, and he tells us that several times he saw Henry walking on the clifftops or the beach with a girl, a fair-haired girl, a bit on the plump side, average height. By girl he means under thirty, a few years under thirty. When he saw her with Henry he had a feeling that this wasn't the first time he'd seen her. Ian asks if he could be a little more specific about her appearance, and Mr Gaskin presses his fingers to his temples,

38

trying to squeeze a memory to the surface. Grimacing at the effort, he looks out of the window. We wait. Eventually he recalls that the girl was with Henry late one evening last summer, on the beach. Henry had his jeans rolled up and was collecting rubbish in a fertiliser bag. Behind him was the girl. She was wearing a purple swimming costume, a bikini, bright purple. Mr Gaskin puts a hand to his brow and closes his eyes, summoning the scene on the beach. We wait a little longer. 'I'm sorry. It's gone. I can't see her face,' he complains, at which Ian lets out a small laugh. Mr Gaskin opens his eyes and blinks at him, confused.

'See the bikini, don't see the face,' Ian explains. 'I can undertand that. I have that problem myself.'

'Oh,' replies Mr Gaskin. 'I see. Yes.' He smiles weakly, before again gazing out of the window.

'This is useful,' says Ian, tapping his notebook. 'Thank you.'

Mr Gaskin follows us to the door in silence, his burden of sadness now increased by the failure of his memory. 'If anything else comes to mind,' he says, 'shall I call the station?'

'Please,' says Ian. He writes down our names and phone numbers for Mr Gaskin, then shakes his hand.

6

Oswald and Son, greengrocers, began trading in 1947, from a shop on the outskirts of Exeter. Forty years later, the business having been left high and dry by the opening of a supermarket half a mile away, James Oswald, son of the son, was forced to shut down. Not long after, a new traffic system narrowed the pavement outside what had once been the Oswalds' shop and clogged the road with cars and lorries from rush hour to rush hour. Marooned in what had become a moribund location, the former Oswald premises were left untenanted for years. The windows disappeared under billboards; the roof began to disintegrate. Then, one Sunday afternoon in November, while stuck in a traffic jam, Alice noticed the derelict shop.

At this point Alice had been working with Katharine Giles for no more than a couple of months. The operation was being run from the kitchen of Katharine's house and a lock-up garage near Katharine's house, an unsatisfactory arrangement but one to which there seemed to be no affordable alternative. Until, that is, Alice saw the shop and decided, feeling the seed of an idea instantly taking root, to take a closer look. She picked off a corner of a poster to peer through the sooty glass; she went round the back and found a small yard and a loading bay. The building had been neglected for so long there wasn't even an agent's board on it, but Alice soon tracked them down and made them an offer: she and her partner would refurbish the shop and pay the rates on it, but would pay no rent; they would have a lease for a year and after that they would be on one month's notice to quit, should a long-term tenant come along. This offer, submitted in writing, was unacceptable. A second letter, elaborating on the humanitarian nature of their enterprise, and for good measure reiterating that the restoration of these dilapidated premises could only be of benefit to the landlords, who at present were lumbered with an asset of negligible commercial value, was likewise rebutted in the fewest possible words.

Then Alice went directly, in person, to the owners of the property, and that was that, because no one, however obtuse or tight-fisted he may be, can resist the ardent goodness of Alice. Confronted with Alice, when Alice's mind is made up, no man could argue for long. When she sits down and looks at you with those unwavering deep green eyes, you know that here is a woman who is sincere and highly principled and absolutely intent on achieving her purpose. And, of course, she's attractive, too, very attractive, which helps in the disarming process. To refuse her would be ungracious. You'd feel that you'd behaved unworthily in taking issue with her, and the landlords duly, rapidly, acceded to her request. It's the same when she's drumming up donations and sponsorship. Nobody ever says 'No' when Alice visits in person. They must dread her visitations, the lovely and implacable spirit of charity.

Before the year's end Alice and Katharine took over the shop, and at the time of Henry's death that's where they were, flanked on one side by a hairdresser who somehow stayed solvent on the revenue from three customers per day and on the other by a boarded-up betting shop. Every morning Alice would set off in their resprayed post-office van to drive around the county or even further afield, gathering discarded books from libraries and colleges and anywhere else that had surplus printed matter to offload. In the afternoon, if she hadn't returned too late, she helped Katharine to sort the haul into packages for dispersal to various wretched zones of the earth, where kids who owned nothing would learn about the world and the English language from out-of-date guidebooks and novels with pages missing, and battered old dictionaries and atlases held together with tape and glue applied by Alice and Katharine and their ever-changing crew of volunteers. It was also Alice's job to phone the regular donors, to cold-call the potential benefactors. Above the desk – a cast-off from the insurance broker in the next street – was stuck a picture of a wizened woman sitting on an oil drum in front of a shack of corrugated iron. The bags under her eyes were like tiny leather purses, but she was only forty years old, said Katharine. She lived in Mozambique and at the time the picture was taken she was learning to read, helped by the books that Alice and Katharine had sent. Now she was running a mobile library, taking books to her neighbours on a donkey-drawn cart. All round the walls there were photographs like this one, displayed like images of the saints. By the door there was one of a pretty eight-year-old. Before school she had to work on her parents' scrap of land; when school was finished she picked up the hoe and the spade again. Of an evening, when the outdoors work was done, she had chores to do in the house, and then her homework, but when the homework was completed she sat down at the table and read to her parents by the light of a kerosene lamp. Her name was Josephine. In the photograph she was sitting at the table, the household's one table, with the unlit lamp beside her, grinning over a ragged copy of *Tarka the Otter*. It came from a man in Appledore, Katharine explained, delighted at the extraordinariness of the book's destiny.

Thousands of books passed through her warehouse every year, and Katharine seemed to know the destination of each one. She was in her mid-fifties then. Her son was a layabout junkie and she was cursed with sciatica, but Katharine's enthusiasm could not be dimmed. Each donation of books was received as a kid would receive a Christmas present, and she packed them up as if the books were as precious as barrels of water. Katharine believed that the day was coming in which everyone would have access to the books they need for their education. What's more, the inequality of men and women would soon be eliminated, all over the world, if not in her lifetime, then within the lifetime of her son's generation. She really did believe this would happen, and to play her part in the realisation of this vision she worked like a demon, earning barely enough to pay the mortgage, with a small surplus for handouts to the freeloading son. We read about gold-diggers: the lusty young girlfriend of the rich and ailing dotard; the errant wife with an eye for the life insurance and a violent boyfriend in tow; the high-maintenance flint-heart, siphoning hubby's bank account until the well runs dry, whereupon it'll be time to snare another sap. These women exist. But a pathological love of cash is predominantly a male vice. For most women, life is not about money. What tends to be important with women is value of a different kind, the value of life itself.

After we married, we lived modestly: small house, boring car, two weeks' holiday a year. As long as we had sufficient cash to cover the outgoings and save a little, Alice was content with that. We were both content with it. And when we began to consider changing our lives, we did the sums and decided together that it was the right thing to do: we could afford it, we should take the chance. And so, in perfect agreement, we determinedly took a wrong turn. Had Alice shown the slightest misgiving about the dip in household income, we wouldn't have done it – and then, two or three years down the line, perhaps we'd have taken a different wrong turn.

One day, in a queue at the supermarket checkout, Alice got talking to Margaret Whittam, and a month later, such is Alice's charm, we were guests at the Whittams' house-warming party. As the party was breaking up, we stood with George at the door of the conservatory, looking out at the garden. 'The job might not be great but it's tolerable, yes? You don't look like a man at his wits' end.'

'It could be better.'

'For ninety-five per cent of people it could be better,' George countered, raising a hand to stay Alice's objection. 'But the time has come to make a change. You feel that. I understand.'

'We both feel it,' Alice interjected.

'Fine, fine. But the job is bearable, for the time being. So my advice would be: don't rush. Think carefully.'

'We have,' said Alice.

'You must see a lot of unhappy people in your line of work,' he remarked, emanating the wisdom of the life-seasoned policeman, though he'd yet to touch forty.

'Nothing but, most days.'

'Well, you'd get a lot more of that.'

'Of course.'

'That's not the problem,' Alice told him. 'He's had enough of just writing out the cheques. And people never see him as being on their side. You're there to minimise your employer's costs, that's how they see it, isn't it, John?'

'Usually.'

'Well, they're right, aren't they?' George commented.

'But he's there to help put things back together, as well. He's not out to rob them, but that's what they think.'

'So you want to be popular, John? Is that it?'

'Not –'

'He doesn't want to be popular,' Alice interrupted. 'He wants to be in a different part of the process.'

'John deals with the aftermath, I deal with the aftermath. We're latecomers, both of us.'

'You know what I mean,' retorted Alice, an undertone of impatience in her voice.

Sipping his champagne, George cast a quick sidelong glance at Alice, an approving glance that was intended to go unobserved. 'You mean catching the bad men.'

'That makes it sound silly. But if you want to put it that way, yes.'

44

George nodded and said nothing, and surveyed the garden with an expression of mild perplexity.

'It's a bit late in the day for a career switch,' said Alice. 'Is that what you're thinking?'

'No. Not at all. It's not too late.'

'So what is it? Tell me.'

Lowering his glass, George turned to regard the insistent and beguiling Alice for an extended moment, meeting her eye. 'Look, Alice. John,' he said at last. 'It can be tough, I know, what you're doing now. Going to see people whose homes have gone up in smoke. Calling at a flat that's been torn apart. Things that can't be replaced, gone for ever. It doesn't make you feel good. It can be distressing. I know. But it's nothing,' he told her. 'Take my word for it, it's nothing,' he repeated, facing the garden rather than us, and Alice's face took on an attentive and slightly fearful and quietly resolute expression, an expression like that which, later, would sometimes appear when the Reverend Beal was on the top of his form, expounding on the ineffable mysteries of God's love. 'How long have you been married?' he asked, as if suddenly starting an interview.

'Going on four years.'

'You seem happy, leaving the job aside for the moment. You and John. You seem very close. Not all couples are. Tell me if this is none of my business.'

'Yes, we're happy,' Alice replied. 'John?'

'Happy. Confirmed.'

'Good,' said George, in full sagacious mode. Father of two teenaged girls, high-flying officer of the law, he drew a long breath and took a last sip of champagne before going on. 'Look, it's a terrific job, don't get me wrong. I wouldn't do anything else. But the things that people are capable of doing to each other,' he went on, directing a scowl at the floor. 'I don't think anything could surprise me any more. The madness that comes over people. The vicious idiocy. It's unimaginable,' he said, turning away, and he wandered off to find a fresh bottle.

The words of this conversation are the gist of it, a reconstruction, not a copy, but those last three phrases were what was said by Detective Inspector Whittam, verbatim. He poured our drinks, chinked glasses. Smiling at the garden of his big new house, he said: 'let me tell you about the day I lost my virginity.'

For more than thirty years these two brothers had lived together, migrating from one pocket of slum accommodation to another in various east London locales before settling in a caravan in the breaker's yard that they ran in Bethnal Green. In the evenings they drank together in a pub across the road from the yard. At six o'clock every evening they'd take their places at their table in the corner and there they would remain until eleven, downing pint after pint after pint, like drinking machines. You'd get a nod out of them, if you were lucky, and hardly a word passed between them. One night, though, they went home and had an argument, over a game of cards. Brother A brought the disagreement to a close by going to bed: his berth was at one end of the caravan and his sibling's was at the other. While Brother A was asleep, Brother B came into his cubicle and struck him a few times – maybe twenty-five times – between the eyes, with a torque wrench. This done, Brother B closed the door and retired to bed, leaving the body of Brother A where it lay. Every evening, through September, October, November, December, Brother B went to the pub across the road. Silent as a bollard he sat next to the void that had been his brother's place, and at night he went home to sleep in his bed, separated from the mouldering corpse by a few feet of space and a very thin wall. 'Gone away,' he replied, if anyone asked, and that was enough to satisfy anyone who could be bothered to enquire as to the whereabouts of the absent man. A few people noticed a smell hanging around the piles of car parts, a sewer smell that was emanating from the vicinity of the caravan, but hygiene had never been the brothers' strong point and nobody was inclined to make an issue of it. So the remains of Brother A were left to dwindle undisturbed until Christmas Eve, when some unexplained mental event induced

Brother B, as last orders were called, to mutter to the woman sitting at the next table, a woman who had never been in the pub before and just happened to be there because she was visiting her nephew and his new wife, 'Get the police.' Thinking they were in the presence of a psychiatric case, and a dangerous-looking psychiatric case at that, the woman edged away. 'Get the police,' he repeated, louder, and then he started shouting. 'Get the fucking police. For fuck's sake get the police.' He burst into tears, but carried on drinking his pint until the police arrived.

The detectives, young George Whittam among them, entered the caravan to find this thing that was halfway to being a mummy, dressed in brown pyjamas, lying on the foulest mattress in Western Europe. 'It was really something special,' George marvelled. 'Most of him had drained away into the mattress, and there were so many dead flies, you could have filled a bath with them.' We listened to his cautionary tale. He described the scene for us so vividly, with such relish: the stink when they opened the door; the brown mulch of a bed with the sticky rind of a corpse lying on it; the demented drunk man stamping on the heaps of flies as if it had been the insects that had killed his brother. We listened and we felt that we were almost there in the caravan with George Whittam, the young constable, as he stared at the bed and tried to stop the shake in his hand. But a case like the deranged brother must come along once in a decade, we told ourselves. There's an element of bravado in the telling of the story too. 'The man who looked on darkness and is not afraid,' joked Alice afterwards, on our way home. And the brothers were from London, after all. London's a different world. Life down here is more sedate. It's not murder or GBH every day of the week. And the satisfactions of justice will outweigh whatever unpleasantness may lie in store. We can handle whatever happens. We love each other. We are happy.

So the decision was made and the reaction to George Whittam's warning was nothing more than a pause, a hesitancy that was soon overcome. But George was right. You can't completely imagine it, and what it does to you is unimaginable – or, to be more precise, we didn't imagine what it would do to us. When you deal with violence and its consequences every week, when every day you're talking to people you know are lying to you, then perhaps it's inevitable that you become a different person. In the beginning it's a performance: you play the part of the hard man, the man with no illusions, the cynic. You learn quickly how it's done. You observe and imitate, but at the outset there's a difference between the role and the real person, between who you are being and who you are. Here's a picture of a girl, can't be older than eighteen, a prostitute, slashed so badly by her punter she was having to hold one side of her face in place when she crawled out of the park on her knees. 'Poor kid,' you say, and you pass the picture on without another word, but your eyes are prickling and you're hoping that the bastard gets sentenced by a judge whose values come straight out of the rule book of Genghis Khan. A couple of years on there's the blistered beetroot face of Evie Challoner, whose boyfriend has doused her with a kettleful of boiling water to make her ugly, so her ex-husband, who wants her back, won't want her back any longer. At this you shake your head, and the weary shake of the head isn't too far from representing what you feel, because the convulsion of pity isn't there any more. 'Christ,' you mutter, and you get on with the work. In fact, you're not so sure what you feel now. It's as though you've spoken your character's lines for so long that you've come to think like him, most of the time, and whenever you're not thinking like him, when you get a pang, you wonder sometimes where it's come from, if you've just slipped out of one character and into another one, the one you used to play all the time. And the home that Alice created and maintained, the pleasant and tranquil and orderly home environment, was intended to be something like a refuge for both of us. It was the place where life was restored to what was dependable and true, a place where the guises of working life were cast off, its contaminations rinsed away.

By agreement we had a house rule: no shop talk in front of Luke. But from someone else he heard the story of the dead man on the beach, and one evening, on his way to bed, he stopped on the stairs and asked, 'Why did someone kill that man?' Sitting side by side on the top step, we talked about Henry for a while. 'Why didn't he have somewhere to live?' he asked. 'Who did it?' He rested his chin on his knees, pondering his father's less than entirely satisfactory answers, not frightened, it seemed, by the thought of the uncaught killer, but unhappy at the unfairness of homeless Henry's death.

It was half an hour or more before Alice came downstairs from Luke's room. 'He wanted me to stay,' she said, taking food from the fridge. 'It's upset him.' There was no sense that blame was being apportioned – there was never that, not until the day of judgement. Rather, it was as though we all had the misfortune to be living in a place with an unhealthy climate, or night-long noise outside. Over the meal there would have been some kind of conversation about Henry, a brief conversation, perhaps with a mention for Henry's mysterious female companion, but there was nothing much to say about the case of Henry and by then it was understood that if nothing was offered, Alice would not enquire. Trusting her husband to do all that could be done, she would prepare the evening's meal, watch the evening's TV with him, and the following Sunday they would go to church together, where Alice would pray and think about Henry's soul, in the belief or the hope that all will be well, that in the end – if not on this earth – the innocent will have their reward.

At 10.30 or thereabouts on the night that Luke was upset, Alice would have gone to bed. On the TV, likely as not, there was yet another report from some hellish zone of Africa: thousands starving, thousands dying of Aids, kids being born diseased, schools set on fire and teachers hacked to death by child-soldiers, the infantry of the Church of Jesus Christ of the Latter-Day Psychos, washing away their sins in the blood of the lambs.

7

A thin broth of sea cloud fills the mouth of the river and through the greyness, here and there, it's just possible to make out where the sky begins, what's hill and what's water, which seam of the mist is a sandbank and which is a thickening of the mist. On the seafront the windows of empty guest houses gleam like slabs of wet slate. Here and there a head can be glimpsed, a hand on a radio, a newspaper being turned, a lampshade in a style that's twenty years old. Kids are skateboarding down the middle of the road and riding their bikes across the putting greens. Names have been spray-painted on the doors of the beach huts. You can stand in the car park and hear nothing but the gasping of the sea. In winter half the town is in a coma.

We call at one of the bigger hotels, and on the afternoon of our visit the register shows that the number of guests in residence is precisely three. The previous weekend a couple from Ontario had stayed for two nights and they'd had the place to themselves. We sit in the manageress's office, noting the names and addresses of all the people who stayed here during the period within which Henry died: that's fewer than thirty individuals to trace, interview and eliminate, a task soon completed. Some of them came here for a break from London, one came for a break from her husband, one was a photographer taking pictures for a travel agent's calendar, one a geologist on a working holiday, one a bibulous clarinettist on the brink of a breakdown. The clarinettist is still on the brink when he's interviewed: he's a jittery wisp of a man, an emaciated five-foot vegan who couldn't bring himself to swat a wasp, let alone kill Henry. None of them could have killed Henry.

Two old blokes are sitting in the hotel bar, mumbling at each other over two-inch Scotches. One of them is our friend Mr Latimer, who slowly finds a match for our faces in the scrambled card index of his memory and greets us with a squint, as if we're approaching from a mile off. We explain our business to his companion and from the depths of his armchair he regards us with eyes that are dissolving in their little puddles of rheum. Gravely as a High Court judge he considers the question of the dead tramp. His chin sinks into the folds of an outsized paisley cravat. He might be falling asleep, so long does he take to formulate a response, but at last he replies: 'No. I'm sorry. Didn't know the chap.' It's as if we'd asked him for the loan of a thousand quid. We take our leave, then there's a tap on the shoulder and Yousif introduces himself, having overheard our exchange with Tweedlepissed and Tweedlestewed.

Yousif is a Lebanese lad, mid twenties, with hair like moleskin and quick dark eyes that betray an excessive eagerness to please. He works as an odd-job man and is helping to patch up the hotel in the comatose months, replacing some skirting boards, doing a bit of rewiring, unclogging the drains and so on. He himself never spoke to Henry, he tells us, but his friend Malak did, many times. Malak worked in the hotel kitchen last year. Late one night, at the end of a long shift, he went out of the back door and there was Henry, grubbing around in the bins. Everyone else had left by then, so Malak went back inside and put together a bag of food for him. They talked for a few minutes, and after that night Malak would make up a parcel of leftovers for Henry whenever he could. When he finished work, he'd leave the food on one of the little dunes, wrapped in foil, for Henry to collect. Sometimes he didn't have to put it in the box, because he'd see Henry on the beach and they'd walk together for a while. Henry wanted to know all about Malak's life and his family, and there was a lot to tell, because Malak had six brothers living in four different countries, and there were four sisters too, at home. 'And cousins, so many cousins,' says Yousif, gesturing as if to raise the spectres of Malak's relatives on the lawns in front of the hotel. 'And they would fire Malak's gun, sometimes,' he adds, securing Ian's attention, which was beginning to slacken. 'It was Malak's hobby. He was a soldier and he likes guns. He has great eyes,' he says, making a finger-pistol and taking aim at the nearest lamp-post. 'Malak had an air rifle, a good one,' he tells us. 'Very expensive. In the morning, early, very early, he went down to the beach to shoot his gun. Sometimes he met Henry there. He went there and sometimes Henry would be there. He would put a small thing, a coin or something, in the sand, and he could hit it from fifty metres, every time,' says Yousif, dumbfounded with admiration. 'And Henry was good. Not every time, but he could hit the coin. He knew about guns.' But how much Henry knew about guns, and how he came to know it, Yousif does not know. Malak himself didn't know much about Henry, because Henry didn't like to talk about himself. He liked to hear about Malak's family but never spoke about his own, and this gave Malak the feeling that none of Henry's people were alive. All Malak really knew about Henry was that his home was on the beach and his full name was Henry Wilson.

'And where's Malak now?' Ian asks.

'He left in September.'

'Do you know where he is?'

'Gone,' says Yousif, with the shrug of a young man who has almost become inured to the perpetual disappointments of life in England. We suspect that Malak was last year's one new friendship.

'Wilson, you said?' asks Ian, writing it down.

As expected, sharpshooter Malak has no official existence: no

National Insurance, no bank account, no forwarding address. He's moved on to some other kitchen and the chances of finding him are vanishingly slim. Malak said he would get in touch when he found a job, Yousif tells us; he promises to let us know if he hears anything.

A full day's footslogging had established little more than that Henry had a degree of expertise in the handling of air rifles, but at the next morning prayers it turns out that Henry Wilson-Ellis-Yarrow-McBain-McCain-McSwain had another skill. A woman named Martha Swinton, in the first week of December, around the fourth or fifth, had been driving out of Knowle when her car cut out and cruised to a standstill. There was heavy fog, and Martha was turning the ignition key over and over again, praying that the thing would miraculously spark into life, when she looked up and saw this wild-looking man looming out of the fog. It was Henry – or rather, it was the homeless man from the beach, as she knew him. Purposefully Henry strode towards the immobilised car, as if he'd been summoned to rescue her, and as he came nearer he was making a gesture that she took to be threatening, before she realised he was miming the action of pulling the bonnet release. Indicating that she should stay in the car, he hoisted the bonnet, then came round to the passenger's side and rapped on the window. Martha wound down the window. 'I need to listen inside,' he told her. This was something of a quandary, being stuck in the fog with this fairly frightening old man demanding admittance to your vehicle, but he waited patiently beside the door and after a few seconds, seeing her hesitation, he suggested that, if she was scared, she could step out of the car as he got in and get back in when he stepped out, so she stayed in the car and opened the door for him. 'Thank you,' he said, but he didn't actually get in, not completely. Instead, he knelt on the road and bent his head into the footwell, placing an ear close to the floor. He seemed to be wearing about a dozen T-shirts, and his clothes gave off a reek of old seaweed. 'Turn the key,' he ordered. Martha turned the key. 'Once more,' he said. Martha turned the key again, and he nodded like a diagnosing doctor at whatever it was he'd been hearing. Then he got out of the car, saying nothing. 'Again,' he instructed her from behind the bonnet. She turned the key and a moment later Henry came round to her window. 'We need a bit of wire,' he told her. 'You don't have a bit of wire, do you? No. Of course you don't have a bit of wire. Why would you have a bit of wire? Right. Wait here.' These words were addressed not to Martha directly but to a point somewhere over her shoulder, as if to a back-seat passenger whose incompetence was to blame for the situation. He loped down the hill, vanishing into the mist. Martha waited and half an hour later, just as she'd decided that Henry wasn't coming back, he reappeared, looking angry. He didn't speak, but went straight back under the bonnet. She could hear him muttering loudly while he worked, perhaps to himself, but perhaps to her as well. 'Turn the switch and the light bulb comes on but what's happened to make it come on? What's the science? Do you know? No, you don't have a clue,' she heard. He was going on about televisions and computers and telephones, and how we don't understand anything. The implication seemed to be that only trained mechanics should be allowed to drive cars. Martha did not take issue. In mid-mutter he interrupted himself with a shout of 'Again!'. The car started and Henry slammed the bonnet with more force than required. He crouched at the road-side, wiping his hands on the wet grass. 'That'll do for a mile or two,' he said. 'Tell your garage it's the fuel pump relay. What's your name?' he asked, quite aggressively, with no pause between the statement and the question.

'Martha Swinton,' she replied and immediately, before she could thank him for the repair, he'd turned his back and was walking away as if there were another car awaiting his attention somewhere in the murk.

Like Henry and Malak playing snipers on the beach, the episode of Martha's car adds a bit of colour to the victim profile, but neither story gets us very far, and as we listen to the report, imagining the scene, we're all thinking the same thing: this case is a runner; Henry will be with us for ever. At a stretch you could argue that Henry's trick with the bit of wire gives some credibility to the tale told to Peggy Thurlow, but you don't have to be an engineer to know what to do when a fuel pump relay is on the blink. And the one fact of obvious significance – that Henry was definitely alive in the first week of December – is superseded within minutes, because one of the lads has spoken to a Mrs Turley, who was visiting her sister on the morning of 9 December – the day of her wedding anniversary, so she remembers the date clearly – and saw Henry sitting on the sea wall. It's the latest reliable sighting we've had so far and we're never to get a later one.

'OK,' says George Whittam, summing up. 'Still among the living on the ninth. Understands motors. Handy with a rifle. Another alias. Is that it?' His eyes have the look of a man facing hours of futile paperwork, but George likes to end with a flourish, and now he lifts a manila folder from the desk and produces the picture, a dozen copies of it. Wearing the *SeaShed* T-shirt and the swimming trunks that Ian bought for him, Henry sits on a boulder, peering at the sea, with one hand on his whiskers in a venerable hermit kind of pose. It's a good photo: a bit arty, but clear. Last night a young woman had phoned, extremely upset, having just heard that Henry was dead. An hour later she walked into Ilfracombe station and delivered the photo, taken by herself last October.

'Fair-haired, plump, average height, twenties?' someone asks.

'Redhead,' says George, as he hands the name and address to Ian. 'For you two,' he says. '*Cherchez la femme*.'

8

The door opens and we're looking at a young woman in grey tracksuit leggings and a baggy grey T-shirt, late twenties, not slim, five-six or five-seven. Her hair, gathered in a twist and secured with a pair of chopsticks, is a colour that some people might classify as red but most would describe as fair or strawberry blonde. We both know at once that we're looking at Henry's walking companion, and at least one of us is thinking it's odd that her face didn't make much of an impression on Tom Gaskin, because it's not the kind of face you see every day of the week. There's something Slavic about the breadth and slope of her cheekbones, and about her eyes, which are narrow and deep-set, and set slightly at an upward angle. The nose, small and somewhat flattened at the bridge, is interesting too, and rather delicate, whereas her mouth is wide and full-lipped, with a distinct ridge above the upper lip, and her jaw is deep and heavy, almost masculine, some would say. Her brow juts out a little, which tends to give her a brooding appearance, and her skin isn't terrific. You couldn't imagine anyone describing Hannah Rowe as pretty, but nobody with functioning visual apparatus could deny that her face has strength, an unusual strength.

She shakes hands with both of us: her grip is strong and her skin surprisingly rough. She precedes us up the stairs to her flat, into a room that has no curtains or blinds. The floorboards are unvarnished and there's just one rug in the middle of the room, a big square of thick chalk-coloured wool with a small square of turquoise inset at one end. There's hardly any furniture: a futon against the wall near the edge of the rug, a couple of leather beanbags, one wicker armchair, that's the lot. A few books are lying on the floor, and there are some shelves of books and cassettes in the corner opposite the futon, above the TV and hi-fi and a tree branch that's propped against the wall, stripped of its bark and as white as veal. The walls are a colour that seems off-white at first, but as the hour passes and the light changes in the room it acquires a tinge that's greenish-grey, and in the centre of one wall there's a row of photographs, each the size of a magazine page. All these pictures show the same thing – a field and a drystone wall – and all were taken from exactly the same place, so the wall runs diagonally across the top right-hand corner, but the images are different, because the light is not the same in any two, so in some the wall is grey and in others black or fawn or even pink, while the field itself is not the same hue of green from one shot to the next. And by the door there are some of pieces of cloth, pressed under glass. They're not patterned or embroidered, like the samples in the *Heidi* house. These are just scraps of material, each dyed a single colour: a blue, a red, a yellow. One of them is black. That's all it is: a bit of black rag. Ian notices it on his way in and you can see that he's instantly decided that we've an arty poser on our hands.

Hannah waves us towards the futon and the armchair. Crossing her ankles, she sits down on the floor, swiftly, easily, and her back is absolutely straight when she's sitting, like someone who does a lot of yoga. For a few seconds she stares into the floor and a profound frown appears, as if she's seeing on the floorboards a picture of Henry. 'So,' she whispers, and she glances up, but at the sky, not at either of us. 'You found him on the second?'

'He was found on the second of January, yes,' replies Ian, employing the tone you'd take with relatives of the bereaved.

'Where?'

'On the beach. Midway between the end of the road and Straight Point.'

She nods, once again gazing downwards. 'And he was murdered.'

'He'd been stabbed.'

Now she begins to pick at a loose strip of wood in the floor, a splinter two or three inches long. It makes a buzzing sound as she plucks it, which she does repeatedly. Tears are budding in her eyes. 'When?' she asks.

'We don't know for certain. Mid December. Around then.'

'So he was out there for two weeks?'

'Possibly.'

'And where is he now?'

'The body's in the mortuary. We need to find the next of kin.' Ian waits for her to respond, but she's pinching at her lip as she regards the sky and there's no sign that a reply is imminent.

Perceiving that we're dealing with someone who's in a less than entirely stable state of mind, Ian quietly clears his throat. 'Your picture. It was taken in October. Is that right?'

'That's right,' she replies abstractedly.

'And when was the last time you saw him? Can you recall?'

Hannah is gazing out of the window, but you can't tell whether she's thinking about the question or counting the clouds. She presses her fingers to her eyes, then examines her fingertips. 'End of November,' she says at last. 'The last Thursday in November.'

'You're sure about that?'

'Absolutely.'

'Can you tell us about his state of mind? Did he seem worried about anything?'

'It was getting colder. He was worried about that.'

'Anything apart from that? Did he say anything about any difficulties he'd had with anyone, any argument?'

'No.'

'He didn't talk about any people he'd seen recently?'

'No.'

'No incident of any kind?'

'No. Obviously.'

'Why obviously?'

'Because I'd have said at the start, wouldn't I? Henry's dead. You want to find out who killed him. I want to find out who killed him. If I had a clue, I'd have said.'

Ian counts voicelessly to five and takes out his notebook. 'So nothing out of the ordinary,' he says, pretending to write. 'Can you tell us anything about his family?'

For a good half-minute Hannah remains silent, sullenly messing with the floorboard, then she shakes her head. 'I don't think he had any,' she says.

'Did he tell you he didn't have any family?'

'The few times he spoke about his parents, it made me think that they were no longer alive. He never mentioned any other relatives.'

'But did he ever actually state that he had no family? Explicitly?'

'No,' she says, dragging the word out, losing patience. 'He never actually said that. Explicitly. I think he was on his own. I think he'd been on his own for a long time.'

'So would you say you knew him well?'

'No. Of course not,' she says, twanging the strip of wood.

'But as well as anyone around here?'

'Possibly. Probably. I don't know. Possibly. If he had any family I think he'd have told me.'

'We heard that Henry was often seen walking with a young woman. Might that have been you?'

'"Often seen",' she quotes under her breath, in a tone of bitter amusement.

'So it was you, do you think?'

'I suppose it was. Who had us under surveillance?'

'You were noticed.'

'I wouldn't say often.'

'What then?'

'From time to time we went for a walk,' she concedes.

This requires from Ian a count of ten. 'You last saw him more than a month before he was discovered, yes?' he continues.

'That's what I said.'

'Would you have expected to see him during that period?'

'No.'

'So you saw him less frequently than once a month, on average?'

'No.'

'More frequently?'

'Sometimes.'

'But in December you didn't have any reason to think something might be wrong?'

'No, I didn't,' she answers, turning to look directly at him for the first time since opening the door. 'I didn't have any reason because I was not here. I've been in London. I went to London at Christmas and when I got back I saw the poster and I brought the picture in,' she says to Ian. 'So you can strike me off the list of suspects.'

'We don't have a list, Ms Rowe,' says Ian, writing. 'What was Henry's surname, do you know?'

'Baldwin,' she says and Ian gives a small wry grin which Hannah, though she's no longer facing him, notices.

'What's funny?' she demands.

'I wouldn't say funny,' Ian tells her. 'Baldwin's about the tenth name we've had for him. We've had Wilson, Ellis, McBain. And Yarrow. We've had others as well.'

Hannah resumes picking at the splinter, one pluck per second. 'Well,' she says with a shrug, 'Baldwin it was. That's what he told me.' Chewing at her lip, in something like a sulk, she looks out of the window, reading the sky.

At this point it should be said that in addition to the track-suit leggings and the shapeless T-shirt, Hannah does not seem to be wearing very much, and Ian is having difficulty, at times, in maintaining a respectful sight line. After the naming of Henry, when Hannah's attention has returned to the world outside, Ian takes the opportunity for another sly appraisal of the comely bosom, and his gaze is continuing southwards when Hannah quickly turns round, as if remembering something she wanted to say. What happens now is that she turns away from Ian, who for most of the next ten minutes might as well be elsewhere, and asks of his colleague, as if out of whimsical curiosity, 'Do you ever speak?'

'I tend to be the listener.'

'Like good cop, bad cop? Talking cop, listening cop?'

'Something along those lines.'

For an instant Hannah comes close to smiling. 'He was nice to talk to, you know?' she says, letting the tears run. 'He was such a nice man.' For a few seconds she maintains eye contact, then her eyes change with a flash of anguish that makes them widen, as if startled by herself. 'Fuck,' she says through clenched teeth, swiping the tears off her face, but you can't tell if she's cursing her own crying or the fate of her murdered friend. 'Fuck. Fuck. Fuck,' she repeats passionlessly, glaring at the wall, at the sky, at her wetted hands. Her fury expelled, she turns back to the favoured policeman, presenting herself as someone who is now ready to talk. And talk she does, at length, as if she's been called as a character witness for Henry Whoever.

It is important to her that we should appreciate his resourcefulness, his toughness, his gentleness, his refusal to complain about the lousy hand that life had dealt him. Despite the kindness of Malak (whose name is invoked like the name of the Good Samaritan), there were days on which Henry ate nothing, but Henry didn't moan about going hungry – he simply remarked on it, as you or I might comment on a day on which the sun didn't shine. In short, indigent yet uncomplaining, Henry had a rare air of dignity about him. Henry was charismatic. Henry was his own man.

'Which is the reason we're here,' mutters Ian, who has been studying a fish tank that stands in a corner of the room, a fish tank filled with clear water and one-quarter filled with shells, crab claws, stones and miscellaneous beach debris, but apparently devoid of fish. 'When he went AWOL, where did he get to? Any idea?' he asks, addressing the side of Hannah's face.

'Last year it was Penzance, during the summer,' she replies, as though the question had been put not by Ian but by his companion. And he was in Plymouth too, on the same trip. Why he'd gone there, how he'd got there, how long he'd spent there, she can't say. When he came back from his travels he usually didn't seem to know where he'd been. Once he was away for a short time, no more than a week, and when she next saw him a bus ticket fell out of his pocket while they were talking, and he picked it up and looked at it as if he'd never seen it before. And a couple of years back, she remembers, Henry reappeared wearing a T-shirt that had come from some car museum, yet Henry was almost certain he hadn't been to any such place.

'Almost certain?' Ian interjects, having decided that the fishless fish tank is evidence in favour of the judgement he'd made on the basis of the black rag by the door.

'That's right,' Hannah responds coolly, again to the non-speaker.

'So he was confused,' Ian summarises. 'Mentally confused.'

'That's not how I'd put it.'

'How would you put it?'

'He was confused when he saw the ticket. When I asked him about the museum. But from day to day his mental state wasn't confused.'

Mimicking the perplexity of the dense, Ian scratches his head, scowling at the effort of thinking. 'You're going to have to run that one by me again,' he says. 'He goes walkabout for a few days and when he comes back here he doesn't have a clue where he's been but his mind isn't confused? I'm not getting it.'

Bestowing on Ian a brief irritated glance, Hannah explains, speaking slowly to the wall behind him. 'When you talked to Henry he wasn't confused. He made sense. He understood what you were saying to him. He answered in sentences. OK? But when he came back from his walkabout, as you put it, he seemed to have lost the time that he'd been away. It was as if he'd been sleep-walking. Make sense to you now?'

'In my experience, when people wake up after sleepwalking they tend to be confused.'

'He was, at first, a bit. But he wasn't confused in the way you meant it.'

'And how did I mean it?'

'On the way to ga-ga. He was more blank than confused.'

'So if you said to him, "Henry, where were you yesterday?" he'd say, "I haven't a clue?" Is that right?'

'He'd remember stuff. Things he'd seen.'

'In that case he wasn't blank, was he?'

'Not entirely, no. He'd remember bits and pieces, but they wouldn't join up. Things would be vague. Like remembering a dream.'

'Sounds to me like he needed medical attention.'

'That's not the sort of help he needed.'

'What sort did he need?'

'Some money wouldn't have gone amiss,' Hannah replies. Asked whether Henry was as vague about the more distant past as he was about the weeks just gone, she confirms that he was and smiles faintly to herself as she says it, as if Henry had cleverly anticipated the problems his vagueness would cause after he'd gone. He once lived in London, many years ago. Sometimes he talked about buildings or places in the city and he'd struggle to see them clearly, because it was so long since he'd been there. He said that explicitly. Did Henry ever name any friends or acquaintances he might once have had? No, there were no names, none that she could recall at the moment. How did Henry come to be homeless, did she know that? She knew that he'd lost his job and that he lost his home as a consequence. What was the job? Henry didn't say. Where was it? Henry didn't say. How long ago? Henry didn't say.

'You didn't ask him?' Ian intervenes.

'If he wanted to tell me more, he'd have told me more,' Hannah firmly replies, as if repeating a rule that Ian had forgotten. 'If he didn't, he'd change the subject. He'd shrug and go quiet, and that would be the end of it.' Again she consults the sky, which seems to bring the recollection of a particular episode with Henry. She is about to speak, then halts herself, narrowing her eyes, putting her thoughts in order. 'With Henry the past was dead,' she says, and grimaces at herself, because that's not quite right. 'It was irrelevant to him. He was lonely and bored a lot of the time, but he never gave the impression of being nostalgic for the life he'd lost. Or hardly ever. There was no bitterness in him. What was gone was gone. He was where he was, and he was making the best of it. But occasionally he'd remember something,' Hannah goes on, offering a rueful smile. She inspects a finger, attending to a speck of dirt caught under a nail before continuing. 'He'd be struck by a memory. It would just seem to hit him, out of nowhere. Little things: what something looked like. A street, a market, a face. He'd be really jolted by it, and delighted, for a while, then he'd begin to get sad and he'd do this,' she says, with a swat of the hand. 'Move on. No dwelling on the past.'

Stifling a yawn that appears rhetorical, Ian closes his notebook. 'Cuts down the topics for conversation, doesn't it? If your past is off the menu,' he observes. 'You say you liked talking to him. What was there to talk about? I mean, it's not as if he'd had an action-packed day at the office.'

The crudity of the question makes Hannah sigh. They talked about the things they could see, she explains. They talked about what she'd been doing since the last time he saw her, about things that had happened in the town, about the weather, the news, the things people talk about.

Ian's notebook goes into a pocket; it's time to wind up. 'But he never named anyone he knew? He saw faces but they had no names?' he asks in conclusion.

'No.'

'Remarkable.'

'That's the way it was,' says Hannah, again not to Ian. She's staring at the photographs of the field with the drystone wall, remembering something about Henry, it appears.

'Well, if you think of anything else, call us on this number,' Ian finishes, depositing a card on the floor beside her knee.

She gives the card a second of her attention. Henry could tell when it was going to rain, she adds. His fingers would swell up and shrink with the changing air pressure. The pulse in his wrists would become so prominent, it was like looking at the flank of a frog as it breathed. He was like a human barometer, never wrong, she says.

The next day new flyers were issued, using Hannah's photograph instead of the fuzzy beach snap, and stations in London were given the new improved mugshot. The response was silence. It felt as if we were lobbing marbles into a bog.

9

One Monday lunchtime we take a message from Tom Gaskin, saying he has some information that might be useful and asking us to drop by his house, whenever was convenient, so as soon as the paperwork is out of the way, around five, we drive over there. As when we'd left him all those days ago, he's sitting at the table in the window, wearing a crisp white shirt, though on this occasion the tie is a stripy blue-and-yellow cricket-club number. When he sees us arrive he gives us a stiff slow wave of the forearm, a tired and polite little gesture, like the wave of a man at a car park barrier greeting the five hundredth driver of the day. You get the impression he's been sitting there for hours, staring out at the sea and the hills.

He seats us around the table, asks if either of us would like tea or coffee, glances at the view from his window, passes comment on the weather. He asks us how the investigation is proceeding and immediately revokes the question, apologising for its impertinence. Then there is no longer any way of delaying. Stroking the backs of his hands, as if trying to rub the creases out of his skin, he begins. 'This may not be of any consequence,' he says, and gives the scratches in the table top a quizzical look, as if distracted for a moment by the problem of how the table came to be scratched. 'Well, you can tell me if it's of any consequence, can't you?' he continues. 'I was sitting here, last Sunday, in this very seat, last Sunday lunchtime. It was shortly after one o'clock. I know that, because the news had just started. On the radio. I was sitting here and I looked over that way, towards where that boat is.' He points steadily towards the horizon, leaving his finger in mid air until we have both looked in the indicated direction. What had caught his attention was a kite, a bright-pink kite, that had come loose and was flying across the beach. Then he saw this young man, a rather unkempt character, walking very slowly, round and round the same spot, close to the sea wall, where Henry sometimes used to bed down for the night. Round and round he went, examining the ground, as though he'd dropped something, then he sat down on the parapet and stayed there for quite a time, looking out at the sea, which was also a bit peculiar, Tom thought, because it wasn't a nice day. Lightly raining, in fact. After that he walked off, around the headland. An hour later he came back and resumed his search of the sand. This went on for another ten minutes or so. Quite odd behaviour, Tom thought, but in itself perhaps not worth remarking on. 'Some folk like the rain, don't they?' he adds. 'I quite like it myself.'

It would be difficult to be more long-winded than Tom Gaskin, and we know that this conversation is going to yield nothing that could not have been relayed to us over the phone. And that's the reason for all the words, to disguise the fact that our presence isn't strictly necessary, not for us, anyway. Tom Gaskin is the loneliest man in town.

'Unkempt?' asks Ian, applying a full stop with an audible tap that he hopes will convey a need for greater momentum.

'That's right. But the thing is,' Tom resumes, dragging his chair closer to the table, 'on Tuesday, after lunchtime, soon after 1.30, I saw the same young man, on a bicycle this time, one of those mountain bikes. He was riding on the sand, and he stopped in the same place and stayed there for a quarter of an hour I'd say, looking around, before he went off towards Straight Point. And again he was gone for an hour or so.'

'Definitely the same person?' Ian enquires. 'I mean, it's quite a distance down to the beach. I don't think I could positively identify someone from this range.'

It was unequivocally the same person, says Tom, and to support his certainty he pulls back the curtain to reveal a huge pair of binoculars on the sill. He used to be a teacher, he explains, a schoolteacher. Biology was his subject, and zoology was always his great love, ornithology in particular. He does a lot of birdwatching, locally and all over the country and abroad, since Helen died, which was eight years ago now, almost. Last year he went to Spain, for the migration, and the year before that as well, he tells us, adjusting the curtains, then he notices the fleeting impatience of Ian's expression. 'I've wandered off the point,' he observes, shaking his head. 'That was always my problem. At home and in the classroom. Always meandering. But where was I?' he asks with a smile for Ian in which there seems to be dismay, bordering on alarm, at his own incoherence.

'Definitely the same person.'

'Oh yes. It was. No question about it. And on Thursday he was there again. The middle of the day, on his bicycle, same place. The same young man. Definitely the same person. Three times within five days, that's what you'd call a pattern of behaviour, isn't it?'

'It's certainly notable,' says Ian, making a note.

Tom waits for the pen to stop moving. 'And four times in a week, that's suspicious, I'd say,' he adds, and is gratified to see the upturn of Ian's eyebrows.

'He was there yesterday?'

'He was. Two o'clock. Same chap. But on this occasion he went that way,' he says, pointing to the path across the High Land.

'Could you describe him?'

Indeed Tom could describe him. Most eyewitnesses can give you two or three points, if you're lucky. Even if they'd had a good clear look, a long look, by the following day it's likely that all that's left in the memory bank is 'blue eyes', 'tall', 'well-built'. And when you bring the suspect in, he has blue eyes all right, but he's five-nine and no more well-built than Joe Average. But he has a finger missing from one hand, which nobody noticed. You could point someone in the direction of a particular person for five minutes, tell them to memorise what they are seeing, and twenty-four hours later not much would remain. Tom, though, he gives us height, narrowness of shoulders, approximate weight and age, hairstyle and colour, colour of jacket, colour of trousers, make of trainers ('the ones with the tick'), colour of laces ('bright blue'), oddity of gait ('hunched, flatfooted, listing'), general demeanour ('very agitated'), size of hands ('unusually large'). No eye colour, but otherwise all you could hope for.

There's so much detail that Ian is struggling to keep pace. 'This is a very precise description, sir,' he says, turning the page.

'Birdwatchers tend to be observant people,' Tom replies, but he lets Ian finish his notes before adding, with a little grin for himself: 'I followed him, you see.'

'You followed him?'

'I did. I was curious. I wanted to find out what he was up to,' says Tom forthrightly, giving each of us a level look.

'And what was he up to?'

'Well, he walked over the headland, to the steps, and he went down to the beach. He walked part of the way to Straight Point, then stopped, and seemed to be searching again. Going round and round in circles. That's what prompted me to call you,' Tom says, and now he reaches back and takes from the sideboard a large-scale Ordnance Survey map. He spreads it open on the table, turning the south side towards us, and places a finger with care on the midpoint of the bay. 'He was standing there. For two or three minutes I observed him and he didn't move more than a few yards from that spot. Looking on the ground, he was, scraping at the sand with his foot. Then he was staring out to sea for a while and after a minute or so it seemed to occur to him that he might be being watched, which is when he saw me.'

'How did he react when he saw you?'

'I couldn't see any reaction of any kind. He seemed to notice me and then he carried on looking at the sea. He didn't move from there,' he says, tapping the map. 'This is where your chap was found, isn't it? So this person might know something,' Tom suggests, almost childishly pleased at the possibility that he may have helped, and we agree that this would appear to be likely. We ask him to phone us right away should another sighting occur. 'Of course, of course,' he replies keenly, looking out at the hill with anticipation, as if it were a stage on which a show was soon to begin. 'If he comes, I'll see him. I have nothing better to do on a Sunday,' he jokes, but he means it, and there's a small fading in his eyes that tells us that he knows that we know that he means it. He allows us to regard him for a moment. We look at him and at the underused room, a room that smells of furniture polish and tedium. It's easy to imagine the Sundays here: read the papers, a cup of tea and sandwich for lunch, an hour or two sitting at the table, watching the hills and the sea, an hour or two with a book before a microwaved meal for one, a bit of TV, perhaps with a glass of something, then bed. Dead Henry and the shifty lad are a godsend for Tom. 'Well,' he says, with a questioning undertone, slapping his thighs lightly, acknowledging that our conversation is concluded while inviting us, tentatively, to share our thoughts with him. We can do nothing more than thank him and ask him again to call us. He gives his thighs another slap, impelling himself to stand.

'Did you find the girl?' he asks abruptly at the door, as though startled by the sudden recollection of what he'd told us on our first visit.

'Yes, we found her.'

Putting his hand over his heart, Tom releases a tremulous breath. 'Oh good, good,' he says, so relieved you'd think we were talking about a girl who'd been kidnapped. 'Can she help you?'

'We hope so,' says Ian. 'We have to hurry, John. That meeting starts at six.'

'Of course. I'm sorry. Thank you for coming by,' says Tom, with a long handshake for both of us.

'And thank you again for the information.'

'I hope it's useful,' says Tom. As we begin to move away, he takes a step backwards into the hall. Under the light bulb the skin of his face looks as thin as a film of flesh-coloured plastic.

'I think it will be.'

'I hope so,' he says. 'I hope so,' he repeats, smiling, disappearing slowly behind the closing door.

The meeting at six is in the pub, with Mary and Rachelle, but the girls aren't there when we arrive. 'It's da poliss,' Josh calls across the bar. 'How's it going? Any breakthrough?' There's no breakthrough, he's told, but as soon as there is he'll be the first to know. Josh pours the pints, smirkingly watching Ian, who's checking his watch every few seconds. 'I'll tell you what you should do,' he says, taking care to place each glass plumb centre on its mat, to crank up the tension a bit. He wipes a scatter of droplets off the bar, as Ian bears the drinks away. 'What you should do is talk to a woman called Hannah Rowe. Lives near here. I can give you the address if you like.'

'Why should we be talking to Ms Rowe?'

'Because Ms Rowe knew the old man, that's why,' says Josh, giving a cheery mock-simpleton's grin.

'And who is Ms Rowe?'

'She did this,' Josh answers, indicating the whole room. 'Painted the walls, the ceiling, the lot. And that's hers as well,' he says, pointing to a picture on a nearby pillar, a painting of the esplanade under mist, with a sea as dark as engine oil behind it. 'Interesting girl. She's very good. Not cheap,' he says, examining the walls, approving the quality of the work, 'but worth every penny.' And here, perhaps, it is intended that an innuendo be heard. It's possible, though, that the tone exists only in the memory of what was said, overdubbed on to it.

Then Mary and Rachelle arrive. 'John's just on his way home,' says Ian to Rachelle, but John stays for another one, and a third.

10

For the best part of twenty years Jim Jackson worked in a timber-yard, but then one Monday morning, blurred by the residue of a weekend's heroic boozing, he lost his focus at an inopportune moment and lopped half of his right hand clean off with a band-saw, and after that, one way and another, he wasn't much good for anything and spent most of the day at home or in the park, drinking and sleeping and drinking some more. In the evenings he might smack his wife about a bit, and from time to time he'd read a bedtime story to his daughter, Jemima, and then, often as not, he'd do something with his daughter that was their little secret and stayed their little secret long after bedtime stories came to an end, until the day Jemima forgot to bolt the bathroom door and her mother walked in and saw Jemima cleaning herself up. So Jim received a hefty sentence and Jim's wife jettisoned his surname and took herself and her daughter off to the other end of the country, where Jemima Kingham, despite the best efforts of her mother, grew into a desperate and highly volatile young woman, given to dicing her arms with razors and fucking any deadbeat who'd share his bag of glue with her. Jemima was a mess, but she knew she was a mess and when, aged eighteen, she found herself pregnant for the third time, she decided she'd see this one through and would do everything she could to make the kid's life a good one.

Jessie, her daughter, was born in February 1971. The father, whose name is lost to us, presented himself at the hospital the day after Jessie's arrival. He put a bunch of flowers on the bed, kissed the baby, sat with Jemima for an hour or two. 'I'll be going then,' he said, giving Jemima a peck on the cheek, and that was the end of his participation in the project. His vanishing was no great surprise to Jemima, nor a great setback, and she knuckled down to the project of raising Jessie alone. She'd do anything to provide for the girl. Saturdays and Sundays were for her daughter; the rest of the week she worked herself stupid. She cleaned other people's houses during the day and cleaned offices in the evening. For a whole year she scarcely saw daylight, putting in nine hours in a basement laundry before going off to swab hospital corridors through the night. 'Trust nobody,' she'd tell the girl. 'Don't owe anything to anyone.' In 1987 she was working in a flower shop from nine to five, in a pub from eight to midnight, and was giving after-hours blowjobs for a fiver. 'Stay away from boys,' she would tell Jessie, and Jessie managed to stay away from them until she was fifteen, when Ryan Tate lurched into her life.

With Ryan too you wonder how much of the script was written for him, long before he came along. Semi-employed brawlers and boozers feature prominently in the roll-call of Ryan's ancestors, and the family tree is richly festooned with convictions for burglary, theft, arson, assault and – in the case of the paternal grandfather – grievous bodily harm, the consequence of a dispute over a bet that ended with a Swiss penknife through the face of the simpleton who had dared to impugn the honesty of the senior Mr Tate. You look at where he came from and you feel they might as well have stamped 'Go to gaol' on Ryan's birth certificate, though you wouldn't have known he'd go as badly wrong as he did. He had one advantage over Jessie: both parents were around. On the other hand, they were present only in the technical sense for much of the time, because Mr and Mrs Tate were the family's elite drinkers, never sober for as long as Ryan could remember. At the time of Ryan's arrest neither parent was in work. His father, Dave, had for years been a man with no visible means of support. Aileen, his mother, had recently been working at a supermarket, a rare interlude of gainful employment that had ended when she was observed waving her husband through the checkout with four unpurchased bottles of vodka in his coat pockets, a routine which had probably been in operation from the day she started the job. As for Ryan, having continued the family tradition by renouncing education at the earliest opportunity, he did a bit of building work here and there, supplementing his income with regular ventures into breaking and entering, and regular spells in custody. He was also a courier for a local dealer, who paid him in cash and dope, and he'd inherited the family predilection for knife work. The Accident and Emergency waiting room should have had a bench named after him.

The third person in this story is Abby Atalay, also aged fifteen. Abby and her parents and her younger sister shared a flat with her childless aunt and uncle, above the kebab shop that the aunt and uncle ran. Money was tight, but the Atalays weren't poor in the way the Tates and the Kinghams were poor, and they were all perfectly law-abiding. An unexceptional, not terribly bright, somewhat overweight and vulnerable kid, Abby was also half-Turkish, which may be of relevance. Nothing ever happened to Abby, until she had the misfortune to go to the same party as Ryan Tate one night, and get drunk for the first time in her life, and let herself get fucked by him. She imagined that this semiconscious coupling might mean something.

Ryan Tate lived less than half a mile from Jessie Kingham and went to the same school, but it seems their paths never crossed, not in any significant way, before Ryan was eighteen. The fateful meeting took place in April 1987, a month after the party, outside the florist's where Jessie's mother worked. Taking a fancy to her, Ryan offered her a cigarette. The cigarette was declined. They talked for a bit. Ryan offered Jessie one of the cans of lager he had in his bag. This too was declined. Ryan then took a rose from a bucket outside the shop, snapped off the moist end and handed the flower to Jessie. Noticing what was going on, Jessie's mother came out to demand payment. Jemima knew about the Tates and didn't like the look of Ryan one bit. To Jemima the eyes of a Ryan Tate were the eyes of a hopeless and very dangerous young man, and she could see in him more than a passing resemblance to her daughter's father. To Jessie, however, the fierce blue eyes of Ryan Tate gave off the charisma of someone who knew how life really was, and the thick violet scar that ran across his jaw didn't do his image any harm either. Her mother, upon being told by Ryan that payment was unfortunately out of the question due to lack of funds, sent him on his way, in a manner that made it clear to Jessie that his banishment was intended to be permanent. Less than a week later, Ryan came across Jessie outside the pub where her mother worked. The following day they had sex in Ryan's flat, in the middle of the afternoon, while his parents snored in front of the TV, pissed out of their heads. Three or four times a week they'd do it, for the next couple of months, always in Ryan's bedroom. Often his parents were at home, and usually they had no idea that Ryan and Jessie were there too.

At around 7.30 p.m. on 17 June 1987, Ryan Tate helped himself to a couple of beers from his parents' supply, then helped himself to a car that some idiot had left unlocked in a backstreet. He drove past Jessie's place and, as luck would have it, she was at home. With money from her mother's purse they bought some more drink. At about eight o'clock they saw a friend of Ryan's, Trevor Driscoll, walking down the street. He got into the car and they returned to the off-licence, where Trevor contributed a six-pack of lager to the evening's intake. For an hour they drove around town, with Ryan swigging his lager as he cruised the high street in the stolen car. They dropped in on another off-licence, so Jessie could buy some more cans while Ryan nicked a half-bottle of whisky. Then, shortly before 9.30, they passed the Atalays' shop and there was Abby, talking to a friend. Since the party Ryan had seen Abby a few times on the street. In Abby's mind perhaps their relationship had a future. Perhaps she thought that there were some issues to resolve and that now might be the time to resolve them. And perhaps she thought that Trevor Driscoll was Jessie's boyfriend. She said goodbye to her friend and climbed into the car. Ten minutes later Trevor Driscoll got out of the car outside his brother's house, and Ryan Tate, Jessie Kingham and Abby Atalay drove up on to Dartmoor.

From here on there are two different versions of events. Ryan Tate claimed that Jessie had known from the start about Abby Atalay, and that there was nothing going on between himself and Abby any longer, but that Jessie — who was drunk by the time they reached the hills — turned on Abby when Abby tried to kiss him. It was a warm night. They'd parked the car and walked a distance, taking the whisky and some beers with them, but as soon as they sat down Abby flung herself at him and the girls had a fight, which ended when Abby got hurt, though why he found himself incapable of keeping the girls apart was something he could never adequately explain. When he saw the blood, and understood what had happened, he panicked. He admitted that. He panicked and he helped Jessie do what she did. Jessie, for her part, said she knew nothing about Abby and Abby knew nothing about her, until they were in the car together, after they'd dropped Trevor Driscoll. The three of them had a huge argument. Ryan stopped in a lay-by and got out of the car, to get away from them, but they both followed him. They were both yelling at him, but Abby was drunk on the whisky and went bananas, so Ryan hit her. Then Jessie just sort of froze. Which is why she did nothing to stop what Ryan then did to Abby.

So one of them, for some reason that we're unlikely ever to know, hit Abby Atalay very hard with a small rock, hard enough to knock her senseless. Not long afterwards they returned to the car and drove until they came to a petrol station. There they are on CCTV: Jessie in the passenger seat, slurping a beer, laughing at something Ryan says to her as he steadies himself against the pump while he fills the petrol can; and Ryan joking with the cashier, unaware that there's a streak of blood on the underside of his arm. Abby, meanwhile, had regained some degree of consciousness and begun to crawl away, but she'd covered only a very short distance by the time Ryan and Jessie got back, so they found her easily enough and cracked her with a rock once more. They then doused her with petrol and set fire to her. In the opinion of the pathologist, Abby was not quite dead at this moment, but a few seconds later she would have been: a lifetime's allowance of pain packed into half a minute. Ryan or Jessie emptied the can over Abby and went back to the car to wait for the fire to die down. Satisfied with their work, they drove the car a couple of miles, rolled it into a ditch and torched it. They then set off on the twelve-mile hike back home.

By midnight Abby's parents had reported her missing. At two o'clock Jessie's mother had phoned the police to say that her daughter had disappeared. Smoke-stained and spattered with Abby's blood, Jessie and Ryan reeled home in the middle of the morning. Within a few hours they were both charged. It took the jury less than an hour to find them guilty, and they only took that long so as not to appear to have rushed the verdict.

Listening to the story of the murder of Abby Atalay, Alice cried. On the kitchen table lay pictures of the killer teens: pea-brained, psychotic Ryan Tate, whose face says he knows that everyone knows he's lying and he could not give a flying fuck what anyone thinks; and pea-brained, confused Jessie Kingham, who looks terrified by what's happening to her and yet, at the same time, not unpleasantly surprised at finding herself notorious. 'They feel no remorse?' asked Alice, peering at their faces, incredulous at their depravity. All that could be said for a fact was that each was claiming that the other was responsible and that neither had expressed the slightest remorse so far. Jessie perhaps was beginning to feel it, however. Soon she'd go berserk with it and take a jump from a second-storey landing, which would break her neck and leave her in a wheelchair for the rest of her life, an outcome that she seemed to accept with equanimity, as a concluding retribution. But with Ryan Tate it was different. You looked at that face and you knew that for him the death of Abby Atalay was no more important than a dog getting run over in the street. That's how it seemed at the time and that's how it's seemed ever since. Jessie Kingham was the one who killed Abby Atalay, he'll tell you, and it's as if he's telling you that Elvis shot JFK and defying you to tell him that he doesn't believe a word of what he's saying. 'There's no one there,' Alice concluded, staring at his face, meeting the challenge of his empty gaze. Ryan Tate was never mentioned at home again. It was soon afterwards that Alice became a churchgoer.

As with violence among the Tates, godliness among the Pierces was something of a tradition, albeit – unlike the volcanic idiocy of the Tate dynasty – a tradition that recently had fallen into abeyance. Great-grandfather Joseph Pierce, the fountainhead of the river of piety, was a much-honoured man of the cloth, for whose son, Julian, the discovery of the same religious vocation would appear to have been as natural a process as the discovery of the desire to walk or speak. With the career of Elisabeth, the first Pierce daughter in three generations, the transmission of the holy gene suffered something of a setback, or so it appeared for a time. Obediently, even willingly devout as a girl, Elisabeth was diverted from the path of righteousness by the experience of university, the study of medicine and betrothal to the unswervingly secular Mr Jameson, a man for whom the *Financial Times* share index was the truest mirror of the real world, just as *Gray's Anatomy* became the touchstone for Dr Elisabeth. Yet the agonised death of her husband, killed by cancer within two years of the birth of their only child, seems to have been the catalyst for an outbreak of faith in the soul of Dr Elisabeth. This faith sustained her for the rest of her life. To her great credit, though, she never preached to her daughter. She never so much as invited her to accompany her to church, and Alice's belief remained dormant for years, until Dr Elisabeth's final illness, when something began to change in Alice, as she would later say, in the light of her mother's selfless preparation for her own death, from cancer also, and several years short of the average span.

On the day of the funeral she went back into the church after the business at the graveside was done. There was motherless Alice alone in the empty church, smaller than life-size under the high stone ceiling. A pillar of sunlight smacked the paving to the side of her, as if the finger of the Lord had fired a shot of revelation in her direction and missed by a couple of yards. Dry-eyed, Alice was looking at the brass eagle on the lectern, at the place where the coffin had rested on its trestle throughout the service, at all the vacant pews, as if imagining the faces of everyone who had been there. She turned and smiled, and there was a sort of shadowing in her gaze, a dimming that never leaves the eyes of some people after bereavement, and never left Alice. But still whatever it was she believed remained covert and undefined for a while longer. The subterranean stream that flowed down from the heights of Joseph Pierce broke into the open only when those two ambassadors of the devil, Ryan Tate and Jessie Kingham, did their worst. There was no discussion, only a quiet announcement of intention: 'I'm going to church tomorrow.' She was happy to go alone, Alice said, as her mother had said to her, and at first she went alone, gradually becoming someone different. A photo of grandfather Pierce, the blessed Julian, occupies the centre of the very first page of one of the family albums, a veritable lighthouse of virtue, radiating probity through rimless glasses, with a dog collar as bright and stiff as a band of ivory and a haircut like the helmet of God's foot soldier.

11

Eventually, a couple of miles along the coast, Henry's possessions are washed ashore, wrapped in a knotted black refuse
sack. His sleeping bag is in it, plus three T-shirts and a zippered
bag containing a toothbrush and a tube of toothpaste.
Everything has been thoroughly doused in brine, but the technicians in the lab subject each item to every test known to forensic science. There's not a shred of suspicious material on any
of the contents, so that's a dead end, but in the same week a
story seems to be emerging, the story of Henry's misdemeanours. A sergeant in Tavistock, seeing the picture that
Hannah had provided, gets in touch to say that he's ninety-
nine point nine per cent sure that our Henry is the same man
as a character he had come across back in the autumn of 1987.
This person had created a disturbance in a post office, a disturbance that was minor but had proved memorable. There was a
queue of people picking up their pensions and this oddball had
worked his way to the front. Aged about fifty, he was wearing
a tweed jacket and a maroon V-necked jumper over a frayed
white shirt, with beige polyester slacks and beige shoes. In his
hand he had a briefcase that had 'Max Planck Institute' sten-
cilled on the side. Whenever a customer had been served, he

used the briefcase to usher the next person towards the counter. He did this again and again, never taking his turn, but then he began muttering to himself, making remarks that sounded as though they might be offensive but weren't clearly audible. A clerk asked him if he was OK, if he needed any help. 'Fine, thank you,' came the reply. 'I'll just wait.' He waited for another quarter of an hour, letting everyone go before him, and the muttering now became louder, a lot louder. Soon he was ranting about how everyone had been brainwashed but he knew what was really happening and he was going to tell the people at the newspapers all about it. He refused all offers of help and he refused to leave. When the police arrived he was in full flow, abusing everyone in sight, telling them they were sheep and stooges. 'It's your psychology that's the problem,' he told the sergeant, before repeating it for the benefit of the rest of his audience. He gave no further trouble, meekly allowing himself to be escorted from the premises and into the car. On the journey to the station he was polite, fairly coherent on the topic of the aggravations of modern bureaucracy, not at all embarrassed by his behaviour in the post office, and seemed somewhat slow on the uptake, which was generally attributed to the effects of drink: it was obvious that he not wholly sober and there were five cans of lager in the Max Planck bag.

The officer who interviewed him in the station recalls a frustrating conversation that seemed to last for hours, with protracted pauses between question and very terse answer. On the subject of the man's identity, he remembers an exchange that was something like this:

'What is your name?'

Silence and staring into space, as though stunned by the question. Finally: 'Henry.'

'Henry who?'

'Arthur Henry,' he replied, in a way that suggested this was merely the first combination of names to occur to him.

'Arthur Henry?'

Another hiatus, as if unconvinced of the plausibility of the name he'd concocted. 'That's right.'

'And where do you live, Arthur?'

'I don't know.' Here he seemed, briefly, to be troubled by his inability to provide a satisfactory reply.

'You do have somewhere to live?'

'Yes.' Pause. 'I don't know.'

'Which is it?'

'I don't know.'

'Think.'

'I do.'

'And where is it?'

'Near here.'

'Are you sure?'

'I think so. No.'

And so it went on. It was only after they had been talking for ten minutes or so that the officer noticed a dark stain on Arthur Henry's trousers, a few inches above the left ankle, a stain that was definitely larger, and darker, after a few more minutes had passed. When his attention was drawn to it, Mr Henry hoisted the trouser leg to reveal a wound on his shin, a deep and septic wound that had been dressed with a wad of toilet paper, held in place with a strip of tape. Refusing an offer of treatment, Mr Henry continued to answer, confusingly and confusedly, the questions that were put to him. By the interview's end it seemed to have been ascertained that Mr Henry was out of work, had recently been evicted from his lodgings, was hoping to find a bed in a hostel that night, had been intoxicated for three or four days, knew nobody whom the police could call to help him out, and would be all right, thank you very much. No charges were brought.

Of greater interest was an incident that occurred in May 1985 in Plymouth, where a station took a call one morning from the headmistress of a nearby primary school. The previous day, while talking to a member of her staff in the playground, she noticed a slovenly middle-aged man sitting on a wall on the opposite side of the road. There was something about him, not just his shabbiness, that made her keep an eye on him. From the way he kept glancing to left and right, she had the impression that he was waiting for someone, but it seemed a peculiar place to be waiting, and from time to time she'd see him stare across the road at the children, and his stare made her feel uneasy. But what worried her most was that when the bell rang, and she was shepherding the children back to their classrooms, the man jumped down from the wall and walked away. And on the day she called the station he had been there again, throughout the play period, sitting on the wall, glancing around and then staring at the children – not at any particular child, but at all of them. She had seen him smiling to himself. The next day, as arranged, she rang the station the moment the man appeared and a constable was sent along to have a word with him. Seeing the constable approaching, the man didn't budge.

'Good morning, sir,' says the policeman.

'Good morning to you,' comes the reply, with an amiable smile. A whiff of beer comes off him, but he does not seem to be drunk. Each fingernail is capped with a deep crescent of black dirt, yet his clothes, though worn through at the collars and cuffs, are clean enough.

'Could I ask you what you're doing here?'

Contemplating his shoes, the man seems to be giving prolonged consideration to his answer. 'Watching,' he says cheerily. 'Just watching.' And then he yawns, so widely you could pop a tennis ball into his mouth if you felt so inclined.

'Watching what, if you don't mind my asking?'

Slow scrutiny of the school buildings and pavement now follows, before, courteously, with a hint of whimsicality, he replies: 'I'm watching the children.'

'And why would you be watching them?'

This requires so much thought that a repetition of the question is needed. 'Because I like to watch children,' the man at last responds, and the baldness of the statement somewhat stumps the constable. 'Don't you like children?'

'Yes.'

'Have children of your own, do you?' the man enquires, taking charge of the conversation.

'Yes.'

'How many?'

'Two.'

'Boy and girl?'

'Two boys.'

'Ages?'

'Seven and nine.'

The man ponders this information. 'Boys get a bad press,' he concludes.

The subsequent silence is a cue for the constable to regain the initiative. 'These children are other people's children, sir. It's not quite the same as watching your own kids.'

This proposition, too, demands an interlude of silent thought. 'Yes,' he concedes. 'I can see that.'

'You've been seen here before, I'm told. Is that the case?'

'It is.'

'Yesterday?'

'Yes.'

'And the day before?'

'Yes.'

'Watching the playground?'

'Yes,' he says, frowning, as if puzzled as to where this line of questioning might be leading.

'I have to ask you to move on, sir. And to refrain from coming back.'

'I understand,' he murmurs, seeming to understand nothing.

'People tend to take a dim view of strangers watching their children. It gives them ideas. The teachers don't like you sitting here. It worries them. They wonder what you're up to.'

'I'm watching the children.'

'Yes, sir. And they would rather you didn't. I would rather you didn't. So if you don't mind –'

Unresistingly permitting the constable to take him by the elbow, the man descends from the wall. With a shake of the hand and without a protest he walks away. The following week he's back, at playtime, sitting on the wall, watching. At a call from the school, the same policeman returns. A strange conversation ensues, recapitulating much of what was said a week before, because the man behaves as though the previous week's warning had never happened, as if he's never seen this policeman before. And, as before, he appears to be slow to comprehend the objection to his presence and departs readily, obligingly, once it has been explained to him. A fortnight passes and he's there yet again, sitting on the wall, watching the kids at play. This time, although the man behaves as if neither of the previous episodes had occurred, and indeed seems perplexed, distressed even, when the policeman insists that they have had this conversation twice before, a warning is administered, threats of custody issued. The man gives his name as Henry Ellis. He is unemployed, he says. He's recently been evicted from his lodgings and is going to a hostel that night. The yawning, the eye colour, the height, the build, the pauses – it's our Henry, of course.

Within a week we hear of another incident. In Honiton, in 1983, a constable spoke to a man who was loitering outside a primary school. Three times in three weeks the local police spoke to him. His name, or the name that he gave, is not recorded, but the description of Henry chimes with what the Honiton police remember of the man's appearance. Some peculiarly wide-mouthed yawning is vividly recalled. The man was out of work, had been evicted from his flat, et cetera, et cetera.

'This fits,' Ian commented, tapping a fingernail on the first photo of Henry, the misty shot of our man on the beach, watching the girls as they trampled down the sandcastle. 'I'm getting a scent.' None of us could deny that it fitted, that a theme was coming through. And so a team starts trawling through the child-molester files, looking for someone born circa 1935–40, perhaps answering to the name of Henry.

12

It's a Sunday afternoon, just past 2.30, and the rain has stopped, giving way to a sky of huge bright clouds and an air in which you can taste a hint of spring. We're clearing the table while Luke is getting his bag packed for an expedition to Eggesford Forest, a treat held over from the previous weekend because of bad weather, and then the phone rings. It's Tom Gaskin, whispering that the suspicious young man has appeared again, a few minutes ago, heading across the High Land. So Alice goes upstairs to tell Luke that the trip is cancelled, and together they wave goodbye from the top of the stairs, the habitually disappointed wife and child.

It takes twenty minutes to get there. Our suspect is pacing around the stones amid which Henry was found and he's exactly as Tom Gaskin described: narrow, gangly, with hair that's sticking up in a dozen different directions, and a plodding, lopsided walk. It's not surprising that the description of him has turned out to be so accurate. What's surprising is his identity: he is none other than Michael Trethowen – Mystic Mike – and in the instant of recognition it seems incomprehensible that Michael Trethowen didn't come to mind as someone whose appearance was identical to the character so precisely delineated by Tom.

This surprise is the cause of a brief hesitation, and in this instant it seems, from the quick turning away of his head, that Michael's impulse, on seeing that he's about to have company, is to hurry off, but then he takes another glance and he too realises that he knows who the other person is, and understands that it may not be in his best interests to make a break for it.

'Hello,' he calls out, over-keen to get his greeting in first.

'Hello, Michael.'

'Mr Donohue,' he says, thrusting his hands into his pockets. He has a look of guilt, but not deep guilt – it's the look of some- one caught shoplifting, at worst. We're ten feet apart, and now he smiles broadly, as if trying out the expression of someone who's glad to have unexpected company on such a fine afternoon. 'What brings you here?' he asks, stepping out from behind the rocks.

'Thought I'd take another tour of the scene.'

He smiles at the sea, which is like a vast expanse of raw iron painted here and there with dabs of mixed pale green and white. 'A fabulous day,' he remarks, and he breathes deeply the aroma of sea-cleansed sand and salt air. You can see his eyes wavering, conscious of being watched.

'How about you? What brings you out here?'

Without taking his eyes off the sea, he shrugs nonchalantly, but then his face changes again, into a doubting wince, as if a taste has come into his mouth and seems sour at first but might not, after all, be unpleasant.

What needs to be known about Michael Trethowen is that he is a young man who has been touched by disaster. When he was eight years old his mother's father, living at that time in Newcastle, County Down, fell ill with pneumonia, so ill that Michael's mother felt it necessary to fly over to be at his bedside. A couple of days later Michael's father went too, leaving the boy in the care of his father's parents. Against expectations, the grand- father recovered. Michael's parents brought the old man home from hospital. The next day, driving on a road outside Newcastle, they were killed outright, in a collision with a tanker. The grandparents adopted the boy and made as good a job of it as anyone could have wished. He was twenty-four at the time of Henry's death and still living at home. As far as we knew, he was a student. When Alice first went to Beal's church, young Michael was already in the congregation, sitting at the back, in the pew where he would always sit, whenever he attended, which was most Sundays. He'd be there before everyone else, reading a book or examining some detail of the building, or pretending to examine it, with an air of absorption that was intense enough to repel anyone who might be tempted to sit within speaking distance. Nobody could listen to a sermon with greater concentration than Michael appeared to listen to Beal's, and he mimed to the hymns as if too preoccupied with profound thoughts to move his mouth in synch with the rest of us. At the end of the show he scuttled out in a rush, before Beal could take up his post for the pastoral farewells. Usually he wore the monastic brown duffel coat (replaced in summer by a light hooded jacket), and the hood always went up as he reached the church door, as if he were putting on some sort of camouflage for the outside world. On a few occasions he held the door open for Alice and she sometimes spoke to him for a minute or two. He seemed an intelligent boy, she said, but very highly strung. Reverend Beal's sermon annoyed him one day, because Beal had misquoted a line from the Bible. It more than irritated him, Alice thought − it seemed to distress him, as if Beal's error were a terrible violation of The Book. Talking to Alice, he couldn't get through a sentence without blushing, and Michael's blushing was very conspicious, because he was a pale-skinned boy, so pale that he looked as if he were standing under a neon light, even on this afternoon, in the light of the pre-spring sun.

Comments are made about the weather, about the biplane that is passing overhead. And then, shaking his head as though there's a bug caught in his hair, Michael remarks: 'He really was rubbish this morning, wasn't he?'

'Who?'

'Beal. He's always rubbish. Complete dead loss. Beal's spiel. You a fan?'

'Not especially.'

'Didn't think so. He does have his fans, you know. His lady helpers, at the vicarage. Heard about them?' he asks, gauging if he has permission to be indiscreet.

'I've heard the gossip.'

'Right,' he says, deciding, in the absence of unambiguous permission, not to risk it.

Now he's slightly off-balance, unsure as to whether he's been rebuked for wanting to spread rumours, so it's time to return to the question: 'You didn't really give me an answer.'

Here Michael does a shiver of his shoulders, as if a cold wind has just passed over us, though the air is still. 'An answer to what?' he replies, briskly rubbing his arms.

'Why you're here.'

Scanning the horizon, back and forth a dozen times, he seems to be choosing between a dozen different lies. 'Here, this exact spot?' he asks with spurious uncertainty.

'Yes, Michael. Here, this precise spot.'

Three or four times more his eyes zip along the horizon blindly. He blows out his cheeks, like a weightlifter preparing to hoist the bar. 'Well,' he begins, but he gets no further than this for a minute or so, genuinely troubled, it appears, by whatever he's thinking. Eventually, after much examination of the sand around us, he asks: 'Do you believe in ghosts?'

'No, I don't. Do you?'

'Not ghosts like haunted-house ghosts. Headless nuns. Ladies in black. That kind of crap. No.'

'What then?'

'Something. I don't know. We can't know, can we?' he says, putting a finger to the bridge of his nose and closing his eyes, his grimace that of someone trying to erase a thought from his mind. 'What do you think? You think we're dead and that's it? Body kaput, end of story?'

'Probably. No evidence to the contrary.'

His eyes are open now and locked into a far-off stare that has no visible object. Gradually he brings his arms up and his hands make slow grasping motions in mid air. 'But there's something here. An interference, in the air. There's interference,' he repeats, accepting that this word will suffice for the time being. 'This is the place, isn't it? Where he was killed. You can feel it,' he says, as his fingers twitch around his face, simulating an electric crackle.

'I don't get anything.'

He looks around, frowning, as though the interference he's talking about is a substance that has a colour and he's puzzled that the traces of it are visible only to him. 'Something nasty happened here,' he says plainly. 'The air's different.' He takes a step away, making swirling motions with his arms, as if clearing smoke from around him. 'Here. Right here.'

The unnerving thing is that Michael is right: it was there, give or take a few inches, that the corpse of Henry was discovered. He couldn't have known this from the report in the newspaper, and after Henry was found no member of the public would have been able to get close enough to see exactly where the body had been. And, of course, by now there's no evidence of any disturbance of the sand. The scene has been erased, yet Michael knows it was here.

Staring into space, eyes motionless, as if listening for the repetition of a faint noise he's just heard, Michael is standing where the photographer, taking pictures of the body, would at some point have had to stand. 'Someone came here, with a knife, to kill him,' he murmurs to himself. 'Why would anyone do that?' he wonders, raising his voice a little.

'I don't know.'

'What could anyone argue with Henry about?'

'You knew him?'

'No,' he replies, shaking his head as if not having known Henry were one of the great regrets of his life.

'So why wonder why anyone would argue with him? For all you know, he might have been an objectionable old bastard.'

This notion prompts an anxious glance and the question, addressed to the air: 'Was he?'

'I don't know. Might have been.'

It takes some time for this concept to find lodging in his mind. 'Yes, I suppose so,' he finally concedes, and then a smile appears, as though at the thought of a well-liked and troublesome relative. Moments later his face assumes the frown of someone struggling with the formation of a complex thought, and he's watching his feet as they draw small circles on the sand. His mouth opens and straight away closes, seeming to shut off words that weren't quite right for what he wants to say, but when he does at last speak, all he says is: 'Man, it's terrible.' He says it in a drawl that sounds like the imitation of some old hippy, a voice that doesn't suit him at all.

'This the first time you've been out here recently?'

'Depends what you mean by recently,' he replies, with a nervous quick shrug.

'This year, say.'

'You mean since Henry?'

'Yes.'

'A couple of times.'

'And before that?'

'Do I come here often?' he laughs, but his laugh is more like an overexcited shriek, the shriek of a girl who's had a few too many. Instantly, hearing the noise he's just made, and afraid that the joke was misjudged, he becomes serious, gravely and sincerely serious. 'I've been here before. Of course. It's near. It's a nice walk.'

'You're here frequently?'

'Not frequently. Occasionally.'

'But twice in two months since Henry was killed. You said twice, yes?'

'A couple of times. Two or three,' he replies, and now, hands pushed deep into his pockets, he's rocking backwards and forwards on his heels, as if on the deck of a boat in a light swell.

'Two or three in two months, after Henry. Why so often? For the atmosphere?'

He casts a sidelong look, gauging the tone of the question. The hands are churning in the pockets and there's a blush on his cheeks. 'Don't really know,' he says.

'You must have some idea. What are you thinking when you set off to come here? It's not as if it's on the way to anywhere. There's obviously something that makes you come here. So, what do you think that might be?'

Again he traces circles on the sand with his feet, seeming not so much guilty as embarrassed at being thought stupid. 'Don't know,' he says, narrowing his eyes as though there's a glare coming off the sea. 'I mean, why do people stop to look at car crashes? You see a crash on the motorway, drivers are always slowing to have a good gawp. They can't help it. Bet they don't know why they do it.'

'This isn't a car crash, Michael. There's nothing to see, is there?'

Here he glances down and his eyes widen, as though seeing stains on the sand. 'No, but there's something here. I told you,' he replies, with a hint of protest in his voice. 'I can sense it.'

'OK, you can sense it. But what's the attraction? What does it make you feel? I don't understand.'

'I don't know. I told you,' he says again, adding a sigh of childish exasperation. His feet are wiping back and forth across the area in which they've been circling, obliterating the marks they've made. 'People write poems in graveyards, don't they? It's the same thing.'

'You're telling me you write poetry?'

'I didn't say that. It just makes me think, that's all.'

'About what?'

He sighs again, less exaggeratedly than before, and his head droops, as if he were exhausted, and beginning to be irked, by the relentless questioning. Staring at a spot in the middle distance,

94

he purses his lips tightly, apparently making one last effort to find an answer that will satisfy. 'Everything,' he says at last, as if confessing to something of which he might feel ashamed. 'About everything. Big things,' he says, making a sweeping wide-armed gesture towards the sea, a self-consciously grandiose gesture, and in that moment he doesn't have the appearance of a suspect. What he looks like is a disturbed young man whose parents were killed when he was a boy and has never recovered from it.

In silence we regard the sea, where a tanker is creeping on the horizon like a slug on a half-mile wall. Every few seconds Michael angles his head to one side, or his lips move in wordless speech, or he nods, as though he's attending to a debate that's taking place inside his mind. 'I don't think Beal believes in God,' he announces, out of the blue. 'Not really believe. Do you think he does?'

'I'd assumed it was a basic requirement for the job.'

'He doesn't,' he states with disconcerting vehemence. 'You heard of Pascal's wager?'

'No.'

'Well, he's signed up for it. You might as well sign up to God, because if you don't, and it turns out he does exist, you have an eternity of hellfire coming your way, but if you do sign up and he doesn't exist, what have you lost? Nothing. You get an eternity of not existing. So you'd be daft not to go along with it. That's the wager, and that's all Beal does. He goes along with it. There's nothing to lose,' he sneers.

'Seems logical.'

'Logic's got nothing to do with it. I'm talking about believing, and Beal doesn't believe. You can tell. He's a salesman, flogging deodorant for the soul. Gives his flock a quick spray every Sunday and sends them on their way. Off you go. Smell nice now. Come back next Sunday for another squirt.' He's angry, inappropriately angry, and seems to be making himself angrier, deliberately, by talking. 'What's it like?' he asks himself. 'What's it like? I'll tell you what it's like: it's like Beal's a salesman for Godcorp plc. His boss is this nice fluffy bloke who wants you to succeed in life and be happy and good, and if you don't succeed in being good, well, maybe you don't have quite so nice a life. Be nice to each other, if you can. That's the message. Try to be nice.'

'Not a bad message.'

'He should be a politician. A councillor, campaigning for bus shelters and a new bypass. That's what he should be doing. If you're given a church to play with, you're meant to be doing more than that. Bringing us The Word. The resurrection and eternal life and all that. But he's lukewarm, and I can't stand lukewarm people. I can't be doing with them,' he says through gritted teeth, and it appears now that perhaps this young man is, after all, capable of something demented. And no sooner has this thought arrived than he adds, smiling with ironic sweetness, 'I'm lukewarm myself.' Eyebrows raised, head cocked, he requests a response.

'You believe it? All that stuff.'

'I don't know,' he says. 'I don't think so.'

'So why go?'

'Because I don't know. To have a think. It's an exercise. A spiritual exercise. The test of boredom,' he says, now trying flippancy, perhaps to rescind what he might have revealed of himself. 'If you can get through an hour of Beal you can get through anything. What doesn't kill me makes me strong. You know that line?'

'No, I don't know that line. What –'

'And why do you go?' he interrupts. 'You're not there every week, are you? I've noticed that,' he says, and it feels like an accusation of frivolousness.

The hope that all might be well with Alice – that would have been part of an honest answer. Instead what's said is: 'I've taken the wager.'

This causes a laugh, or the sound of a laugh, a sound that emerges from his expressionless face like a bleat from the horn of the trumpet. 'No, you haven't. That's not true.' He makes another laughing sound, which ceases in an instant, as if his larynx has been stoppered. 'Why do you think the others go?' he asks.

'Never thought about it. Maybe they can't resist the magnetism of the blessed Beal.'

'No,' he replies, taking the idea seriously. 'I'll tell you why some of them are there. The school. That's all it is. They want their kids to go to the church school and so they're putting in the pew-hours. Some of these people would join the Tonton Macoute if it improved little Miranda's chances of getting on in life.' Frowning deeply, he considers a long rippled bank of sand, as though seeing there the faces of Beal's reprehensible flock. 'Mr Bywater,' he then announces, as though he's just spotted Mr Bywater walking towards us. 'You know him? Sits in the second row. Bald. Horrible beard.'

'Sure.'

'He's having an affair with another woman. I saw him coming out of a house in the afternoon and it wasn't his house. This woman gave him a kiss. I saw them,' he says with the tense little giggle of a child who's played a malicious joke on someone and is half sorry for it. 'I saw them in a car together as well. A week ago,' he adds, by way of conclusive evidence. 'You watch his wife next Sunday. She knows he's up to something. She gives him these glances when he's not looking. The woman's in a terrible state,' he asserts passionately, as if Mrs Bywater had confessed her intimate sufferings to him. He glares at the sea, and his whole face is suffused with a blush of furious indignation. He's wearing a jacket like a tracksuit top, but with about a dozen zips in it, and now he undoes one of the zips and reaches into the pocket, pulling out a postcard. 'Look at this,' he orders, shooting an arm out sideways. On the card there's a detail from a painting: it's a demon lurking in a cave, gnawing his claws and boggle-eyed with rapture at the arrival of a new shipment of the sinful. 'That's what we need. A Last Judgement on the wall, right in front of you. Every church should have one. No messing about. Do as I tell you or

97

you'll boil for ever after. Threats are the only thing that works.'
Like a mechanical boom his arm withdraws, taking the card back
to the pocket. Grimly, chin haughtily raised, he surveys the cliffs
behind us as if, condemned by him, Mr Bywater has just been
dispatched through a fissure in the rock into the lake of everlast-
ing fire. He's rocking backwards and forwards on his heels and
toes, as tense as a runner waiting for the starter's whistle. This
is a very unusual boy.

Now, if you ask George Whittam to name half a dozen people
he respects, the odds are that Vincent O'Brien, the racehorse
trainer, will be one of the chosen few. George knows his horses.
He appreciates the patient skills of the great trainer. But George's
respect for Vincent O'Brien has a major element of fondness to
it, and this fondness was born, he will tell you, when Mr O'Brien
was asked, in a TV documentary, what it was that he looked for
in a colt or a filly. Why had he had so much success in detecting
the grain of greatness in these unformed animals. In reply, he
didn't talk about bloodlines or proportions or musculature.
Instead, he came over all lyrical about the eyes. When deciding
if he should take a young horse on, he takes hold of its head and
gives it a good long look in the eye, and that tells him all he needs
to know about its potential. For George Whittam, likewise, the
eye has often been crucial, as it was in the case of Maggie
Tenterden, the occasion of Whittam's first major truth moment.

Two days after her twelfth birthday, Maggie went to meet a
friend in a nearby street, and she never came back. The estate on
which the Tenterdens lived was what you would call a close-knit
community. Everyone wanted to help. People put pictures of
Maggie in their windows, searched every alley and walkway,
checked every bin and abandoned car, combed the parks and
wasteland on the edge of the estate. From breakfast to midnight
relays of neighbours took it in turns to comfort Maggie's parents
and sisters. Nobody did more than Vernon Tenterden, the eldest
of Maggie's cousins. Every day he was at his aunt's and uncle's
house, making tea, answering the phone, fending off the

reporters. He went from door to door, making his own enquiries, just on the off-chance that people would tell him things they wouldn't tell the police. One afternoon, George Whittam and a colleague went to the family's flat to give them a briefing on progress and to ask a few questions. A whole posse was waiting for them: the parents, a grandmother, two of Maggie's aunts, four or five neighbours and a pair of cousins, Vernon among them. An anonymous caller had rung in to say that he'd seen a girl who looked like Maggie walking beside a road in Dartford. The girl was wearing a pink top like the one Maggie had been wearing on the day she disappeared and was with a boy, a West Indian boy, tall, aged perhaps fourteen or fifteen. The call was probably a hoax, George counselled them, but did Maggie have a friend who fitted this description? Did the family know of any reason Maggie might have gone to Dartford? The mother stared desperately at George and pressed her hands to her face, as if Maggie's life depended on her being able to think of something that would explain why her daughter might have been in Dartford with a black boy. When she started weeping, Vernon, sitting on the arm of the settee, put a cup of tea into the hand of his aunt and shot a doleful glance George Whittam's way, and in that split second George knew, absolutely knew for a stone-solid fact, that Vernon had made the call, that the call was a hoax, that Maggie was dead and that he was looking at the man who had murdered her. Within twenty-four hours they found the girl's body, wrapped in a quilt in Vernon Tenterden's lock-up garage.

But looking into the eyes of Michael Trethowen is a far from straightforward operation, because he has a flickery gaze that never rests, and when you do get a glimpse you don't seem to see the same person from one minute to the next. He's supercilious; he's as shy as a ten-year-old; he's sunk into a twenty-second gloom; he's struck by a secret idea that pleases him immoderately; he's seized by contempt, perhaps contempt for himself. He talks like three different people in the space of three sentences. One moment it's a ludicrous idea that these weedy arms could have done the damage that killed Henry, and the next moment the lad seems half mad, in need of treatment, capable of doing anything. He calls Henry 'the stiff on the cliff', then the Reverend Beal is a 'fuckwit', then it seems that any second now he's going to cry, but he doesn't cry – he makes a remark about some story he'd read in a magazine about a batch of Roman coins being found in a bag of potatoes; and then we're back to church, with a monologue, the longest of the session, on the subject of a brilliant sermon he heard last year, a fantastic performance it was, so much better than anything that fuckwit Beal could come up with. For a good five minutes Michael becomes the inspired preacher, drunk on his own eloquence, regaling the beach with the instructive tale of the bright young man who had a good career, plenty of money, an expensive car, expensive apartment, everything he could desire. He worked hard and played hard, drank fine wines, chased and seduced many beautiful women, thinking of nothing but himself, his pleasure, his success. In time, though, he came to see the falsity of the life he had been leading. He married, he had children. He became a good father. He was a good husband. He made himself a better man, but still he was not living in Christ. Still he had not repented. Still he had not accepted the grace of Our Lord. And then one day – a delicious day, a day like today – he came home from work. He kissed his wife, he kissed his children. He went up the stairs to his bedroom and in that room, without warning, Death struck him down. In the blinking of an eye he was struck down, and now he was damned, for he had not accepted the grace of Our Lord. 'Tomorrow you might die,' proclaims Michael, waving his arms around in his imaginary pulpit, giddy with speech. 'This very hour you might die. As surely as the dawn, Death is coming. Death is ready for you. Death is ready for you, my friend, but are you ready for Death?' And for an instant he stares as if to say: 'It's you I'm talking to. This question is meant for you.' But he's smiling now, as if we're friends who meet every Sunday afternoon, on this beach, for a chat about the week's events.

It's not easy to think of what to say, and before anything can take shape Michael has asked: 'What are you thinking?'

'About Henry,' is the lie that offers itself.

'What about him?'

'His life. What his life was like.'

'No,' says Michael flatly. 'You were wondering what on earth I'm talking about and what I'm doing here. That's what you were thinking. Weren't you?'

'No. I wasn't.'

'You were,' he insists. 'And it's not a coincidence that you're here when I'm here.' He scans the sand, as if someone might be spying on him from behind a rock. 'Well,' he says, pulling up a cuff to look at a watch that isn't there, 'it's time I got going. Will that be all, officer?' There's resentment in the lift of his upper lip, while from his eyes it seems he thinks this is an immensely witty way to conclude. Dismissed, he strolls a few yards before turning to deliver his parting shot. 'For what is your life?' he demands, pointing in accusation, grinning at the confusion of his audience. 'It is even a vapour, that appeareth for a little time, and then vanisheth away.'

He ambles off, flat-footed, toppling to starboard, his arms swinging disjointedly from the shoulders. Twice he glances back and then he's running in a lopsided lope, ducking his head with every other stride, as if dodging stones.

13

A few months before Henry's death we were at the Whittams' for a meal, along with an employee of Margaret's and the woman's limp little husband, a man whose name – like his wife's – is now lost from memory. At some point the limp little husband was reminiscing mistily about a place he'd visited as a boy with his parents and sisters, a castle somewhere in France, and this gave Rebecca Whittam a cue to start talking about a friend of hers who had made them play a game that was a version of *Desert Island Discs*, in which you had to pick ten memories to keep you sane on your desert island, instead of your top ten records. 'Would the French castle get into your top ten?' she asked. 'Possibly, possibly,' the husband replied. 'Top five?' Anticipating that this might be heading into deep waters, Margaret tried to intervene, but was ignored by her daughter.

The husband assured his hostess that he didn't mind answering. 'Possibly,' he said to Rebecca, with the smirk of someone who is about to reveal more of himself than might be wise.

'Number One?'

'No, no,' he bashfully responded and his wife suggested to him, with a horrible simper, that the day of their wedding might take the prize, and it turned out, astoundingly, that her guess was right.

For as long as her sister was living at home, Rebecca had been the shy one, the moody one, the one who preferred to stay in her room when guests were in the house. Brighter, prettier, always articulate in the company of adults, Monica occupied centre stage with ease, while Rebecca – with occasional eruptions of jealousy, but more often a little in awe, it seemed – settled for the role of reticent sidekick, to whom Monica might turn, once in a while, for verification that something had indeed happened as she had told it. As soon as Monica had left for university, however, Rebecca was a girl transformed, as if confidence were a substance that was floating within the house and Monica's allowance of it had now become her own. Overnight, almost, she acquired a way of looking at people that was as remarkable as her father's, but quite different. Someone could be subjected to George Whittam's forensic gaze and remain unaware that they'd been seen through. Vernon Tenterden, for one, seems not to have felt the instant in which George skewered him. With Rebecca, on the other hand, you were disarmed by a gaze that made full use of the directness of youth, and bold dark eyes, and tear ducts that seem to make it unnecessary for her to blink more then once every five minutes. When she wanted to, Rebecca could give you a look that told you that this was a girl who valued honesty above all else, and requested, or demanded, your honesty in return for the promise of hers. On this particular evening, by a slow, long-delayed blink, plus a curt little nod, we knew that Rebecca deemed the spouse of her mother's colleague to have failed to fulfil his obligations under the terms of this treaty of reciprocal frankness. She turned to her father, who declined to nominate a first-choice memory, but told her, taking the scrutiny of her eyes full on, that he'd be happy to be left with the recollection of his life as it was today.

'Full marks for diplomacy,' his wife commended him, raising her glass.

'Crawler,' said Rebecca, raising hers, and then she turned to us, requiring something considerably better than she'd been fobbed off with so far.

Alice said, not unexpectedly, that the day that Luke was born would be in her top three, and a moment later decided it might in fact be her Number One. Then it was the turn of Mr Donohue, who was honoured with the full-power gaze, and what he chose was a very hot day in July, in France, six years before: 'A perfect day.' Rebecca, with a severe smile, requested more information, but Alice, as was clear from the way her thumb scratched at her napkin, wanted the subject closed, because she was imagining that it would take only one more sentence to reveal to everyone, in explicit detail, the episode her husband had in mind, as clearly as if the scene had been projected on to the wall directly from the interior of his head. So what was offered to Rebecca and the rest of the company was a platitude of fine foreign weather and young parenthood, a rewrite that deleted the crucial specifics, so as not to embarrass. But had the answer been given without omission, this is what it would have been. We're in a small stone cottage on a farm in Brittany, on a broiling July afternoon. Upstairs we have a bathroom with a mighty cast-iron bath and one huge bedroom, which has an iron-framed bed, an ancient mirrored wardrobe and no other furniture. The window of the bedroom opens on to an orchard and the sea beyond it, half a mile away, and below the window is the roof of the disused shed that's attached to the cottage. Luke is asleep in his Moses basket on the bed and Alice is sitting on the windowsill, naked, with her feet on the hot tiles of the sloping roof. Her hair is coiled up, and there are little streaks of sweat on her back and down her side. Behind her the leaves of the orchard are white; the grass is white and the sea is the bluish-white of new steel. The room smells of beeswax and sea water and warm straw. Luke is splayed on his back in his basket, arms thrown wide, as if sleep has knocked him over. Alice's eyes are closed and she is leaning forward into the heat, her wrists crossed on her thighs. Her skin is like soft marble in the full sunlight and is a pale apricot colour where the shadows fall. Even now she has a modesty, a gorgeous modesty and self-possession, as if she were not naked but wearing clothes too fine to be seen. She is perfectly, untouchably beautiful. Hearing the latch, she turns and smiles, seeming as happy as it's possible to be, because she's in the life she wanted, which was our life, the three of us – and that's the moment, that's the memory, a scene that seems, now, to have arranged itself so that it will always be remembered, and revisited more than any other memory of Alice.

In everything Alice did she had a characteristic style, but a style that didn't seem to be something created consciously to make an impression. The poise of Alice's manner, of her bearing, was uncontrived, a sort of demure grace that you could believe had been with her since she was a child. And there are no photographs of small Alice in a mess or in a foul mood. Here's Alice in the playground with baggy-socked school friends, standing within her own microclimate of serenity, looking as if she's been dressed for the shot two minutes before. At the zoo with her father, aged seven or eight, she radiates the presence of a tiny celebrity with whom her father is having his picture taken. Here's Alice at fourteen, having skipped the lumpen years of adolescence and moved directly into small-scale womanhood. And here's Alice aged twenty-three, photographed in Flat 3, 126 Tesset Road, by the man she would soon marry.

Tesset Road was a nondescript avenue of patched tarmac, cracked paving stones and disintegrating Victorian houses, nearly all of them divided into flats, with a row of low-budget shops at its midpoint: a Chinese takeaway, a hardware shop, a barber's, a newsagent's, an insurance broker and a launderette. The peeling blue door next to the launderette opened on to a hallway that always had a slurry of uncollected mail on the floor, and from there a staircase of crumbling lino conducted you, past windows that were slathered with the greasy dust of two decades, to the door of Alice's flat. Here, immediately, the dirt and racket of Tesset Road was replaced by the air of clarity and calm that Alice had created in those three small rooms. The furniture was sparse and tasteful and made to last, because Alice believed – always believed, even when she had more money and space than was available when she lived at number 126 – that it was better to buy one well-made thing than three of inferior quality. A black leather and chrome sofa took up most of one wall: it was made in Germany more than twenty-five years earlier, looked almost new and was bought for a pittance at an auction. The frosted-glass table and Italian chairs also were bought at auction, for next to nothing, and in the bathroom there was single long shelf of frosted glass, which supported a small array of expensive-looking bottles and jars, like a miniature exhibition of perfumery and cosmetics, but arranged for no other eyes but her own.

If a thing could not be done well, Alice would rather not do it. Her friends drove clapped-out old cars until they could afford something half-decent; Alice cycled everywhere, until she'd saved enough for an immaculate second-hand Audi with full service history. Her friends would make do with a dirt-cheap package holiday to Torremolinos if that's what it took to get their annual dose of the sun; Alice would go without a break, so that next year she could spend a fortnight in Granada in a decent hotel, on her own if need be. Alice enjoyed eating at restaurants, but when we moved here she found that nowhere within half an hour's drive came up to scratch, and so for a few years, until Peter and Marianne Jevons came to the rescue, we rarely ate out. Within a week of Pescheria's opening we were there, at what would become the regular table, at the widest of the windows, overlooking the sea. Had Alice designed the place herself it could not have been more to her liking, with its scrubbed floorboards and walls of whitewashed wood, and fabrics all in tones of oatmeal and chalk. On every table stood a slender little vase and in every vase there was a single flower, the table's solitary dash of piercing colour. It was like a chapel of fine food and whenever Peter or Marianne came to your table they spoke to you with a solicitude that was priestly. They were Alice's kind of people: unostentatious, diligent, devoted to their work and to each other, and civil to everyone, even the high-handed Londoners who expected a snappier mode of service than the Jevonses provided.

Soon after the session with Michael Trethowen on the beach it was Alice's birthday, so we went, of course, to Pescheria. And one of the things we would have talked about was Michael Trethowen, because the previous Sunday he'd sidled up to Alice after the service and started up a conversation about the weather and then about her husband, who had been harassing him, as he put it, half jokingly. What was more, Mr Donohue didn't think much of the Reverend Beal. Didn't rate him at all – did she know that? Alice didn't know that, and doubted if it were the case. It's true, Michael insisted. Mr Donohue thinks Beal's a disgrace. And then, claiming to have remembered some pressing errand, he was off, mission accomplished. So we talked for a while about Michael and agreed that the boy might benefit from talking to a counsellor of some sort. We talked about the Reverend Beal and agreed that sometimes his style was a little too smooth. But mostly we talked about Luke and his progress at school and about the summer holiday, which Alice wanted to book in the next few weeks, to give Luke something definite to look forward to, not like last year's debacle, with the Portuguese villa that turned out to be only half built and downwind of an evil-smelling factory. We found ourselves reminiscing about previous holidays we'd enjoyed, with and without Luke, and here it became difficult not to think of Henry as Hannah Rowe described him, swatting the past away whenever it pestered him. And inevitably Henry himself came into the conversation, along with the young woman, unnamed, who used to walk with him and was sure he was completely alone in the world, and had admired him for his fortitude. We agreed, as we'd agreed before, that neither of us would have lasted long if we'd had to live as

Henry lived. The incident of the bus ticket was mentioned: Henry staring at the ticket in the palm of his hand, clueless as to how he came to have it in his pocket. Had living rough ruined his mind like that, we wondered, not for the first time, or did he end up living rough because his mind wasn't right? 'To think he was once somebody's little boy,' said Alice, taking her empty glass by its stem. 'I look at Luke and I can't help thinking that a mother once looked at Henry in the same way.' She watched the wineglass revolving in her fingers. 'I hope she died,' she said. 'I mean, it would be terrible, to just lose touch. To have him drift out of your life.'

'He might not have drifted. She might have booted him out.'

'I suppose,' she murmured, still watching the swivelling glass. 'You think I'm being sentimental, don't you?'

'No.'

'I'm sorry,' she said. And at that moment, as she put the glass down, her eyes took on a sorrowing cast: for outcast Henry perhaps, or for a world in which a harmless old vagrant gets murdered, or maybe merely for us.

Before the main course had been finished, the day's headache had appeared, a bad one. We were home before ten o'clock, somewhat earlier than expected, and as we closed the front door there was a flurry in the living room that was noisier than Rebecca alone would have made. When we go in, Rebecca is standing in front of the TV, aiming the remote control at it, and on the settee there's a chubby and very pretty girl with shaggy black hair and kohl-darkened eyes, dressed all in black. 'This is Jessica,' says Rebecca straight away. A bottle of wine and two glasses are on the coffee table. Jessica is almost bent double, knees clamped together, hands clamped to her ribs, as if trying to squeeze herself down to a smaller size. The head of a tattooed snake can be seen in the gap between T-shirt and jeans.

'Hello, Jessica,' says Alice, and Jessica smiles queasily.

'Luke's been a dream,' Rebecca reports brightly. 'In bed at eight on the dot. Not a peep out of him.'

'He was worn out,' says Alice, opening her handbag for Rebecca's money. 'Thank you.'

'There was a film that Jessie wanted to see but her mum and dad were watching something else so Jessie phoned to ask if she could come over to watch it here,' explains Rebecca in a single breath. 'I said it was OK.'

'Yes,' says Jessica, almost doubled over now, as if in the throes of severe stomach-ache.

'I should have phoned you to ask but I didn't think you'd mind. Was that OK?'

'Of course. It's fine,' says Alice, looking at the TV, which is showing some sitcom.

'It wasn't any good,' Jessica interjects. 'The film.'

'It was rubbish,' Rebecca confirms, and she gives Jessica a quick look of abashed amusement. Then she notices Alice's glance at the coffee table, and a flush of apprehension passes over her face.

'I brought it,' Jessica volunteers. The girls watch Alice as she lifts and inspects the empty bottle. 'It was rubbish as well,' adds Jessica. 'I had more than Bec.'

'I only had a glass,' Rebecca verifies. 'Not even that much. You won't tell my folks? They let me have a glass at home but –'

'It's OK,' says Alice, smiling, which brings Jessica out of her crouch. 'Really. It's fine.'

'It was my fault,' says Jessica.

'It's OK,' Alice assures her.

Jessica turns and bends over the arm of the settee to pick her jacket off the floor. Her T-shirt is very tight and as she twists, it can be seen that the clip of her bra is unfastened. Rebecca, in the same instant, observes that the undone clip has been noted and reacts with a beseeching glance. In the car she scarcely utters a word, engulfed with embarrassment, while Jessica, sitting alone and mute in the back, stares out of the window as if being driven through a town she's never seen before but is nonetheless of almost no interest. We stop outside Jessica's house. In the front garden there's a tree with what appear to be small kites or flags hanging from some of the branches, and in the middle of the lawn there's a low pile of scrap metal. 'Thank you, Mr Donohue,' says Jessica, opening the door. 'See you tomorrow, Bec.'

Rebecca nods, looking at the mound of scrap. But she can't help herself: once Jessica is out of the car she has to watch her, all the way to the front door. As soon as we pull away she starts talking. 'You won't tell my parents that Jessie came round, will you, Mr Donohue?' she asks. They don't approve of Jessie, she explains, because she's always getting into trouble at school and they don't think much of her family either. Jessie's sister had a kid before she left school and her mother's a tree hugger who does all these therapies with twigs and flowers and crystals. 'Jessie was born in a pond in the garden,' says Rebecca, laughing, but with pleading eyes. And Jessie's father makes gates and railings in wrought iron, but he's an artist really, or he thinks he is. That's what the pile of scrap is for. 'You won't tell them, will you?' she asks again. 'They'd go mental. They just can't stand her. But she's really interesting. You can see she's interesting, but they don't get it.' Then her eyes are making a demand rather than an appeal, and she gets the promise she wants.

Back home, the bottle had been emptied and dropped in the bin, the glasses washed and dried and put away, the coffee table wiped. 'What did you say to her?' asked Alice.

'Thanks for babysitting. Goodnight. See you soon.'

'You didn't say anything about her friend?'

'Didn't think it was necessary.'

'I don't like the idea of people we don't know being in the house when we're not here.'

'She seems a nice kid.'

'If she'd asked, I wouldn't mind.'

'It's no big deal, is it? It's not as if they'd got slaughtered, is it? She's a responsible girl.'

110

'That's not the point. It's the principle. We don't know anything about the other one.'

'Well, we know that Rebecca likes her a lot. And vice versa.'

'Meaning?'

'They're in love.'

'What?' Alice asked. She had been going around the room, repositioning photographs and vases and books by a fraction of an inch, as if the presence of uninvited Jessica might have knocked things a little out of place, but at this she stopped and looked up, as though hearing something break.

'They're girlfriend and girlfriend. It's obvious.'

'Not to me.'

'Well –'

'But she has a boyfriend. What's his name? Tom.'

'That's as may be. Now she has a girlfriend. You didn't see the looks between them?'

'Clearly not.'

'If you'd been in the car, it would have been obvious, believe me.'

'Why?'

'It doesn't matter. Little signs.'

'Just looks?'

'And a few other things.'

'Such as?'

'It doesn't matter.'

'Such as?'

'Jessie's bra was undone, for one thing. That was fairly unambiguous, I thought.'

'You were looking at Jessica's bra?'

'It came to my attention.'

'It's not funny, John.'

She regarded the blank TV screen, as if coming to terms with something unsettling that she'd learned from a programme that had just finished. 'I'm going to bed,' she said at last, touching fingertips gingerly to her forehead.

With Alice there were never any major arguments, not a single full-blown row until the day it all fell apart. It was as though someone had left a window open somewhere in the house, just slightly ajar, and bit by bit the whole place was getting colder. That's what it was like.

14

The team working on the sex offender files had yet to find a match for Henry. Every door in town had been knocked on, and nobody had come forward with any new information since the day Hannah Rowe walked into the station. So it was time to invite Ronnie Houghton back in.

Ronnie is quietly thrilled: cometh the hour, cometh the man from the *Echo*. The constabulary have run into a cul-de-sac and without the assistance of Ronnie there's little chance of finding a way forward. We're not giving him much more than we gave him first time round, apart from the mugshot, but he's not complaining. By his tight-lipped resolution he wants us to appreciate that we're setting him a challenge, a challenge to which he will rise, because it's the mark of a star reporter that he can make a story out of thin material. Reading his notes at the end of the briefing, he assumes the face of a general studying a map of the battlefield, seeing his strategy taking form. PUZZLE OF TRAGIC HENRY we read on page three, above the photograph that Hannah took. Going for maximum pathos, Ronnie reports that mystery is deepening around Henry the enigmatic beach man, Henry the forgetful wanderer. He mentions that he was seen in Tavistock and Plymouth and Honiton, but there's no mention of any loitering in the vicinity of school playgrounds – we didn't tell Ronnie about that angle, because you couldn't expect much help in reconstructing the CV of a suspected child fancier. The story appears in the Friday edition, and takes up a good half of the page. Come Monday, we've had no calls. Not one.

The following Friday it's the turn of the regional TV news. Henry the mystery man is granted a one-minute slot, between a bus jammed under a railway bridge and the hundredth birthday of a lady from Buddleigh Salterton, widow of a hero of the Somme. For just five seconds Henry's face fills the screen, but that does the trick. Before the weather forecast is over the phone is ringing and within the next twenty-four hours we hear from a dozen people who once had some contact, or think they might have had contact, with Henry. A woman remembers that one afternoon about three years ago, in Launceston, a man who looked like the man in the picture helped her to get her baby's buggy on to a bus; he seemed in a bad way, she said, but he was surprisingly well-spoken. Another caller, from Wadebridge, recollects a man who slept rough in a small park at the end of her street for a few weeks one summer, four or five years ago, and she's almost positive that it was the murdered man. Around the same time Henry was spotted in Newquay by a Mr Wylie, a milkman, who distinctly recalls seeing a tramp who closely resembled Henry. Several times in the course of a single month he saw him: the man wore a filthy blue suit and was always charging along the street, swinging a leather briefcase. In Taunton, five years previously, an inebriated Henry stood in the middle of the road, shouting abuse at the passing traffic and waving a map in the air. This incident happened within half a mile of the bakery owned by Mrs Edie Bullamore, who for a period of about six or seven weeks would give any unsold loaves to a homeless man who had a strong Bristol accent and was definitely Henry.

For the years 1985 to 1988 we have no fewer than twenty-eight sightings, in various parts of Devon and Cornwall, of someone who was almost certainly Henry, and for the summer of 1989 there's a glut of sightings in Plymouth and all over southern

Cornwall, between the second week of June and the last week of August. He was walking very fast, nearly all the callers say, and he was wearing a lot of T-shirts. A Mrs Erskine, working in a fish and chip shop in St Austell in August 1989, saw him pass her door half a dozen times in a single afternoon, as though he were doing laps of the town. He thanked her very politely when she gave him a bag of chips, then put the chips in his briefcase and hurried away, never to be seen again.

All of these people are interviewed, and none of them gives us anything meaty, none except Mr Ged Ormorod, who for more than thirty years ran a newsagent's shop in Ilfracombe. He opened his shop every morning at 7 a.m. and every morning for a period of some eighteen months, from the autumn of 1979, within a few minutes of opening, as he was unfurling the awning of the shop or putting the billboards out, he would see a man walk past, the same man every morning. There was nothing particularly remarkable about the man's appearance: he was middle-aged, perhaps in his mid forties, quite thin, bearded, around six feet tall. What made him memorable was the punctuality of his arrival, the speed at which he walked and the fact that, although he and Ged must have greeted each other on more than five hundred occasions, their exchanges never progressed beyond 'Good morning' multiplied by two. 'Never earlier than five past and never later than ten past, and always too busy to pass the time of day,' said Ged, studying the photo of Henry, making himself absolutely certain that Henry and his man were identical. Rain or shine, seven days a week, Henry hastened by, nearly always in jeans and a denim shirt, though in the event of serious rainfall he might wear also a flimsy plastic jacket, and once or twice, on the coldest days, he took the precaution of wearing one denim shirt on top of another.

For a year and a half he was a feature of every morning, and then one Wednesday he wasn't there any more. Thursday and Friday came and went, with no sign of him. He was gone, but Ged Ormorod did see him again, one more time, on a hot July afternoon in 1984. Turning out of a side street close to the harbour, Ged was forced to a standstill by a gang of schoolkids disembarking from a coach. He sidestepped and found himself face to face with his lost acquaintance, if acquaintance isn't too strong a word for what Henry was. It was unmistakably the high-speed walker, even though he was somewhat thinner than he used to be and his beard was a little more ragged, and he was wearing a shiny and very dirty blue suit, buttoned up despite the heat, and a blue tie with a grubby white shirt. For a few seconds Ged Ormorod stared, then he smiled, but no smile came back. In fact, nothing came back, not the slightest sign of recognition. In a state of some confusion, Ged initiated their first and only conversation. 'Well. I wondered where you'd got to,' he said, or words to that effect.

The man in the shiny blue suit looked at him as if he were trying to decipher some graffiti scrawled on a wall. He was sweating heavily and a trickle of grey water, emerging from behind an ear, was making its way towards his collar. 'Do I know you?' the man asked. The question was blunt, but quietly put, with no sense of bafflement, as though what was being asked was something like: 'If I go down this street, will I come to the post office?'

Ged explained that he ran the newsagent's shop. 'Just down there,' he said, pointing, beginning to wish that this encounter hadn't happened. 'You used to go past, every morning, when I was opening up.' The man looked along the seafront, and then, still unenlightened, at Ged. 'About three years ago?' Ged added.

The man's face formed the smile of a polite person who has been waylaid at a bus stop by someone he's never seen before and is being given some information that's of very little relevance to anything in his own life. 'Did we speak?' he asked.

'We sort of said hello to each other. Most days,' Ged replied.

Here the man furrowed his brow, as you would frown to feign involvement in a story that's of no interest at all. 'Most days?' he repeated.

'That's right. Around seven o'clock. A few minutes after.'

Now the man seemed to go through the motions of consulting his memory. 'When was this?' he asks. 'Three years, you said?' It was a very busy stretch of pavement on which they were standing and Ged was aware that the two of them constituted something of an obstruction, but the man seemed not to notice, nor even to feel the knocks against his shoulder. Stock-still he stood, as if standing in an empty field.

'That's right,' said Ged.

For a few seconds, in a plausible simulation of perplexity, the man in the blue suit scratched at his beard, then he shrugged, casting off whatever thoughts he'd been having. 'No,' he concluded. 'No. I don't think so. It couldn't have been me,' he said, making it sound as if he were refusing an offer of charity. Steadily he gazed at Ged, and under this cold and self-certain gaze Ged started to doubt what he had known to be a fact. It was, he said, like being transfixed by a hypnotist who has you believing your hands have turned green and he's the Archbishop of Canterbury.

And so Ged ended up apologising. 'I could have sworn. But I must be mistaken.'

Graciously the man smiled. 'That's all right,' he replied. 'There must be a lot of people who look like me.'

Ged smiled in response to this, partly because this man, trussed up in a filthy blue suit on a sweltering summer afternoon, did not appear to be disingenuous in maintaining that his appearance was in no way out of the ordinary. 'Sorry to have bothered you,' said Ged.

'Not at all,' said the man, and he walked off, very quickly. It was indubitably the same person and Ged didn't know what to think, because the two explanations for what had happened – that this person really did have no memory of their fairly recent and very numerous encounters, or that for some unfathomable reason he was lying, and lying with absolute conviction – were both hard to accept. But thirty or forty yards away the man looked back and aimed at Ged a glance that seemed hostile, and hostile in a way that made it seem much likelier that he had in fact known all along who Ged was.

It wasn't only outside his shop that Ged had seen this character. One afternoon, driving to his daughter's house, he noticed a fine old Mercedes being raised on a jack outside a garage, and a moment later he recognised the man operating the jack. On a couple of other occasions he drove past the garage, and there was his man. Once he waved to him from the car; the reaction – or rather, the lack of it – appeared in retrospect to be a preview of the meeting on the street. The garage closed some years ago, but it didn't take long to trace the former owner, Mr Irwin: he lived in a house on the other side of the street. Shown the photograph of our Henry, he confirmed that he'd employed him for about a year. His name was Henry, he said – Henry Wilson. Mr Wilson had appeared at the garage one day, asking if there was any work. He seemed keen and genuine, but there wasn't anything going. Next week he came back: same question, same answer. The week after he was there again. He'd smartened himself up a bit. First time round he'd had a beard; now he'd had a shave. Still no work, though. He kept coming back, every week, same day, same time. In the end he happened to show his face on the day after one of the mechanics had quit without warning, so Mr Irwin took a chance on Henry, cash in hand, no notice on either side. A good worker, he turned out to be. Dependable, kept his thoughts to himself. A grim bugger, but talented with machines. Never needed to look at a manual: just straight in, sort it out. There was no chat in him at all. Nobody ever heard him talk about his family or anything outside his job. Except once, one of his workmates kept going at him, in the pub on a Friday after work. Henry would go for a pint on a Friday, just the one. But this workmate could drink four pints in the time it took Henry to finish his one and he kept going at Henry to tell them something about himself. He wouldn't let up, and eventually Henry revealed that he'd been married and that it hadn't worked out. He made it clear that this was all he was going to say, but the pestering continued for so long that Henry became angry, so angry that it looked as if a fight might break out. In the end Henry walked out, leaving half his drink on the table. They didn't even know where he lived, until Henry for some reason let himself go on a Friday night and drank a skinful. He was paralytic, so one of the lads put him in a minicab and went with him, to make sure he was OK, and that's how he got into Henry's bedsit, which was a really weird place, because it was as if nobody lived there. It was very neat: nothing left lying around, no pictures anywhere, nothing in the way of personal touches. You looked around and you saw nothing that belonged to him. The most characterless flat in Britain, it was. You'd have thought he'd moved in yesterday. Soon after that there was an incident with a customer who said his car had been damaged while it was in for a service. It was nonsense: an altercation happened and Henry lost his temper. He was waving a spanner at the man and had to be pulled away. Afterwards, before anything could be said, Henry announced he had to leave. A handshake and that was it – Henry was gone.

And that's the sum of what we learn from the man who was Henry's boss for more than a year, but at least we can set to work tracing the workmate who seems to be the one person in Ilfracombe who knew where Henry lived, and perhaps, somewhere, there's an ex-wife to find as well.

15

It's been a day of paperwork and no progress, and now, late in the afternoon, it's raining so hard that water is tumbling out of the gutters in gouts, and the trees and the road are making a roaring noise with all the rain that's hitting them. Standing at the door, waiting for it to open, it's as if a cascade of pencils is falling point-first on to our heads. 'Bleeding hell,' says Hannah, laughingly amazed. She's barefoot, and wearing jeans with rips in the knees and a top that has a breaking wave and *SeaShed* printed on it, similar to the T-shirt that we found on Henry. For a few more seconds, before stepping aside, she enjoys the spectacle of the deluge and the two saturated policemen.

In the living room she takes our coats and inspects them quizzically, with a show of intrigued revulsion, as if pretending they're pelts of an unidentified species. 'Sometimes waterproof just isn't enough,' she comments, bearing the coats away.

We don't speak while she's out of the room, but Ian raises an eyebrow at Hannah's unexpected good humour. For this visit he's taking the role of the silent partner, and he's getting out his notebook when she comes back in, carrying two small towels, which she throws to us.

Waiting to take the towels back, she says to Ian: 'I think we got on each other's nerves, last time. Am I allowed to say that?

I'm sorry. But you rubbed me up the wrong way, somehow. Which is easy to do at the moment.'

'Of course.'

'With all this business, you know? Henry. I'm upset about it. It's all I can think about. I've not been sleeping well, so I was a bit –' and she makes a snarl, finger-claws extended, then pauses, aware that's she's talking too much, too quickly.

'We understand,' Ian assures her, but Ian makes his mind up fast and he's never going to like her. We return the towels.

'OK,' she says, with a quick smile and a puff of relief at having resolved this issue. She clutches the towels to her chest. 'Coffee? I'm having one. This place is too cold, isn't it? I knocked the thermostat down by mistake and it takes ages to warm up. The boiler's on its last legs.' She puts a hand flat on the radiator, first at the top, then lower down. 'Getting there, slowly,' she says. 'Anyway, coffee?'

'Thank you,' says Ian, and this is just about the last thing he says for the best part of half an hour. We look around the room. A record is spinning on the deck and the empty sleeve is lying open on top of it: it's a bossa nova album, and on the shelves there's a lot of Spanish music, or South American, and a fair amount of reggae, a minority taste in this part of the country. The books don't reveal much, though: novels you see in every station bookshop, a few thrillers, a book of aerial photographs of Britain, some popular science and psychology, three or four travel guides and half a dozen books on plants and wildlife. A laptop, on the floor, has a spreadsheet on screen, and next to it there's a video of some BBC nature programme. Since our first visit the fishless fish tank has been moved to the floor, but it's still a quarter filled with claws and shells and stones, under clear water.

'They died,' says Hannah, bringing three mugs of coffee. 'The fish. They all went belly-up at Christmas.'

'All?'

'Six of them. All at once.'

'Really?'

'Really. No. Of course not. I'm having you on. There were never any fish. Just a load of rocks and stuff. For effect. I like the look of them in the water. It brightens them up.' She tilts an eyebrow in mockery of this foible of hers, then places one mug beside the futon, which Ian takes, and another by the wicker chair. 'Sit, sit,' she orders. Having closed down the laptop, she swings one of the beanbags against the wall and sits down, cross-legged. The soles of her feet are blotched with white paint. She looks towards the windows. The rain is hitting the panes so hard it sounds like the rumble of a huge drum. Noticing a spot of paint on her forearm she licks a fingertip and rubs at it. Told that we saw her picture in the pub, and liked it, she rubs harder. 'How did you know it was mine?' she asks.

'The barman told us. And you painted the room as well?'

Looking up, she seems to consider, for a second or two, how she should take this answer. 'Why ask, when you know?'

'I did really like the picture.'

'Thank you,' she says. The subject closed, she takes a sip of her coffee. 'You said you had more questions. About Henry.'

So we go through the list of places through which Henry's wanderings took him in the summer of 1989. Taunton he might have mentioned to her, Newquay too, and Plymouth she's already told us about. She's told us everything she knows about what sent Henry to the towns he walked through, which is nothing at all. Launceston, St Austell and Wadebridge: she never knew he was at any of these. Tavistock? He never made reference to Tavistock, as far as she can remember, but she might have forgotten. She's not discernibly engaged when told that he lived in Ilfracombe for a couple of years, that he worked in a garage, was a skilled mechanic and just took off one day, without so much as a good-bye, but there's a reaction, a touch of the tongue to her bottom lip, at the news that he was known there as Henry Wilson, not Henry Baldwin. His silences and evasions might never have both-ered her, but some mental retuning is required for the idea that

Henry might have lied to her, just as he lied to all those other people who knew him by another name. And when she hears about the newsagent's later encounter with Henry, she can't help but register, by the smallest tightening of the eyelids, that this story surprises her a little. 'Henry in a suit,' she says, trying to smile. 'I'd like to have seen that.'

'But what's interesting is that last look back. This man didn't know what to think until then. Either Henry was faking, or he truly had absolutely no idea who this person was. But when he looked back, that tipped the balance towards the idea that Henry knew him. And we wanted to ask you what you thought.'

'I couldn't say. I wasn't there. Perhaps Henry didn't like him.'

'That's a possibility. But most people wouldn't go through the rigmarole of pretending not to remember.'

'Most people don't sleep on cliffs. Most people don't spend all summer walking.'

'Point taken. But when Henry went on his walks, when he came back, you said that he didn't know where he'd been. Right?'

'Sometimes.'

'OK. Sometimes. But was there ever an occasion when you weren't altogether convinced? Did it ever seem possible to you that he was putting on an act?'

'Why would he do that?'

'I don't know. But was there a moment when you wondered that he might be putting it on?'

'No,' she replies, plainly, not defensively, seemingly saddened rather than offended that anyone should propose such a notion.

'Not once?'

'Never.'

'I have to say that I don't really get it. He goes meandering all over the place for a month or two, and when he gets back here it's as if nothing has happened in the interim. All wiped from his mind. I'm struggling to accept this. We all are.'

At this Ian contributes a nod. 'It wasn't all wiped,' says Hannah to Ian's averted face. 'He'd remember parts of it. I told you.'

'I must have misunderstood. I thought you said he had no idea where he'd been. Blank, not confused, wasn't that it? The bus ticket –'

Perhaps, thinking it wasn't terribly relevant, she hadn't explained as carefully as she should have done, she says, but now she clarifies: some incidents, some scenes from his wanderings did stick in his mind, but often weren't accessible to Henry's memory, or not to his conscious memory. Ask him where he'd been the week before last and in all likelihood he'd not be able to recall. But weeks later, spontaneously, something might come back to him. One day, for example, passing a shop with Hannah, he saw a postcard that stopped him in his tracks. What the picture showed was a ruined wall on a promontory high above the surf. Henry removed the card from the rack and turned it over to read the photo credits. 'Tintagel,' announced Henry, as if to say that this, of course, is the answer to a crossword clue that had stumped him a day or two ago. He displayed the picture to Hannah. 'Down there,' he said, pointing into a corner of the picture, 'there's a cave through the rock. They call it what's-his-name's cave. What's his name? You know. The wizard.' Hannah had to provide the name of Merlin. 'That's him. That's where I was. Tintagel.' With Hannah's help he worked out when it was that he was at Tintagel. 'July. I was at Tintagel in July,' said Henry, pleased to have settled the issue, but more for Hannah's sake, she felt, than for his, and that was the end of the subject, now that it was settled. A sticker on a car's rear window – 'Lovelly Clovelly' – revealed to Henry his whereabouts a month or two before. Overhearing two women talking about the huge waves at Bude reminded him that he'd seen huge waves there too. And so on and so on, and in each instance, it would seem, it was as though Henry was content that something had been slotted into its rightful place, but this rightful place seemed to be an almost abstract concept, because he showed no significant emotional response to the recovery of these missing days. The rediscovery of his own past affected him no more than finding a missing button would do – or rather, this was the case with his recent past. When memories of more distant days occurred to him, however, he often appeared jolted by them, to use a word that Hannah had used in our first interview, a word she still thinks is the best one. The postcard of Tintagel brought him to a halt, but an easy halt; when a moment from his deeper past resurfaced spontaneously, he might react as if smacked about the head by an invisible hand. Several times he actually clutched his brow with both hands, covering his face. You'd think that a migraine had struck him, but when his hands came down he would be smiling broadly, as often as not. Walking above Littleham Cove, they saw some crows being chased in the air by seagulls, a sight at which Henry stopped, staring beyond the birds. He sat down and dipped his face into the basin of his palms. 'I saw something remarkable,' he said eventually, lowering his hands, and Hannah wasn't sure if he was talking about what he'd just seen in his mind or an event long gone, which he remembered as having been remarkable. What the crows and seagulls had sparked in his brain was a sunny morning in a town to which he could not attach a label. He was in a street of identical houses, semi-detached houses with bay windows and white pebble-dashed walls, and there was not a car or person moving on the street. To his right there was a park of yellowed grass, behind railings, and he was standing underneath a tree, on a dusty and sticky patch of pavement, when a screech made him turn round and there, flying down the centre of the road, directly above the dotted white lines, at head height, was a heron, pursued by a dozen crows, which were swooping around it as it flew. Perfectly straight the heron flew, all the way down the long wide street, into the sun. With an arm held out straight, directing Hannah's gaze towards the phantom bird, Henry watched the heron again fly into the sun, smiling as the vision shrank out of sight. Late one afternoon, rain almost as heavy as the rain of this evening had ceased as abruptly as a hydrant turned off, and been followed by brilliant cold sunshine that had made Henry see a hill that he'd seen as a child, a distant hill that looked in the light of sunset like a vast mound of thick green cloth, but what age he'd been on the day of this remembered sunset he didn't know, nor did he have any idea where the hill might have been. An aroma of pine sap sent him back, with dizzying immediacy, to some woodland in high summer, where the sunlight, coming flat through the wood, picked out beads of amber sweat on the bark of the trees and he could smell again the warm musty matting of pine needles on which he'd been treading.

Henry's fits of memory, that's what Hannah calls these episodes, and you'd think, listening to her talking about them, almost reliving them, that she's talking about time spent in the presence of someone famous, or a poet. Describing the rain-soaked hill, she moves her hand in small undulations, as if to stroke the plush green fabric that Henry had imagined. It's touching, her devotion to him, the vividness with which she remembers him, but it's almost inconceivable that a man could experience episodes such as these, in which fragments of his childhood returned to him with the force and precision of the present, yet not once reveal anything factual, anything usefully factual, about his life. Too much in thrall to Henry the mystic, Hannah must have forgotten the workaday details, or not paid them much attention at the time. Asked again if Henry ever let slip anything about himself, she answers demurely, as if this is more a philosophical debate than a murder investigation: 'These things were about himself.'

'But you know what I mean. About his life. His life story. It's hard to make anything coherent out of what you're telling me. I'm finding it hard, let's say that. Here's this man who's no sooner done something than it's wiped from his mind, yet he's so overcome by the flashback of a walk in the woods that he needs to lie down for a minute to recover. He remembers trees but he can't remember any people. I don't get it.'

'He could remember people. I never said he couldn't.'

'OK. But nobody with a name attached.'

'That's true, I think,' she says, with a floorwards frown to signify a verifying check of her memory.

'And we know nothing about his family. No facts.'

'Lots of facts. Little scenes, images. Bits and pieces.'

'But no information. Like where they lived, if his parents are alive or dead?'

'I told you. I'm sure they're dead.'

'That's your hunch.'

'You make it sound as if I'm being obstructive. I'm not.'

'No. It's just –'

'I told you,' she says, and for an instant there's a glare in her eyes that indicates the presence, suppressed, of a spectacular temper. 'It wasn't appropriate to ask. He's a lot older than me. If he'd wanted to tell me he'd have told me. And this sadness used to come over him, after he'd remembered something. I wasn't going to pester him. I already told you. He had to explain what he'd remembered and then he wanted rid of it. I've said all this.'

'I'm trying to understand what was going on in his mind, that's all.'

'I didn't say I understood him.'

'But you must have wondered?'

'He was who he was. He wasn't a puzzle to be solved,' she says, her attitude close to condescension.

'Well, he is now.'

At this rejoinder, spoken more cuttingly than intended, she looks away, at the door, and a movement of her jaw gives her face the sullenness that we saw during our first conversation. 'Sorry he wasn't more helpful,' she mutters to the wall. 'I'm –'

'Didn't it strike you as odd that he went on these long walks, promptly forgot all about them, but never forgot where to come back to? He entirely forgets the man in Ilfracombe, but doesn't forget you. I'm assuming you didn't have to introduce yourself all over again, or am I making a false assumption?'

'No.'

'So you can see why this is a problem, can't you?'

'Are you trying to imply something?'

'Not implying anything. Just suggesting that it's odd. It makes him seem more like a homing pigeon.'

'A neat comparison,' she comments, and here we get a look more caustic than anything she threw at Ian before.

'You prefer the idea of sleepwalking. I remember. OK. So we say it was as if he went away on a big sleepwalk. Sleepwalkers somehow don't get lost. They find their beds again, just as Henry came back to the beach. But sleepwalkers set off at a certain time in the night. A switch is thrown in their brains and off they go. So why did Henry walk?'

'I don't know.'

'He never explained what triggered it? Never made any remark about it?'

'Why should he? It's just something he did. It was what he did. Most people go on holiday in the summer. Henry walked.'

'That's the reason behind it then, you think? A break from routine?'

'Maybe he liked going for long walks. Maybe he went loopy every year. Perhaps he wanted to see Tintagel.'

'And then forgot all about it.'

'Look, I don't know. What would you like me to say? He just wanted to get away. Will that do?'

'Everyone, all the eyewitnesses, describe the same thing: he's walking fast, so fast you'd think someone was after him. This isn't just someone going for a ramble around the county. And why all the different names? Was he scared of somebody?'

'Christ,' she whispers, shaking her head slowly. 'Man on the run. But only in high season.' She looks up, and her eyes have the fixity of someone who is about to reiterate an argument for the final time. 'You didn't know him. I knew him. The names were just a game, I suppose. Henry wasn't running from anyone.'

'He never mentioned that he had a wife?'

At this news Hannah becomes very still, cradling the mug in both hands, her face immobile, projecting a steady, assessing gaze.

'No,' she says, maintaining her stony scrutiny. 'He didn't mention that. Who said he was married?'

'His employer, in Ilfracombe. Henry told him he used to be married and it hadn't worked out. He changed the subject quickly. A touchy subject, apparently.'

'He's sure?'

'He's sure that's what Henry said.'

'Well,' she shrugs.

'So he never alluded to a wife? Ex-wife?'

'To the best of my admittedly not infallible recollection, he did not,' she replies with a thin, sarcastic smile, and then the scrutinising gaze returns, intensified by a slight squinting. 'Why do you tell me this?' she asks. 'I get the feeling you're testing me out. Do you think I'm keeping something from you? I'm not. There are things I haven't told you, but they're not of any relevance. I have dozens of Henry's memories stored away. Do you want to hear them all? A runaway horse, a labrador that wouldn't stop howling. Want me to list them all? If you like, I will. It'll bore you witless, but I'll tell you. Gladly. I'm not holding anything back. "He never mentioned he had a wife?" What's that about? What's the game? You know he didn't tell me.'

'I thought you might like to know. I know you're not –'

'And why would I like to know?'

'OK. I'll put it another way. I thought you should know.'

'Why?'

'Because he was your friend.'

She nods, meaning merely that this utterance has been heard, and for a few seconds longer the measure-taking look is sustained. 'This is nonsense,' she pronounces. 'Utter nonsense. You're scoring points. You're trying to upset me. He did it first time,' she says, with a jerk of the chin towards Ian, who doesn't look up from his notebook, 'and now you're having a go. I don't know why, but that's what you're doing.'

There is an impulse to apologise, but instead what is said is: 'No, that's not it. The idea is to talk about him as much as

129

possible. The more we talk about him, the more we'll learn. When you think about someone, when you try to remember everything about them, sooner or later you get stuck. Your thinking goes into a tunnel. But just keeping talking about them and you can take yourself by surprise. The words might trigger something. Without thinking, it suddenly pops into your mind.'

'So you want to hear about the siren that wouldn't stop? Is that what you're saying?' she says, one eyebrow cocked in ridicule. 'I tell you about the runaway horse and bingo! Oh yes, come to think of it, he was a bigamist. That's how it works, eh?'

'Memory is tricky.'

'Wise words, officer.'

'We all overlook things. I've known people, people who've been burgled, who couldn't remember what's gone missing. There's a gap on the shelf, but they don't know what used to be in it. Things they've seen and used day in day out. Things that have become so familiar, they've stopped seeing them. I've known people completely misdescribe a person they've known for years.'

'I'm not forgetting anything crucial about Henry, believe me.'

'But you don't know, do you? By definition.'

Peering into the dregs of her coffee, she gives this idea not a second's thought. The rain streaming on the windows, however, receives prolonged observation.

This has been badly misjudged and to make it worse there's one more issue to raise. 'We're nearly done. There's one last question we have to ask.'

'Fire away,' she says, again examining the contents of the mug.

'Did he ever say anything, or do anything, that made you think, if only for a moment, that he may have had a thing about children?'

'I don't understand,' she answers, with simulated obtuseness.

'Young children. Did he ever behave towards children, talk about children, in a way that struck you as inappropriate?'

'Like, did he try to give sweets to kids on the beach? Did he have a thing about Mothercare catalogues? Was he a dirty old man? What are you talking about?' A reddening appears with a stare of anger, but at the same time a rim of water is swelling in each eye.

'We've had some information –'

'What? He used to hang round the school gates?'

'Yes, I'm afraid. A man who seems to have been Henry was cautioned outside a primary school. More than once.'

'"Seems to have been".'

'It was Henry.'

Eye to eye she stares, as if to test the quality of this statement, then the intensity of her gaze slackens by a fraction, withdrawing. 'No,' she says coldly, 'he wasn't in the habit of accosting children. I can't recall us ever being anywhere near a child. No.' When she blinks, dislodging tears from her eyes, she lets their trace remain, as if to wipe it away would be to admit to being hurt. It's empty by now, but she raises the mug to her mouth and at the same time gives a glance that seems to say that she had expected better. She puts the mug on the floor. Again she watches the rain on the window-panes. She's not going to say anything.

'I'm sorry.' The words might as well have been spoken to the wall, for all the response they get. 'This is difficult, I know. But we have to pursue every possibility. Someone killed Henry. We want to find the person who did it. As much as you do.' She nods, chewing non-existent gum. 'We're going to find the person who killed him.'

'I should hope so,' she says, to the windows.

It's time to go, but another remark gets made. 'Your T-shirt. Henry had one just like it, didn't he? Did you give it to him?'

'Yes,' she says, fleetingly giving her attention. 'Why?'

'An innocent question.'

'I gave him my cast-offs,' she says, as though her actions were an example of a general attitude towards Henry that merited scorn.

'He needed them.'

Ignoring this comment, she stands up. 'We're done?' she asks.

'We are.'

At the door she pauses, looking down the hallway. 'I've been trying to help,' she protests, turning, in a brief resurgence of anger that has helplessness and grief in it.

'I know. You liked him a lot. We understand that.'

'Yes, I did.'

'This thing about the kids, it might be nothing. But you need to –'

'Your coats,' she says. With this, and a weakly bitter smile, she leaves the room. She's gone for somewhat longer than it should take, and when she comes back she has the composure of exhaustion. 'Still sopping,' she says, passing our coats over.

'Don't worry,' says Ian.

And then she says, pointing to the windows: 'Look at that.'

The sea, shining over most of its extent, is the grey-black of graphite, flecked here and there with silver, and the sky is a great sagging blue-black mass, a huge stew of plum-coloured clouds, with a thin strip of bright lemon underneath it, lining the horizon. It's memorable, not for itself but for Hannah's face, for the momentary expression of joy at the sight of the sea and the sky.

16

It doesn't take long to locate Henry's bolt-hole in Ilfracombe.
Now the temporary home of an unemployed welder and his girlfriend and their five-month-old daughter, it's seen half a dozen
changes of occupant since Henry's day, and the population of the
immediately surrounding premises has been similarly mobile. The
one fixed point in the street is flat four of the building opposite,
the residence of Mr and Mrs Fratton, who remember very little
about their one-time neighbour. Kept himself to himself, he did,
Mr Fratton relates. Never seemed to have visitors, says Mrs
Fratton. Never saw him with anyone. Wasn't unfriendly, not as
such, but he wasn't an inviting sort of man. Wanted to be left
alone, that was the feeling you got from him. Mr Fratton, working night shifts for the best part of a year, would often pass Henry
in the street. You could set your clock by him, he said. If Mr
Fratton reached home at 6.45, he'd see Henry leaving. But did
Mr Fratton ever actually conduct anything that might be termed
a conversation with his neighbour of two years? No. Do door-
to-door enquiries in the immediate vicinity of Henry's ex-dwelling
yield anything new? They do not. Some recall seeing him on his
way to work or back, but nobody ever passed a word with him.
Once again dead Henry disappears, a wraith of fading memories.

We do, however, discover the origins of the notorious blue suit.

A Mr Bob Vaughan, having belatedly seen, in a dentist's waiting room, Ronnie Houghton's second story, gives us a call. In 1977 Mr Vaughan opened a dry cleaner's in Taunton. The incident with Henry happened in 1982, he remembered, because he'd been in business five years when he decided it was time to smarten the place up. Between the counter and door of the shop Mr Vaughan had a rail of unclaimed clothes for sale – anything left for longer than three months went up there. One day he saw this man peering through the window at the rail of homeless clothes. For perhaps a minute he stood outside, staring, as if trying to remember if one of the shirts hanging there might once have belonged to him. The following day he reappeared and again spent a minute peering through the window, but this time he came in. He was wearing jeans and a denim shirt, both of which had lost almost all their colour and were beginning to fray, but they were moderately clean, unlike the footwear – a pair of scuffed black moccasins that hadn't seen polish or brush for a very long time. The hair, likewise, was in need of attention – so dense and tangled and greasy, in fact, that at first glance, seeing the man looking into the shop, Mr Vaughan thought he was wearing a beret or cap. There was another customer in the shop and the man went over to the rack, where he lifted a suit that had passed the three-month tariff only that week and proceeded to examine it very closely, turning the sleeves inside out, checking the lining of the pockets and so on.

When the other customer had left, the man carried the suit over to the counter. A mighty yawn – a real jaw-cracker – preceded the man's first words, which were spoken in a voice that was surprising. A well-off voice, it was, and the words themselves were surprising too. 'I find myself in a predicament,' he said, or 'in a quandary', or something along those lines. Without embarrassment, stating his situation as though describing the situation of a third party, the man explained that he needed a suit for an interview, and the blue suit on the rail would do very nicely, but his present circumstances would not permit him to pay for it.

This was the way he spoke: 'circumstances would not permit'. His manner of speaking was strange and it was strange that a person who seemed, from his speech, to be of a fairly comfortable social status should find himself unable to afford twenty pounds for a second-hand suit, or even be interested in buying a second-hand suit for that matter. He then asked if he might do some work 'in lieu' – pronounced not 'in loo', but the French way. There was no work. Margins were tight, the laundry was in effect a husband-and-wife operation. They needed only a part-time helper and that position was taken. 'I understand,' the man replied. He put the suit back on the rail, thanked Mr Vaughan and closed the door softly behind him.

A week later he was back, asking whether the situation vis-à-vis the part-time post had changed. It had not, and was not likely to in the foreseeable future, Mr Vaughan told him. Nonetheless the man kept coming back. Every Wednesday for six or seven weeks, on the stroke of three o'clock in he'd walk, with his blanched denim outfit and his half-dead moccasins and his flat hat of hair, enquiring after the hypothetical job. It was awkward, having to deal with this man in his mid forties who was as persistent as a schoolkid, coming back every week, as if he'd forgotten that it was only seven days ago that he was turned away. In the end Mr Vaughan relented and offered him some work, helping to repaint the shop and the back rooms. They began on a Saturday, as soon as the shop closed, and worked together through the evening until after midnight. Early the next morning they picked up the brushes again for a stint that ended up lasting the best part of a day. Mr Vaughan's helper, who gave his name as Henry Palmer, worked like a maniac, refusing to take a break for food, gulping a coffee while racing the paint roller up and down the wall, as if a stopwatch were running and he wouldn't get his reward if he dawdled. If Mr Vaughan had allowed him to, he'd have worked right through the Saturday night and kept going until he was finished. They had the radio on, as it soon became clear that Mr Palmer wasn't much of a man for chat, but he did

135

let slip a few details about himself. He had separated from his wife and fallen on hard times, when the factory where he'd been employed went bust. He'd been a machinist, a lathe operator, but he fancied trying something different now, a desk job of some kind. Though he'd written a lot of applications, he wasn't having much luck. He needed to smarten himself up a bit, he'd concluded. He told a story about going to see someone about working on the phones in an office, but when he got there they turned him away without giving him a chance to open his mouth. The next day he repeated the story, but it wasn't exactly the same, second time round. Some detail contradicted something he'd said the previous evening, which made Mr Vaughan wonder.

Many of the things that Mr Palmer told him didn't altogether fit, and of course the voice and the lack of money didn't quite match. For one thing, the wife's name changed: Emma or Gemma one day and something different the next. There were discrepancies regarding how long he'd been out of work. He was staying with his brother in Taunton, he said, but the brother's name took a few seconds to occur to him, long enough to convince Mr Vaughan that for some reason he was being spun a tale, though he couldn't quite imagine why someone should bother to invent a brother for the benefit of a someone he didn't know from Adam. Taciturn, hard-working and not to be taken at his word, that was how Mr Vaughan summed up his two-day assistant. A harmless fantasist, you could say. In the small hours of Monday morning, three or four hours before the shop was due to open, Mr Palmer took his suit, declined an offer of breakfast and took his leave.

So that's the story of the suit, another inconsequential instalment of the life of vagabond Henry. While a team was tracking down any adult male Palmers who might have been resident in the Taunton area in the early 1980s (several were found, none of them a brother of Henry), the investigation of Mystic Mike was assigned to Geoff Salter and Chris Davies. The relationship between Geoff Salter and Ian Mowbray was not ideally smooth. For one thing, doughy slow-lane Geoff disliked his colleague's modus operandi. Bloody Mowbray carried on as if every waking moment of his life were an audition, that's what Geoff thought. Perceiving quite quickly that Ian was smarter than him, Geoff also let it be known that he found something comical in his colleague's blatant ambitiousness. Furthermore, having a small-eyed, jowly, ninety-per-cent-finished kind of face, Geoff probably envied Ian's clean-cut features. He also harboured a certain tenderness for Mary, which didn't help.

One evening, in the week of Mr Vaughan, Geoff joins us in the pub, chiefly so he can bother Ian, who is not finding it easy to disguise the fact that he resents not having been given Mystic Mike (the closest thing we had to a credible candidate), but ostensibly to tell us about an incident that's just happened down on the beach. He was walking by The Maer when he saw this bonfire and a gang of kids round it, about a dozen of them. Some of them were drinking and a couple were nowhere near legal, so he decided to have a word. Most of them scarpered the moment they saw him, but a few – the older ones – stood their ground. There were some smashed-up pallets and a cricket bat on the fire, and beside the fire they'd made a mound of sand, with the front half of a broken surfboard as a headstone. Someone had drawn a wreath of flowers on the mound and scrawled beneath them: *The Unknown Cunt – RIP.*

'Not funny,' says Mary, and Geoff agrees that it isn't funny, instantly expunging the smile from his face, but Ian laughs, for the purposes of outflanking Geoff by maintaining a show of cordiality towards him, even though there's a risk of increasing the tension that has lately arisen between himself and Mary, who is of course pleased that gormless Geoff is the one who's been put on the trail of the possibly dangerous headcase, but on the other hand has begun to tire of Ian's moaning about Geoff's good fortune in being handed the aforesaid headcase, and in addition has become a little tetchy about Ian's perceived – but disputed – fondness for Rachelle, who this evening is not with us.

'What the fuck else ever happened around here?' one of the

kids had said to Geoff, upon being told that they weren't show-ing appropriate respect for the dead. 'Fuck-all since the Vikings.'

Mary is not entertained by this either, but Geoff can't help himself once he's embarked on a story: he turns on the tap and out it comes in a gush. But Ian's laughing and he knows the kid in question, a lad who fancies himself as a hard case but is more a whiner than a hooligan. You look at him and you see someone packed with advance resentment for all the injustices that life will inflict on him – that's Ian's line, or words to that effect, and this gets a smile out of Mary, and out of Geoff, who is wishing to Christ that he'd said something like that, and so to compensate for his slowness of wit he shares with us his latest discoveries in the screwy world of Mystic Mike. This ploy fails to provoke any visible irritation in Ian, who now places a hand on Mary's thigh, whence Mary removes it, as though lifting a greasy rag. With this slight upward movement on the tension gauge, it's time to get another round.

And who is at the bar, starting his shift at this very minute? It's Josh, and right away he wants to know if we've talked to Hannah yet. Told that we have, he asks: 'And?' He seems to be expecting to hear something that might amuse him.

'And what?'

'What did you think?'

'About what?'

'About her.'

'What we think about Ms Rowe is neither here nor there.'

'But was she helpful?'

'Yes. She was helpful.'

He lines up the glasses and begins to pour. Directed at the light in the centre of the ceiling, his face has an expression that's intended to advertise the fact that he's thinking of something that's related to Hannah and is very much to his advantage. With a wry little smile for his secret thoughts, he puts the first filled pint on the bar and says: 'But her father's a total arsehole.'

'I'll take your word for it.'

'He's an art teacher. Does summer courses for daubers: all these old biddies with their watercolour sets. Carries on like he's Michelangelo reincarnated, but the old girls love him. Five hundred quid a head plus VAT? Screaming great bargain. Packs them in, he does.' Shaking his head at the idea of Mr Rowe, muttering about the prat in a cravat and his semi-senile fan club, he pours the rest of the drinks. He takes the money, laughing to himself, but when he hands back the change it's the opportunity for a direct, tight-browed, deep-thinking stare. 'Know what I think?' he asks. 'I'll tell you. Her and that old man. Hannah and that Henry bloke? It's all to do with her father. It was a father thing, what she had with him. That's what it was. Explains a lot, it does.'

'Does it?'

'It does.'

'A lot about what?'

Here a pause occurs, as Josh perceives that he is rapidly losing what remains of the goodwill of his audience. 'Well. You know.'

'No, I don't know, Josh.'

'Her and Henry. It was unusual, yes? That's all.'

'We're not investigating Ms Rowe.'

'No, I know,' he says, taking a step away, one hand raised. 'I didn't –'

'Your opinion of Mr Rowe has been noted. Thank you. Unless you're suggesting that we interview Mr Rowe in connection with the murder. Are you suggesting that he might have killed Henry?'

'No. Of course not.'

'Good.'

'OK. I shouldn't have said anything,' he says, but for an instant there is a defiance in his eye, a look that's about Hannah, and it's like being called a fraud and having a mirror held up to your face to prove it.

17

This year's Easter sermon, Beal's springtime pitch for Godcorp plc, is notable for its melancholy little refrain, deployed to punctuate his inventory of the past year's bad news. Earthquake in Iran: 'What hope is there, what hope?' Massacre in Monrovia: 'What hope is there, what hope?' War in Kuwait: 'What hope is there, what hope?' Eyes uplifted, he gives voice to our collective despair. Unspeakable bloodshed in South Africa, bombings by the IRA: 'What hope is there, what hope?' The dreadful event so close to home: 'What hope is there, what hope?' He sighs the phrase like a lullaby for our grieving souls. He pauses, forcing a smile, a smile overburdened with humility, a smile of benevolent admonition. We are invited to meditate upon our sins. With a slow sideways sweep of an arm, he introduces the effigy on the cross, our judge in the court of heaven, our hope. 'The risen Lord,' he whispers, in a swoon of unworthiness.

In the second row, Mr Bywater is raking his beard, and his wife, when he's not looking, is giving him the glances of a woman betrayed. Michael Trethowen, brow profoundly furrowed, scrutinises the crucified Christ as if there's something about Him that doesn't quite add up, but he can't define precisely what it is. Alice, however, sits in imperturbable contemplation, gazing into the flowers that have been set on the altar steps. The sunlight shines on the dark wood of the pews and the rough stone walls; birds are chirruping in the graveyard; we can taste the juicy spring air. The church, it must be said, would be a pleasant place to pass half an hour, if only Beal were elsewhere.

At the end of the show Michael stays in his seat, fiddling with the buttons of his coat. We're out of the church before him and have reached the corner of the street when his voice behind us says: 'Hello, Mrs Donohue.' His face, already hectic, reddens more deeply at Alice's smile. 'Actually,' he goes on, before Alice can speak, 'it was your husband I wanted to speak to. Just for a minute. There's something I –. Just for one minute. Would that be OK? I'm sorry.' Alice says goodbye and Michael, pressing his knuckles to his mouth, distraught at the thought of having disrupted our day, watches her until she is out of sight. 'You don't mind? You're sure it's OK?' he asks, overdoing the politeness. 'Only a minute, that's all,' he repeats. A moment later, having been reassured that the time can be spared, he ceases the histrionics. 'This way,' he says, pointing in the opposite direction, as if there's something worth seeing down there. Then straight away he's talking about Beal. 'What did you make of that, then?' he asks, and without pausing for a reply he gives his verdict on the sermon, which he thinks could be summarised as: 'Let's move on, good people; let's forget Henry.' This is perhaps unjust, an idea to which Michael gives approximately three seconds' thought before embarking on some skit about the resurrection, with St Peter at the pearly gates offering the blessed souls a catalogue of pictures, showing themselves at every stage of life from birth to death, so they can pick the look they'd like to wear for ever in heaven. It's a tricky problem, Michael allows, and he can understand Beal's haziness on the issue. In Italy somewhere there's a big painting of the resurrection and it's really hilarious, he says, with no hilarity in his eyes. The saved are coming out of the ground like shoots of grass and they all look terrific: they're twenty-five years old, all of them. It's like a big stage, with these well-honed bodies popping up through the floor, but

141

in the wings there's a gang of skeletons, and the skeleton at the front seems to be complaining to one of the fully formed nakeds. 'Any idea where my skin's got to?' Michael wheedles, one hand arched tenderly on his chest. We've turned right, then right and right again, and are nearing the back of the church.

'This is what you wanted to talk to me about?'

At this he shakes his head and makes a sound that's perhaps intended to be a laugh, but is more like the sound made by someone who's taken a light blow to the belly. 'Of course it's not,' he says, coming to a stop. The shoulders sag, the head bends forward, implying a pretence abandoned. His attention is fixed briefly on a garden hedge, then he turns. 'I wanted to apologise,' he says. 'I told your wife what you said about Beal. That you didn't think much of him. I'm very sorry. I had to get it off my chest. That I'm sorry, I mean. Not what you thought of Beal. I'm really sorry. I shouldn't have.' The voice is plausibly contrite and the posture too (one shoulder hunched; hands squirming together) might be convincing. The eyes, what's more, are expressive of contrition, as is the pursing of the lips, but the blinking is all wrong. People blink in phase with what they're thinking and what they're saying, but Michael's blinking is an event of the face alone, like a bad actor whose words are mere speech, with no link to anything underneath. It should be: 'I don't know why I did it [blink]. I was talking to your wife and it just came out [blink]. I wasn't thinking [blink]. It was wrong of me [blink] and I understand if you're angry [blink]. Has she said anything about it [blink]?' But the script delivered by Michael is something like: 'I don't know why I did it. I was talking to your wife and it [blink] just came out. I wasn't thinking. It was [blink] wrong of me and I understand if you're angry. Has she said [blink] anything about it?' Awaiting a reply, he looks again towards the hedge, but he's not looking at anything.

'No. Not a thing.'

This elicits a tiny jerk of the head, a turn arrested at its beginning. 'Good,' he says. 'I'd hate to have caused any trouble.'

142

'You didn't cause any trouble at all.'

'Good,' he repeats, coming to terms with the probability that he's not going to be asked why he talked to Alice. 'Good. I'm glad.'

We know by now that the mind of young Michael is as unsettled a place as it appears to be. Exceptionally gifted, stubborn and prone to bouts of deep gloom, that's how his former head-master characterised him to Geoff Salter and Chris Davies, and the picture given by his tutors at the university was much the same. Engineering was his subject, and from day one he was picked out as a first-class student. When Michael was in buoyant form he absorbed textbooks the way other students absorbed beer, and in lectures he took fairly rudimentary notes because he had almost faultless recall of what had been said. Essays seemed to cost him no effort. His ingenuity in problem solving was astounding, his appetite for work inexhaustible. But his mood was volatile, and at least once a term he would plummet into a depression that might last a few days or for weeks on end, and when he was in one of these troughs he was incapable of making sense of anything. He'd sit in the library all day, with a book open on the desk in front of him, never turning a page. He'd not miss lectures or seminars, but it was impossible to get more than a couple of words out of him. The essays kept coming in, but were far below his customary standard, and deadlines were missed. He had episodes of great anger as well, directed inwards usually, but occasionally vented on his less able colleagues – in other words, almost everyone was a potential target. Once he became so frustrated with the cumbersome thought processes of one hapless student that he burst into tears; another day he screamed and stormed out of the room. At the best of times his social skills were negligible. He lived at home, was rarely seen in any of the common rooms and never in the bar. There were no ex-girlfriends to interview, but Geoff did trace a girl who once went to the cinema with Michael. He insisted on paying for her, walked her home at the end of the evening, thanked her for accompanying him and that was the end of their romance. A sweet boy, she said he was, but he lived in a world of his own. Or not quite of his own: he was devoted to his grand-parents, she remembered, and sometimes would rush home from lectures to cook a meal for them.

At the start of the autumn term of the third year, he fell sharply into one of his depressions, but this one didn't lift. Come the Christmas break he was still unreachable and when the spring term began he seemed worse. He was talking to himself during lectures, muttering about the incompetence of the lecturer, or talking nonsense. There was an incident in a workshop, when he deliberately burned his hand with a soldering iron. One evening he had to be talked into leaving the library at closing time. He was seen standing motionless in the car park, in torren-tial rain. Then, as suddenly as it had started, this episode came to an end. Once again he was churning out the top-grade essays, devouring books at a gluttonous rate. By Michael's standards he was positively chatty. Once in a while he could even be persuaded to come along for a coffee. Now it was full steam ahead to top marks, that's what everyone thought, but they were wrong. In the middle of a seminar he announced that he was leaving and promptly walked out. He'd done this sort of thing before, so people assumed he'd meant that he was leaving the room, but it turned out he meant leaving the university, for good. The pres-sure was getting to him, he told his tutor. It was true that he'd missed several weeks of teaching during this last bout, but he'd caught up, as he always had caught up, and now he seemed to be sailing through his course work. No, Michael insisted, he was going to crack. He made it sound as if this was something he'd made up his mind to do. It took three or four sessions to cajole him into staying, to see how things went. Michael duly went into a nosedive. When the summer term began he was missing. His tutor called at the grandparents' house, where he found Michael sitting in a deckchair in the garden, with a blanket wrapped round his knees, like some geriatric invalid. He appeared cogent enough and noticeably less morose than he'd been when he was last at the university, but he was adamant that he was in no state to resume his studies. Underneath the deckchair was a small stack of hi-fi magazines. This was all he could read at the moment, Michael said, apologising for being so listless. They discussed the possibility of his returning the following year. Michael seemed keen to come back, but he never did.

His grandparents didn't attempt to persuade him to reconsider, nor did they try to get to the bottom of his reasons for quitting: he was unhappy at the university and that, for them, was sufficient reason for him to leave. Geoff's reading of the situation was that they had raised Michael – if 'raised' isn't too active a verb in this context – as if in the belief that one day his parents might return to the land of the living in order to reclaim their son, and they wanted to be able to hand him back as little changed as possible. A nudge on the tiller every now and then, that seems to have been their method, a method of culpable irresponsibility, as far as Geoff was concerned, though he and Chris found it hard not to warm to Mrs Trethowen, a scatty old lady with huge grey eyes and sleeves stuffed full of tissues and an approach to sentence construction that was something close to free association. 'A quirky chap. Always has been,' she declared with a giggle, before embarking on a medley of self-interrupted recollections that were evidently intended to support this assertion, but instead left Geoff thinking that, although he'd lost the thread a few times, 'quirky' seemed to be a flattering translation. 'A thoughtful boy,' she concluded, in wonder-struck pride, having described a child whom others might describe with precisely the opposite adjective.

Money was not a problem in the Trethowen household. Old Mr Trethowen had made a tidy sum as a structural engineer, his wife was the only child of a prosperous farmer, and their son and daughter-in-law had both become partners in a successful architectural practice. In the year he went to university Michael had inherited most of his parents' not insubstantial estate. To

Michael's fellow students there was no visible sign of the fattened bank balance: he dressed messily, he didn't own a car, he didn't go away during the holidays. The cash was spent at home, first to fund the building of Michael's shed and then to fill it.

The shed stands behind a screen of laurel at the end of a lawn that's just a yard or two longer than an Olympic swimming pool, and it compares to your average garden shed in much the same way as an Armani suit compares to an anorak. Designed by a partner in his parents' firm, it's the size of a six-car garage and made mainly from expensive wood, but with one wall entirely of glass, with a glass door set into it. Through this wall you see a wide steel bench, spotlights, tool racks, a couple of computers, a scattering of circuit boards and bits of wiring. This is the nerve centre of Michael's one-man business, an enterprise founded during his student years. He repairs and modifies hi-fi equipment, but this is a sideline to the main business – the creation of the T-Blok amplifier, Michael Trethowen's ever-evolving, sod-the-cost contribution to the home entertainment industry. A prototype of the mighty T-Blok – two hefty lumps of raw aluminium wired to a pair of speakers (also manufactured by Michael) with woofers as big as buckets and a half-tonne CD player built by an American pen pal – stands at the far end of the shed, on steel tables welded by Michael's own hand, and is operating at high capacity on the afternoon Geoff and Chris come calling. Mrs Trethowen has to wave through the glass wall to get her grandson's attention, and when Michael opens the door this deluge of sound comes out, as if he's got a couple of church choirs in there, singing at the top of their voices.

It's a stupendous racket, as Geoff remarks to Michael, bellowing to be heard, and this gets things off to a good start. 'Sit there,' Mike yells eagerly, waving at the old Chesterfield that stands in the centre of the shed, aligned towards the speakers. Standing beside his amplifiers, Michael closes his eyes, grinning in ecstasy, swaying slightly, as though standing under a waterfall. 'Forty separate parts to this!' he shouts, amazed. 'Forty voices!' Giddily he stoops to turn the volume down. 'Listen,' he says. 'You can hear them distinctly. Forty! It's incredible.' He points at the speakers, smiling encouragement, but Geoff isn't counting the voices: he's studying the decor. On to the walls above the music system are pinned dozens of pictures in neat rows. They look like cartoons and many of them seem to feature explosions or fighting, but it's difficult to make them out from where Geoff and Chris are sitting. 'I made these,' declares Michael, patting the amplifiers to divert their attention from the wall. He turns the music down and reels off some technical specifications of his handiwork. Feigning comprehension, Geoff kneels to examine the impressive hardware. Through a mesh in the top of one of the aluminium boxes he sees wires glowing orange. 'Valves,' says Geoff, accenting the surprise, and Michael rewards his guests with a layman's guide to the superior sonic qualities of the old technology. Impressed, Geoff again surveys the wall behind Michael's head. The cartoons are Japanese and are full of huge-breasted saucer-eyed teenies in ripped shorts, being menaced by drooling gunmen and half-human machines. One picture seems to show a car-load of buxom schoolgirls being raped by robots. In another a knife is being pushed through a boy's chest and the blade is emerging through his back like a shark's fin.

'Look at this,' says Michael, ejecting the CD. He ushers Geoff and Chris to one of the computers, where the T-Blok brochure is displaying quotes from satisfied customers ('This gear is truly awesome!') and a review from a magazine that Geoff has never heard of ('stunning transparency . . . smoothly delivered power'). For twenty minutes or so Michael holds forth on the genesis of the T-Blok, the unacceptability of ninety-nine point nine per cent of hi-fi equipment on sale in Britain, the vileness of digital recording, his never-ending personal quest for aural purity and naturalness. At first he sounds like a harmless crank, bringing us the good news that through high-end audio engineering we shall be redeemed. By the end, spouting about noise pollution,

147

air pollution, the triviality of modern life, with the wall of cartoons behind him, he's become a dangerous obsessive, a fascistic geek. 'There's nothing as good as vinyl,' he pronounces. 'For true sound, real living sound, vinyl murders digital every time. But vinyl's dead. In the cause of convenience, it's being killed. The tyranny of the mediocre, I tell you. Can't fight it. Got to beat them at their own game. You have to make digital sound like analogue, yes? It's the bloody Dutch,' he says, leaning forward to impart more forcibly the truth of the conspiracy he has uncovered. 'They invent the cassette, the abomination of abominations. Then they give us the CD, tinned food for the ears. They hate music. That's what it is. They can't hear properly. It's all that pornography and drugs. Dulled their senses. It's the only explanation,' he says, and Geoff can't tell if he's joking or not.

Michael's grandmother now appears at the door, bearing a tray of tea and biscuits. She knocks, waits outside until summoned by a wave from the young master, then comes in and sets the tray down on the floor beside the Chesterfield, in a space cleared of magazines by Michael. 'There you are,' she says, and backs away, as if she's merely the dear old housekeeper. The interruption gives Geoff and Chris their cue to get down to business. In collaboration with George Whittam, they've invented a suspect for the killing of Henry: a man in his thirties, thick-set, crewcut, white, with a prominent tattoo of an anchor on his right forearm. This man was seen on the beach several times in early December, and is known to have asked two witnesses, on different days, if they'd seen Henry around. Geoff would like to know if Michael has seen anyone matching this description. Michael has not. 'You visit the beach quite regularly, I believe. Is that so?' It is so, Michael readily confirms. In that case, Geoff would like Michael to let us know if he should ever see anyone who might be this man.

'Wilco,' answers Michael, giving a snappy salute. There's nothing in Michael's response to these questions that could be taken as an indication of a troublesome conscience. 'So how's it going?' he asks and Chris hints that the net is closing: we've unearthed some promising material for the labs to analyse; there's been a crucial call from a member of the public; there have been some developments that we, of course, are not in a position to disclose. Not one word of it is true, and none of it seems to cause Michael the slightest concern. On the contrary, now that he's vented his opinions on the foul state of music reproduction and the corruption of the world in general, he could hardly be more relaxed. He nods gravely, gratified that the labours of Geoff, Chris and their fellow officers are proceeding towards a satisfactory conclusion.

But an hour later Geoff emerges from Michael's shed-lab convinced that this is our man and that it's only a matter of time before he owns up. This is because, after Geoff and Chris had concluded their summary of our fictitious progress, Michael – reclining almost horizontally, with the tea cup supported on his belly and his eyes trained on the ceiling – drew a deep breath and revealed, calmly, but with the air of a man unburdening himself of a secret that he has kept hidden for years, that he could perfectly understand why someone might murder a stranger. 'To do something irrevocable,' he murmured, seeming now to be thinking aloud. 'It would clarify everything. You take a life. After that, you are a murderer. That's what you are,' he said, and it was as though being a murderer was as marvellous as being a man who had walked on the moon. 'Your life is utterly changed, and definite. So many accidents go into making you who you are, but to do something like that, it makes you entirely responsible for yourself. You've made yourself.'

'And unmade someone else,' Geoff countered.

Michael looked at Geoff and, seeming neither to see nor hear him, smiled. 'I can understand it,' he said. 'I really can. So easily.'

And now, walking past the back of the church, Michael's at it again, positively inviting suspicion. We've finished talking about the gaffe with Alice, the cringe has been superseded by

149

Michael's day-to-day lurch, and we're exchanging banalities about the weather, football, whatever. We're into the postlude of our conversation, but then he says, as if reporting to his probation officer: 'I'm going to the beach. Are you going?'

'Not today, Michael.'

A ruminating silence follows. His lips are pressed tightly together and his eyes are doing a rapid scan of the pavement. Then there's a sly sidelong look, as theatrical as the earlier hand-wringing, and he mutters: 'It was quite a clever thing to do, though, wasn't it?'

'What was?'

'To kill him on the sand.' It's said with a silly little mischievous grin, like a kid who's said something rude and is hoping that he'll get away with it by smiling.

'Clever's not the word I'd pick.'

'No, but you know, the wind blows over it, the tide comes in, there's all your footprints gone. Not going to be any fingerprints, are there? Not like in a house. No spots of blood, bits of hair and all that stuff. All gets washed away, doesn't it?'

'You'd be surprised, Michael.' He doesn't flinch at this, just as Geoff's kiddology didn't get a reaction, but it's worth pursuing the point. 'Every crime that's committed, the person that did it takes something away from the scene. And leaves something behind. It's a fundamental law.'

Michael gives a ponderous, professorial nod, approving the elegance of the formulation. He wants to talk about stains. 'When someone stabs a person to death with a knife, some of the victim's blood would get on to them, yes?'

'Very likely.'

'Henry's killer would have been sprayed with blood, and blood is hard to clean, is that right?'

'That's right.'

'Very hard.'

'Harder than you'd think. Boiling won't do it. Bleaching won't do it. There's always a trace. Always that tiny particle of

150

evidence.' Still there's not the merest observable flicker of disquiet. 'There was this individual, in the States. Killed his wife, put her body in the freezer, then cut it to pieces once it'd frozen solid. Just to make sure, he put the pieces through a wood-chipper and chucked the bits into a river. A sack of meat-sawdust, that's what he'd made of her.'

'And?' Michael urges, wide-eyed with what's intended to be horror but is closer to delight.

'The FBI got the machine from the tool-hire company and took it apart.'

'And?'

'And they found a few slivers of varnished fingernail and some hairs that matched hairs from the wife's hairbrush. Divers went into the river and they found some more material. Not much more than mince, but they got a little lump of thumb-pad out of it, enough to take a print off. Eleven stone the woman had weighed, and all that was left was a couple of ounces of nail and skin and hair. But it was all they needed. They caught him.'

He simulates retching and the next thing he says, breezily, as though we'd never stopped talking about sport, is: 'I'd better get going.' We shake hands, and as we step apart he does a disgruntled frown. Something remains on his mind. He stares at the sky, assessing the advisability of speaking, then he says: 'PC Plod has been round to see me. You know that, I assume?'

'Who?'

'Sergeant Salter. Have you to thank for his company, do I?'

'No.'

'I think I do.'

'Well, you're wrong.'

'Not the sharpest tool in the box, is he?' says Michael in sympathy. 'But do give him my regards.' He walks away, scuffing his feet on the pavement as he goes. A dozen footsteps on, he stops and half turns. 'You used to be an insurance man, didn't you?' he calls.

'That's right.'

'Your wife told me. I've got a good one for you. "Invest now in real Insurance." INRI: "Invest now in real insurance." Good, yes?' He presents a face of innocent glee, then there's one of his shrieking laughs. ''Bye now,' he says with an American accent, then he jogs towards his bike.

18

The flow of new information in effect dried up and there came a week in which there was just one fresh item. It was supplied by a Mrs Fiona Appleton, of Plymouth, who rang to tell us that she believed she might have had an encounter with the dead man several years ago, around 1974 or 1975. It was a summer morning when this incident happened, around seven o'clock. Mr Appleton was away on business. The sun had been up for a couple of hours and Mrs Appleton was a poor sleeper whenever her husband was not at home, so she got out of bed, had breakfast and busied herself with a bit of housework. She was dusting the windowsill in the front room, she remembers, when she looked out and saw a man sitting on the kerb outside their house, on the other side of the road. His age, she'd guess, was in the region of forty and he was very dishevelled. He had his head in his hands and was gazing in the direction of the house. Three or four supermarket carrier bags sat on the pavement beside him. Mrs Appleton continued with the housework, but the man did not budge. Head in his hands, he glumly gazed upon the house. She thought about calling the police, but the man seemed so downcast that she decided, in the end, to go out to him, to find out if he needed any help. The man looked at her as she came down the drive. Seemingly feeble with fatigue and dejection, he did not move as she approached him. The bags, she now saw, were stuffed with clothes and newspapers. She stood in front of him, in her house-coat, duster in hand, and the man looked her up and down. He seemed so miserable that she couldn't take offence. In fact, the way he looked at her made her feel as if she wasn't really there, as if he wasn't seeing her properly. Then he looked at the house again. 'I'm sorry,' he said at last. The words were spoken meekly, as if to someone in a cinema who's come along and told you that the seat you've just taken has been reserved for someone else. That's all he said. 'I'm sorry.' Stiffly he stood up and walked away. End of incident. If this was Henry, it's his earliest appearance, the oldest fragment of Henry's existence. And that, we thought, was the sole significance of the incident outside the Appletons' house.

But we were getting calls from Tom Gaskin, a lot of calls. Every time Michael Trethowen made a pilgrimage to the crime scene, we heard about it from Tom, and the frequency of Michael's attendance had been increasing since Easter, as the weather brightened and the days grew longer. Then the tone of Tom's reports changed, after the Sunday afternoon on which the strange young man came sauntering up Tom Gaskin's road, like a tourist doing some casual sightseeing on a Paris boulevard, and then, catching sight of Tom at his window, waved at him, as if he could hardly believe his good fortune in finding him there, though the young man and Tom had never exchanged as much as a single word. For a minimum of fifteen seconds he stood on the pave-ment, smiling and waving, but the smile then vanished and the waving became sinister: dour-faced, the young man began moving his arms in wider and wider sweeps, as though cleaning very large imaginary windows. Seeing Tom withdraw from the window, he stopped in mid wipe, as suddenly as a machine disconnected from the power, and walked on, taking the High Land path.

Next week, on the Thursday, he reappeared outside the house, but on this occasion he didn't break stride, instead hailing Tom in passing, like an old friend who often happens to be passing this way. On the following Tuesday he was there again, and again there was a variation in the performance: as before, he did not slow down, but now there was something insanely rigid about his grin and the waving was almost frantic. A week later, at lunchtime, Michael was back. This time he came to a halt, waving as if trying to attract Tom's attention, though he'd had Tom's attention from the moment he came into view. After a few seconds the waving turned into beckoning – he was pointing towards the beach, apparently inviting Tom to join him there. Worse: as Tom put down the paper he'd been reading, the beckoning hand turned into a fist and the young man began to mime the act of stabbing someone in front of him. Pinching the tip of his tongue between his teeth, he did the stabbing action over and over again, giving Tom a merry, waggle-headed smile, like a clown growing desperate with an unresponsive audience, and this made Tom Gaskin very nervous, so nervous that a house call was needed to calm him down.

We sit in the armchairs, well away from the window, and he keeps looking around the room as if he's begun to suspect there might be cameras hidden in the corners. 'Did someone tell him I'd reported him?' he asks, leaning forward, his hands meshed, his eyebrows and the skin round his eyes fixed in a half-mask of anxiety. 'I'm not saying you told him. I know you wouldn't. But he must have found out.'

'It would seem he knows you've had an eye on him, yes. But no one from the station would have told him.'

'Are you sure?' he asks, as respectfully as his unease will allow.

'As sure as I can be, yes.'

'But not absolutely sure.'

'You can never be absolutely sure, Mr Gaskin. But it's unlikely, I'd say. Extremely unlikely.'

For a moment he gazes woefully into the carpet, fiddling with his cufflinks as if they were worry beads. Even though he didn't have a millimetre of fat to lose, he seems to have shrunk since the previous visit. The cuffs of his shirt, like cylinders of pure white card, hang loosely from his wrists, and his collar too has an inch or two of slack. 'It's upsetting,' he says.

'It's not pleasant, I know.'

'Can't he be arrested? It must be against the law, what he's doing. Surely. Isn't it?'

'We can warn him to stay away, certainly. Do you want us to do that?'

Perusing the pattern of the carpet, he considers the offer, but gets lost in a labyrinth of unpalatable choices. 'I don't know,' he says. A thumb is working the back of a finger. With a glance he seems to request help in clarifying his dilemma.

'I think he'll stop of his own accord, sooner or later. Sooner rather than later. But why wait? If we speak to him, he'll stop right away.'

'It might make him worse. He seems to have a grudge against me. Lord knows what would happen.'

'He'd stop, I assure you.'

'You can never be absolutely sure,' Tom replies, forcing a tenuous grim smile. 'You said so yourself.'

'Well, OK. Sometimes you can be sure. He'd stop.'

He looks out of the window, perhaps trying to picture the view without the malign young man in it. Nowadays he's having difficulty sleeping, he says. And he's hardly eaten these past few days, he adds, as though reporting something shameful, like bankruptcy. 'I don't know,' he muses. 'If he stops doing this, he may do something worse.'

'He won't.'

'He might already have done something worse.'

'It's possible.'

'He might break in here.'

'He won't do that.'

'I'm scared.'

'I can see why you would be. I wouldn't be happy if some little creep was doing to me what this one's doing. But we're watching him. He knows we're watching him. And now we'll tell him

156

to lay off. He's not going to get up to something then, is he? If anyone so much as touches the handle of your back door, he's suspect number one. He knows that. Only an idiot would try something else.'

'He behaves like an idiot.'

'He's not, believe me. He might not have all four wheels to the deck, but he's not an idiot.'

'Whoever killed that poor man was something nastier than an idiot.'

'Granted.'

'And it could be him. It could, couldn't it?'

A dispassionate recitation of theory is called for. 'Let's say, Tom, for the sake of argument, that this person, this young man, is the man who killed Henry. Whoever killed Henry is a criminal of a certain type. There are species of killer. You can classify them like animals. The man who stabbed Henry isn't the sort who's going to break into a house and murder someone. Drugged-up burglars do that, once in a blue moon. Henry wasn't killed by a drugged-up burglar. People get killed at home by people they know. Family, nearly always. This boy doesn't know you.'

'Yes, he does.'

'He recognises you. That's as far as it goes.'

'Far enough, I'd say.'

'He's winding you up. It's a kind of game for him. Not a funny game, I know. Very unfunny. But this boy isn't a danger to you, Mr Gaskin. I'm absolutely convinced of that. He's a nuisance, but he's not a danger.'

Extended examination of the carpet ensues. Though the contortions of his brow are relaxing a little, he can't persuade himself to accept that he's safe, but he seems to have lost the will to protest.

'Is there anyone you could stay with for a few days? He'll stop plaguing you, as soon as we give him a caution. I guarantee that. But it might help you to get away for a day or two. Get him out of your mind. When you get back he'll have gone.'

'You can't warn him off the beach, can you?' he says, with a small, wan, one-second smile. 'I'll still see him. He'll still be here. It makes you feel like a prisoner in your own home,' he says, looking at the pictures on the mantelpiece.

'I can imagine. But we'll have a word with him and the situation will improve. And I think it would be a good idea for you to get out of the house for a couple of nights. Just for a weekend. It'll help.'

Again there's a polite approximation of a smile, expressing regretful rejection of the proposal that has just been made, and his next words, spoken after another slow perusal of the mantelpiece photographs, are the words we expect. 'There isn't anybody,' he says, stating the situation simply as a fact, not as an invitation to sympathy.

'Nobody at all?'

'Not near, anyway.'

'How far's not near?'

'Canada. There's a cousin in Vancouver.'

'That's not near.'

'No,' he says. A picture hangs above the sideboard, an old-looking black-and-white photograph of a dozen people standing on a flight of steps that descends from wide french windows to an area of bright gravel. It's to this picture that Tom has now turned his attention, and as he squints at it his face acquires a hint of mischief. 'But in his case,' he adds, 'it's about the right distance. That's him, the Vancouver cousin,' he says, rising quickly from his seat to tap on the glass above the face of a cheery and underfed gentleman, aged about forty, whose suit is drooping at the shoulders and whose hair, brilliantined and unparted, gives off the shine of a ball of wet granite. Beside cousin Bob stands a portly lady who is holding a parasol aloft and smiling like a woman who has been holding her pose for too long. This is Sylvia, Bob's unfortunate wife. One morning, a little under a year after this picture was taken, Sylvia waved her husband off to work and that turned out to be the final exit. The following week the bailiffs were at the door. Cousin Bob, they explained, had debts. He owed a vast amount to a business partner, a man whose name was completely unknown to Sylvia. That was in 1958. She went to live with her parents. A couple of years on, a letter came from Canada: Bob was deeply sorry for what he'd done and begged her forgiveness. He'd done all right for himself in Canada and wanted her to come out there. He'd make it up to her, he promised. They'd live in comfort for the rest of their days. The letter went in the dustbin. Once a month he wrote and they all went into the bin, unanswered, until Sylvia fell ill. She wrote to him saying that she didn't want to hear from him again. But the letters kept coming, sometimes with a cheque in them, then Sylvia died. Bob flew back for the funeral, at which he let slip, in the process of getting plastered with Uncle Ernest, that he had two children by a woman he'd met in Vancouver. 'That's Ernest,' said Tom, indicating the man nearest to the camera. 'Fancied himself as the wit of the family,' he explains, as the roguish set of the hat and the artfully dangling cigarette might suggest. One by one Tom identifies the members of the clan: his sisters, Janey and Rose, his mother and father, his parents' brothers and sisters, and the perpetually ailing Great-Aunt Gladys, who always gave the impression that everyone in the family had in some unspecified way let her down, including, so it appears, whoever was taking this snap. 'All gone now, except Bob and me,' says Tom and then, pointing to the one face that remained unnamed, he said with simple pride: 'And that's Helen.'

For fifty-four years they were married, and here she is, in picture after picture, her face softening over the decades and then becoming leaner, but in every photograph, however many faces may surround her, she is recognisable in an instant by the openness of her smile, a smile that seems to denote an uncomplicated and affectionate nature, a propensity to be amused, a complete lack of vanity. In middle age she stands on a steep beach of egg-sized pebbles, smilingly bedraggled in the rain, next to Tom and in the midst of his birdwatching pals, each of whom is sporting a pair of binoculars as big as two pint glasses. Here, some years before, she lounges on a bank of grass, holding hands with Tom, and in the next picture she's in her late twenties, larking with friends on an open-topped tram. Here she's a teenager, wearing a halter-neck top and capacious shorts, perched on an iron balustrade, with her hands on her knees and her feet on the saddle of a tandem, and then she's an old woman, reading in the chair from which Tom has just risen, giving him a look of loving reprimand. We move along the row of photographs, and every photograph has its brief story, and by the third or fourth picture, as if catching Helen's smile, he's smiling too, his anxiety overridden for as long as he views his gallery of happiness.

'Fifty-four years,' he repeats, modestly gratified by their achievement. 'We had a good life together. Never sick, either of us, not really sick. Very lucky, we were. "I feel poorly," she said to me one morning and she stayed in bed, and that night she died. One day of illness and that was it. Eight years ago. We had a good life. Very good,' he says, and the softness in his voice seems to speak not of regret but of a tenderness for someone living. The gallery ends with Helen, twenty-ish, parting the leaves of a weeping willow to step out into the sunlight, on the bank of the river where they used to go rowing. For half a minute, not speaking, we look at the laughing face of his dead wife-to-be. 'Children would have been good,' he remarks, 'but otherwise life couldn't have been better. I had a good run.' Then there's a light, barely palpable, pat on the elbow, and he says: 'You must be going.'

At the front door he pauses, hand on the catch. 'So you'll talk to him?' he asks.

'We will, Tom. Don't worry.'

'Easier said than done,' he says, and already the lines are deepening again on his brow.

'We're watching him.'

'Thank you.'

'He's not going to do anything.'

'I know,' he says, though he can't quite believe it. When he closes the door, the chain is threaded through the loop straight away and the bolt is thrown too.

By now it's early evening, around six o'clock. Mary will soon be in the pub and we've arranged to meet her there. The pub does not, at this moment, hold much appeal: the mood that's descended with the closing of Tom's door requires a walk and no company for a while. What would have been the elements of that mood? It was unlikely there would be any reason to call again at Tom Gaskin's house, once Michael Trethowen had been sorted out, so there was a sense, in leaving, that the old man was being abandoned. There was certainly also an element of affection for Tom and the kindling of a posthumous affection for Helen, transmitted by her husband and by his photographs. The example of the Gaskins' marriage, their exemplary half-century, might have instilled a consciousness, tinged with self-pity, of having failed. And a feeling of loneliness was brought away from the house, passed on by Tom and inhaled with the air of the underused rooms. The day had been warm and it was warm still, with a subtle and tepid breeze. The low-lying sun shone across the sea, laying a road of lush orange over the water, and the sandbanks in mid stream were ridges of tarnished gold. Scores of small white clouds were moving slowly inland, like a huge island of ice breaking up. Perhaps climate and scene were both conducive to an indulgence in sadness, the sort of sadness that inclines you to a suspension of will, to a torpid receptivity. Families were coming off the beach, heading back to their hotels. On the sand lay two black-haired girls, both pretty, possibly Spanish or Italian. They were lying on their stomachs, smoking, turning the pages of their magazines as they talked. The narrowness of the space between them, and the way one of the girls took a lighter from her companion, without looking, were proof of a deeply rooted friendship. All these things might have had a bearing on what follows.

Less than five minutes' walk from this part of the seafront

161

there's a house that has a hedge cut into the shape of a dolphin. A woman is standing outside this house, by one of the windows: she's wearing a white overall and large plastic goggles, with a blowtorch in one hand and a blade in the other, scraping paint from the window frame, and this woman is Hannah Rowe.

At the squeal of the gate she looks round, and her reaction is the slightest pursing of the lips. She turns off the blowtorch and pushes the goggles up into her hair. 'I haven't remembered anything,' she says, with a wince of annoyance, 'if that's what you're going to ask.'

'OK.'

'I'd have phoned if there was anything.'

'I know.'

She holds the blowtorch out from her thigh, in a loosely closed hand, and there's a truculence to her gaze and stance. 'Was it what you were going to ask?'

'I would have asked, yes. Probably. But I was just passing.'

She looks down the street to left and right. 'OK. And where's your friend?' she asks.

'Meeting his girlfriend.'

'He has a girlfriend?'

'He does.'

Today she's wearing trainers that seem to have been spattered by the contents of about two hundred different paint pots. She's looking down at the trainers but seeing something else, and a lopsided smile appears. 'Quite something, isn't he?' she remarks, then she imitates, very well, Ian's high-intensity woman-melting stare. 'Anything new to tell?' she asks. 'What about the wife? Henry's wife. Supposed wife.'

'We're still working on it.'

'Aha,' she comments, with a bob of the chin, expressive of self-vindication.

'We're not even sure what name to be chasing. His, I mean. The surname.'

'And she might not even exist.'

'She might not.'

A mild frown appears, as if an anticipated argument has expired, disappointingly, before it could properly begin. She shifts her weight, straightening one leg and flexing the other. 'Any more school-gate stories?'

'None.'

'No dodgy behaviour I should know about, as a friend?' she asks, putting a mordant stress on the final clause.

'No. A few more sightings. Nothing vital.'

'So you've stopped by to tell me there's nothing to tell me,' she says, rubbing her chin with mannish roughness, in a parody of puzzlement.

'Well, there is a suspect.'

Instantly her attitude ceases to be an attitude. 'Who?' she asks in a low voice, her look unguarded.

'I can't say.'

'Why not?'

'He's not been charged.'

'Is it someone from here?'

'Really, I can't tell you. If he's charged, I'll let you know straight away. But as things stand –'

'I've understood,' she interrupts, leaning back against the sill. With a thumb she smooths down a spike of charred paint, and another. 'Thank you,' she adds, with a direct glance, and the words seem genuine. Somewhere in the vicinity there's a bird that's making a call like the squeaking of thin wet rubber, like balloons being tied. Hannah peers at the bush in which it seems the bird is hiding; we both do.

'Are you doing the whole thing?'

She looks askance at the façade of the house and appears to be wearied by the sight of it. 'Doors and windows, front and back. Strip, repair, prime, two coats.'

'Just you on your own?'

'Just little me.'

'Take you long, will it?'

'A week. Five days.'

'Nice to be out in the sun.'

'I infer that you think you could do it quicker.'

'No. Takes me five days to put up a shelf.'

'Is that so?' she says, as if this blatant untruth could scarcely be of less interest.

'Do you resent it? Doing this. This kind of work.'

'Why should I resent it?'

'Might not be what you really want to do. If you had the choice you wouldn't be here, would you? You'd rather be a painter painter than a house painter, no?'

'I do have the choice, and I'm here.'

'You know what I mean.'

'This is what I choose to do,' she replies with the firmness of someone rebutting a slight on her character. 'I make decent money. I'm my own boss. I work when I want to. I like it.'

'But presumably you have to do it as well? To buy time to –'

'I enjoy it,' she says. 'I don't know why you think that's so remarkable.'

'I don't. I just had a sense that you weren't enjoying it that much.'

'Today I'm not. I'm having an off-day. You don't have off-days?'

'Of course I do.'

'Well, there you are,' she says, crossing her arms emphatically. 'Don't jump to conclusions.'

'I didn't think I had.'

'I told you,' she says. 'I have things on my mind.'

'We're aware of that.'

There's an infinitesimal hesitation before she says: 'Are you?'

'Yes, I am.'

'Didn't seem so last time.'

'You think about Henry a lot. I know that.'

She rolls her eyes, making a show of incredulity at the fatuousness of this statement. For several seconds she holds the skyward gaze, at the same time releasing a long breath, denoting patience being maintained in the face of provocative stupidity, but the breath lasts too long and the gaze wanders a little, from which it's evident that her reaction is in part a way of averting tears. 'Yes, I think about Henry a lot,' she says, then something, in all likelihood the face of her audience, makes her reconsider the tone. In the pause that follows she places the blowtorch and blade carefully on a sill and brushes a little mound of singed debris off the woodwork, before recrossing her arms in a posture that signifies not truculence, but rather frankness. 'I miss him,' she says with a shrug, as though excusing an outbreak of sentimentality.

'I'm sure you do.'

'And if I don't miss him, who will? That's how I feel. The day I stop thinking of him, that's the end of him. Who else cares that he's dead?'

'I do.'

'But not in the same way.'

'No. Probably not.'

Hannah's response is the nod and weak mouth-only smile of a bereft woman receiving well-intentioned but insufficient words of consolation. She lowers her head. A few seconds later, pressing the heels of her thumbs into her eyes, she emits a rising moan of self-impatience.

At this point, with Hannah weeping, what suggests itself is the story of Ian and Henry and the bathing trunks. 'Ian will remember him too. He had dealings with Henry, after some busybody lodged a complaint. He was skinny-dipping. Henry, not Ian.' This doesn't raise as much as a rudimentary smile, but she looks up and listens to the story, and at Henry's fastidious refusal to don wet clothing she allows herself to laugh.

He was a tough old bugger, impervious to the cold, she says, by way of introduction to her own tale of Henry and the beach. One Sunday afternoon, in February or March of last year, they were walking along the water's edge when they noticed a large piece of cloth, pink, turning in the foam of a wave, three or four waves out. It was a striking sight, this patch of bright pink material swirling around in the sea, and they watched it for a minute or two. Suddenly, without a word of warning, Henry set out to retrieve it. The sea must have been freezing, but he waded right in. The water was thigh-high where he fished out the shirt. That's what it was: a football shirt, pink with black trimmings. Henry scooped it out of the water, wrung it out on the beach and presented it to Hannah. 'Here you are,' he said, as if they'd been ambling along a shopping street and the shirt was something she'd seen in a window and taken a liking to. 'I'd better go and change,' he said, indicating the sopping old jeans, and with that he was gone, back to the rocks.

'Palermo.'

'Sorry?'

'Palermo. Pink and black are the colours of Palermo's football team. Could have fallen off an Italian boat. Or off an Italian seaman.'

'Suppose,' she agrees, disinclined to follow this line of speculation. She's looking again towards the bush where the invisible bird is still squeaking, and a pensiveness swiftly overcomes her. It must be Henry she's thinking of and there's some complication in her thoughts — it appears not to be simple nostalgia for his company that is occupying her. Momentarily she narrows her eyes, as if to make out something minuscule on the paving stones, then, with a blink, she reawakens to an awareness of herself and of being observed. 'I have to get on,' she says, reaching for the blade.

'Sure.'

'Thanks for the update.'

'We'll keep you posted, like I said.'

'For the story too.'

'OK.'

'And for not being horrible,' she says. Taking a lighter from her pocket, she turns her back.

In some experiment in the States, psychologists recorded on

166

videotape five hours of interviews with psychiatric patients, to analyse what we might call the speech of our faces. So they sat down and noted every significant visual change, every distinctly meaningful face. What these patients were saying was often simple, but when the psychologists had finished they found that they had identified six thousand different expressions. Six thousand expressions in five hours of talking: that's a shift of meaning every three seconds. A single frown might be an act of three or four episodes. You can't describe these episodes precisely, not without sounding like a coroner, but you can see them and read them, or note them at least. And when Hannah says 'For the story too', there's a movement of an eyelid, a contraction of a fraction of a millimetre, that seems to say something new, but it's gone so quickly it's impossible to be certain that it was there.

She's scraping away at the paint, and she doesn't look back.

19

The reputation of George Whittam is based on two talents above all: the soul-searching eye is the first; the other is his silence. He's adept at misdirection too. His boss, when he was starting out, impressed him with a talk about magicians, about the magician's sleight of hand: the misdirection of attention was what it was all about, he told him, and we can learn a lot from that. When you question a tough case, you create a fog of words, you advance by moving backwards and sideways, you get to the heart of the matter by irrelevance. The lesson wasn't lost on young George. A suspect might talk to him for hours on end and never guess what he's getting at, until it's pointed out that a comment made in passing at eleven o'clock doesn't quite tally with a comment made in passing at four, and that the answer to this contradiction itself doesn't match up with a remark made at nine. But when the verbiage doesn't do the trick, he'll deploy its opposite, his speciality: the industrial-strength silence. If need be, he can be as silent as a dead man and stay that way the whole day long. You could put him up for a head-to-head confrontation with an iguana and the iguana would start talking before George did.

He is an intimidating man: six-foot two, fifteen stone, meaty hands and refrigerated blue eyes. From the look of him you'd think that this is a man who relishes activities that are strenuous

168

and involve a sizeable serving of pain: rugby, boxing and so on. And you'd be right. He does follow rugby. He used to be a rower until a slipped disc confined him to land. But he has another passion, every bit as keen as his love of hairy-chested sports, and this one is the key to his proficiency with silence: he loves musicals, or, to be more precise, he loves American musicals of a certain vintage. If a classic Broadway production has ever been recorded, George Whittam has that recording on his shelves, and lodged permanently in his brain as well. At a moment's notice he could sing you – off-key – the whole album of any show by Rogers and Hammerstein, Cole Porter, Irving Berlin, any of them, from start to finish, every note. And that's the secret of the brain-crushing silence. He's sitting there, giving the villain the infinite sub-zero stare, as if he's looking through a window at a vista of lakes and mountains that's boring him rigid. The recipient of the stare has come through an afternoon of talking without being lured into self-contradiction. No flaws have been identified in the alibi. But he's exhausted by the effort, and under the pressure of Whittam's silence he begins to have doubts. Soon he's thinking, 'He knows something. What did I say? What's he got on me? Who's talked? What've they told him? What the hell's going on in his head?' And what actually is going on inside George Whittam's head? Songs from *My Fair Lady*, that's what. He's playing the whole show to himself, and when that's done he'll listen to another one, and then another, until his cell mate starts to talk and tells him what he wants to hear.

But with Gary Quinton neither the ordeal by conversation nor the ordeal by silence is working. Mr Quinton was born and raised in Lambeth, worked as a bouncer and debt collector for a few years, picked up a couple of convictions before doing time for grievous bodily harm, and on his emergence from prison headed south-west, where he was soon pursuing a vigorous career in the recreational drug distribution industry. A high-IQ psychopath, it takes him a couple of years to carve out a lucrative territory for himself, filtering the proceeds through the bank accounts of a hundred phoney companies and terrified sidekicks. He pays other people to do the muscle work for him now, and it's proving very hard to nail him.

Around the beginning of March we hear that Keith Guillory, one of Quinton's closest associates and a man not previously known for his maritime interests, has rented a fishing boat for a few weeks, a boat that's seen, soon after, cruising up and down the river and crawling along the coast in a manner that very much suggests reconnaissance. In April, at the Quay, Guillory is photographed with Gary Quinton and an unidentified younger man, who takes the boat upriver when the discussions are done, leaving the other two to go their separate ways. Something is about to happen, that's obvious, then a week later there's a call from a young woman, hysterical, saying someone's been killed. When the police get to the house, the young woman's running around on the pavement, pulling her hair out, literally. She's as high as a kite and the only coherent statement they can get out of her is that she won't go back into the house. Inside, there's another woman lying, unconscious, on a bed of filthy pillows in the living room, surrounded by tin-foil trays of cold curry, and in the kitchen, chained to the cooker, is the lad from the boat, also unconscious, with his legs splayed in a puddle of blood. Someone had taken a blade, or several blades, one of them a hacksaw, to various extremities. He wasn't going to die, but he could forget about learning to play the violin, and walking in a straight line was going to be a bit of a challenge in the short term, come to that. We go looking for Guillory, but Guillory has gone missing. Gary Quinton is duly pulled in for a chat.

This happens on a Friday morning; in the evening we're having a meal at the Whittams' house, and Quinton's name inevitably comes up. 'He guesses that we've been watching him,' George tells Alice, 'so right at the outset he admits he'd met the lad. Peter Jellico is his name and he's met him just the once, at the Quay. Never saw him again after that. What's Guillory doing with the boat? Fishing, exploring the river. Any idea where Guillory might have got to? Not a clue. It's bollocks. Complete and utter bollocks. He'd lie to his own reflection, that bloke,' says George with a rueful shake of the head. 'But he's so good at it. Ninety solid minutes of non-stop lying, cool as you like. A fucking devil, but a brilliant liar.'

Mouth wide open with exaggerated shock, Rebecca claps her hands to her ears.

'Language,' says Margaret, distributing the coffees and whiskies.

'*Pardonnez*,' says George, with a penitent bow to his daughter. 'But credit where credit's due. You've never known anyone lie like this guy can lie. You tell a lie,' he says to Alice, 'and you'll give yourself away, even if what you're saying hangs together and makes perfect sense. You'll be looking down more than you should, touching your face too much, your voice will go up a bit, your smile will last just that fraction of a fraction of a second too long. Not Gary Quinton. He looks you right in the eye and lies his head off, hour after hour, without ever tripping himself up. It's amazing. He's a poisonous scum-sucker, don't get me wrong about that. Evil ratbag of the first order. But he's a kind of genius.'

'You don't mean that,' says Alice, stirring her coffee.

'Oh, I do.'

'No, not genius.'

'OK. Perhaps not a genius. But it's a real gift he's got. A phenomenal memory, if nothing else. You have to remember a lie in a way you don't have to remember the truth. A lie has to be sustained, you need to keep reminding yourself of it, like remembering a whole play, and if you get one line wrong, at any time, the whole play falls apart. But the truth just lies there, takes care of itself. You can't recall all of it, of course you can't. But there are a hundred different ways of getting to it, things that lead you to it. Off the top of your head you can't remember what you did last Wednesday, but Thursday you can remember, and that gives you a ladder up to Wednesday. The truth of one day knits in with

171

the truth of other days in all these directions. Yes?' he asks, clasping his fingers in front of his face to demonstrate the mesh of facts.

'We got it, Dad,' says Rebecca, but her father is looking only at Alice, who glances at his hands and nods.

'The truth is a web, see? Nothing stands on its own. One truth is connected to others. But the lie stands alone. It's supported only by the liar's mind, by his memory, and ultimately the liar's memory will let him down, nine hundred and ninety-nine times out of a thousand. I've spent an hour or two with someone I shouldn't have been with, just say,' he proposes to Alice, with a wink for her husband. 'Margaret asks me where I was. "I was with Harry. We bumped into each other outside Boots. We had a coffee at that new place in Fore Street." Six weeks later Margaret asks again. What time was it? Originally I said two o'clock, now I say three, or I hesitate, just a split second, but it's the give-away. It's not the hesitation of someone trying to remember what time it was. It's someone trying to remember what he said, and that looks different. It sounds different. But with Gary Quinton this wouldn't happen. If he made up a story a year ago, it's still there in his head, in all its ramifications. Quinton's virtual world. He's an artist, you could say. And an evil fucking bastard who should be dropped down a mine shaft without a helmet.'

'Second warning,' Margaret announces, and as usual George pays no heed to her, or so you'd think. This is the part she plays, the civilising influence, disregarded by the cantankerous spouse, but she doesn't mind the swearing and he does moderate the profanities at home, under her influence. Margaret admires her husband and he in turn admires her. Possessing an excellent head for figures, she's the boss of the domestic economy as well as of her own thriving little company, supplying high-grade kitchens to all corners of the county and beyond. Tough-minded, clear-sighted, always purposeful, a respected boss, she runs her business and her husband likewise runs his, and they esteem each other for it.

'I tell you, Alice, the guff this man comes out with,' continues George. 'He's become interested in boats. Going to take classes, he is. Learning about navigation and all that. He'd always wanted to sail boats, when he was a kid in London, but the poor wee mite never got to see the sea. When he heard what had happened to the lad from the boat, he was disgusted, he was. He does a very good disgusted. We tell him that we've busted this dealer in Plymouth and he's been telling us some interesting things about Gary Quinton's network. Then the shutters come down. Not playing any more.' His hand chops at the table top, making the cups chatter on the saucers.

Margaret, holding her cup down as if against the tremors of an earthquake, gives Alice a small smile and raises her eyes to the ceiling. The monologue has been addressed mainly to Alice and one reason for this is simply that Alice's face is an extremely rewarding face to talk to. There is a pleasure in being regarded by Alice, a pleasure only partly aesthetic. Another reason, almost certainly, is that George senses that all is not perfect with Alice and her husband, and that her husband's work is the root of the problem. Over the past year or so he's seen her becoming more self-enclosed, and he's seen this happen before, many times, with colleagues' wives, this withdrawal that comes from a feeling of exclusion. The hours are long, the commitment intense, and this can cause difficulties at home. 'If you're not careful, you raise a wall around yourself,' that's what he'd said to us, years back. So when he directs his talk at Alice he's trying to break down that wall, to bring her into the team, and perhaps also he makes a particular effort with Alice because Alice is a person one would want to be liked by, and he can see that she doesn't like him as much as she once did, a dwindling that may be due to her holding him in some way responsible for the life she now finds herself living. But this isn't what Alice thinks. She and her husband alone are responsible for where they are, but it's true that when she looks at George Whittam she sees personified a world she often wishes we hadn't entered, and it's true that Alice isn't keen on

173

George Whittam. She was never very keen on him: he's too blunt and robust for her liking, and too fond of his own charisma and the mystique of the job that he does, and the more he's tried to win her over, the less keen she's become.

'My patience is limitless', he goes on, 'when it comes to dealing with people like this, but this one is special. He's got a brain of stone. He's not saying another word until his lawyer arrives and in the interim he'll make himself as blank as the sky for as long as I'd like to gaze at him. And who's his lawyer?' he asks the table at large, and he pauses for a gulp of Scotch.

'Mr A,' Rebecca answers brightly, as though on cue.

'Mr A,' echoes her father. 'Gary Quinton has retained the services of Roland Ackerman. Slimy, cash-besotted Ackerman. The twistiest little bastard in Christendom. If –'

'Third and final warning,' Margaret interrupts.

'No, but the man's a weasel. A mercenary weasel. Another hoodlum to get off the hook, another holiday in the Bahamas.'

'It's his job to serve his client's best interests,' Rebecca tells him. 'Someone's got to do it.'

'Quinton's as guilty as f—.' At Margaret's bulging glare George bites his lip. 'As guilty as Herod. And Ackerman knows it.'

'How do you know he knows?' asks Rebecca.

'Because he's not an imbecile and only an imbecile wouldn't know it. A blind, deaf imbecile. Three men on a boat. One vanishes, one gets cut up. Last man standing is Gary Quinton. QED.'

'But you said yourself that Mr Quinton is an accomplished liar, did you not?' Rebecca parries, taking on the pomposity of the defence brief, warming to what has become her customary role of opposition to her father. 'Good enough to deceive Mr Ackerman.'

'Ackerman knows more than we know.'

'Yes, but what he knows may just be more lies.'

'No.'

'You can't be certain that Mr Ackerman's not acting in good faith.'

'Ackerman and good faith don't belong in the same sentence. Aiding villains is what he does. Wealthy villains. He coaches them. I tell you, we've had characters who can't string three words together, left to themselves, and after a session with Ackerman they're talking like Winston bloody Churchill.'

'So he gives them a bit of help. Why not? They're being grilled by the professionals. A slip of the tongue might get them into trouble. If I was up against you lot I'd want some coaching. Must be terrifying.'

'Not as terrifying as having one of Gary Quinton's gorillas standing in your kitchen.'

'But', says Alice, almost in a whisper, tracing a shape on the table with a fingertip, 'even if Mr Ackerman is corrupt, everyone is entitled to a defence. Even Gary Quinton.'

'Innocent until proved guilty,' adds Rebecca.

'Other way round with this lad.'

'But if you have a case against him, surely Mr Ackerman isn't a problem?' asks Alice, now glancing at George.

'He's a problem because he stops us getting at him. He gets in the way.'

'I don't see it,' Alice quietly perseveres. 'You say Quinton's not going to confess to anything, with or without Mr Ackerman. So he's not really in the way. And however much he coaches his clients, he can't alter the facts. It's down to the police and the prosecution to compile the evidence, isn't it? The truth is independent of Mr Ackerman.'

'Exactly,' says Rebecca, giving Alice a smile which has a grain of tentativeness, a millisecond of vulnerability that can be explained by the evening that she was discovered with Jessica, an episode that also accounts for Alice's inability to meet her eye. Deflected, Rebecca turns back to her father. 'So what happened after the lawyer showed up?' she asks him.

'Thank you and goodbye.'

'And now?'

'Now we have to find Guillory sharpish and in the meantime

we don't let Quinton out of our sights. And we hope that the lad in ward seven and his girlfriend start to get a bit more co-operative, because at the moment they're in denial. Scared shitless. Sorry – witless. As you would be, if you'd annoyed Gary Quinton.'

'You'll plug on,' says Margaret.

'We'll plug on and we'll drag him to court, and we'll hope to Christ we get a jury that can follow the plot.'

'Oh sweet Mary and Joseph, not juries,' groans Rebecca, chancing another smile for Alice, but this one too is wasted and her groan makes no difference to her father, who is off on another solo run, complaining about jurors who make their minds up the moment the defendant stands up, and jurors who wake up only for the closing statements and even then have problems grasping the simplest concepts. And Alice takes issue with him, as she takes issue when he turns his complaint into a tirade against barristers and the way they identify the one or two half-bright members of the jury and work on them to win their vote, like contestants in a talent show, and the way they work on the slightest shred of doubt, the tiniest possibility of doubt, and magnify it out of all proportion. 'It's like declaring a house unfit for human habitation just because there's a patch of rot in the bathroom window,' he says. Alice does not accept this idea either and George withdraws it, because, however strong the urge to share his thoughts might be, he'd rather not be in conflict with Alice. Hoping to alight on an aspect of this topic in which he might find Alice more sympathetic, he takes a sideways step, expressing a dissatisfaction, a dissatisfaction shared by many in his line of work, with the rules of evidence, the disabling definitions of what is and isn't admissible. 'If juries knew what we knew, you'd get a different outcome, a lot of the time,' he tells her.

'Like knowing Gary Quinton's guilty?' suggests Rebecca, pre-empting any intervention from Alice.

'A jury decides if they think a man's guilty or innocent, and sometimes you know they've got it wrong and we could have told them things that would have changed their minds, but we can't.

We know they've got it wrong, the judge knows they've got it wrong.'

But for Alice the fallibility of justice is inevitable, whatever the system. It's more than inevitable, it's a good thing. We should be aware, always, that perfection is impossible, she says, and for a moment there's a risk that God is about to be brought into the discussion. Better that one guilty man goes free than an innocent man gets imprisoned, Alice insists, and Margaret, unseen by Alice, gives her a look, as she has occasionally before, that has something almost wistful in it, as if Alice represents something she has through necessity lost.

'But we'll nail Gary Quinton,' George concludes. His daughter, standing behind him, puts her hands on his shoulders and receives a kiss on her fingers. 'He's a grade-A lowlife and we're going to have him, Alice. I can promise you that.'

This promise was made with some force, a vehemence attributable less to Alice's resistance to seeing things as he sees them than to the stagnation of the search for Henry's killer. Only once in the course of that evening was Henry referred to. 'It was never going to be easy,' Margaret remarked in the kitchen, as the others were taking their places at the table. For Margaret, it seemed, Henry was already registered as a lost cause, a debit to be logged in the ledger of her husband's career, where it's cancelled out by the vastly more numerous entries in the credit column. For her husband, on the other hand, no unsolved case could ever be written off. It was an ineradicable blemish, a chronic pain. 'Some nights he won't come to bed,' Margaret confided. 'He sits downstairs, watching rubbish on television, brooding. Last week he was wandering around the garden at two in the morning. He actually feels guilty,' she said, pulling a face to signify incomprehension, helplessness, despair, love – none of them genuine, except the last. She could have been playing the part of the artist's wife, bemoaning the torments of creation. 'We'd best steer clear,' she advised. 'Don't mention the mad boy.'

Michael Trethowen had been invited to the station, so he could

177

be warned away from Tom Gaskin and for George to check him out. 'What's with the street theatre outside the old man's house?' George starts off, to which Michael answers that he'd like to know what's with the old codger's private investigator routine, a smart-arsed response that does nothing to ingratiate him with his questioner. 'What makes you think he's watching you?' asks George, restraining the urge to escalate the conflict without further delay.

'You'd have to be blind not to see him and I'm not blind,' says Michael. '*Au contraire*. Someone should tell him the lenses catch the sun. It's like having a beacon flashing up there. So stupid.' Circling his eyes with looped fingers, Michael laughs.

'Granted that Mr Gaskin has seen fit to use his windows for the eccentric purpose of admiring the view,' George goes on, 'the question remains: what makes you think it's you he's watching?'

Here Michael discloses that, several months ago, he was followed by the old man. 'I went down on to the beach and he was creeping along behind me.'

The beach is a public domain, George points out. 'Just because he happened to be there at the same time as you, going in the same direction, it doesn't mean he was following you.'

Michael, becoming irked, repeats that he was being followed. 'He was practically walking in my footsteps,' he says, at which point George suggests that perhaps there might be a touch of paranoia here. This duly sparks a flash of anger. 'It was a piss-miserable winter's day, there was no one else around. Nobody. Just me, him and a whole lot of landscape. I stop, he stops. I move, he moves. He was following me. It was so obvious.'

Now George takes a short break, to consider the face across the table, as if studying an artefact he's been offered at a price he considers too high. 'So you got it into your head that this old man was keeping tabs on you,' he resumes, 'and you thought you'd get your own back by putting the fear of God in him.'

The fear of God makes Michael snort. 'I thought I'd suggest that he might back off,' he says.

'A heavy-handed way of going about it,' George proposes. 'Was the mad slasher number strictly necessary?'

Michael smiles, as if being complimented on the power of his performance. 'He seemed a bit slow on the uptake,' he says, which prompts George, not missing a beat, to recount some of the ill-considered remarks that Mr Trethowen had made in the presence of officers Salter and Davies. 'Is that an accurate account of what was said?' George enquires.

'More or less,' Michael agrees.

And the next question, uttered through a mask of bulldog truculence, is: 'Did you kill Henry?' This produces another laugh, albeit a laugh with markedly less energy than the first. Having allowed the last curl of Michael's smile to flatten, George asks, with the pitying half-smile of a man who's dealing with a simpleton who doesn't comprehend the gravity of the situation in which he finds himself: 'Why did you kill Henry?'

'I didn't,' says Michael, grimacing at the proposterousness of the idea.

George, sighing, wipes a hand slowly downwards across his face. 'So what's all this crap about killing him? You said you could understand why someone would kill him. Yes? You said that?'

Michael confirms that he did indeed say that he could understand why someone should kill someone else. 'Presumably you can understand it too,' he goes on, rallying, 'otherwise you wouldn't be in this job.'

As if allowing the validity of this witty riposte, George cocks his head to the side and looks Michael in the eye. 'You said it would be an interesting thing to do,' he reminds him. Those were not his exact words, says Michael. 'You tell two of my officers that it would be an interesting project, to murder someone in cold blood,' George continues evenly, 'and then you express to a third officer your opinion that it would be a terribly clever idea to slaughter them on a beach. And now you're prancing around outside this old man's house, waving a knife in the air.'

Michael shrugs. 'An imaginary knife,' he says, which provokes in George another instantaneous change of gear.

Now in wrathful mode, he stands up and bends over to press down on Michael's shoulders. 'Look, son,' he says, giving him the driller eyes, 'you'd be well advised not to fuck with us.' He feels a small shudder in Michael's body. 'Look at me,' he says. 'Look at me. Why did you kill Henry?'

'I didn't kill Henry.'

'Was it an interesting experience? Did it live up to expectations?' Michael's face is beginning to quake and George keeps hammering at him. 'Why did you kill Henry?'

'I didn't.'

'Why did you kill Henry?'

When he takes the clamps off Michael's shoulders, the lad is shivering as if he's naked in a blizzard. He's in tears; his mouth is wobbling like a kid's. 'I didn't,' he keeps repeating. Dissatisfied with what he's hearing, George slumps back in his chair. From the look he's giving the lad, you'd think this was someone he'd borne a grudge against for years. After a couple of minutes of silence, Michael says that we can search his place if we like.

George contemplates the hanging light bulb for a long time. 'Yes,' he tells him, 'we might take you up on that offer.'

After his tête-à-tête at the station, Michael refrains from troubling Tom Gaskin. He refrains from being seen in public at all. Weeks pass before he reappears at church. When he does at last return he has a cowed look, as if fresh from his humiliation at the hands of George Whittam. Hunched forward, he gives Beal's sermon his fiercest attention; he ignores everybody in the congregation, even Alice.

180

20

More than half a year has passed since the day Benjamin Kemp and Milo went for their walk on the beach and we have no clearer idea of who killed Henry than we did then, though Geoff Sàlter, from time to time, tries to revive the candidacy of Michael Trethowen. Our ideas about Henry aren't advancing either. In Ilfracombe the cloth has been wrung dry: he might as well have lived there for two weeks rather than two years for all the impression he's left behind. Work on the files continues to be fruitless. If Henry was a child molester he was a molester with no form, as far as we can see, and he doesn't seem to feature on any register of missing persons compiled anywhere between Land's End and the Shetlands. Nobody in all of Britain is missing Henry, it would appear, except Hannah Rowe.

The beach is filling up, the seafront shops are doing a good trade, the weather's fine and life is back in full swing, minus Henry, a subtraction of almost nought. Geoff Salter, relieved of the surveillance of Michael Trethowen, is transferred to a case that has self-solver written all over it. A young woman has been throttled with a pair of her own tights and left for dead in her flat. She can describe the man clearly, but doesn't know his full name: she'd met him that night, in a pub in Plymouth, and he'd said his name was David. He'd driven her back to her place and they were going to have sex but he'd had so much to drink that he couldn't manage it, and then he'd become violent. She can remember the pub they'd been in and what time they'd left, and his car: a Mazda sports car, silver. And there they are, the victim and her two best friends and David, on the pub's CCTV, chatting at the bar at 7.49 p.m.; and there are the victim and David, minus the friends, sitting at a table at 9.55 p.m.; and there are the victim and David leaving together at 10.26 p.m. Cameras at three different sets of traffic lights show a silver Mazda crossing Plymouth between 10.40 p.m. and 10.50 p.m. with someone very like David at the wheel in one shot and someone very like the victim alongside him in another. A neighbour, posting a letter, saw a silver Mazda being parked in the victim's street shortly after 11 p.m.; some time between 11.30 p.m. and midnight the couple in the flat below heard a woman scream. The owner of the silver Mazda is not at home when Geoff comes calling and neither is he at work: he'd phoned his manager, suffering a nasty bout of food poisoning, courtesy of a dodgy Chinese. There it is, in a single paragraph: the whole story done and dusted.

The pursuit of Gary Quinton is now taking up a lot of Whittam's time. In a Plymouth backstreet there's the wreck of a BMW that used to have bronze-tinted windows until someone applied a brick to the glasswork, prior to letting an incontinent dog have a frolic on the seats. A few dozen strokes of a sledge-hammer have been given to the body panels, for an impressive moon surface effect, and a garnish of brake fluid has interestingly enhanced the paint job. An ice pick has been taken to the tyres as well. The owner, though unhappy with the condition of his vehicle, is reluctant to pursue the matter. He has a record for dealing, but supposedly is straight now. All roads lead to Mr Quinton.

When the team allocated to Henry is downgraded to two part-timers it's time for the Donohues to take the long-awaited holiday. The villa that we've rented is within a short walk of a wide, curving bay that's lined by a narrow beach of soft and clean sand, but for most of the day you need a firewalker's feet to stroll on the beach. The heatwave is into its second week when we arrive and only on day eight of the fourteen does the temperature begin to fall, and then only by a degree or two each day. It's so hot, cars driving past the house leave tracks on the tarmac and the mountain that looms over the bay seems to tremble all day. An hour's slathering with sun cream precedes the morning's visit to the beach, where we pitch camp amid the pines and bushes that screen the beach from the road. At first it appears that we've hit upon a spot known to only a select band of holidaymakers, but then they become visible, lurking in the shade: every twenty or thirty yards, along the full crescent of the beach, there's a little encampment of foreigners, gazing at the sand and the burning water, like the survivors of a shipwreck. Very few people risk a long dose of sun, but each day we find ourselves within waving distance of an ancient chestnut-coloured German couple, who place themselves midway between the water and the perimeter vegetation, and arrange their leisure equipment – two huge para-sols, two huge snowy towels, two huge plastic crates of food and chilled drinks – with the precision of scientists laying out an experiment. Permanently naked they lie all day on their towels, rolling out of the shadow to sunbathe, rolling in to read. They wave to us as we dash towards the water and they smile with a gracious condescension that gives the impression they've been here the whole summer.

The sea is as smooth as a pool of honey and the dazzle makes it impossible to turn your eyes sunwards. Face-down we float, the three of us, watching small brown fish moving across sand that's as bright as paper. That's all there seems to be in the waters of the bay, these gangs of small drab fish, however far out we swim. For most of the day we stay close to the trees. In the beach café, on the second morning, Luke meets a Belgian kid, whose name turns out to be Luc, a coincidence that puts the seal on their spontaneous alliance. For hours Luke and Luc play in the thick-ets, returning to base only for water. Alice sunbathes on the boundary of the shade. 'Relax. Please,' she says, half opening an eye as she swipes an arm across the sand to level it. Occasionally a boat edges into the bay and stays there for an hour or two, shaking like something seen through fire. Tiny figures leap from the stern, making no sound as they hit the water. When the boys aren't yelling there's no sound of any kind: no birdsong, no insects, no people talking, as though the heat has stunned everyone and everything into silence. After fifteen minutes of reading, Alice is asleep. Once in a while someone might break cover to spring to the water, but there are whole hours in which nothing moves on the beach, except the rolling German nudists.

In the early afternoon, however, someone materialises out of the haze at the far end of the beach. Cheap jewellery is what he's selling and every woman on the beach is treated to his patter, even the ancient German. 'Hello,' he says to Alice. The husband gets a bow, but he talks to Alice as if she were on her own. He's not leering at her and not quite flirting, but the smile transmits an honest male appreciation of what's in front of him, and the appreciation is tolerated, as it wouldn't have been, perhaps, a year or two ago. He's a lad in his mid twenties, with dyed blond dreadlocks and a blurry look to the eyes, as if last night's drugs haven't quite worn off. Despite the silly hair he is a very nice-looking specimen, with a plumb-line nose and a jaw like a set square. 'Oh lady, please,' he says, in a softly wheedling voice that has a transatlantic tinge to it, suggesting that he's learned his English from American TV. 'Just look. For a minute. One minute.' Silver necklaces dangle from a well-muscled arm, displayed against the background of fat-free and hairless torso.

'No, thank you,' says Alice. 'Not my kind of thing,' she says, because she'd never tell him to go away and neither would she lie and say we've come to the beach without cash. From a soft leather bag he hoists a fistful of beads made of plastic-looking stone. 'No, really. Thank you,' says Alice. Another scoop in the bag brings out an array of rings that could have fallen out of a bubble-gum machine. 'I'm sorry,' says Alice. 'I really don't need one.'

Crestfallen, beach boy starts putting his wares back into the bag, slowly. He looks at Alice with dewy eyes, shaking his head. 'But I need you to buy one,' he says, and plaintively he extends a hand in which a silver bracelet is nestled. Patiently he waits while Alice inspects the item. Like a semi-naked footman, head bowed, he doesn't say a word, and within a minute he's closed the deal. With meek gratitude he accepts payment of the asking price, then backs away, as though withdrawing from the royal presence.

'Katharine might like it,' says Alice. 'And he won't bother us again now.' But the next day he pays us a call, and the day after. The day after that, spotting him at long range, Alice takes to the sea, but he wades in after her, raising a rope of necklaces above the water. 'I've bought all I'm going to buy,' she tells him, but it makes no difference. Nothing short of a shovel to the face is going to deter this lad. Next day he again appears in the midst of the vibrating air. 'This isn't funny any more,' says Alice, sitting up, holding her bikini top in place. The elderly owners of a Dutch-registered camper van, this morning's new arrivals to the beach, are getting the spiel, fifty yards away. Watching the newcomers as they smile and shake their heads and smile, Alice whispers, 'We could always try having sex. Now, I mean. Pretending. We could pretend to be having sex. It might get rid of him.' The light-heartedness of the idea lasts a couple of seconds, then there's a taut moment, an exchange of looks in which Alice's eyes seem to convey a tenuous hope and a questioning, as though she's saying that she might be able to believe that, by an exertion of will, we could recover our younger selves, and is asking if she is alone in this belief, as she feels she might be, though she is trying to suppress that suspicion. The response, a smile, is evidently equivocal, or worse. Seeing no reassurance in it, Alice glances away, into the sun, which shocks her eyes shut. Beach boy, having waited at a respectful distance until we were done, pads through the sand. With an envious smirk for the lucky husband, he homes in on Alice again. 'No,' she says, so sharply that he veers away without another word.

Luke and Luc are having a good time together. They snorkel shoulder to shoulder and take turns to bury each other in sand. In the undergrowth they construct a hideout from boxes borrowed from the café. One morning there's a knock on the door, at half-past seven: it's Luc, wanting to know if his friend is ready yet. Forty-eight hours later Luc has gone, with no warning. For most of that day we are occupied with the consoling of Luke. Our opinion of Luc is soon revised unfavourably in the light of his thoughtless departure. The fugitive is consigned to history and Luke surveys the beach from his cardboard lookout, on the watch for a new playmate. The ancient naked Germans are with us still, as is the vendor of tat. Having amiably rebuffed him for a few days, the Dutch contingent succumb to the pressure and invest in a necklace, only to find that this earns them an even more persistent visit the following afternoon. Again they buy some-thing, as they do on every subsequent day. Jewellery boy gives us a wide berth, granting Alice a proud terse nod on his way to the Germans. The Dutch woman holds the day's purchase aloft for us to see and shrugs helplessly. No children come to the beach. Luke wants to go home; he wants to see his friend Terry. Father and son take a walk to the rocks at the end of the beach. We find a few crabs, of uniform size and colour. They cling, immo-bile, to small overhangs, dabbed lightly by tiny waves.

'Why did that man want to live outdoors?' asks Luke, and we talk about Henry for a while, and how people might come to be homeless. Luke reports that Luc had said that if you peered into the eyes of someone who had been murdered, you could see the picture of the person who had killed him. At being told that this isn't true he sighs and looks down at the rocks, as if logging another disappointment on to the tally of the holiday. We watch the rock-coloured crabs doing nothing. Luke's boredom becomes a grudge against the whole bay, so we drive to see a ruined fort, a fort more ruined than expected, but big and impressive in its way, for an hour or two. Skinny lizards are to be seen panting on the broken walls. Lots of yellow butterflies are limping through

186

the air. Back at the beach, the owner of the café is visited by friends who have a dog that swims, and this brings about some improvement in morale. Luke swims with the dog; we all swim with the dog. We throw a ball for the dog: Mum chucks it with all her might straight up in the air and it comes back down a foot away, which gets a laugh; Dad chucks it halfway to Turkey, and this gets applause. Luke and Alice wrestle in the shallows and skirmish with the dog. The sun blazes; the sky is immaculate azure; the sea water is as clear as air; everyone is laughing. This is a picture of happiness, and that's what it feels like: a picture of happiness.

The dog departs and boredom fastens itself on to Luke like a headache. He needs to look at something, he explains, and there's nothing left to look at here, now we've done the fish and we've done the crabs. Inland, not far, there's the ruin of an ancient palace. We drive to it, up into the hills, past groves of wizened trees with leaves that shine like scraps of greaseproof paper. On the ramp of the car park there's a broken fan belt that turns out, on closer inspection from Luke, to be a flattened snake. The palace is a very ancient palace and very ruined: not one of the walls is taller than Luke and it takes a lot of imagination, more than any of us can muster, to see a residence of any sort there. Luke wanders through the dusty maze of crumbling stone, searching for something of interest, and Alice takes about twenty photographs of Luke among the ruins, frowning at rooms that look like sheep pens. Nearby there's a museum of stuff dug up in the vicinity of the palace, which we decide to visit because it will be cooler, if nothing else. It's just a couple of rooms, a small warehouse of venerable junk: cases of old pots, bits of battered metalwork, some slabs of painted plaster. Near the entrance there's an artist's impression of the hall of the palace, as it would have been: it looks like the foyer of a Las Vegas hotel, with some mini-skirted wrestlers mooching about. Guidebooks in hand, half a dozen other tourists are trudging around, putting names to things, understanding nothing and having next to no pleasure.

Alice moves slowly through the museum, reading almost every label, as if the collection has been put together just for her and it would be discourteous to hurry. Meanwhile Luke goes from case to case, giving each display a ten-second search, as though in a reptile house in which every animal is turning out to be asleep. Room one is soon done with. He disappears into room two and has been gone for five minutes when he comes running back in. 'Dad,' he says with a pull on the shorts, 'look at this.' He leads the way to a cabinet of pottery and points at the scene painted on the outside of a big red jar. A huge-headed giant, slumped against a rock, has raised a hand to remove from his eye a long pole from which six or seven little stick-men are swinging. 'What's going on here?' asks Luke, pulling a face of gleeful revulsion. The caption is not a great deal of help, but Alice arrives and can make enough sense of it to satisfy Luke. He moves on to the adjacent jar. 'That's Hercules wrestling a lion,' Alice explains. 'And there he's holding the whole world on his shoulders. That's him killing a dog with three heads, and wrestling with a lion. I don't know the story. I'll look it up when we get home.' Luke completes a circuit of the jar before striding back to the first room, leaving us looking at the painted jar, but not really looking.

We follow, to see him standing in front of a fragment of painted wall, arms folded, head cocked. A young woman and her boyfriend, both blond and tall and twenty-ish, probably German, stand beside him, arms folded too, and as perplexed as Luke. 'What's happening?' he shouts at them, making the young woman start. 'What's this about? Who's the lady?' demands Luke, at a slightly lower volume. The young woman frowns in consternation, as though Luke were a goblin that had just popped out of the ground, but her boyfriend lowers his guidebook and says to Luke, mock-solemnly: 'Little man, I do not know for sure, but this person I think has been turned into stone.' He smiles commendingly at Alice, who now crouches beside Luke, putting an arm round his shoulders, and together they ponder the half-obliterated scene on the wall. Alice points at something and speaks to Luke, and Luke in response nods seriously, fixing his gaze on his mother's eyes. Leaving, the young man passes a hand lightly over Luke's hair. Alice and Luke give the painted wall another minute, then she whispers in his ear and they move on, hand in hand.

At the end of the beach there's a restaurant, a shack with an awning out front, over a platform of bleached wood. After the trip to the museum and palace we eat there, as we do most evenings. And the conversation is the same as it is most evenings:
'How's yours?'

'Good. How's yours?'

'Fine.' The food is the same every night: thick slabs of cheese and slices of tomato, a bony fish from the freezer, but it's fine. It's a nice place to sit, with the vast darkness of the bay before us and the street lights of the town miles away to the left, shimmering in dark space. Beyond the light of the restaurant the water is liver-purple, merging into a blackness in which we can just make out the different blackness of the hill that separates the bay from the sea. The far-off engine of a fishing boat can be heard; its single red lamp, so faint that after each blink it has to be found again, is creeping towards the open sea, moving out from the town. Between the tables and the water there's twenty feet of sand, where Luke can play as soon as he's finished his food. He sits on the sand, raking the beam of his torch back and forth, hoping for a glimpse of some night creature.

Alice says she thinks Luke has enjoyed being here, on the whole, but that two weeks of beach has been too much for him. It's a pity that Luc went, she says, and that the museum was so dull. We agree that next year we should look for somewhere that has good beaches and interesting towns nearby – Spain, perhaps. And when we get home, we could get a book of Greek myths and legends for Luke, because he seems to like the stories. Some of them he knows already, or parts of some of them: he guessed that the thing hanging on a tree, which Alice thought was a gown, was in fact the Golden Fleece. The waiter takes the plates away. Luke has gone down to the water's edge and is scanning the shallows with his torch. Vigilant as a guard in his watchtower, he makes a visor of his hand, shielding his eyes from the restaurant's lights. 'He's a good kid,' says Alice. 'We've been lucky.' This is said in the tone of a reminder of what's important, and a glance that suggests that the reminder should not be necessary. The shaft of light turns upright, as Luke plants the torch in the sand so he can take off his plimsolls. 'Just the shoes, OK?' calls Alice. Not turning, Luke responds with a hand raised over his shoulder. He's taken half a dozen strides when Alice calls, 'No further.' Shaking his head in exasperation, Luke points the torch downwards, showing his legs in air from mid-calf up.

As regularly as the rays of a lighthouse the torchlight sweeps back and forth on the green-grey water. Just beyond the reach of the beam there's a ripple, a fish breaking the surface, and Luke aims the light towards the source of the sound, leaning forward. Alice says quietly: 'Are you here?'

'What do you mean?'

'You're thinking about Henry, aren't you?'

'No, I'm not.'

'I think you are.'

'He's there, but I'm not thinking about him.'

'A fine distinction,' she says, with the smiling sigh of a woman reconciled to her situation, or almost reconciled.

'I'm not thinking about Henry.'

'About what, then?'

'Nothing in particular. Just looking. Watching Luke.'

In the mouth of the bay, near where the horizon must be, three rows of white dots appear: a cruise ship easing towards the port. The noise of its engines reaches us as a low-pitched pulse, like the throb of a washing machine. We follow its progress, until its lights become confused with the lights of the quay and the streets around. Luke has been standing perfectly still in the water, the extinguished torch held close to his chest, entranced by the ship, as if the sight of it were as amazing as the sight of a whale. Now he's walking back to us: 'I'm tired,' says Alice, though it's not late.

When we get to bed she reads for an hour. 'Goodnight,' she says, before a small kiss, then she turns off the lamp on her side. Within minutes she's asleep, and in sleep her face changes, becoming the unworried face of several years ago, and the smell of pine sap in the room brings memories with it, of the room in France and Alice at the window. Asleep, Alice smiles. Above us the rafters creak, cooling. The shutters are open: the moon, almost full, hangs above the mountain, illuminating an excerpt of jagged horizon. Every few minutes a lorry passes along the coast road. Alice's smile broadens into a smile that sometimes Luke can elicit, and only Luke; she murmurs a word.

Some nights she dreams of a town that exists only in her dreams, though she recognises parts of her town from real places she has seen. Often she finds her dream-self in a wide windswept hilltop square that's paved with large smooth slabs and bordered by ornate, crumbling façades, like the façades round the square in some village in Portugal, by the sea, where we once sat for an hour drinking lemon juice. Down the hill from the square stands a church in which there are elements of three or four buildings she can name, combined with things she has no memory of having seen. The door of this church is of dark heavy wood, like the door of Beal's church, and she knows that when she passes through it there will be, to her left, a long chapel, like a corridor, covered in blue paintings that glitter in candlelight, and always there's a service being conducted in this chapel, a service she can hear but never see. She approaches the church by an elegant bridge that's like a bridge in Venice, but it spans a fast-flowing river, and to get to the church she has to go along a cobbled alleyway where a walled garden is spilling out through a breach in the bricks. Every time Alice dreams of her town, she'll see all these things: the church, the bridge, the fat cobblestones, the overspilling garden. And in the heart of the town there's a mirrored arcade that has an old-fashioned French café in it, a café with small round tables and a zinc bar. The arcade is crowded with people who move like actors on a stage and don't seem to notice her as she weaves through them, as if she's a ghost, but a contented ghost. Wherever the dream starts she knows how to make her way to the arcade, and when she's had her coffee there, sitting close to a young girl in a green silk dress that she's sure she's never seen in reality, she'll walk through streets that change from dream to dream, as if taking shape around her as she walks, but inevitably lead to the church and the hilltop square, and always, during this part of the dream, she'll find some new feature of the dream-town: a fountain in a deserted courtyard, a huge glass hall, a field hung with drying bedsheets. She says it's a wonderful sensation, when she realises that the dream that's now beginning is a dream of her non-existent town, and that she'll soon be seeing the beautiful chapel and the mirrored arcade, and things she's never seen before.

Perhaps that was happening when she smiled: she was recognising where she was. And when Alice in her sleep murmured a word, as if to someone she was pleased to meet and had expected to meet, perhaps she was in her dream-café, with the girl in the green silk dress.

21

Back in the real world, the moron who tried to strangle his one-night stand has been run to ground in a Lake District B&B. He was about to begin his breakfast when the local constabulary came creeping into the dining room, and his face, they said, instantly turned the colour of turkey meat. Presented with the evidence by George Whittam, he decided to make an argument of it. He wouldn't deny he was with the girl. But it was an accident, a really horrible accident, a game that went out of control. She liked rough stuff, he would have George believe. He had to make out he was strangling her when they were doing it. It made it more exciting for her. But the knot slipped and got too tight, and he was trying to get it off her neck but she was thrashing about and making it tighter, and next thing he knew she'd gone blue and stopped breathing. Why didn't he cut the tights off her neck? Why didn't he make any attempt to resuscitate her? Why didn't he call for an ambulance? Because he thought she was dead and he just froze. He was looking at her and he thought she was dead, and the only thing he could think of doing was to do a runner, because who would believe him? 'Certainly not me,' said George, 'and nobody else in his right mind.' The gaze was activated.

The accused, feigning the distress of the wrongly disbelieved, buried his face in his hands. 'I wouldn't have hurt her,' he moaned, 'I really liked her,' and he did this expression that was meant to look like a spasm of grief, but he couldn't quite bring it off. What he looked like was a slob who'd just missed an open goal in a Sunday morning pub game. He hadn't shaved recently, but scratches were visible through the stubble on his cheek and neck: two sets of broken tracks descending from jaw to neck. Was trying to claw his head off part of the game? 'Like I say, she liked it rough.' His eyes, said George, were switching from side to side as if he were looking out of the window of a fast-moving train.

On the same day, an hour or two after George has finished with the strangler, Lynn Paisley walks into the station. She was down on the beach with her kids and a friend and the friend's kids, and they all went for a swim, and when they came out of the water their purses had gone. A family further up the beach had seen a lad acting suspiciously around their things: a swarthy-looking lad, about twenty, with greasy hair, green sweatshirt and jeans. Lynn Paisley is the fifth person to report a theft from the beach since lunchtime and the second to describe a swarthy-looking lad in a green sweatshirt. 'You mean sort of gypsy-ish?' the sergeant prompts her, quoting the earlier description.

'I couldn't say. I didn't see him,' says Lynn, and at this point her attention is diverted by the poster on the wall, the one with Hannah's picture of Henry. She thinks she recognises the face, and while she's giving the sergeant her name and address and a list of what's missing, she begins to remember an episode from years ago, in the hospital. She sees, approximately, a man's face in her mind, a face that resembles the one in this picture, and as she stares at the poster the face that she's remembering becomes more like the one on the poster, and the face on the poster becomes more like the one that she's remembering. By the time she's finished dictating her friend's details, she's as sure as she can be. 'I think I met him,' she says, and within the hour she's being interviewed.

194

She's a large and soft-contoured woman, wearing a capacious lilac smock that falls to her ankles. Her feet are clad in big sensible sandals, also lilac, and her hair is a pinned-up swirl of russet, with streaks of a darker red here and there, and plentiful threads of grey. Her expression at rest is a smile that speaks of a generous nature, while the eyes, in their stillness, seem to advertise a clear-mindedness and certainty of purpose. This is a woman who does not waste time and has faith in her own judgement, you feel. She's probably a staunch person to have as a friend and is someone you'd rather have on your side than against you. Sitting with her ankles together and hands clasped lightly on her lap, she adjusts readily to finding herself cast into a police investigation. She asks for a minute to have a think, and inspects the picture of Henry that we've put on the table. Ready to begin, she gives us a smile and a nod, like a singer to her accompanist at the start of a concert. She's a nurse, she tells us. This feels right. If you woke up in a hospital bed and Lynn Paisley was the first person you saw, you might feel a bit less unhappy about your situation. She works in Southampton. It was in Southampton that she came across Mr Palmer. The month in question, she works out, must have been February 1977, because it was shortly before her brother's daughter was born.

For half an hour or more she talks, with scarcely a break, remembering details as she's speaking and bringing them smoothly in. She begins with a Friday evening, when this man was brought through from Accident and Emergency. He'd been found lying in an alleyway behind some shops, unconscious and quite badly knocked about: there were cuts on his face, lesions on the torso and legs, a wrist was broken and a couple of ribs were cracked. Nobody managed to get much information out of him in the hours after he came round, other than that his name was Henry Palmer and he'd been in a fight. Addled by concussion and a considerable volume of alcohol, he took quite a while to remember his name and he seemed unsure about his age: forty, he said at one point, thirty-nine some time later. He appeared to be several years older than that. How he had come to be in the alley, and who had set about him, he wasn't able to say, though it seemed to be established that only one assailant was involved. That night he slept for almost twelve hours.

Lynn was close to his bed when he woke up. He regarded the cast on the broken wrist, then raised a hand to his face. A finger found a line of sutures; he pressed the wound firmly, apparently insensible to any increase in pain this caused. He pressed on each cut and examined the bruises on his chest, and he seemed, thought Lynn, to be satisfied by the extent of his injuries. One eye was almost closed by swelling. With the good eye he looked at Lynn, then he said, as if apologising for being there: 'It was my fault.' She asked him what he meant exactly, to which he repeated: 'It was my fault. I'm sorry.' He turned away, 'as if ashamed. More than ashamed – mortified,' says Lynn. 'He closed his eyes. Perhaps the pain had got to him, or he was thinking about something. Whatever it was, I felt my attitude towards him changing. I had this sudden rush of sympathy for him.' Seeing a reaction from Ian, she pauses and gives him a look of a sort we're used to giving out, not receiving. 'I know what you're thinking,' she tells him. 'I was there to look after him. I should have been sympathetic from the start. And I was, but not entirely, if you want the truth. Because right off you could see he was a drinker and my father was a drinker. I don't like what it does to people. So I have a prejudice. Shouldn't, I know, but I do. I wasn't very well disposed towards Henry at first. I thought: it's a Friday night, here's another duffed-up drunk. And we're used to the morning-after remorse. But there was something unusual about this one. It came from the depths. Really from the depths,' she says, placing a clenched hand over her heart.

Later that morning she asked Henry what had happened to him. He wanted to know what he'd said to the doctor last night. She told him: there'd been a fight, that's all. He couldn't tell her any more, he said. 'Can't or won't?' she asked.

196

'Can't,' he replied and she left it at that, though she knew he'd meant 'won't'. When she asked him if there was anyone he'd like the hospital to contact, he said: 'No, I don't think so. Thank you.' Then he fell asleep.

'Where do you live, Henry?' she asked him later.

'Not far,' he replied, but this time she pursued the point, and from Henry's reluctance to be specific about an address she concluded that there was no address to be specific about. It had been a possibility that he was homeless: he was severely under-fed, had dirty fingernails, and his hair and beard could have done with a wash and trim. His clothes, bundled in a bag, lacked fresh-ness. But a multitude of unhygienic, ill-tended single men had passed through Lynn's ward over the years, so it wasn't absolutely certain, in her eyes, that Henry was a down-and-out. He slept for hours, that first day.

Late in the afternoon he woke up and, seeing the windows darkened, called out to the nurse on duty: 'Is it morning?' The answer – 'It's nearly five' – seemed to distress him, as did the sight of the man lying in the previously unoccupied bed beside him. Bewildered, he tried to get up, and fell. 'Tell the other one I've thought of somebody,' he said to the nurses who helped him back into bed. By 'the other one' he meant Lynn, and 'some-body', she learned the next morning, was Gemma, his ex-wife, who was living in London, as far as he knew. He hadn't seen her for a while but he would like her to know where he was.

At this Ian emits a small cry of revelation. Gazing ceiling-wards, he raises his hands in an attitude of thankful prayer, a performance regarded by Lynn with a serene, detached curios-ity, as if she were watching through a window. 'This is good,' he explains. 'The wife. We knew she exists, but we've never found her. Never even had a name.'

'Ah,' Lynn responds, with a damping tone. 'You have a name, but you don't have a wife. Not as such.'

His ex-wife's name was Gemma Simpson, he said, and she'd been living in Hindmans Road, East Dulwich, the last time he spoke to her, which was three years back. The phone directory had nobody of that name listed in that street. Informed of this, Henry now provided a rather important piece of information that he'd forgotten to mention before: four years ago, Gemma had married a man called Petridis. 'And there was indeed a Petridis in Hindmans Road. But Henry had been a bit careless with his terms,' says Lynn, as if she's talking about an amusing small misdemeanour committed by one of her children. When Lynn asked if she was speaking to the former Gemma Simpson, and then if Gemma was once married to a Mr Henry Palmer, the woman reacted as if this were an accusation.

'No,' snapped Gemma.

'I'm sorry,' Lynne replied. 'I thought you were married.'

'You thought wrong.'

'Oh. Henry said you were.'

'Well, we weren't.'

'But you knew him?'

'What's it got to do with you?'

Lynn explained who she was and told her what had happened to Henry. 'I'm sorry to hear that,' Gemma responded with about as much emotion as you might express if someone told you that it rained all last week in Aberdeen. At the suggestion that Henry might benefit from a visit, Gemma made it clear that she didn't want to know. 'I haven't got time for this,' she said, putting the phone down.

She would tell Henry that she hadn't been able to get an answer, Lynn decided, but there was no need, as it turned out, because he didn't ask about Gemma. However, he began to act strangely later that day, after the phone call, so strangely that one of the nurses wondered if he might have had a stroke. There had always been a deliberateness about the way he spoke, which Lynn had attributed to the after-effects of the assault, or to the cumulative effects of alcohol, or both. Now there was a definite sense of a time lag between thought and speech, a delay in which it seemed, sometimes, that words changed or went astray somewhere along the route from brain to mouth. 'One day I'll end up walking to Moscow,' he said, and the next instant frowned, perplexed by what he'd heard himself say. 'Can you hand me that thing?' he asked, pointing to the chair. 'What thing? The newspaper?' With a rictus of anguish he stared at the newspaper. 'Yes, that's the word,' he said. At lunchtime she turned her back on him for a moment and he started jabbing the fork into the base of his thumb. 'My hand's half dead,' he told her, as though his hand were not part of his body. Knocking a fist on his ribs, he remarked that he was aware of a pain, but wasn't sure if the pain was his. A doctor took a look at him and decided that he hadn't had a stroke.

A second call to Gemma was no more productive than the first. 'Not my problem,' she said. Told that Henry didn't seem to have any friends, she commented: 'Amaze me.'

'Is there any family?' Lynn asked. No, there was no family. Lynn disclosed her suspicion that Henry was homeless.

'But you don't know for sure,' was Gemma's response.

'Pretty well certain.'

Here there was a pause, the merest interval of hesitation, before Gemma replied: 'I'm sorry to hear that.' She revealed that she was pregnant and didn't feel too good in the mornings. A visit from herself wouldn't do any good anyway, she said. 'Tell him I said hello,' she finished, cutting Lynn off in midsentence.

People came across Henry in various parts of the hospital. He appeared in the foyer and in the café, wearing his pyjamas. He was seen standing in the corridor, staring at his reflection in a window, furiously, as if he were being followed by his double. He was found wandering into the children's ward. Next morning he wasn't in his bed when breakfast was brought round. A porter found him in the hospital garden, sitting on a bench, gazing at the sky. His fingers were scarlet and the seat of his pyjamas soaked with melted frost. Asked what he was doing, he looked around the garden, bemused, as if he'd just been woken up and couldn't understand where he was. Back in bed, he stared for hours at the ceiling, in a trance.

Increasingly concerned about Henry's mental state, Lynn made a third attempt to persuade Gemma to come down to Southampton. Henry seemed very confused, she said. She told Gemma about the incident in the garden. 'Christ Almighty,' Gemma sighed, a sigh that was ninety-five per cent resentment. Another twenty minutes and she'd agreed, after complaining about expense and childcare arrangements and morning sickness, to get on the train.

She arrived at midday, striding into the ward with the air of somebody who had come for a very specific purpose, on which she was determined to waste as little time as possible. The pink velour top – stretched over a five- or six-month belly – was memorable, as were the spiky eyelashes and the tight-set damson-coloured lips, but what struck Lynn first was how much younger than Henry she was: late twenties, you'd have guessed. 'I'm looking for Henry Palmer,' she said, as though she'd been summoned to take him home from a police cell. When Lynn introduced herself, the response was a sharp nod and 'Where is he?' Henry had made an effort to improve his appearance: his face had been scrubbed, and he'd run a wetted comb through his hair and beard. Seeing Gemma, and taking note of her thickened waist, he waved to her and smiled as broadly as the bruising would permit. Gemma, on the other hand, was shocked at Henry's appearance. 'I wouldn't have recognised you,' she said, without affection.

'It'll go down soon. No damage done,' said Henry, fingering the stitches.

'Not what I meant,' said Gemma, staying where she was, at the foot of the bed, while Henry eased himself upright and wrapped a dressing gown round his shoulders.

They left the ward, walking two feet apart, not talking to each other until they were in the corridor. That was the last of Gemma. 'Gone then, has she?' asked one of the nurses when Henry returned.

'Aye,' he replied, lightly, as if the visit had been of no importance.

'Nice of her to come down,' suggested Lynn.

'Yes, it was,' said Henry, smiling. And then, after a minute of silence, he said: 'It seems like a hundred years ago.' There was a wistfulness to the remark, a feeling of resignation, but no sooner had he spoken than he put his hands to his head and shook it violently, as if to unblock his memory. 'I need a drink,' he said.

'When you're out of here,' Lynn replied. The next day he announced that he was going to sit in the garden for a while. He dressed himself, hobbled out of the ward and just kept going. 'That's it,' she says. 'We never saw him again.' Once more she contemplates the photograph of Henry, questioningly, as if in the slender hope that the face might provide a clue as to why he acted as he did. In a murmur she asks: 'He lived here?'

Ian gives her the gist of the story: Henry's bivouacs on the beach and The Maer, the peregrinations, the body in the sand, the miscellany of names. On the top page of his notes: 'children's ward' is underlined, and while we're talking to Lynn he's sketching circles round the phrase. When Lynn asks if we're finished he springs to his feet to shake her hand and thank her earnestly. He almost runs out of the room.

Gemma is not at home, so Ian leaves a message. A week later – she's been on holiday – she gets back to us. She sounds as Lynn had described her. The news that Henry is dead is received with something less than grief. Within ten seconds she seems to absorb the fact of his decease and come to terms with it. She wants to know why we need to talk to her.

'Because Henry was murdered.'

Another ten seconds are required for this information to be processed. 'What's that got to do with me?' she asks.

'We're building up a victim profile. We're speaking to everyone who knew him.'

'What, everyone?'

'Everyone we can find.'

'I don't know.'

'You don't know what, Mrs Petridis?'

'What's it got to do with me?'

It takes the best part of five minutes to make her understand. 'OK,' she says at last, as if she has a choice in the matter.

22

Nicholas Zalygin, returning home to 47 Corbett Road on a Sunday night after a weekend with his parents, was taking the front-door keys from his pocket when he heard, from inside, what sounded like a bath running. This was troubling in itself, because Donald, his co-tenant and boyfriend, had left the previous morning for a friend's house, where he had intended to stay for a couple of days. More troubling still, the bathroom light wasn't on. For that matter the whole house seemed to be in darkness. As Nicholas opened the door, the sound became immediately too loud and too near. He turned on the hall light and what he saw, instead of the staircase, was a cascade of water, like something from an ornamental garden. He looked towards the kitchen: huge curls of wallpaper were lying on the floor and where the doorway should have been there was a screen of falling water. He took a look inside the living room. Treading on the carpet was like walking on thick wet moss, and the light wouldn't come on. Water was streaming from the lampshade in the centre of the ceiling. Another waterfall was spattering on the sofa.

Upstairs, Nicholas's bedroom had been wrecked. Huge plates of sodden plaster were lying all over the room and water was coming through the ceiling in half a dozen places, most heavily above the bed. The mattress was bowed into a canoe shape by the weight of water it had absorbed. Tracing the flood to its source, Nicholas found that the pipe that fed the tank in the loft, directly above his bedroom, had become detached, and was pumping water at full pressure into the roof space. His first move was the logical one: he shut off the mains supply. Next he assessed the situation. It did not strike him that it was inadvisable to allow the continued coexistence of electricity and copious quantities of water. Wires were fizzing in the walls, but Nicholas didn't hear them. He left the power on. The priority, Nicholas reasoned, was to get the house dried out. After that, the salvage operation could get under way. It was mid-November, cold and drizzly. This is perhaps why Nicholas, rather than throw the windows open, decided that the acceleration of the drying process could best be effected by making sure all the windows were tightly shut before cranking the central heating up to maximum. He switched the boiler to twenty-four-hour setting, rang Donald and drove off to join him.

Upon hearing of the disaster, Donald was of course dismayed. He was not, however, dismayed by Nicholas's emergency measures. On the contrary, he thought Nicholas had done the sensible thing, as did Donald's friend. It occurred to none of them that it might not be a good idea to create a closed microclimate of Amazonian heat and humidity in a house that was now awash with water-borne spores, to say nothing of what had been lurking in the carpets, on the walls and in the furniture, awaiting an opportunity to propagate. No, in a consensus of doziness they applauded Nicholas's strategy and concurred that it would be best to stay away from Corbett Road for a few days, leaving the radiators to do their restorative work.

On Friday Nicholas and Donald went home. Standing at the door, they became aware of a sweet and pungent mustiness in the air, something like the smell that comes off a place that hasn't been inhabited for years. They opened the door and a thick hot fume of rot and stagnancy flowed over them. A thin grey fur now covered the walls. Meaty little yellow mushrooms were growing on the carpet. A sky-blue fuzz bloomed here and there on the ceilings and on the stairs some bone-white growths had sprouted. With every footstep the carpet oozed rank grey slime. Nicholas's bed had become a fungus farm, and everything in his wardrobe had acquired stripes and badges of luscious turquoise.

Before the insurers arrived, Nicholas and Donald did some clearing up. The waterlogged bed and various lengths of slime-covered carpet were heaped in the back garden. Their books, now largely reduced to sludge, were shovelled into bin bags and deposited on to the lawn out front, between a semi-dissolved old armchair and a sofa that had become host to some spectacularly florid growths. There, beside the sofa, was where the loss adjuster was crouching, poking through the bin bags, estimating the value of the books that had gone into the making of this slurry, when Alice Jameson, on her way back home, having finished a half-day at the office, stopped at the gate and, seeing the wreckage, asked: 'What happened?' She put her hands to her face, as if these ruined things were the possessions of close friends, though in fact she knew nothing of Nicholas and Donald. Together we toured the reeking house. Smiling with ambivalent fascination – amazed by the spectacle and appalled on behalf of the numbskull tenants – she gazed at the profusions of multicoloured mould, and that's how it started.

The story of how John met Alice was often told. It had even been told before in the Whittams' garden, on the evening of the house-warming party, when for Margaret it was a tale about the curious workings of fate, bringing us together through the fortuitous combination of a faulty water pipe and some outstandingly silly people, whereas what her husband heard was the comical rout of the culpably stupid by the ineluctable forces of nature, the triumph of the microbes over dim humanity. Now, on a warm summer's evening in the garden of the Whittams' house, the story was told to Rebecca. We'd been standing around for a while, in a group of about a dozen, admiring George's spatula technique at the state-of-the-art barbecue that had just been installed on the edge of the patio. There had been some desultory talk of Henry, but already the murdered tramp was halfway to being folk-lore. Geoff Salter was there, with Muriel, standing next to the newly-weds from across the street. 'Short engagement, ours was,' said Geoff, locking a hand on Muriel's shoulder in a gesture that was meant to signify enduring conjugal love, but rather suggested an officer making an arrest. 'Met at a Christmas party, married by Easter. Weren't we, love?' he said, eyes widening with the remembered fire of first love, then he hauled Muriel closer to kiss her heavily on the mouth. Released, Muriel smoothed her dress, gave a small smile to Alice and raised her eyes heavenwards at her husband's disregard for decorum. 'Got yourself some Madeleys there,' said Geoff, pointing to the row of swollen, tight-skinned sausages on the grill, prompting laughter from himself and George. 'Shall I tell them?' he asked George.

'Please, no,' Muriel objected weakly, with no hope of success. 'There's a time and a place for everything,' she said, and her heedless husband explained to the newly-weds that he had once come into contact with a gentleman by the name of Mr Madeley, who had lived alone and had the discourtesy to top himself in the middle of a heatwave, in a poorly ventilated south-facing room.

'Not a large man, when he was alive. But a couple of days at low heat and it was a different story. By the time we found him he'd gone up like a balloon with all the gas in him. Someone brushed against the body, whereupon Mr Madeley exploded. Went off like a bomb,' said Geoff, with jubilant flying-apart gestures of the hands for added emphasis, spilling beer into the roses. 'Bits of him on the curtains, on the ceiling, all over us,' he chortled. 'Mr Madeley's message from beyond the grave: "Fuck off and leave me alone, you bastards."'

The newly-weds, at a loss, lifted their glasses in unison, though the wife's was empty. Muriel offered them a smile of impotent apology, the smile of a woman who has been similarly embarrassed too many times to count. 'Lovely,' she said, stroking Geoff's head as you'd stroke the head of an overexcited pup. 'Thank you so much for that, dear.'

'We've heard worse,' commented Rebecca, as her father, straight-faced but eyes smiling, punctured the sausages one by one, delivering a sharp single jab to each. Warned by a glance from Rebecca that we might be about to hear worse, Alice caught the eye of another guest and detached herself from the periphery of the group with a gliding sidestep that was unobserved by most.

Some time later we're in the kitchen, rinsing glasses, looking out on the garden, where Monica – back home for the summer vacation – is enchanting a claque of half-cut male mid-lifers with her mercurial intelligence and abundant areas of exposed female firmness. Alice has succeeded in manoeuvring the newly-weds away from Geoff, who is waving a beer aloft in each hand and regaling a pair of young women so relentlessly that one of them has been struck with facial paralysis, while the other is sending eye-transmitted Mayday signals in Alice's direction every five seconds. Geoff, reaching the punchline, erupts into laughter; the paralysed woman, after a delay, manages a queasy grin.

'Why does he do this?' says Rebecca. 'It's always the same. Has a drink and starts thinking he's a comedian. Every time. But of course, as we know, comedians are really very sad people. On the outside they smile, but deep inside they're blue,' she mocks, at the reflection of her face. 'Are comedians who only think they're comedians even sadder than real comedians? Is Sergeant Salter a sad man? His wife seems to like him and he seems to like his wife. Work issues, then. Must be work,' she proposes chirpily, turning to present a troublemaker's grin. 'Is that it? The career flightpath not taking the route he'd imagined? What do you think? Or can't you say? No, you can't. Of course you can't.' Out in the garden she'd been drinking fruit juice, but now it seems likely that something stronger has been taken. 'But two beers at once, that's not good, is it? I mean, it might indicate something. Or am I talking out of turn?'

'Most of us like a drink from time to time.'

This is taken as intended, as a reminder of a specific evening. A deflection of the eyes is followed by a self-correcting pause, then she says, 'True, but not as much.'

'Maybe. He likes a drink. It gives him pleasure.'

'And gives them pain,' she says, with first a nod towards Geoff's audience, then a sideways glance that is quickly withdrawn but followed at once by a glance that's sustained for a moment longer, searching for, and finding, an assurance that she has not over-stepped the mark and put at risk the tacit pact that exists between us. She lifts a couple of tumblers from the suds and turns them under the running cold water.

Mrs Newly-wed, so delighted by a remark just made by Alice, touches Alice's forearm lightly and bends towards her to whis-per. Waving a segment of chicken on a two-foot fork, George hails the husband, who replies with a rubbing of his fatless belly, an unconvincing mime of satiety.

'Good job your wife's here,' says Rebecca. 'I wish I could do it, but I can't. The chit-chat.' She winces as if struck on the back of the head, nearly dropping a glass. 'That sounds terrible. You know what I'm saying. The diplomatic stuff. Keeping things tick-ing along. Your wife's brilliant at it. Monica can do it. I'm useless.'

'Ditto.'

Washing and drying glasses, we watch Alice and the newly-weds at their small talk. Even if it were to be revealed to her in a flash of clairvoyance that, as in fact will prove to be the case, she'll never come across these people again, Alice would conduct herself in exactly the same way. She'd give them all the time they would like from her, however much tedium it entails.

On the patio Muriel Salter, discreetly as a waitress, extricates the empty beer cans from his hands in passing and replaces them with a single full one, without disrupting the flow of her husband's monologue, and gets a pat on the behind in thanks. 'I don't see the attraction. I know I shouldn't say it, but really. Not my idea of Mr Right,' Rebecca pronounces, then hears herself and laughs. 'Well. You know what I mean. Your wife wasn't impressed, was she?'

'Mr Madeley has exploded once too often.'

'Just once? Lucky woman. About the twentieth time for me.' And this is where Rebecca, looking at Geoff Salter and his wife, asks: 'So how did you meet, you and your wife?' The question is casually put, but the implication – that this is another partnership she cannot understand – is unmistakable even before she blushes. 'None of my business,' she says. 'I shouldn't have asked. Pretend –'

'No. I'll tell you. It's a good one.' So, in reaction to Rebecca's presumptuousness, the story of the brainless tenants of 47 Corbett Road is told again, to oblige her to picture Alice – the too fastidious, too refined wife of Mr Donohue – walking through rooms that stink like a summer swamp, fascinated by the rampaging fungi.

'Amazing,' says Rebecca at the end, unamazed, picking up the tray of clean glasses, an action in which can be read a scepticism about what she's just heard, a scepticism which partly explains why, when's she left the room, the half-hour in the Corbett Road house is kept in the mind, is held there, tenaciously, like a charm, or a memento. And there's another reason for holding on to the memory of Alice in the flood-damaged house.

After the conversation with Lynn Paisley there had been an impulse to tell Hannah Rowe what we had learned, an impulse that recurred but was overridden easily enough, just as thoughts of Hannah Rowe, occurring sporadically in the course of the days in Greece, had been quashed with no great difficulty. Two days before the gathering at the Whittams' house, however, the impulse was there again, and more forcefully than before, so that it now felt necessary to relay the gist of Lynn Paisley's statement, almost as if this episode from Henry's life were an item he'd bequeathed to Hannah in his will and had to be handed over. It was at the beach that this happened, the part where Henry's body had been found. There was no definite purpose to being at the beach that afternoon. Perhaps what was at work was a half-baked notion that contemplation of the death site, or at the death site, might in some way bring clarity, that some hitherto overlooked connections might make themselves apparent, like one of those pictures with an image hidden in the middle of a morass of swirling colours that you stare at for hours and see nothing, then suddenly it's there and you can't comprehend how it was ever missed. And the bay was gorgeous in the light and the warmth of early evening. Uncovered by the retreating tide, the sand glowed bronze at the water's margin, and the sea was dotted with sails that might have been placed there for maximum picturesque effect. Three or four big clouds hung over the horizon, white with tinges of apricot. Even the seaweed looked good, draped on the rocks like cloths of emerald baize and black plush. It was in this context that the idea of talking to Hannah reappeared.

There was time, while the phone was ringing, for anticipated disappointment at her not being home to be joined by hope that she wouldn't answer, but she did answer, saying 'Hello' as though to someone who calls every day. She would be at home for another fifteen minutes, she said.

A canvas bag rests against a wall. A large pad of paper protrudes from it and there's a tin of watercolours in a side pocket. Hannah stands beside the bag, leaning against the wall, arms crossed, to hear the news. She's already put on a jacket, ready to go out. 'So?' she asks.

'It's looking like there's no wife.'

An eyebrow flexes. 'That's the news? I told you there was no wife.'

'But there was a girlfriend. A long-term girlfriend. He was in hospital once and he told the nurses he had a wife, but she turned out not to have been married to him. This might be the woman he was talking about in Ilfracombe. I'm interviewing her the day after tomorrow. She's in London.'

'That's it?'

'That's the essence. There's a bit more, if you want.'

210

'How much more?'

'Five minutes should cover it.'

She's smiling to herself as she looks at her watch. 'OK,' she says, and still leaning against the wall she listens, eyes narrowing from time to time, as if trying to picture the visit of Gemma, pyjama-clad Henry in the frozen garden, Henry impaling his own thumb with a fork. (Henry straying into the children's ward is omitted from the report.) 'Nice woman,' she comments. 'Lynn, that is.'

'Very.'

'But you don't know who put him in hospital?'

'No.'

'Well,' she says, picking up the bag, 'thanks for telling me.'

'I'll let you know if anything comes of the girlfriend.'

'Thank you.'

'You're in a hurry.'

'Not a hurry, no. But I have to get going,' she states, and she moves towards the door.

Nothing else is said until we're outside, at the gate. Gathering her hair back and guiding it through the loop of an elastic band, she tilts her head and says: 'You look as if you have a question. I'm going this way,' she adds, pointing towards the sea, and we start to walk. 'You don't have a question?' she asks. We're walking quickly, side by side.

'I don't get it, with Henry.'

'Neither do I.'

'No, I mean what it was about Henry. I still don't get what it was about him. The nurse took a shine to him. You took to him. What was it?'

'I already told you.'

'He was nice.'

'Yes, he was nice. Why do you think that's ridiculous?' she enquires, looking straight ahead, maintaining a good pace.

'I don't.'

'That's not how it sounds.'

'So he was nice. But tough.'

'This is stupid. You can't say why you like someone, can you? You just do.'

'Have a try. I just can't quite see him in my head. I need more. Say anything that comes to mind. It all helps.'

This provokes a doubtful scowl, but her reluctance is momentary. 'Well,' she says, 'he liked being alive.'

'Most of us prefer it to the alternative.'

'Do you want me talk or don't you?'

'Please. Yes. Go on.'

'He loved being alive, OK? That better? He was like a kid a lot of the time. Things excited him. Just the sight of what was around, the sounds. And he had this air of melancholy too. And that was part of it, part of his appeal. Not sad about something in particular. Melancholy. You felt that he'd always been like this. He loved being alive and he'd always been melancholy. Are you happy with that?'

'Any more?'

'He was honest.'

'Up to a point. He wasn't too honest about his name.'

'Here we go again. The name's not important.'

'It's important to us.'

'It wasn't important to me. His real name could have been Fernando Tampax for all I care. You asked me why I liked him. I'm answering your question, all right? He was honest. To me he was honest. He told me what he was thinking. If he didn't want to talk he'd say so: "I don't feel like talking." And that was fine.'

'OK.'

'He was sometimes lonely and he was sometimes bored, and he would tell me when he was. But he wasn't needy. He didn't make claims on me. He would just say it: "Today I'm lonely." As a simple statement of fact: this is how I am today.'

'He didn't complain. I remember.'

'You're doing it again.'

'What again?'

'There's a tone.'

'No, there isn't.'

'There is. You can't hear yourself,' she said, striding on.

'He was lonely and you felt sorry for him.'

'No. Yes. No. A bit. Sometimes he was lonely and sometimes I felt sorry for him. But I liked spending time with him and I think he liked spending time with me.'

'Still don't get it. He told you what was on his mind, right? He was honest with you.'

'That's what I said.'

'But he didn't tell you much about himself. Next to nothing, in fact.'

'What's the problem?'

'When people talk they talk about themselves, most of the time.'

'Well, there you have it. Henry didn't. Maybe that's your answer. That's why I liked him. What interested him was what was outside himself and that's what made him interesting. He said interesting things.'

'About what? The news? The weather?'

We're at the seafront, waiting for a gap in the traffic. Scanning the street slowly, as if searching for someone in particular, she says: 'I don't think there's much point continuing with this. I found the things Henry said very interesting, some of them. OK? Perhaps I'm an idiot. Possibly you'd have found him boring. I don't know.'

'Of course not. All –'

'You make me feel that I have to justify myself for being interested in him.'

'That's not –'

'I'm sorry you find the idea ridiculous.' The road is clear now, but she makes no move.

'I don't.'

'Yes, you do.'

'Give me an example.'

213

'What?' she demands, angrily wiping at an eye.

'Give me an example of something he said.'

'So you can make fun again?'

'No. I want to understand. Just one example. Think of it as a swap. I've given you Henry in the hospital.'

'I've already thanked you.'

'Come on. Anything.'

'I can't think.'

'Just a small scene for me to imagine. One minute, that's all it'll take. A little bit of Henry in his own words. Please.'

'Why?'

'I said.'

'You want to understand.'

'That's right.'

'You want to understand Henry.'

'That's right.'

Face to face now, she presents a gaze that is wry and unpersuaded, then, with the sigh of someone making a last concession, she lets the bag slip from her shoulder and on to the pavement. 'OK,' she says, and draws a long breath. 'Henry and the sea,' she begins, indicating the estuary with a theatrical sweep of her arm, as if a curtain had just risen to reveal the vista. 'Some days he would stare at the sea for hours. He'd be there in the morning, on the wall, and when I came back from work he was still there, the very same spot. Hadn't moved all day. The next time I spoke to him I told him I'd seen him and I asked him what he'd been thinking about, watching the sea for so long. And what he said was that he wasn't sure if he had been watching it. Not his exact words. But that was the essence of it.'

'Meaning? That he'd been bored, or was hypnotised by it? What —'

'No, that's not it,' she says, smiling down at her hands, which are cupped and slightly parted, as if to pass across a fragile and valuable object. 'He might have been bored. He must have been, off and on. But what he meant was that he didn't know who or what had been doing the watching.'

'Lost me. But it's reminding me of something.' After fifteen seconds or so, despite the distraction of Hannah's expectant scrutiny, the connection is made: it's Lynn, telling us about Henry thumping his own ribs, experiencing the pain that might not have been his.

The response to the story of Henry and his disassociated pain is a disconcerting stare, as if she were trying to read tiny print on the eyeballs of the person in front of her. 'He could feel it but he couldn't feel it? I can't really . . . What –?'

'Some sort of short-circuit in the brain. Processing error, something like that.'

'God,' she murmurs, and she frowns at the pavement for so long it begins to seem that she might have lost track of what she was talking about, but then she lets the thought go and her face comes up, now unlined. 'But this wasn't a short-circuit,' she resumes. 'This was an idea, a clear idea. I just didn't grasp it straight away.'

'I'm still not grasping it.'

'OK,' she says, as eager as a young teacher with a class of bright kids. Again she waves an arm at the water. 'You look at the sea. Your brain, through your eyes, sees the sea. But do you look at the sea? Is there a person called you who is doing the looking? From the brain, from the chemicals and the electricity in the skull, comes a command to the eyes and the eyes move and you call this looking. You will yourself to look at the sea, or that's what you think, or you think you think, but the idea is just a spark in the tissue. The brain thinks, and one of the things it thinks is that you are you. There's not a person called You inside your head, telling the brain what to think. You come after the spark. That's all you are. Yes? It's terrible, when you start to think about it. If you can say that. I mean, if that can be said.' She smiles sympathetically at what she takes to be a perplexity that replicates her own initial reaction to Henry's conundrum, a perplexity that is renewed, fleetingly, in the expression of her eyes. 'How about that?' she asks, lifting the bag. 'Will that do? Convinced now?'

'That will do. It's interesting. Very.'

She squints, assessing the quotient of sarcasm, and appears to find none.

'Really, it is.'

The look, making sure of its assessment, lasts for another four or five seconds. 'OK. In that case I'm glad to have helped. I'm going that way,' she says, pointing in the direction of the clock-tower. We shake hands briskly.

Frequently, usually at night, usually as the slide into sleep began, faces appeared as though of their own accord, mortuary faces, most of them: the sardonic grin of Carl Banham, self-poisoned with strychnine; the soft, all-accepting smile of Jeannine Shepard, dead at twenty with enough heroin in her bloodstream to kill her four times over; the face of Keith Hathaway, howling as though he still felt the pain of the knife-thrust that did him in; and Henry's dissolving head, of course. And now, among the dead faces, there was the face of Hannah Rowe. Before the day of the walk to the seafront she had already appeared a few times, but not many, and had been easily turned away. But afterwards it was different, and the apparition of Hannah became as persistent as a lie about yourself, a lie that you can't get out of your mind, and then you begin to understand why you can't get rid of it. 'For the story too,' she would repeat, and 'You want to understand Henry', with an emphasis on the name that perhaps was heavier than her voice in reality had given it.

When Luke was a baby, night after night Alice would come awake in the small hours and be on her way to his room a second or two before the crying started. The arrival of the dead faces too, she seemed to sense unconsciously – not every time, but often enough for it to seem uncanny. Rising to the surface of sleep, she would slide a hand across the pillow and whisper a few words. Sometimes she'd wake up fully and we'd talk, in the dark. By the year of Henry's death, though, things had changed, and whenever her hand did slip across the bed, which was rarely, her eyes would not open and she would hardly ever speak. But once, on a night when many of the faces had been present, and Hannah's most of all, there was the slightest touch of Alice's hand and it felt like a reproof, a summoning back, which brought to mind the house in Corbett Road, ten years before, and Alice beside a grey-streaked wall, astonished, a hand to her mouth. On a hook behind the door there was a dressing gown, originally white, now lichen-grey, with a collar that had turned the colour of spinach. She regarded the dressing gown for a long time. 'I shouldn't be here. This isn't right,' she said, and in the next instant we looked at each other, and that was when it happened: the flash, the spark, the truth moment, whatever you want to call it. Or that's what Alice used to say: 'It was in that room. You did something, a sort of nod. And that was it.' But now, in the remembered room, all that happens is that Alice regards the dressing gown and walks through the doorway, taking care not to touch the walls.

23

The Petridis residence is a compact three-bedroom terraced house, double-glazed in pseudo-leaded style, repointed and repainted recently, and fronted by a snow-white waist-high fence that once enclosed a small garden, a room-sized space that has now been paved as a parking bay. The neighbours on one side still have a garden, a mess of shrubs and grass that cannot have seen shears or mower within the past year. On the other side, behind a fence that isn't quite as well maintained as the Petridis fence, there's a bed of gravel with big terracotta pots on it, half a dozen of them, artfully spaced on the stones, and each with a single small feathery-leaved bush sprouting from it. There are no flowers to detract from the elegance of the wispy mini-trees, but the periphery of the Petridis carport is a welter of blooms, spilling from overpopulated flowerbeds and hanging from baskets on the walls. Reds and dark pinks and purples and lilacs predominate, a colour scheme that continues inside, but toned down a degree or two. The three-piece suite is a dusky kind of pink and so are the curtains, and the cushions are the colour of plums. The lamp-shade, shaped like the head of a tulip, is white glass with a pink-ish tint and the walls are of a similar shade. On the unit to the side of the TV stand photos of the family, framed mostly in purple plastic. Behind the settee there's a large print (maroon-dyed wooden frame), showing a tranquil aquamarine sea, with pots of geraniums on a pink brick wall in the foreground. Gemma herself – wearing a peach-pink top with her jeans and red canvas shoes – maintains the colour co-ordination, and the effect is a little unsettling, not just because of the all-embracing red-pink-purple theme, but because all the furniture and furnishings (the carpet, the cushions, the curtains – everything, even Gemma's clothes) give the impression of having been bought at the same time, from the same place. It all matches and it's all almost new. Ian dubs her Mrs Catalogue.

Neat and trim, Gemma obviously puts some effort into staying in shape: not too much (there's a small amount of mid-life yield around the midriff), but enough to keep her a few years ahead of the game. The haircut – a short, sharp bob, enhanced dark brown – suits the cut of the face: the whole arrangement of brow and nose and mouth and jawline has a lot of straight lines in it, creating an ensemble that's designed for argument rather than ingratiation. The teeth are impressive too: white and straight and perfectly symmetrical, they make a contribution to the demeanour of efficiency and charmlessness. (She's a receptionist at a dental surgery, we discover.) The shelves, though, display evidence that there is a sunny side to Mrs Petridis. There she is with Mr Petridis (we assume), dancing on the deck of a cruise ship, with a crown of flowers on her head; there she is at a theme park, grasping a handrail as she howls; there she is with her girls, wrestling on a river bank. With us, however, she's not sunny at all, and it soon becomes clear that, twenty years on, she's still nurturing a grievance against Henry. And we, as the men who have brought him back into her life, are a legitimate target.

We've come a long way, but the hospitality doesn't extend beyond allowing us to park our backsides on the settee. More than an hour we're talking to her, without as much as a rumour of a cup of tea. 'Nice house,' remarks Ian, favouring our host-ess with his sincerest smile, and Gemma looks at him as if he's just made a remark in Swahili. When he hands her a copy of

Hannah's photograph, she takes it as relucantly as you'd take a writ. 'That's Henry last year,' Ian explains. Gemma holds the picture into the sunlight and is perfectly unmoved as she examines the face. She could be looking for a crack in a saucer. 'That's your Henry Palmer?' asks Ian.

'Never was my Henry Palmer,' she replies.

'But the same man as the man you knew?'

'Might be.'

'You're not sure?'

'It's similar. I think it's him,' she concedes, handing back the picture.

'You can keep it.'

'No thanks,' she says, removing a hair from her sleeve.

Again we go over what she was told on the phone: how the body was found, what little we know of Henry's life, the difficulties of the enquiry. 'Then we heard about you,' says Ian.

Gemma blinks at us, as if trying to decide if she can be bothered to respond, then says: 'What about me?'

'That you were with Henry. That he referred to you as his wife.'

'Not to me he didn't.'

'OK. But –'

'Not to no one else neither.'

'Except the nurse,' Ian reminds her, knitting his fingers, a sign that already he's come to realise that this afternoon may require an overdraft on his reserves of patience.

'Yeah.' Gemma shrugs. 'Well. Maybe.'

'So we can conclude that you remained a person of some significance to him,' Ian goes on, unfurling the fingers, as though elucidating a simple equation for the benefit of an underpowered student. 'And that being the case, it's possible that you can help us to build up the profile.'

'The what?'

'The victim profile.'

'Right,' she says.

'So we'd like you to tell us everything you can,' says Ian,

leaning forward to peer at her face, as if looking down a fox-hole that may or may not be occupied.

'A long time ago,' she says.

Ian makes a show of taking out his notebook and pen, ready to transcribe the great narrative that is about to commence. 'You met Henry when?' he asks, squandering another smile. '1968?'

'Don't know, not off the top of my head. About then.'

'And you were with him for how long?'

'What's "with him" mean?'

'Let's say from first date to break-up.'

She takes her time working out the answer and, having worked it out, waits a while before giving it. 'Three years. And a bit.'

'And you lived together for how much of that time?'

'Too bloody long,' she says, and here we turn a corner, or at least, from this moment on, talking to Gemma is not constantly as arduous as shoving a two-ton safe up a hill. Only a Trappist would describe her as talkative – half a dozen words per sentence and one sentence per answer, that's her preferred span – but at least she doesn't lapse into morose non-compliance after every utterance. That phrase – 'Too bloody long' – is like the first wasp of a swarm flying out from its nest, one by one.

She met Henry when she was twenty years old, a couple of weeks after her birthday. He was thirty, she tells us, as if this discrepancy between their ages, in hindsight, reveals the inevitab-ility of the failure of their relationship, though Henry's seniority doesn't seem to be an issue in what follows. They met in a pub in New Cross. Two or three nights a week she'd go there with friends, and then at some point, she doesn't know when, Henry began to appear, and before too long he was there, at the same table in the corner, reading his newspaper, every night she went there. Occasionally they'd exchange a look, but there was noth-ing in it, not for Gemma, anyway. For months they never spoke, then she had a boyfriend and wasn't going to the pub any more, then they broke up, and next time she went to the pub Henry said to her: 'I was wondering where you'd got to.' That was the start of it. 'I get caught by Henry on the rebound and he was no bloody use either,' she says, but Ian, pointing out that she and Henry were together for a while, coaxes a few concessions out of her. He looked OK, she admits; nothing special, but all right. And he wasn't pushy, she'll give him that much. 'He didn't come on to me. I went for him. That's a laugh, isn't it?' she says, with the nearest thing to a smile we'll see all afternoon.

'Do you have a photograph of him?' Ian asks.

'Somewhere, maybe.'

'We could do with one. It might help.'

'Help who?' she wants to know.

'Might jog some memories,' Ian tells her. 'We'll makes copies and send it back to you. I'll give you a receipt. Would you mind?'

'You want me to get it now?' she asks, as though she'd been asked to go out in a blizzard to buy a pint of milk.

While she's away, we give the room some attention. The photos of the daughters interest Ian more than the pictures of their mother, particularly the photos of the older girl. In the middle of one of the shelves there's a shot of her sitting on the bonnet of an Audi with a 1989 plate. She's a pleasant-looking kid, with wavy dark shoulder-length hair, but unfortunately the paternal genes have come out on top in too many departments, landing her with mighty eyebrows and a nose that needs a lot more space than her face can give it. 'What's her name?' Ian asks Gemma the instant she reappears.

'Myrto,' she answers. She sits at the table and removes the lid from the shoebox she's brought.

'And her sister?'

'Anna.'

'So Anna's thirteen?'

'Fourteen.'

'And Myrto's what, seventeen?'

'Nineteen.'

'Really?'

'Really,' says Gemma flatly, as she takes a wallet of snaps from the shoebox.

'You don't look old enough,' says Ian.

'So I've been told,' says Gemma, leafing through the contents of the wallet. If she'd looked up she might have noticed Ian inspecting again the face of Myrto and, a moment later, the pensiveness of his expression becoming lighter as, his calculations concluded, he arrives at a theory. 'This one?' she asks, turning a washed-out colour photo towards us. In front of a rust-pocked blue Mini stands a man in jeans and an oil-smeared T-shirt, a well-built man, with thick, sinewy forearms and a boxer's neck. His hair, cut in a weirdly level fringe at the front, hangs lankly at the sides, partly covering the upper reaches of an incoherent beard, a folk singer's sort of ill-managed chin growth. Round-eyed and grinning, he is wielding a spanner in a fist, as if it's a bone he's just wrestled from a Rottweiler.

'This is Henry?' asks Ian, taking the photo.

'My first car,' says Gemma. 'That's why I kept it.'

'So he wasn't entirely useless. Or is the picture misleading?'

'That was his job. He fixed cars.'

When Gemma met Henry he was working for a garage in Lewisham, one of a succession of shitty jobs for various half-legal employers, most of them in the same line of business, though occasionally he worked as a builder. It was all cash in hand, the work he did, and getting hold of the cash tended to be a struggle. Whenever Henry left a job he was usually owed money, and Henry was often leaving, for one reason or another. He worked three months for one outfit and never got a penny: he turned up for work on the Monday and the padlocks were on the gate. The Lewisham outfit was one of the worst. The cars it kept on the road weren't even fit for scrap and Henry's pay was always weeks in arrears. 'And the place he was living in,' says Gemma with a nauseated sniff. 'A hovel. Ten bedsits in the building and about a hundred people in them, and Henry the only white face. He had hardly any stuff, not even a telly,' she says, revealing for an instant what may be a granule of sympathy for her erstwhile lover. 'Not worth it. Buy it on Monday, it gets nicked on Tuesday. I went there once,' she goes on, sickened by the picture that's formed in her mind. 'And I mean once. Never again. So he was always coming to me and in the end he stayed, I suppose.'

'Just stayed? For a couple of years?'

'Yeah. He just stayed. That's how it feels. Don't know how it happened,' she says, making it clear that the conundrum of herself and Henry is a problem of history, and problems of history are of very little pertinence to her life.

'I gather he didn't look much like this when you saw him in hospital,' says Ian.

'Course he didn't. He'd been done over, hadn't he?'

'Mrs Paisley says she was surprised when she discovered his age.'

'Who?'

'The nurse who contacted you. Lynn Paisley.'

'Oh.'

'She thought he looked a lot older than he was.'

'So?'

'Did it strike you that he looked a lot older?'

'He looked like shit.'

'That must have shocked you.'

'Not really. Don't remember. Don't think so.' Blankly she shrugs at Ian, pursing her lips in indifferent apology.

A barely visible rocking of Ian's left foot betrays a rising anti-pathy. After consulting his notes he makes a show of adding a line or two, a trick that sometimes introduces an element of unease into the proceedings, and a little unease is often produc-tive. On Gemma, though, the fakery is wasted. Waiting for Ian to finish whatever it is he has to do, she directs her incurious gaze at the dead TV screen. 'Just to clarify,' he resumes. 'You and Henry split up in –?'

'He buggered off in 1971.'

'Spring, summer –?'

224

'November. Early November.'

'OK. So it was only a little over five years later when you saw him in hospital. And in that time he's gone from looking like this' – he holds up the photo – 'to looking like shit.'

'No.'

'Your words, weren't they?'

'Yeah.'

'You've lost me.'

'It wasn't five years.'

'November 1971 to February –'

'He came back.'

'You saw him again?'

'That's what I said.'

'And this was –?'

'About a year later.'

'And you saw him where?'

'Here. He was out in the street, swearing his head off. Pissed, of course.'

'He used to drink?'

'You could say that.'

'His drinking was a problem?'

'Not for him it wasn't.'

'But for you it was.'

'One of the problems,' she says, and she gives the air an uppercut.

'You mean –'

'Oh, yes. Not at the start, to be fair. But in the end he was handy. Very handy,' she says, throwing a more forceful punch.

'So he was violent,' Ian goes on.

'Yeah.'

'And when he appeared again, was he violent then?'

'Didn't have the chance. I called the police.'

'What exactly did he do?'

'Told you. He stood out there, swearing.'

'He was swearing at you. Is that all?'

225

'He was swearing at the house.'

'So you didn't talk.'

'No, we had a few words.'

'Specifically?'

'He said he wanted to come back and I said there wasn't a chance. He said: "There's something I want to say to you." And I said to him: "And there's something I want to say to you and all: piss off." Then I called the police.'

'That was all?'

'I can't remember. It's not important. Wasn't important then and not important now.'

'Do you know where he'd been in the meantime?'

'Not a clue.'

'What about when you saw him in hospital? Did he say what he'd been doing for the past few years?'

'Didn't ask.'

'Did he give you any indication of his circumstances?'

'Didn't say. I don't remember. He was skint. That's about it.'

'And his injuries. Did he say what had happened?'

'Been in a fight.'

'So we believe.'

'So. He'd been in a fight.'

'But you don't know any more than that?'

'If I did, I've forgotten.'

'Mrs Paisley told us that he was behaving peculiarly.'

'Nothing new there, then.'

'He seemed confused. Detached from himself. Did he seem that way to you? As if he'd got lost. Something like that.'

'How about playing for sympathy?' Gemma proposes. 'How about taking the piss?'

'Mrs Paisley thought that something seriously strange was happening inside his head.'

'Good for Mrs Paisley.'

'The doctors thought so too.'

'Obviously they know best.'

226

'You think they were wrong?'

'He was a conman. All that staring into space. The "Where am I?" bollocks. Henry's speciality. The man was an arsehole. You don't need a doctor to tell you what was wrong with his head,' she says, miming the pulling and downing of a pint. 'You want sympathy for Henry Palmer, you've come to the wrong place, I'll tell you that much for nothing.'

'When you say you'd seen it before '

'Well, I had. He could turn it on. You want to know why I wasn't impressed? I'll tell you,' she says, and now Gemma's version of Henry begins to fit, roughly, with what we knew.

Gemma's Henry, like Hannah's, was prone to periods of absence, from which he would return with no good account of where he had been and no explanation for his wandering – or rather, no explanation that satisfied Gemma. For a year or so his timetable was as regular as that of any office worker: leave home at eight, back home around six, or rarely more than half an hour later. He changed jobs a lot, but the routine stayed the same. He seemed content with life at home. At weekends they'd go up to town, see a film, go for a drink. Sometimes they'd drive out into the countryside. It wasn't exciting, but it was a better life than a lot of people have and an improvement on the relationship she'd had before Henry came along. Henry never sponged off her, she'd say that much for him, and he didn't want things his own way all the time. But then he started to change: nothing drastic, just a gradual darkening of his mood. He was never much of a talker, but even so it was noticeable that he was becoming more withdrawn. He was happy to do whatever Gemma wanted to do, except that 'happy' is the wrong word, because nothing truly made him happy. Nothing made him happy, nothing made him angry, nothing seemed to get his blood racing. He didn't seem depressed, just lukewarm about everything. He was aware that he wasn't quite himself, but he told Gemma that he'd soon snap out of it. He didn't snap out of it. Her flat had a tiny garden and he'd pace around it for a whole hour, as if it were a miniature prison yard. Then the sleepwalking began. She'd wake up in the morning to find that every light in the house had been turned on, or all the drawers had been opened during the night, as if Henry had been looking for something in his sleep. Once she was woken by someone pounding on the front door: she reached out to wake Henry but Henry wasn't there, and he wasn't there because it was Henry hammering on the door. Stark naked, he'd sauntered out of the flat and then found himself, freezing, outside the neighbours' house. As a kid he'd been a sleepwalker, he told her. There was no reason to worry. But he seemed tired a lot of the time, perhaps because he was never getting a decent night's sleep. He was having bad headaches and had this feeling of pressure on his head all day. It was like wearing an iron hat, he said, but he wouldn't listen when Gemma told him he should go and see a doctor. 'It'll go,' he kept saying, but it wasn't the headaches that went – it was Henry. One evening he hadn't come home by eight. Gemma rang his boss, who hadn't seen him all day. For the best part of a week there was not a word from Henry, then he reappeared on the doorstep one night, the worse for drink. 'I had to get away,' he said. He was sorry if he'd upset her. He'd been in a hotel for a few nights, but where the hotel was he couldn't say, and neither could he explain why it hadn't been possible to call her.

Convinced that he'd been on an almighty bender, Gemma could hardly bring herself to talk to him. Taking his punishment without protest, without any attempt at a defence, Henry ate alone, slept on the settee, worked extra hours at the new job that he'd found within a week or two. In the end they patched things up and Henry was on his best behaviour, for a while. They went on holiday together, to Cornwall, and had a good time. But before long there were signs that trouble was in the offing. He began to go quiet again. When they went to the pub he'd sometimes drink a pint or two more than usual, then he was having the extra couple every time. They had arguments about his drinking, about the lousy jobs he kept taking. He wasn't stupid – he could have been doing something better, but he just wouldn't make the effort. The sleepwalking started again. One morning she thought they'd been burgled during the night, but it had been Henry going mad, turning the place upside down and then coming back to bed, asleep all the while. When the headaches started she said to him: 'I don't want you doing a runner again. You pull that trick once more and you're out.' Henry duly went missing. A whole week this time: Monday to Monday. As before, his departure was unannounced, but on this occasion he did remember to call home. He rang from a service station on the M6 and wanted her to believe that he wasn't altogether sure how he'd come to be there. Anyway, he was on his way home now, he said, and put the phone down before she could tell him to save himself the trouble. When he arrived, the script was the same: he'd just had to get away, not from her but from everything, from himself most of all. 'Who went with you up the M6 then?' she wanted to know, and he didn't have an answer to that one. His clothes stank of pubs and his eyes were the colour of salmon. She didn't want an explanation from him: she had an explanation and she wanted him out. Henry pleaded for one last chance: he'd cut down on his drinking, he'd find a better job, he'd go and talk to the doctor about his problem. They reached a truce rather than a reconciliation. For a few months Henry did drink less, but his next job was in yet another dodgy garage, and he never made it to the doctor's surgery. 'I'll go next week, I promise,' he was always saying, but somehow he could never find the time. He could find time for a quick pint on the way home, though, so Gemma told him she wanted him to look for somewhere else to live. He was looking for a flat, or so he said, when the cycle started again, with the difference that a dose of domestic violence now came with the sleepwalking and the headaches and the rising alcohol intake. 'I'd had enough,' says Gemma, rubbing her eyes as if exhausted by the mere memory of life with Henry. 'I told him to fuck off and leave me alone, and that's what he did. Went off to work in the morning and that turned out to be goodbye.'

'So the next time you saw him was a year later, when he turned up in the street?'

'Correct.'

'In all that time you never heard from him either?'

'Nothing. Not a word.'

'I can see why you don't remember him fondly,' says Ian.

'I prefer not to remember him at all.'

'We won't keep you much longer,' he assures her.

'Thank you,' she replies with a chill grimace of a smile.

'When he reappeared, did he give any indication of where he'd been?'

'Yeah. There was an indication he'd been down the pub.'

'Yes, but I mean did he say anything about where he'd been in the interim?'

'Could have been on the moon for all I care.'

'I appreciate that, but was anything said, that you can recollect?'

'It wasn't what you'd call a conversation.'

'OK. So he didn't say anything about where he'd been? Nothing at all.'

'That's right.'

'What about friends or family? Did no one hear from him?' asks Ian and this gets a laugh, if laugh is the right word for the outrush of air that emerges from a mouth that's forming a shape that might technically be classified as a smile.

'What friends? He didn't have any friends, only mine, and they were never wild about him.'

'And family?'

'None on his side.'

'Absolutely nobody?'

'Nobody I knew of. His father did a bunk when he was a kid. His mother died years back. Buried in Nunhead. We went there once.'

'So was he from this area?'

'Yeah. Round here somewhere.'

'OK,' says Ian, his eyebrows raised in exaggeration of his pleasure at this information. 'This is interesting,' he says, making a note with great deliberation. 'This changes the picture. Now, is there anything you can tell us about his life before you knew him?' he asks, but Gemma has almost nothing more to tell us.

'To give him his due, it wasn't a big deal with Henry. He didn't bring any baggage with him,' she says. 'And didn't take any with him either,' she adds unsmilingly.

'Is there anything else you think we should know? Anything at all?'

Gemma's gaze travels towards the open window, as if tracking the flight of a fly. 'No,' she says. 'I think we're done.'

We rise together. 'Thank you for your time,' says Ian. 'We'll get the photo back to you within the week.'

'No hurry,' she says, moving doorwards with some alacrity.

Taking one last look at the photos on the shelves, Ian remarks: 'Henry and children.' Although she almost certainly hears this, Gemma, by now in the hall, makes no response, but she steps back into the room to find out why we're not following. 'Henry and children,' Ian repeats, as if stating the subject of a documentary he'd once seen. 'We were told that Henry liked children. And Mrs Paisley said he was delighted that you were expecting a baby,' he says, though Lynn Paisley had said no such thing.

For four or five seconds Gemma looks at him, trying to work out what he's getting at, then, with a blink like the falling of a guillotine blade, she cuts the thought off. 'Not as I recall,' she answers.

'You mean you can't recall if he was delighted or you recall that he wasn't?'

'I mean I can't remember,' she says, unlatching the front door. 'But whoever told you Henry liked kids, they don't know what they're talking about. He couldn't stand them. Talk to my sister if you like. When she came round here with her two, he'd make himself scarce pretty sharpish. Ask her about Uncle Henry.'

231

We don't take the sister's details. 'Well, thank you, Mrs Petridis,' says Ian, giving his hand, which she takes as if there's something deformed on the end of his arm, and she closes the door so quickly she almost clips our heels.

24

Peter Jellico is not telling us what he knows, and he knows we know he's not telling us what he knows, but he's sticking to his story: Guillory and Quinton rented the boat to go sea fishing; he got sliced up because he owes a lot of money to someone; and this someone is in no way associated with Messrs Guillory and Quinton. The look of terror is fixed in his eyes like a photograph, and from the way he grips the arms of the chair you'd think this interview was taking place on a ledge of rock a thousand feet above the sea. 'You help us clobber Gary Quinton and we'll look after you. Believe me, we'll look after you,' says George, arms spread generously, trying to make it sound as if what's on offer is the opportunity of a lifetime. 'You'll get money. We'll relocate you, and your girlfriend, miles from here, wherever you like. You'll be protected. You'll be safe. You have my word for that,' he says, giving him the sustained gaze of unflinching integrity, but a promise from a policeman is worth nothing against a promise from Gary Quinton: the terrified eyes, seeing only the image of madman Quinton, do not change. We could present him with a suitcase of banknotes and a fortified palace on a Hawaian island and it would make no difference: the only way we would get Peter Jellico into the witness box would be to threaten him with something even worse than Quinton will give him if he talks.

Two weeks after tottering out of hospital, Peter and his girl-friend load up a van and drive away, in search of a new life of penury and addiction beyond the range of Quinton's radar. And in the same week we hear that Guillory is back in town and has taken temporary possession of a motorboat. Steered by Jellico's replacement, this vessel is observed shuttling up and down the river and nibbling along the coast, in the manner of its predecessor. Then we lose sight of it, and the next thing we know is that wreckage is being washed ashore at Slapton and Keith Guillory, paying cash, is compensating the owner for the loss of his motorboat. The owner isn't complaining.

Meanwhile, the dental records of Henry Palmer turn out to be a match for the teeth of our corpse, so whereas we were fairly sure that Lynn Paisley's patient and Gemma Simpson's boyfriend and our Henry were identical, we now know for a fact that Henry Palmer and our Henry are the same man. But there is a catch, which is that Henry Palmer, loving son of Jessie Palmer (born 10 June 1909; passed away 22 March 1966; buried in Nunhead cemetery), is not the same man as Gemma Simpson's Henry Palmer, because Henry Palmer the loving son of Jessie Palmer is alive and well and living in Hackney. There is some dismay at this latest transformation of avenue into cul-de-sac, but nobody is greatly surprised. Neither does anyone think there's much point in telling Gemma Petridis that her unsatisfactory lover was even less straight with her than she had thought.

Aspects of the earlier life of Henry are withheld from Hannah, too. Nothing is said about his penchant for physical force and the strength of Gemma's dislike is understated. Retold for Hannah, the separation of Gemma and Henry is the inevitable drifting apart of a young woman and an older and somewhat eccentric man, whose eccentricities were exacerbated by a weakness for the bottle. That Henry Palmer wasn't Henry Palmer is accepted with wry affection, as if the amassing of various names was just her old friend's quaint pastime. We talk about the symptoms that presaged his disappearances. 'Sleepwalking, who knows?' she says. 'Headaches, not as I remember. I don't think there were any clues that he was about to strike off for the hills.' Standing by the open window, she turns to look intently towards the sea, verifying that her recollection is accurate. 'None that I noticed, anyway,' she says. 'He just went.' The subject of Henry's drinking, a subject with some potential for conflict, is quickly passed over. 'All I can say is I never saw him drunk. Or I never noticed he was drunk. But I'd have noticed, I'm sure. Perhaps he got blitzed on days when I didn't see him. I don't know. But if Henry was an alcoholic, he was in very good shape for one. I don't think he was drinking. I really don't. Perhaps he couldn't afford it. Perhaps something happened to make him give up. I don't know,' she says, with a smile, to herself, of mild regret.

She would have been spending the evening alone and she conducts herself as though nothing has been changed substantially by the arrival of company. No effort has been made to present herself. Bare-legged and barefoot, she's wearing a denim skirt that's tattered at the hem and a black T-shirt that's no longer true black. Two or three minutes seem to pass before she speaks again. Leaning against the wall, she gives the impression, as she watches the sea, that this is what she would have been doing anyway, just watching the sea as the sun slides into it. A warm, sweet, saline air is coming into the room. On the houses there's a varnish of buttermilk sunlight.

'So where now, with Henry?' she asks.

'Another appeal maybe. We can use Gemma's picture.'

'A twenty-year-old photo. I doubt that's going to do much.'

'You never know. Stranger things have happened.'

'Never say never,' she replies, and a corner of her mouth lifts by a fraction of a millimetre. 'Slow and steady wins the race.'

'We'll keep slogging away.'

'I'm sure,' she says, in such a way that it may or may not be a compliment. For a minute or so she surveys the gardens below and at some point a keenness enters her gaze, as if she's come to suspect that something in what she's seeing might be in some way different from its appearance yesterday, but can't work out what the difference is. Then she says: 'But you're not telling me everything, are you?'

'About what?'

'Your visit to Gemma. About Henry.'

'I'm telling you everything I can.'

'I don't think that's true. I think you don't like the sound of him very much,' she says, but not in reproof.

'It's neither here nor there, what I think. I didn't know him.'

'No,' she agrees. Again she surveys the streets, but distractedly now, until her gaze stops at the garden of the house next door. The neighbours' loft is being converted, and there's a pale patch in the centre of the lawn, where the builders had stacked the timber and tarpaulins. 'Yellowgreen,' she remarks. 'There's not a proper name for it. We have all these names for the nice colours, the red and blue zones of the spectrum. Cobalt, azure, turquoise, ultramarine, aquamarine.' There's been almost no eye contact so far, but now, as she recites the names, there is. She ticks off the names on her fingers: 'scarlet, vermilion, crimson, carmine, claret, cerise. But yellowgreen is a displeasing colour. Sickly, seedy, rotten, pissy. So it doesn't merit a name.' She and Henry devised a game, she says. If they saw something that was a particularly striking colour, they'd try to think what it was like, where they'd seen that exact tone before. Henry was brilliant at this, of course. Nine times out of ten he could find a match in seconds. 'The best one', she says, with that gleam of joy, 'was a sunset. It had just stopped raining. It had been pelting all afternoon, and there were these thick purple clouds all over the sea, with streaks of dark red and indigo and deep pink in them. And Henry got it right away: the underside of your tongue. That was what it looked like. Perfect.'

'That's good.'

'"That's good" isn't what your face is saying.'

'No, it's good.'

'But —?'

'He remembers where he's seen colours before, but he can't remember where he's been.'

'Here we go.'

'No. But it's strange. That's all I'm saying.'

'You don't like him.'

'Not true.'

'OK. You're fed up with him.'

'No.'

'I think you are.'

'Sometimes it feels like trying to catch steam in a net, but I'm not fed up with him.'

'OK,' she says, as if unconcerned, and a few seconds later, abruptly, she starts talking about the doctor whose house she's redecorating this week. 'She told me this story, and I thought of you as soon as I heard it,' she says, closing the window. 'I'm having a glass of wine. You want one?' she asks, and as we go through to the kitchen she retells this story about Mr Wiggly and the primary-school kids. One morning it's announced to the class that they'll soon be getting a visit from someone called Mr Wiggly. Mr Wiggly is a very funny man, their teacher says. She tells them what Mr Wiggly will look like: he's got eyebrows like caterpillars and huge blue shoes and a shiny silver waistcoat, and he'll have balloons attached to him, all over his jacket. Next morning, the teacher gives the kids the same speech. Coming soon: Mr Wiggly, the funny man. He'll have eyebrows like caterpillars and huge blue shoes and a shiny silver waistcoat, and there'll be balloons all over him. Every morning, all week, the kids are given this build-up. Any day now you'll be seeing Mr Wiggly, with his balloons and caterpillar eyebrows and blue shoes and silver waistcoat. At last, today's the day. The kids are beside themselves with anticipation. Mr Wiggly is in the building, the teacher tells them. Any second now, he'll be here. The door opens and in walks this man who looks like a random bloke off the street: ordinary jacket, ordinary shirt, ordinary trousers, ordinary shoes. Standard issue eyebrows. 'Hello, children,' he says, 'I'm Mr Wiggly.' From his pocket he takes a packet of balloons. He blows them up and hands them out. When every child has a balloon, Mr Wiggly tells them it was very nice to meet them, but he must now be on his way. He has other schools to visit. Goodbye. A few weeks later a different teacher asks them if Mr Wiggly came to see them. Oh yes, answer the kids, he was great. What was he like? He was funny, the kids reply, and every one of them describes Mr Wiggly in the same way: he had eyebrows like caterpillars and huge blue shoes and a silver waistcoat, and there were balloons all over him.

'Well?' she asks. 'Interesting?' And in the next breath, and in the same tone of pensive amusement, she says: 'Are you sure you know what you're doing?'

'With what? Henry?'

The immediate response is a mocking face of bright-eyed innocence. 'You're married,' she says.

'Yes.'

'So I'll ask you again: do you know what you're doing?'

Here there is a pause, and perhaps also an expression indicative of concentrated self-scrutiny, though none is taking place.

'Answer?' she demands.

'What about you?'

'I don't. But for me that's not a problem. I'm on my own and I'm happy that way. But if you haven't thought this through, we'll stop.'

'I can't say I've thought it through.'

'OK,' she says decisively, with a quick smile of good-humoured acceptance, as though the subject had been nothing more consequential than a proposed walk to the beach. From the fridge she takes a half-full bottle, which she empties into two large glasses. 'Cheers,' she says, passing a glass and touching it with hers, and glancing away from each other we find ourselves looking at the picture – a photograph from a magazine – that's tacked to the wall beside the fridge. It shows a sunlit corner of a courtyard, with weeds sprouting through dry earth, and a doorway in which a single tall flower rises. A dozen clay pots of various sizes and shapes are lined against one of the walls, which is bare stone from halfway up, while the flaking plaster of the lower half is painted with a grassy landscape that's hard to make out. On the other wall there's a clearer painting, of a lion pouncing on to a running bull. 'You been there?' she asks.

'Not to my knowledge. Where is it?'

It's Pompeii and she was thirteen when she went there, for a day. She peers at the row of bare clay pots, seeing memories of that day in Pompeii. 'It was wonderful,' she says, her eyes widening as though seeing snapshots of the holiday. Before that trip she'd had this image of the Romans as a grimly effective race of soldiers and road-builders, ploughing across Europe by the most direct route possible, making laws and smiting barbarians left, right and centre, and feeding Christians to the lions for light relief. 'And then I saw all this,' she says, raising her glass to the picture, 'and I realised I didn't know a thing. The colours – it was amazing, just amazing.' She describes a house where the red of the walls was so vivid you'd have thought it had been painted twenty years ago, not twenty hundred years, and the rooms were decorated with beautiful scenes, like scenes from a play that you couldn't understand. 'And it was so hot. Unbelievable,' she gasps, stunned anew by the remembered heat. There were stepping stones across the main streets, she recalls, and when she dribbled some water on to one of these stones it had evaporated straight away, as if the drops had sunk right through the stone.

We leave the kitchen and in the hall we stop at a picture of Hannah, a few years younger, laughing on the bench of a rowing boat, with her arms round an attractive black-haired young woman, who is giving the camera a deranged grin as she unbuttons, or pretends to unbutton, Hannah's shirt. This is Sophie, her best friend ever since they were at school together. Sophie was smart and a bit of a handful, and she couldn't wait to get away from home – not that she didn't get on with her parents, but the pace of life here was driving her wild. She went to university in London and that's where she's stayed, but somehow

Hannah and Sophie are as close as ever. When Henry died, that's where Hannah was: staying in Sophie's flat in Hammersmith. 'And I saw Conrad too. My brother. I always see him at Christmas. That's him,' she says, pointing to a photo of a scowling lad on a mountain top. 'That's him as well, and those are my parents. Divorced, ten years ago.' Her mother lives in France, running an estate agency that's mainly for Brits buying holiday homes; she's far happier now. Her father's an art teacher; he lives in St Ives; Hannah gets on with him better than with her mother; she gets on better with his wife than she does with her mother.

Up there is an aunt, with a couple of cousins. She moves from picture to picture, accounting for all the people in them as if to a dinner party guest who has asked for them all to be identified. No flirtation is going on, and there's too much detail to this inventory of friends and family, as Hannah knows. We're enacting a pretence of mere acquaintanceship, perhaps in the knowledge that this is nothing more than a diversion that will end soon, with us returning to where we were, on the brink of the precipice, or perhaps in the hope that, in this interval, some consideration of consequences might take place and attraction be allowed to weaken a degree. But the door of her bedroom is ajar and in the gap, in shadow, can be seen a chest of drawers with a mirror and an assortment of bottles and jars on it, and one of these things in particular, one of these attributes of Hannah, transmits an aura of intimacy: a small clear flask of perfume, with its stopper upturned alongside.

Clouds are congealing over the sun and the walls of the living room have deepened to a colour that's distinctly grey. She mixed the paint herself, she says, scooping the slew of sketchbooks off the futon, and then we're talking about Henry again. Some days she doesn't accept that he's dead. She finds herself thinking like a child, as though death is an incident that we'll get over, as though there'll be an opportunity to start again. 'This doesn't make sense, I know,' she says. 'I know he's dead but I don't quite believe it. You can't really think about death, can you? Do you think about death? You must do, in your line of work. Do you?' she asks, but there's no time to answer, because she has to pass on something that Henry once said to her. It was a Sunday, a cool and radiant morning in early spring, and they were sitting on the beach when church bells began to ring, and the next thing she knew she was on the verge of crying, because she couldn't bear the thought of there being days like this, in the future, that she wouldn't see. She told Henry that the thought of being obliterated from the world was too much for her, and his response was that she won't be obliterated, because people will remember her. 'Death is no big thing, that was Henry's line,' she says. 'When we're alive we have all these experiences in our brain, this accumulation of experiences, and when we're dead this particular bundle of experiences isn't in the world any more, but others take their place. We have an idea of who we are, then we die, and another idea of who we are takes over. Or a hundred different ideas.'

'You were convinced by that?'

'Not remotely.'

'I'd rather be forgotten and see a few more radiant Sundays.'

'Same here. But Henry wasn't bothered about dying. He really wasn't bothered,' she repeats, staring into the wine as if into a crystal ball from which enlightenment akin to Henry's might rise, but instead she's becoming upset. 'Need a pee,' she says. As she stands up, she notices a glance at a sketchbook that has fallen open. 'Take a look, if you want,' she says.

Rocks and hills and buildings and boats in the harbour fill the first dozen pages, all of them drawn rapidly, roughly, in thick smudgy pencil, but after a double-page sketch of cliffs there's Hannah herself, depicted in a tangle of fine lines, frowning fiercely, followed by Hannah in a marginally better mood, and Hannah from the waist up, solemnly naked, and then there's a face, more approximately drawn, that looks somewhat like Josh. Overleaf the same lad is there again, but this time the pencil work is detailed and it's certainly Josh. On the next page it's his turn to be naked, face down on a bed, and the sight of him causes a feeling that's like being taken out a short distance on the backwash of a wave, knowing the next wave will finally drop you on the beach.

Hannah brings in another half-bottle, refills her glass and deposits the bottle on the floor. Lounging against the windowsill, she watches the appraisal of her work.

'The cathedral, yes?'

'Yes.'

'And where's this?'

'Lyme.'

'And who's he?'

'Tim. Sophie's boyfriend. Sophie's then boyfriend.'

'OK.'

'If you carry on you'll find Sophie. Same hour, same bed.'

'And this one? I think I recognise him. Josh McKee?'

'Yes.'

'OK.'

'You knew about him. It's not a surprise.'

'No.'

'You don't seem pleased.'

'I wouldn't say that.'

'So what would you say?'

'Can't quite imagine it.'

'Imagine what?'

'You and him.'

'Well, there's an easy answer to that. Don't try,' she says, giving her attention to the view outside, unconcerned.

There's more Josh, more self-portraits, more boats, Sophie naked, an old couple sitting on a bench. 'Is Henry in one of these?'

'No, he's not.'

'You never did Henry?'

'No.'

'Why not?'

'Never seemed appropriate. Not that sort of friend, I suppose.'

'But he knew you can draw?'

'Yes.'

'He saw some of these?'

'If not those, others. Yes.'

'But you never thought of drawing Henry?'

'Might have thought about it. Never did it,' she says, with a look that translates as: 'I won't ask again: do you know what you're doing?'

'I find that odd. He'd have been a good subject, I'd have thought.'

'Well,' she says, shrugging. As the end of the sketchbook is reached, she finishes her glass. 'I know what you're thinking,' she says. 'The curtains. You're wondering about the curtains. I hate curtains. Dust gatherers.'

'What's wrong with blinds?'

'I like the light. And no one can see in anyway,' she says, stepping away from the window.

25

The face of the younger Henry, detached from Gemma's picture and freshened up, appears on station noticeboards from Kent to Cornwall, and its appearance gives rise to a small blizzard of London sightings, all of which quickly melt away, leaving us with a few tiny drops of almost useless knowledge. In several cases the chronology is vague, but it seems to be established that Henry was sleeping rough in central London in the early and mid seventies. A former traffic warden is seventy-five per cent sure that it was Henry who used to sleep in the back doorway of a shop on Oxford Street, some time in 1972 or 1973, maybe 1974. A lecturer at King's College, the only witness to be certain beyond all doubt that the person he remembers is the man on the noticeboard, reports that Henry was to be seen nearly every day walking round and round St James's Park during the summer of 1974, when the lecturer, then recently graduated, was working as a deckchair attendant. The manager of a shop near Waterloo Station recalls a vagrant who used to storm up and down the street. A woman who used to serve soup to the homeless in the West End says that someone very like Henry was sometimes in the queue when her van pulled up in Northumberland Avenue; she's the only one of the other witnesses who ever spoke to him and their dialogue appears to have consisted of the same five words every time: 'All right, dear?' and 'Thank you.' In 1972 he's outside Gemma's house; three years later he's in Plymouth, apologising to Mrs Appleton; and from all that time in between, we have him speaking just two words, 'Thank you', and it's possible it wasn't even Henry speaking them.

No paper trail was left behind by Henry's cash-economy existence with Gemma, and it's beginning to feel as though the enquiry's last hope died at the grave of the unrelated Mrs Palmer. So the policy now is to admit that we're floundering. Displayed together, the two faces of Henry – Gemma's and Hannah's – get a sneeze-and-you'll-miss-them showing on local TV news bulletins in the south, accompanying an appeal from George Whittam. 'If there's anyone out there who knows anything about this man, especially the last few months of his life, we're very keen to hear from them,' he says, in an interview that's given only a little less airtime than the obligatory heart-warming final segment: a chat with a woman whose cat has miraculously survived being locked in a supermarket freezer. Though he's already concluded that Henry isn't, after all, going to be the story that catapults him into the pages of the national press, Ronnie Houghton comes in for a briefing and duly runs another story: BEACH MURDER – POLICE BAFFLED. There's a remote chance that this admission might produce something. It's not unknown for a killer, having achieved by assiduous crime-scene hygiene the first objective of confounding the cloddish forces of law and order, to embark on the riskier game of tormenting the enemy as a further demonstration of his superior intellect. Bragging notes might arrive in the post; there might be calls from phone boxes, disclosing facts known only to the police and the perpetrator; an item removed from the victim might now materialise. Sometimes the villain appears in person at the station, eager to help, offering a bogus piece of information.

In this case, however, the guilty party isn't playing any games. We get a minor rash of sightings in various parts of Devon and Cornwall: one in Launceston, another one in Truro, a couple of

Plymouths, a Tavistock. All of them describe a tramp in a hurry, but none of them adds anything to the picture. Hundreds of thousands of people must have seen George Whittam on the news, and of all these viewers just one – Mrs Yaxley, from Southampton – gets in touch to report anything more substantial than a glimpse of Henry moving at five miles per hour.

Mrs Yaxley is absolutely sure of the date of the incident: Samantha, her daughter, was in her final year at her primary school and it was during the autumn half-term break, so that makes it October 1976. On the morning in question, Mrs Yaxley was waiting for the mother of one of Samantha's school friends to arrive: Samantha was going to spend the day with this friend, while Mrs Yaxley was at work. It would have been around 8 a.m. Mr Yaxley had already left, about ten minutes earlier. Samantha was running up and down the stairs, gathering toys for the day. Every few minutes she'd rush out into the street, to look out for the car. Finishing her make-up at the bedroom mirror, Mrs Yaxley looked outside and saw this character lurking by the railings of the allotments on the other side of the street. Skulking in the shade of the trees, he seemed to be studying Mrs Yaxley's house or her neighbours', and her first thought was that he was a burglar doing reconnaissance. They'd moved into the house only a few weeks earlier, and someone had told her that burglars often strike houses where the owners haven't yet settled in properly, but then she noticed the nylon holdall and decided it was a far-fetched idea, that a burglar would be standing there, across the street, with his bag of housebreaking tools between his feet. Nonetheless he was behaving suspiciously and his appearance did not make a favourable impression: his hair and beard were bedraggled and greasy, no charity shop would have accepted his coat, and his toes had broken through one of his shoes. At the slam of the front door Mrs Yaxley saw the man look towards where Samantha must have been standing, then he picked up his bag and walked away, quickly, so quickly that it seemed likely he'd suddenly become aware of being watched. Not until he was out of sight, and Samantha had come inside, did Mrs Yaxley go back to getting ready for work.

Five minutes later Samantha called out that her bag was packed and she was going to wait in the street, and Mrs Yaxley returned to the bedroom window. She saw Samantha standing on the pavement, gazing at the man with the holdall, who was standing a couple of feet in front of her daughter, smiling at her. Seeing this, Mrs Yaxley rapped the glass so hard she thought she might crack it, and the man, after glancing up, touched Samantha's hair before turning round and striding away, not with the air of a man who had been chased off, but rather like someone offended and leaving on his own terms, which made Mrs Yaxley even angrier. She hurried downstairs and out into the street, but by the time she reached Samantha the man had gone. 'What did he say to you?' she asked her daughter, and the answer, as you'd expect, was that he wanted to know her name. And, despite remembering what her parents had told her time and time again about talking to strangers, Samantha had told him her name. 'What else did he ask you? He put his hand on your head and he said something. What did he say?' demanded Mrs Yaxley. Samantha began to cry, but she was crying not because of anything the man had said to her, but because her mother was so agitated. All the man had said was 'Goodbye'. He seemed nice, said Samantha, but he smelt of mud. Neither Samantha nor her mother ever saw him again.

On the very day that Mrs Yaxley phoned in, Oliver Bywater decided it would be a bit of a lark to go sailing with half a dozen old friends from university, only one of whom had even the faintest idea how to handle a wind-driven vessel. The plan had been to creep along the coast for a couple of hours, never straying beyond hailing distance of the shore, drop anchor for lunch, then creep back to harbour. Part one of the plan was executed more or less as intended, even if a solo paddler in a canoe would have made better progress than this mob did. One of the gang had just landed a grotesquely well-paid job with a German bank in London and to celebrate his success some champagne had been loaded on board. A quantity of this champagne was consumed at lunchtime, which might have been a factor in the chaos of the afternoon. They were blown backwards; they drifted further and further out; half the team was feeling seasick or worse. Two hours past the time they were scheduled to be back on dry land, they were still miles from port and discipline was going to pieces. The wind was picking up as well, and it was not coming from the most helpful point of the compass. A gust almost capsized them, dumping one of the crew in the water. No sooner had he been fished out than another gust caught them, and because someone hadn't done his job properly, and Oliver Bywater wasn't paying as much attention to his environment as he should have been, an untied yard swung round at great speed and clouted him on the head, fracturing his skull and knocking him, senseless, into the sea, from where he was retrieved so inefficiently that further injuries were inflicted in the retrieval, and mouth-to-mouth resuscitation was needed. Fortunately they'd packed the flares, but it still took a long time to get Oliver to hospital, and now he's in intensive care.

Enjoined by the Reverend Beal to pray for the recovery of Oliver Bywater, Alice closes her eyes, and her eyelids clench in the fervour of her prayer. Less fluent than is customary, Beal seems to be improvising. Once or twice he stumbles over his words. He appears genuinely troubled by the misfortune of the Bywaters and they appear grateful for his caring. Of the two, Mr Bywater is the more obviously distressed, perhaps because guilt is at work as well. We all stand and Mr Bywater rises last, as though lethargic with woe. He stares over the top of his hymn book, not even pretending to sing. His wife, however, is taking strength from the experience of being here. When she sings her gaze goes up, as though seeing hope perched on the rafters, and at the end of the hymn she breathes deeply like someone at the summit of a hill. The church is full of sunlight today, and the smell of it alone – a perfume of lilies and warm wood and beeswax, with a faint element of grass sap – would do anyone some good.

The service is over. The Bywaters, arm in arm, stay in their places and Beal sits down beside them. The lifeless face of Mr Bywater seems to say that prayers will make no difference, nothing will make any difference – his son is going to die. He looks at Beal's hand as it settles on his shoulder and he nods like a puppet. Beal dispenses comfort equally to each, then takes his leave with a sorrowful smile and a bow, and Mrs Bywater adjusts her husband's tie, a gesture of pure tenderness. Having for once not rushed out of the building, Michael Trethowen is only now slipping out from his pew. He glances at Mr Bywater and his lips form a shape which, given a few seconds more to ripen, would become a sneer. Alice, on her way to the Bywaters, passes Michael in the aisle and he nods to her, which he's done a few times in recent weeks, albeit grudgingly. But today is the day that Michael Trethowen decides to re-establish verbal contact with the Donohues.

Pinned to the noticeboard inside the door is a notice of a choir concert. 'One not to miss,' Michael mutters to himself, just loud enough to be overheard, and then, turning round, he asks: 'How have you been?' The question is put with an awkwardness that is perhaps meant to be that of a friend trying to initiate a reconciliation after a foolish falling out.

'Fine. And you?'

'Good, good. I'm good.' This is followed by some rueful contemplation of the notice. 'Will you be going?' he asks, jabbing a thumb at it.

'I may be busy.'

'Same here,' he says. The door of the church is open, but when Michael looks in that direction he seems to see something barring his exit. 'Business is good,' he says.

'Glad to hear it.'

'Surprisingly good. Took an order from Japan last week. A guy in Tokyo.'

'Coals to Newcastle.'

'Yes,' he says, making a smile that involves only the lower

249

reaches of the head. 'I suppose so.' In this pause his eyes swerve towards the nave, in such a way as to make it an immediately persuasive idea that the reason for this conversation is that he's waiting for Alice to join us. 'And what about Henry?' he enquires circumspectly, as if wary of causing offence.

'What about him?'

'I saw your boss on the news,' he says. 'Thoroughly fed up with things, by the look of it. A day away from giving up.'

'No.'

'No?'

'No. Nobody's giving up.'

'Despondent. That's how he looked.'

'If that's how he looked to you, that's how he looked to you.'

'It was.'

'OK. I'm not going to argue about it.'

'And I'm not going to argue either,' he says, with the tense smile of a man talking to a friend who will not admit to a major problem in his life, a problem of which everyone who knows him has long been aware. 'A tough man, that Mr Whittam,' he adds. Seeing Alice coming towards us, he presents to her a face that's all goodwill and delight, as if he has not set eyes on her for months. 'Hello, Mrs Donohue,' he says, and for the first time ever he doesn't blush when she speaks to him. He would have us believe that the misfortune of Oliver Bywater has affected him deeply. 'One moment's inattention,' he says, eyes narrowing at the awfulness of it, and he clicks his fingers in front of his face, then winces in self-reproach at the inappropriateness of such a gesture in such a place. 'The parents,' he goes on, adopting an impressive frown of solicitude. 'How are they?'

'They're bearing up,' Alice replies, not quite ridding her eyes of their quizzical cast at Michael's renewal of communication.

'Good,' he says, 'that's good.' Reassured, he smiles into the space between us and we look at him, and this goes on for half a minute or so, until Michael, smacking his thigh with too much force, announces that it's time to get back to his soldering iron.

250

'Can't keep Mr Shibasaki waiting, can we?' he says, and he shakes Alice's hand (Alice's only) before lurching off. At the doorway he steps sharply to the left, as though to avoid an invisible obstacle.

He's an odd boy, we agree, and we talk a bit about Michael and about the Bywaters on our way to pick up Luke. We've left him with Kim and Martin Vanes, parents of best friend Terry, and when we get to the house the boys are up the tree in the garden, shouting from the wooden platform that Martin built for them in May. So fine for climbing, with its dense and strong and wide-spreading branches, this tree was what clinched the boys' friendship, even though at the time they were too small to tackle anything except the limb that sagged to within a foot of the lawn. It was an elephant's trunk, this thick drooping branch, and they would hang upside down from it, making it sway with their weight, and afterwards, sitting on the grass, they would contemplate the challenge of the tree, plotting the routes they might take through the leaves in the months to come. The platform, lodged in a crutch around the two-thirds point, is their current limit, decreed by the mothers. Often, by way of protest, the boys make a show of planning the final push to the summit, and that's what they are doing this afternoon. Through the french windows we watch them: Luke is waving a silvered plastic sword that glints in the sun; from the small cardboard box that they've hauled up there, Terry takes a pair of toy binoculars and uses them to study the topmost boughs. With a great deal of pointing, Terry makes a proposal, to which Luke attends closely, nodding gravely. They laugh, and the binoculars are aimed downwards, in the direction of the windows, attracting a wave from Kim, at which the boys in unison turn their backs. We go through to the front part of the living room.

A couple of minutes later, thinking she's heard something amiss in the garden, Alice returns to the windows and, overly alert to the possibility of mishap in the aftermath of Oliver Bywater's accident, lets out a yelp, because Terry has ventured a short crawl along a branch above the platform. She goes out to talk him

251

down. Standing close to the edge, Luke remonstrates with his mother, who waves him to step back. Rolling his eyes, he retreats a step; rolling his eyes likewise, Terry reverses down the branch. 'He's looking more and more like Alice, isn't he?' Kim remarks. Every time we see her she says this, and it's true. Luke's mouth resembles his mother's more than ever; the curve of his brow is Alice's; he has acquired a way of looking at his father that has something of Alice in it, a way which, for a son, and a son so young, has too much observation in it. Kim is an immensely pleasant woman. She's a good wife, a perfect mother, and we have never had anything to say to each other. This is the moment for the bathroom.

At the top of the stairs there's a tall window, from which the boys can be seen. Facing in opposite directions, they lean forward, with hands raised to shield their eyes, in the posture of lookouts in the crow's nest. Terry, catching sight of his friend's father at the upstairs window, points with the telescope he's holding, and calls down to left and right, as if alerting the crew to the sighting of the enemy. He tugs on Luke's arm to make him turn and see.

26

'Look at it,' Hannah orders, scooping a palmful of the stuff from the floor of the tank, and she holds it up, like a jeweller presenting an expensive necklace for inspection.

'It's sand.'

'No,' she says, in the tone of a patient teacher whose patience is being tested to its limit. 'Look. It's not sand. Look carefully,' she urges, but her face – the eyes trained avidly on what she's holding, the lower lip nipped between her teeth – is far more interesting than the sludge she's holding.

'Nice sand.'

'You're doing this deliberately, aren't you?'

'Very nice sand.'

'It's not sand. Ordinary sand is weeny bits of worn-down rock, OK? This is not worn-down rock. Look properly. See?' she demands, thrusting her hand closer. 'Shells. Zillions of broken shells.'

'I see.'

'No. Look. There's only one place in the whole country where you'll find a mixture like this. These shells aren't from British waters. They're from the Caribbean.' It's a quirk of the Atlantic currents, she explains. The shells are carried right across the ocean, getting pulverised in transit, before being dumped on this one narrow beach on the northern coast of south-west England. 'It's wonderful. Unique. A tropical beach in north Devon,' she says, stroking the damp sand in her palm as though it were the fur of some delicate small animal. 'Dozens of species in this stuff, all mashed up. Look closely and you'll find every colour you can put a name to. Go on. Get your nose right in there.'

Inspected from a range of six inches, the rough brown powder is indeed transformed into a stew of multifarious colours. There's a lot of white grains, and various reds, greys, yellows. One splinter of shell is golden, another lime-green. 'Blue. There's no blue.'

'It'll be in there somewhere,' she replies, irritated, and she stirs the pat of shell-sand until she finds it: a fleck of royal blue, not much bigger than an ant's head. 'You're meant to be impressed. If you want me to stay sweet', she says, 'you'll be impressed.'

'I'm impressed.'

'But you didn't know about it?'

'About what?'

'Barricane.'

'I'm a policeman, not a whatever you'd call it. Beachologist.'

'It's famous. And near.'

'Not famous enough for me.'

'Henry was impressed.'

'Of course.'

'Is that called for?'

'Meaning: from what you've told me, I could imagine Henry getting a buzz out of being shown shells by you.'

'You're making fun of me,' she says. A moment earlier she was teasing, but now her face is registering a wounded indignation.

'No.'

'Making fun of Henry, then.'

'No.'

'Well, I didn't show him, anyway. He knew about it already. He'd been there.'

'So this wasn't one of his mystery tours? He remembered this one.'

'He'd slept at Barricane.'

'OK.'

'For months. Before he ever came here. Is that all right with you? Satisfactory explanation?'

'More than satisfactory. Thank you.'

'I'm so glad.'

'Was he ever here? In this flat?'

'No, he wasn't,' she answers, letting the shell-sand slide back into the water. She rinses her hand and dries it on her jeans, wiping it half a dozen times – more often than is necessary – up and down her thigh.

'Never?'

'Sorry, I wasn't clear. No. As in "No". As in "Not ever". To put it another way: No.'

'Did it never come up? I mean, he knew you lived somewhere in town, presumably. Didn't he ever ask you where? He must have wondered.'

Lips pressed tight, she picks at the floorboards. A mocking smile begins to appear, implying a reply that isn't going to be spoken, then her expression hardens. 'You're jealous,' she says. 'You have a wife and you're jealous of a dead man. There's a word for that.'

'Hypocrisy.'

'That's the one,' she cries, with a clap of her hands, then she leans forward to add a kiss, but the thought concerning Henry has not left her. All evening it's with her, and when she looks away from the table, casting a quick glance in the direction of the hall, it's not difficult to read what she's thinking: her friend was sleeping on the beach, all through the winter months, while she was living here, alone, in a flat that has room to spare.

After the meal she starts a spat about Josh, whose comely physique adorns the pages of more than one sketchbook. 'You're obsessed with him,' she says, moving as if to take the drawing away, but making no effort to seize it. 'You have to be a bit of a voyeur, I suppose, in your line of work. Is that what it is? Taking a peep at my past? So we had sex. You knew that from the start. You want to know if it was good sex? It was. Not a lot more than that, but good sex.'

Josh McKee is an intermittent nuisance, but Henry is always with us. Visible from her bed, a piece of pink cloth protrudes from a bag that's tucked behind the wardrobe. It's the Palermo shirt, and it's wrapped round a gruesome little porcelain doll with crimson cheeks and a crimson dress, and a cube of pink and lime-green fibreglass that looks like a lump of fossilised jelly. These too were gifts from Henry, and from the swerve of her eyes when she says this it seems that, as suspected, there may have been complications to Henry's friendship. 'Not infatuation, no,' she says firmly, but with an undertone of sadness. Maybe, she concedes, there was an element of attraction; some time later, this possible attraction is confirmed as a definite fondness, a fondness that once or twice proved awkward. 'Just for a moment,' she adds, but the change of the pitch of her voice, the slight constriction of her throat, says something different, while the cast of her eyes recalls her gazing out of the window as Ian asked her when she'd last seen Henry.

Sometimes it's as if Henry is the departed mutual friend who brought us together and tribute must be paid to him whenever we meet. No walk on the clifftops can pass without his name arising. Fine weather makes her think of Henry; bad weather makes her think of Henry. We're sitting on the rocks, late in the day; streamers of tangerine cloud fill the sky; a warm wind is whipping a smoke of dry sand off the beach. Clasping her ribs, Hannah makes a whimpering sound and says she feels almost too well. Henry, it turns out, once pulled off his T-shirts and howled at the sun; sometimes, he explained, he simply felt too well.

And he's even there on the evening that would come to be remembered more richly than any other evening with Hannah. We've looked at Barricane and driven on to Ilfracombe in a downpour. For half an hour, parked not far from the harbour, we shelter in her van. The rain on the roof is making a din like coffee beans in a grinder, and the water running down the windows makes them look like melting plastic. Then, as suddenly as the closing of a stopcock, it stops. The flooded roads and pavements, reflecting the last of the light, are matt silver, a brighter colour than the sky overhead, which is a blend of various densities of grey. We walk up the winding path to the hilltop chapel. 'We've got an hour,' she says. 'Let's enjoy it. Let's just sit here.' And, 'You mustn't leave your wife. I don't want you to leave your wife. This is an affair. It's good for both of us, but it won't go on for ever.' The clouds are like a dark grey scum on a lake of tar, and all over the sea there's a low, shapeless surf. It's like shavings of ice, she says. The sea beneath the foam is black, except in one place, in the wake of the boat that's now setting out from the harbour, churning up a trail of jade. Later, exactly the same green appears in a long slot of sky between the clouds and the horizon. One afternoon, says Hannah, she and Henry had been at Straight Point and they'd seen dolphins near the shore. She'd made some comments about the intelligence of dolphins, the way they communicate with each other and with humans. It would be wonderful, she'd said, if we could decipher the sounds the dolphins made, and to this Henry had responded: 'If they could talk, we couldn't understand them.' This, it would appear, is an observation of such profundity that embellishment would be superfluous. She stares at the sea for a while before turning for a considered response, but it's impossible to meet her gaze, because what is prompted by the supposed wisdom of Henry, as relayed by Hannah, is not a deep thought about the language of dolphins, but instead a momentary withdrawal, and then something too incoherent to be termed a thought: it's rather a confusion of notions to do with what makes her so attractive, with the idea that who Hannah is and what Hannah says – what anyone is and what anyone says – might in some way not be the same thing, with the idea of love being often love at first sight, because what's desired is in the face, in the eyes, in the way she bears

257

herself, because the essence of her is there, not in the words of philosophical Henry, admiringly repeated. When the strip of green on the horizon widens, and a stain of blood-orange leaks into it, the grip of her fingers tightens. 'God,' she says in a gasp, 'look at that. Fuck. Fuck.' Second by second her kiss changes, like the speaking of a long wordless sentence.

On the way down the path, in darkness, she announces, as if in the face of an objection, that a client has cancelled so she's going to London next weekend, to see Sophie. They'll be going clubbing, she says, and this provokes, absurdly, a spasm of jealousy, a jealousy that temporarily overrides all consciousness of guilt. It's as though there are now two lives in parallel, rather than a single life in which infidelity is happening.

27

The map of Henry's meanderings has fifty or sixty pins and labels on it, and some days it seems there might be a pattern to be discovered amid the scatter. On several occasions Ian returns to the idea that Plymouth must be the key to it. 'This means something,' he says, scrutinising the city's outcrop of tags. 'We've got him here in 1975 and 1976, and again in 1985, 1986, 1987. Ten years apart. A place he comes back to.' But we've got him all over the area in 1986 and 1987, and what's remarkable about a man returning to the only real city in the region? Henry was reliant on handouts, so it would have been more remarkable if he had never been seen there. And of course you're going to receive most reports from the location that has most people. What of all the days for which we have no trace of Henry's movements? Perhaps this map, showing only the memories of citizens who are not merely observant and unforgetful but public-spirited too, omits what matters most. Perhaps wholly different patterns would emerge if we had a day-by-day trace of Henry's whereabouts, and the patterns that we're seeing at the moment would disappear within the web. It's like reading tea leaves. If we're so inclined, we can find a significant cluster between Dartmoor and Bodmin Moor. He's seen in Barnstaple on two occasions and the later of these is precisely one year after the earlier, to the day. Is this significant? Run a thread between outcrops of multiple sightings and an emblem of order appears: a nicely balanced triangle with Crediton, Honiton and Tiverton at its angles. Extend it to Taunton and you have a diamond, which probably also means nothing. Coffee in one hand, sheaf of statements in the other, feet resting on a pile of printouts, Ian scans the map, awaiting illumination. He rereads our notes until he's too bored to go on. He flaps a batch of them in front of his face, as if to shake an answer out of them. And one day, on a Wednesday afternoon, his answer arrives.

We are at our desks, watching an altercation that's taking place in the yard. Chris Davies and Kieran Balfe are glaring at each other from opposite sides of a car. Balfe opens the door, closes it again, slams a hand on the roof, then Ian, lifting a page from the nearest pile, murmurs: 'Mrs Yaxley. Something's been bugging me about her.' He ransacks the papers until he finds the Yaxley interview. Three or four times he goes through it and a wary smile appears on the last reading. He eases back in his chair, pressing the page against his chest. Davies and Balfe are driving away. As soon as they've gone, he places the sheet on the desk, delicately, as if handling a priceless old document. 'An idea,' he says.

'Proceed.'

'Mrs Yaxley, OK? What happens there? She looks out the window, sees Henry on the other side of the road. Doesn't much like what she sees. He's a burglar, casing the houses, that's her first reaction. She watches him for a while. Her daughter goes outside and Henry looks her way. He removes himself from the scene.'

'He knew he'd been seen.'

'Possible. A bit later, Samantha's outside again. Her mother sees Henry talking to her and makes her presence known. She smacks the glass, Henry runs. Correction: doesn't run. He strolls away. So why was he there?'

'To talk to the girl.'

'OK. But why?'

'Cute kid.'

'So he's outside her house, eight o'clock in the morning, on the off-chance she'll come out to play.'

'School holidays. There's a good chance she'll come out.'

'But he's loitering right outside.'

'Not quite. Lurking under the trees.'

'OK, but she saw him plainly enough. People are going to work. He'll be seen. If the idea was to accost little Samantha, it's a peculiar way to go about it. Stake out the house. Stand there in full view of anyone who happens to look out.'

'Perhaps he just wanted a peep.'

'He came back, though, didn't he?'

'He wanted another look.'

'He came back and he spoke to her, virtually on her doorstep. Why do that?'

'Paedophiles take risks.'

'And paedophiles are devious bastards. This isn't devious, is it? The opposite of devious. If getting at little Samantha was the intention, why do it there?'

'It was half-term. Home was the only place he was guaranteed to see her. And we know he wasn't much of a man for dis- cretion. He didn't go in for much in the way of camouflage at the schools, did he? Sat on a wall gawping, as I recall.'

'True. And he didn't talk to any kids at the school playgrounds either. We have only one case of Henry actually approaching a child, and that's Samantha Yaxley,' says Ian, cocking an eyebrow to invite his colleague to make the deduction that he himself has already made, while his smirk says he's confident that his colleague won't make it.

'So?'

'So, what if we're making an error of classification? We're putting the incident with Samantha Yaxley in the same category as the incidents at the Plymouth school and the school in Honiton. And Henry straying into the children's ward. Dirty old man and his liking for little kiddies. It's the obvious connection. But maybe it's the wrong connection. Maybe there's another category: Henry and houses. Forget about Samantha for a moment. There's a precedent for what happened at the Yaxley house and it has nothing to do with little girls,' he goes on, at which point he stops to forage through the box file on his desk. 'Here,' he says, displaying the crucial document for an instant before snatching it back. 'Mrs Appleton, Plymouth, a year before Mrs Yaxley. Delete the kid and the similarities jump out. Mrs Appleton is doing the housework; she looks out of the window; she sees someone we think is Henry – are sure is Henry – camped outside the house; she leaves the house; he looks at her, he looks at the house, apologises, scarpers. You see my point?'

'I see a similarity. I don't see a point.'

He's getting so much pleasure from this, he has to stand up and start playing to the one-man jury. With a forefinger he pins the Yaxley report to the desk. 'Mrs Yaxley doesn't actually say she saw Henry talking to Samantha. He was standing in front of the girl, smiling at her. But when Mrs Yaxley banged on the window he wasn't talking, not at that moment. He might already have said what he wanted to say. He could have been leaving before she intervened. Not saying he was: he could have been, OK? When Mrs Yaxley first saw him, he was watching the house. And when Samantha came out, he took one look at her and walked away. If he was there to ogle Samantha, why bugger off as soon as he sees her? And why come back five minutes later? Why take the trip round the block?'

'To get a grip on himself. He'd got overexcited.'

'Maybe, maybe. But what if this little girl wasn't who he'd expected to see? He's surprised by the sight of her, goes away to sort out his thoughts, comes back to make certain. Samantha's mother asks her what the man said to her, and she says, "He asked me my name."'

'"Hello, little girlie, what's your name, then?"'

'Sure. But what if that's not quite the question? What if it goes like: "Hello, what's your name?" "Samantha." "Samantha who?"

"Samantha Yaxley." And then he clears off. He's backing away from Samantha when her mother spies her, because the kid's already told him what he wants to know. He wants to know who lives there, in that house. He discovers it's the Yaxleys and he leaves, because it's not the Yaxleys he's after. What did she tell us? They'd not been in the house for long. He was after the people who'd been there before.' At risk of hyperventilation he pauses, hand raised to forestall any spoiling of his conclusion. 'OK, OK,' he continues. 'Cut to our woman in Plymouth. Mrs Appleton. Same situation: beginning of the day, Henry's sitting outside the house. He's there for a while, watching. Owner of the house emerges, Henry takes a look at her. Matches woman to house. Exit Henry. What does he say to her? One thing: "I'm sorry." As in: "Sorry, it's not you I'm looking for."'

'That's pushing it.'

'It fits. Come on. I've got something here.'

'If you're looking for someone at home, the normal procedure is to knock on the door and ask.'

'Perhaps that's what he would have done, sooner or later. But he's not what you'd describe as presentable, is he? He's a mess. So he gets there in the morning and just hangs around, waiting.'

'Why the house visit? He couldn't check the phone book?'

'I don't know. They're ex-directory? Fancies giving them a big surprise? Some reason or other. Don't be an arse. I'm right. You know I'm right,' he says, brandishing the phone like a trophy.

Within a minute he's left a message for Mrs Yaxley, who returns the call at lunchtime and what he hears has him mouthing hallelujahs at the ceiling. At the time of the encounter with Henry, the Yaxleys had been at that address for less than a year. They'd bought the house from a Mr and Mrs Ellis, and Ellis, of course, was one of Henry's guises: Miss Leith believed his name was Henry Ellis, and in May 1985, in Plymouth, it was Henry Ellis sitting on the wall by the playground. As for Mrs Appleton, she too had not been in her house for very long when Henry came calling. Her vendors were the Rillings, who had bought the place back in 1968, also from a Mr and Mrs Ellis. It takes a matter of hours to track down the Ellises: they live in Southampton, within a couple of miles of their old house. After the dead end of the Nunhead grave, we're at last closing in on Henry's family, or so it seems.

Mrs Ellis tells Ian she is not aware of any Henry on her husband's side of the family, but there are so many Ellises she may have forgotten some of them, or never known of them in the first place. She promises to ask her husband when he gets home, so Ian rings again in the evening. No, says Mrs Ellis, there's definitely no Henry in the family. They do have a Harold though, a distant cousin, so distant they have no idea where he lives nowadays. Given Henry's predilection for aliases, there's a chance that Harold and Henry are one and the same person, but cousin Harold has not been seen for the best part of thirty years, so Henry cannot be Harold, unless for some reason he abandoned his quest for the Ellises after the chat with Samantha Yaxley. 'Could you describe Harold? As much as you can recall,' Ian requests, willing himself to believe the implausible, but a moment later he's banging a fist on his forehead. Cousin Harold was five-foot three or five-foot four the last time they saw him, and the wrong side of thirty as well. Thus, barely a minute after it arose, the mirage of Harold-Henry vanishes, yet the fact remains that the Ellis name is in some way a connection between our man and the two houses, and the Ellises are a populous clan, so our Henry's face might be hiding somewhere in the family albums. Only at the end of the conversation does Ian reveal anything of the circumstances of Henry's death. The following day we're off to Southampton.

There's a nervousness to Bridget Ellis's manner as she takes us through to the living room, but it's a nervousness that has the quality of a permanent constituent of character, like the fastidiousness that's made manifest by the neatly combed and lacquered grey hair and the nicely matched black slacks and dark-grey roll-neck top, on which there's not a single fleck or loose hair. She's fifty or thereabouts, waistless, tiny – no more than five-one – and walks with a light and rapid and bouncy step, as though her tendons have been made a bit too short for her heels to make substantial contact with the ground. Her husband, on the other hand, is a good fourteen inches taller than Bridget, and when he gets up from the sofa he rises with the strong slowness of a middle-aged man who used to be athletic before the joints began to misbehave. Bridget, leading the way, talks at the pace of a horse-racing commentator; her husband, one senses, is a man of few words. When we come into the room, he says nothing, but gets up from the sofa to switch off the cricket, then sits back down and crosses his arms. 'My husband, Patrick,' says Bridget, and he raises a hand for shaking. He has fingers that could bend pennies. His sweatshirt, rolled up to the elbows, reveals Bridget's name on a tattooed scroll that's winding round a scarlet heart.

On the coffee table, between Patrick and the television, lie a dozen photo albums awaiting our attention, but we never get to open them. 'This is the last picture of Henry. From last year,' Ian begins, laying the print on the table. Mrs Ellis is taking a pair of glasses from the table, so it's Pat who examines it first, and when he looks at it he seems confused, like someone who's just waking up and not altogether sure of where he is. He takes the second photo from Ian and passes the first one to his wife.

'Can't say I recognise him,' says Bridget.

It's apparent that Ian is indeed on to something, because the moment Patrick Ellis focuses on the younger Henry he blinks and turns aside, taking a long breath, as if a fume of ammonia has wafted over him. Wiping a hand across his mouth and chin, three or four times, he hands the picture to his wife who, after a first look from arm's length, takes off the glasses again and brings it closer to her face.

'Oh,' says Bridget, and it sounds like the understated expression of a huge disappointment.

Patrick, looking at his wife, places a hand on her knee. She does not take her eyes off the photograph. 'We know him,' says

Patrick, still looking at his wife, awaiting a fuller reaction from her.

Bridget's gaze is wandering over the picture of Henry, as if she's gazing into a mirror and wondering, in resignation, how all the years have gone so quickly. 'His name isn't Ellis,' she says, and she lets her husband take the picture from her hand. He pushes it back across the table, and now she turns to look at him and curves a hand over his.

Sombrely bemused, Patrick regards his hand and his wife's as they lie cupped together on Bridget's knee, then a tremor appears in the centre of his lower lip and he says to us, rising to his feet, 'Excuse me.' He closes the door as gently as a father leaving the bedroom of his sleeping child.

The stairs creak and Bridget proffers a lifeless smile. She looks towards the ceiling, listening, but there's no sound from upstairs. A minute passes like this and then, seeing Ian about to speak, she says, in a voice that has the calmness of exhaustion: 'His name is Ivor Clifford. That's who that is. He killed our daughter.' She spends a few seconds brushing something invisible from the table top and then, as if addressing a phantom listener who is seated beside us, she tells us what happened.

Katie was their first child, and she was killed on 18 April 1964. She was four years old, nearly five. For much of the morning it had been raining, but soon after eleven the sun came out and Katie went outside to play. At the time there was an area of open ground opposite their house. It had been marked out for new houses, but the work had been held up and the land had become overgrown. On the far side a fence and a screen of trees separated this area from a park, but the fence was missing half its staves, so the children only had to cross the one road and then they could walk all the way to the swings and slides, across the waste ground. But beyond the park there was a busier road and, although she was told never to go anywhere near it, this was where Katie was killed, by a car that Ivor Clifford was driving. He was going too fast, but his lawyer got him off: the road was still slippery from the rain and there was oil on it as well, he argued; Katie ran out so quickly; the sun in the rear-view mirror might have dazzled him. 'But he was driving too fast. He wasn't paying attention and he was driving too fast,' Bridget says, not with rancour, but with the plainness of someone who has reached an accommodation with unerasable pain. A neighbour came running to tell them there had been an accident, but Katie was already dead when Patrick reached her. Clifford had smashed himself against the steering wheel and was slumped in his seat. He didn't move when the police and the ambulance arrived, and neither did Patrick. 'He wouldn't let go. He just sat in the road, holding her,' she says, then she stops. Stroking her neck, she searches the air as if seeking words there. Her lips part and close again, and it's a while before she resumes.

'When Clifford got off, Pat went berserk,' she goes on. 'Effing and blinding at the jury and the judge and the lawyers. They were going to lock him up if he didn't calm down. When we came home, he was too furious to talk. That went on for ages. He'd break things, throw things. He put his fist through a window one day. He kicked a hole in a door. We got this letter from Clifford, saying how sorry he was. He could have said he was sorry every day for the rest of his life and it wouldn't have been enough. Pat went mental when he read it. Tore it up before I could see it. I thought he was going to demolish the house. After that he was too miserable to be furious. At weekends he was spending hours at the cemetery. He couldn't be bothered with anything else. He wanted to be dead, he kept saying. When he went to bed he was hoping he wouldn't wake up again. He's a driver, HGV, but he had to give up work because he was always taking too long on the road. They never knew when he was going to turn up. In the end we had to get away. We couldn't be in the place where it happened. It was killing him,' says Bridget. 'And me,' she adds.

So, four years on, the Ellises left Plymouth and moved to Southampton, where Patrick found work with another haulage company and where, eleven years after the death of Katie, Lauren was born. Had it been Bridget's choice, they would have tried for a second child sooner, but it was hard for Patrick to come round to the idea. 'It was impossible for him, to start again without her.' Bridget explains, glancing towards the door, listening for her husband. 'And he thought he couldn't cope. With all the strain of it. Once you've lost a child, you're never quite right, you know?' she says, requesting our understanding, though the bereft wistfulness of her eyes and the staunch set of her lips say that it's impossible to understand, to understand fully, unless it's happened to you. 'You're thinking something could go wrong any moment. When Lauren was little, he'd sit by her cot for hours when she was asleep, like her heart would stop if he wasn't there. We were both on edge, all the time. It's got better, but we're still like that, a bit. You hear a siren and your heart's going a hundred to the dozen, know what I mean? If she's out and the phone rings, sometimes you jump a foot in the air. "Oh God, something's happened to Lauren," you think. That's her. That's Lauren,' she says, pointing to a picture of a girl in a blue school blazer, revealing braced teeth between tense lips. 'Pat says that when she's grown up and people ask her what her parents were like, she'll say that they stared at her a lot. That's what she'll remember about us.' We laugh with her, but Ian's gaze is straying in the direction of a photograph in an alcove beside the fireplace. Observing this, Bridget confirms that the girl in the pink dress and white ankle socks is Katie. For a few seconds all three of us look at the dead girl. She appears to be four years old, nearly five. Standing on a lawn that's faded to the colour of cardboard, she grins as she presents a cat to the camera, clutching it under its front legs so its head is getting shoved into folds of fur and the hind paws are dangling almost to the grass. To her left there's a long segment of chequered dress, a woman's leg from knee to shoe, and a hand, fingers spread, descending from the corner of the frame.

We look away, taking our lead from Bridget, and she gives us a small smile, a defeated smile that means she cannot find anything to say, but also tells us two things more: that her life has had no easy days since the day Katie died; and that there is something she's withholding.

'We're sorry to have brought it back,' says Ian, ending an interval of silence.

'No, no. Don't worry,' Bridget replies. 'It comes back on its own.'

The next lull is broken by Bridget. 'We won't be needing these, then,' she says, picking up the photo albums. She takes them over to the sideboard and puts them in a drawer.

The floor above us squeaks, at which Ian says: 'We would like to talk to your husband for a minute, Mrs Ellis.'

'Do you have to?' she asks. 'Pat can't bear to talk about it. Really, he can't.'

'We understand, but we do have to talk to him. We'll keep it brief.'

'Everything Pat knows, I know. Any questions, I can deal with them.'

'But the letter from Mr Clifford, you said you didn't see it.'

'Not the actual letter, no. But I know what was in it. Pat told me what it said.'

'Yes, Mrs Ellis, but nonetheless we do need to have a word with your husband.'

'I don't see why,' she says, seeming to think that we might change our minds if she keeps up the resistance.

'Mrs Ellis, we appreciate that this is distressing and we don't want to make this harder for you, but we have to talk to him. So if you could get him?'

'I don't see why it's necessary.'

'Please.'

'Right you are,' she says, unpersuaded, 'I'll get him.' She scratches her head to signify puzzlement at our insistence, and shrugs, overstating her bafflement, and so betraying an unease that does not appear to be wholly attributable to her concern about her husband's state of mind. Slowly she climbs the stairs, then we hear the rumble of their voices through the ceiling, followed by a lengthy pause before their descending tread. Patrick Ellis comes into the room alone.

'Mr Ellis, we're sorry, but we have to ask you a couple of questions,' Ian tells him once he's seated, to which his response is to spread his hands in a gesture of enforced compliance. Sitting with his arms crossed loosely and his eyes wilfully deadened, he has the demeanour of a man who has already told his side of the story and sees no need for further talk. 'We believe that you received a letter from Ivor Clifford, several years ago,' Ian continues. The consequent movement of Patrick's head is too slight to be unambiguously a nod of agreement. 'Is that the case?' Ian asks him.

'Correct.'

'This was some sort of apology, yes?' The response to this is feebler than a snort of contempt, as if to say that Clifford's letter does not even deserve the effort of strong comment. 'And you destroyed this letter as soon as you'd read it.'

'Correct.'

'Because you didn't think he was genuine?'

'I couldn't care less if he was genuine.'

'OK. Because you hated him.'

'Correct.'

'You could never forgive him.'

'Correct.'

'And you still can't?'

'Correct.'

'And you think you never will.'

'Can't see into the future, can I?'

'But you feel you won't ever forgive him?'

'Would you?' he asks. A tension is showing in his arms now, and in his eyes a stolid truculence is coming to the fore.

'I don't know. I can't imagine it,' says Ian, but the sympathetic phrase passes without acknowledgement. 'This letter,' he resumes, 'can you recall, was there an address on it?'

'There wasn't.'

270

'You're sure about that?'

'Absolutely,' Patrick states, and here a change occurs in the intensity of his focus, a change that indicates that he knows what we want him to say and is about to say it. 'If there was an address, I wouldn't have ripped it up.'

'What would you have done?'

He lifts his head an inch off the back of the seat and says to us, as though explaining a point to a pair of imbeciles: 'I'd have gone to wherever he was and I'd have shoved the fucking letter down his throat and when I'd done that I'd have kicked his head in. That's what I would have done.'

'You'd have killed him?'

'Very likely.'

'That's what you think he deserved?'

'He murdered our girl.'

'He caused her death.'

Disdaining to answer, Patrick gradually twists his neck to left and right and left, as if to ease a cramp, then gives us a look that suggests it would be best for all of us if we let the subject rest now.

'Did Mr Clifford ever write to you again?' Ian asks.

'No.'

'Never?'

'No.' With a card player's studied impassiveness he takes our sceptical gazes.

Ian is speaking for both of us when he says: 'But I think it's possible that you encountered Mr Clifford again. I think it's probable.'

'Do you?' says Patrick heavily, but the appearance of weary indifference is compromised by a double blink.

'I do.'

'OK,' he says.

'OK what?'

'OK that's what you think.'

'And is it true?'

271

'When would this have been?'

'Some time after you moved here.'

'OK,' he says again, his tone that of someone considering a cash offer that's not as good as he'd hoped for, but might be the best he can get.

'To be precise: February 1977. I think that maybe Mr Clifford tracked you down and tried to speak to you.'

He stares back at Ian, obdurate for a few seconds more, and then, cornered, he gives him a quarter-smile, condescendingly impressed. 'OK,' he says, raising his hands.

'So what happened, Mr Ellis?'

'We had words.'

'What did he say to you?'

'I can't recall. I wasn't listening.'

'And what did you say to him?'

'I can't recall.'

'You can't recall?'

'No.'

'But you can remember what happened?'

'He was at the depot gates. I told him to fuck off.'

'I think you might have put it more strongly than that.'

'I think you might be right.'

'You had more than just words. There was a fight, wasn't there?'

'I wouldn't call it a fight,' he says. Since he admitted to the meeting with Henry his replies have all been instantaneous and blandly delivered, and this answer is too.

'What would you call it?'

'I wouldn't call it a fight,' he repeats.

'Mr Clifford was quite badly injured.'

'Was he?'

'Yes, he was.'

'I didn't look, to tell you the truth.'

At around this point, perhaps a moment sooner, Bridget soundlessly comes back into the room. She hesitates at the door and then, having ascertained what we're talking about, she crosses to the sofa and sits close to her husband. With an air of resolute loyalty she takes his hand and only now does she look up at us.

Patrick kisses her hand and does not release it. 'You think I killed him?' he asks us, merely curious.

'Did you?'

'No,' he says, then he trains on Ian a look of glowering honesty, a look that is maintained until he sees that his word has prevailed. 'But I'm not going to make out I'm sorry,' he goes on. 'So someone killed him. What do you want me to say? It's a tragedy? I can't. I don't care. I don't feel good and I don't feel bad. I don't care that he's dead. Nothing will bring her back. I didn't kill him. I could have. I would have. But I didn't and you can't do me for wanting to kill him.'

'No, Mr Ellis, we can't.'

'He has nothing to do with it,' Bridget tells us, clutching at Patrick's arm as if she thinks we might take him away. 'You believe him?' she asks and tears spring into her eyes when we answer her.

As soon as he's in the car, Ian starts banging his head on the steering wheel. 'Fuck fuck fuck fuck fuck,' he moans. 'For a minute I thought we had it. But it's not him, is it? He put Henry in hospital, but he's not our man.'

Often, when a couple lose a child, the grief does not draw them together but instead destroys them. Discovering that there can be no consolation, no release from the anguish of it, each comes to understand that we are essentially alone and that's how they end up living. The Ellises, though, have come through it, and we're both glad when we have the proof that Patrick Ellis is not our man. The records of the haulage company for which he works show that Patrick Ellis was driving through France and Germany during most of the period in which Henry must have died, and for the rest of the time he has so tight an alibi that only if he'd had a private plane at his disposal could he have dropped into our part of the world to kill Henry. But although we haven't caught Henry's killer, we've caught Henry. Within days of our visit to Southampton he at last has an official identity, complete with National Insurance Number and birth certificate: he's Ivor Wesley Clifford, born in Brierley Hill, in the West Midlands, on 5 July 1938, to Isaac Clifford (born 1913) and May Patricia Clifford, née Riley (born 1918). Isaac Clifford died in Normandy in 1944, we soon discover; but the former May Clifford is still alive.

28

The facts of the case, as presented by the defence to the satisfaction of the jury, are that at 11.45 a.m. on 18 April 1964 a movement of the air caused a body of cloud to shift in a northerly direction, thereby permitting the sun briefly to shine directly on to the stretch of Shackleton Road along which Ivor Clifford then happened to be driving, and to flash in the rear-view mirror of Mr Clifford's car, momentarily disrupting his vision, so that for a crucial second or two he was unaware of the presence of Katie Ellis, who had darted out into the road from between two parked cars with such suddenness, and so close to Mr Clifford's vehicle, that it is unlikely that, even had his sight not been impaired and the road conditions not been worsened by a mixture of standing rainwater and a quantity of engine oil, Mr Clifford would have been able to reduce his speed from something in the region of 27 or 28 miles per hour to zero in the space available to him. If it had not been for that small atmospheric event, that little gust of wind, the lives of the Ellis family would have continued more or less happily, and Ivor Clifford would perhaps have remained Ivor Clifford for the rest of his days.

'I'd go to pieces,' she says, having heard about Katie, and for a minute, sitting in a corner of her living room, she contemplates the grain of the floorboards, pressing her palms to the side of her face, shaking her head at the immensity of their loss. She presses fingertips to her eyes and utters a sound that's like a whispered scream. 'Doesn't bear thinking about,' she says, and then, as she stares across the room, her thoughts turn from the suffering of the Ellises to the suffering of Henry. To Hannah the death of Katie Ellis is the key to the life of Henry, the remorse-crippled indigent. She admires and cannot understand his perfect secrecy; she cannot understand why she never guessed that something like this might have been the answer. It all makes sense now: a narrative is bestowed on Henry's previously incoherent existence and it has the clarity of tragedy. Guilt drove Henry away from Gemma and guilt drove him back to her; guilt drove him to drink and sent him in search of the Ellises; unassuageable guilt in the end drove him half mad and erased much of his life from his mind, leaving nothing but scraps flitting in the breeze of his brain. Hannah's Henry is a character from the Middle Ages, a contrite wanderer, a saintly sinner in search of rest, scourging himself along the highways and byways of England.

We meet most days for an hour or so, sometimes at her flat, sometimes at the house of a client. For the Petersons she's painting the hall and landing and main bedroom, for which they've chosen a combination of pale yellow and pale orange that Hannah fails to persuade them to reconsider. 'Love in a giant sorbet,' she says, unbuttoning her overall. From the back bedroom of the Petersons' house you can see, at the bottom of a large terraced garden, a blue-walled outbuilding with a short steel chimney. It's a pottery studio, says Hannah. She painted it last year and Henry dropped by one afternoon to see how she was getting on. 'He sat in the garden for most of the morning, watching the paint dry,' she jokes, and as always there's a sadness at the mention of Henry, but the sadness passes quickly and in its place there's something akin to reverence, which makes it difficult not to tell her what we know about his misdemeanours. But – as would later be proved – her belief in the character of penitent Henry would withstand the revelation of unpleasant facts and the only consequence of

276

telling her everything would be disagreement, so nothing is said. 'See you tomorrow,' she says, with her customary coolness at parting, closing one segment of her day before moving on to the next.

That evening, at home, we might not have talked about Henry at all. His episode was drawing to a close: we had found out who he was and we had found the next of kin, so we could hold the funeral soon; maybe one day his killer would be caught. The death of Katie Ellis had been lamented. There was little more to say. Ian and his not wholly baseless self-satisfaction was the subject of the conversation, such as it was. LCA Mowbray was what Geoff Salter had taken to calling him: Lights, Camera, Action. 'Witty. For Geoff,' Alice remarked, uncharacteristically acerbic, not looking up from her plate. Luke was brought back home by Martin Vanes at 7.30. We began a new bedtime book, a version of King Arthur and the Knights of the Round Table.

At the sword in the stone we agree to call it a day. 'So he's got superpowers?' asks Luke. 'Like Batman and Superman and Spiderman? So that means nobody can ever kill him?' At lights out he's lying with his head in the centre of the pillow, staring at the ceiling, pondering the powers of the once and future king.

Alice is sitting in her armchair with a jacket draped over her lap. She's holding a sleeve and is looking at the jacket as though it's a pet that's died.

'Luke OK?' she asks.

'Fine. Do you want a coffee?'

She twists her mouth, as if being called upon to answer a difficult question. 'No,' she replies, frowning at the sleeve, 'I don't think I do.'

'Sure? I'm making one.'

'Sure,' she says and she waits three or four seconds before adding: 'John?'

'Yes?'

'There's a paint mark here.' With a peevish movement of the lips that seems to indicate that the damage to the fabric is her only concern, she displays the little streak of pale orange paint on the inside of the cuff.

'Must have brushed against something.'

'You don't know what?'

'I don't.'

'Difficult to brush against wet paint with your wrist and not know about it,' she comments, yet still it seems possible that the stain alone is what is troubling her. 'It's going to be hard to shift. It's not emulsion,' she says, rubbing at the mark with a wetted thumb. 'And an unusual colour. I'd have thought you'd have noticed.'

'So would I.'

'Not like you to be so careless,' she says, an observation that prompts the thought that this tick of paint may be taken as evidence of the actions of an idiot, or of a man who wanted, unwittingly, to be found out. And no sooner has this thought arisen than Alice, dropping the sleeve and looking up, says: 'Well?'

'I don't know where it came from.'

She dips her head and narrows her eyes, as if in some doubt as to the identity of the person who is standing before her. 'Are you having an affair?' she asks, but in the tone in which she might ask if any work had to be done this evening.

'No.'

'Are you having an affair?' she repeats, in the same stressless voice.

'No.'

'Are you having an affair?'

'No.'

'But you've been seeing a lot of that girl, the one who knew Henry? What's her name?'

'Hannah Rowe.'

'You've been seeing her.'

'We've talked to her, yes.'

'I don't mean you plural. I mean you singular.'

'Yes, I've talked to her.'

'Several times.'

'A few times.'

'She must have a lot to say.'

'She does, yes. She's our main source of information.'

'But none of it seems to be of much use, as far as I can see. Still at square one, aren't you?'

'You never know what's going to be useful.'

'So whenever Hannah Rowe wants a chat, you'll come running.'

'No. If we get new information and we need to check it against what she remembers, we'll talk to her.'

'You mean: "I'll talk to her."'

'I will, or Ian, or both of us.'

'And the poor girl earns such a pittance that she doesn't have a phone? Or is a face-to-face interview an absolute necessity?'

'Sometimes it is.'

'And the fact that she's an attractive young woman is entirely coincidental, of course.'

'Who said she was attractive?'

'You did. First time you spoke to her. You said she was attractive.'

'She's our chief source. She knew him better than anyone.'

'Where did the paint come from?' she asks again, as relentless as a prosecutor.

'I told you. I don't know.'

'Don't lie to me,' she says, almost soothingly, as one might say: 'Calm down.'

'I really don't know. It could have been there for days.'

'It hasn't been there for days. It's appeared since this morning.'

'Well, I don't know.'

'She's a painter. A house painter, yes?'

'Yes.'

'She paints; there's paint on your sleeve.'

'Alice, I don't know where it came from.'

The use of her name strikes Alice like an insult that might have been misheard. She blinks, very deliberately, three or four times, then, with an inhalation that's suggestive of a revulsion almost mastered, folds the jacket loosely and deposits it on the floor. 'Why are you lying to me?' she enquires, and in her eyes there is only a tolerably painful curiosity.

'I'm not.'

'I wish you wouldn't lie to me. What you've done is bad enough, but you're making it worse.'

'I'm not lying to you.'

'I'll ask you again: are you having an affair?'

'No.'

'Are you having an affair?' she repeats once more, like a recording of herself.

'No.'

'Why do you keep on lying?' she asks, her bewilderment that of a parent in conflict with a recalcitrant teenager.

It's like beginning to lose your balance on a tightrope and deciding to make a dash for safety, though you know, underneath the impulse to run, that the platform is a pace or two too far away and you're going to fall. 'I'm not lying. I don't know what else I can say.'

'You could try the truth.'

'I have done.'

'She's an attractive girl.'

'She's not unattractive.'

'And you're sleeping with her.'

'No, I am not.'

'You are. What's the point of lying? If you could see what I'm seeing you'd stop it. If you could see your face.'

'Alice —'

'Look at me. Are you having an affair with that girl?'

'No.'

'You're lying.'

'I'm not.'

'Someone saw you together.'

'Who?'

'Someone. It doesn't matter.'

'It does matter. What did they think they saw? Who was it?'

'It doesn't matter, John. I know. From the way you are, the way you've been. It's so obvious. Did you really think I wouldn't notice?' Only now does she falter. In bitter exasperation she glances aside and her lips form words that are not uttered. Then, quietly, as if to herself, she says: 'I think you should leave.'

'What?'

'I think you should leave this house. Go somewhere else. Wherever. I want you to leave. I don't want to live with you.'

'But –'

'I can't ever trust you again, John.'

'Look –'

'I want you to go,' she says, at last raising her voice, with a flare of fury in which, for an instant, appears a semblance of the vivacity of Alice when we were younger.

Some hours later there is a confession, but a tactical one. 'You slept with her once? That's what you want me to believe? And you think that would make it all right?' she replies, her face hardening into something close to loathing. She does not cry. Not once, in the subsequent days, does she allow herself to be seen in tears.

Implacable in the execution of justice, she discusses the separation as if it were little more than a matter of moving some furniture from one place to another. We agree what we should tell Luke and on what day we should tell him. We're sitting in the kitchen, in the middle of the afternoon, and Alice is gazing at the garden, as though looking at a picture of a place in which she once lived. 'I hope you'll think she was worth it,' she says and she goes to the sink, to pour into the kettle enough water for a single cup.

29

About thirty armchairs, high-backed and high-seated, upholstered with greasy rose-patterned fabric, are set out in a ring, spaced like the numbers on a clock dial, with a gap in the circle for the TV. It's two o'clock on a late summer afternoon, but the room is darkened by the bushes between the windows and the main road, so the lights are on. The decor makes you think of a conference room in a cheap motorway hotel: the lights are neon strips; the walls are the colour of oatcakes; the carpet fudge-brown. To brighten the place up a bit, however, someone has taped to the walls some dauby paintings of flowers on large rectangles of wrinkled paper, the sort of artwork you might see in a primary school. Two men and three women are sitting in the room, each separated by at least one vacant chair. Nobody is talking, or reading, or doing anything except sit. They look as though they have been told to sit there and wait, without being told what it is they're waiting for. There's some activity on the TV screen, but the picture is bleached out by the neon glare. Another resident comes in, advancing inch by inch with the aid of a frame. A nurse overtakes him and takes up a position by an empty chair, ready to guide him to his berth. The seated five are watching him as you might watch a cloud pass across the sky. Close to the door crouches a large toy dog with long nylon fur, the colour of overchewed chewing gum.

'Mrs Yarrow must be in her room,' says the supervisor and she leads down a corridor that's carpeted with the same heavy-duty brown nylon as the communal room. Between every pair of doors hangs a framed print of an old map, evidently bought in bulk, as every print is the same size and every frame the same design. From one of the bedrooms comes the voice of Dean Martin; next door an old man is swearing in a querulous yell, while a young woman soothingly repeats his name: 'Mr Smyth; Mr Smyth; Mr Smyth.' The supervisor halts outside the room of Mrs Yarrow. 'We ask them to keep the door open, but she never does. She likes to keep herself to herself,' she says before knocking, and smiles indulgently at Mrs Yarrow's quirkiness.

A strong voice calls 'Come in,' as if summoning us into a doctor's surgery, and when we step into the room we step into the gaze of Mrs Yarrow, whose eyes are trained on the door, over the horizon of half-moon glasses. Wearing a crisply pleated blue dress, of a design that might have been fashionable some time around 1950, she's sitting in a wing-backed chair at the window with a book open on her lap. Her hair, perfectly white and as thick as a thirty-year-old's, is held from her face by a puce velvet-covered band, and a necklace of pale red beads lies loosely on her throat. 'One of you will have to sit on the bed,' she says, gesturing with her left hand at the bed and at the chair that's tucked under the writing desk. Her right hand, curled on the book, does not move and the right side of her mouth has the appearance of being dragged down by an invisible hook. The right eyelid also has fallen slightly, but her eyes are very clear and frank, and the skin around them is soft-looking and only lightly lined. Having placed the book on the table to the side of her chair, she adjusts the position of the lifeless hand, setting its fingers in a loose curl, and when everything is in order she says, 'Ivor, then. Tell me.' The set of her face and a small upward movement of her chin indicate that she expects nothing but bad news of her son, and is prepared for the blow of it, and requires us to be direct, so Ian tells her that he has died, that he died at the end of last year. He tells her that someone killed him.

Nothing in her expression changes as she listens and when Ian has finished speaking she says nothing, but instead, with no loss of self-possession, detaches her attention from us. Putting a finger to her temple, she seems to contemplate the death of Ivor as one might contemplate the death of an aged and distant relative.

'We're sorry it's taken so long to trace you,' says Ian, and we go on, taking turns, to give her a summary of the challenges presented by the man we knew as Henry. We recount the list of aliases, we describe his wanderings, the peculiarity of his memory, the circumstances of his life in his final years. We tell her about his living with Gemma, and working at the Ilfracombe garage, and his friendship with Ms Rowe. None of it affects her greatly, it appears, and she has no questions. Nonplussed by the absence of demonstrated emotion, Ian introduces a personal perspective, with the tale of Henry and the bathing trunks, and at this she smiles, but barely, as though at an anecdote that has been heard too many times before and was never very amusing to begin with.

'A fight, was it?' she asks.

'We're not sure. It seems improbable.'

Mrs Yarrow looks out at the garden, apparently undecided as to what she should think. The garden comprises half a dozen small flowerbeds and a few shrubs and silver birch saplings on islands of grass, and a flat path that winds round them, with a bench under the boughs of one of the birches. In the vicinity of the bench an old man is standing. A raincoat hangs off him like a dust sheet thrown over a standard lamp, and ankles as jagged as cobbles of flint are on show between his trousers and his sandals, but he has a full head of springy grey hair that was dyed nut-brown at some point in the fairly recent past, and now the dye has almost grown out, leaving dabs of brown here and there on the grey, like the plumage of a young owl. His arm shakes with the effort of raising his walking stick off the ground, as though to remonstrate with someone who is blocking his way, and he stares in the direction of the garden wall in consternation, even when the nurse touches his hand and gently brings the stick down. 'Every day the same,' remarks Mrs Yarrow, the flatness of her voice suggesting a compassion that has been blunted through overuse. 'Has his lunch, goes out into the garden and forgets where he is. Every day the same palaver.' Sitting on the bench, the nurse talks to the old man and strokes his sleeve, and he nods, beginning to understand.

Watching the scene outside, Mrs Yarrow says, in the tone of a formal statement: 'I was not a loving mother.' Sternly she regards the hand in her lap, reflecting on what she has just said. 'I was not a loving mother,' she reiterates, content with the self-description, 'and Ivor was not a loving son. Which came first, I couldn't say. I know that I tried to love him and never quite managed it. I hoped he couldn't tell, but perhaps he could. Who knows what's going on in the minds of small children? I did everything a mother is supposed to do. Maybe it was my fault. Perhaps he could tell right away that I didn't really love him, before he could say a word. But I don't think so. I went through the motions of loving him and I'm sure it was convincing. Like any mother, I put my boy first. I was with him all day. But there was always a coldness about him. When he cried, holding him didn't make much difference. He cried until he'd had enough of crying. He never much liked being fussed over and he didn't much care for the company of other children. That's how he was. Ivor was Ivor, I think, right from the start. We were given him and he was given us, and neither of us thought it was a satisfactory arrangement.' She glances at us, as though to check we're keeping pace with her dictation, then turns back to the garden, which now has no one in it.

'But he was an easy child, compared to many,' she resumes, slowly kneading the damaged hand. For the first six years he was a well-behaved little boy: remote and too quiet, but easily managed. 'Law-abiding' is the phrase on which she settles. But when Ivor was six years old, his father died and after that his behaviour began to change. Ivor and Isaac had not been particularly close – the war had kept them apart for a lot of the time, and Ivor's relationship with his father, whenever they were together, was indistinguishable from his relationship with his mother – but the removal of his father from his life seemed to give Ivor grounds for a grievance against the world, an inextinguishable grievance vented in the direction of his mother on a daily basis. 'Spiky, very spiky' is how she characterises him. 'It was like having a small and bad-tempered lodger in the house,' she says with a grimace of reluctant amusement. 'So between the ages of six and twelve Ivor evolved from being unlovable to being positively unpleasant, and from the age of twelve to the day he left home, seven years later, he doggedly consolidated his unpleasantness.

Frank Yarrow, May's second husband, for a long time tried his best to get along with his stepson. Mild-mannered by nature, he began by giving Ivor a lot of leeway, treating him almost as an equal in the household, never raising his voice, no matter how provocative the boy might be. Eventually, however, even he tired of Ivor's insolence, the laziness, the tediously frequent hints by which the boy would impress upon his stepfather that life at home had been happily harmonious before his mother's remarriage. Frank began to assert some authority, but tactfully, at first. Ivor let it be known that he was obedient only because it suited him to be so, and if ever he was spoken to in a way that offended him – and he was easily offended – he would sulk for days, or answer back. Once, asked to clean out the grate, Ivor said 'Do it yourself,' and Frank slapped him on the face for that. Afterwards, for a whole month, Ivor refused to look his stepfather in the eye and spoke to him only when spoken to.

Fishing was something Ivor seemed to enjoy, as far as they could tell. 'He was often at the river, put it that way,' says Mrs Yarrow. Fastidious in her efforts to remember her son truly, and to describe truly what she remembers, she presents each sentence clearly, unhurriedly, within brackets of brief silence. Ivor was also interested in Grand Prix and motorbike racing (pictures of cars and bikes covered the walls of his room), and he would spend hours making drawings of animals from a book that had belonged to his father. Other than that, nothing much seemed to give him pleasure. He didn't like where he was living: he didn't like the house, he didn't like the town. He gave the impression that he felt he was owed something better, for some reason – perhaps because his father was dead. One day he'd go to live in London, he said, because London was a place where things happened. In that case, Frank reasoned, he needed to make more of an effort at school. Education was the way to make a better life for himself. To this advice Ivor responded, inevitably, by absenting himself from school, sometimes bodily, every day in spirit. His marks had never been good, because Ivor wasn't that bright, but now they became appalling. 'It goes in one ear and out the other,' was the verdict of his teachers. He was quite open about playing truant. 'I didn't go to school today,' he'd say, then he'd sit down to receive his ticking-off from Frank, which he'd take with a silly grin on his face, as if listening to a nice man who was talking to him in a foreign language. Asked where he'd been when he should have been at school, he'd say he'd been walking. Usually he'd offer no more detailed an explanation. 'Just walking,' he'd reply, with a helpless shrug, unable to comprehend why this explanation did not suffice. Some Saturdays and Sundays he'd be out all day, and his socks often had small hard discs on the soles, where blisters had burst.

As soon as he could, Ivor left school to work in the steel mill. 'Long gone. It's a shopping centre now,' Mrs Yarrow adds, as though the passing of the mill and the unravelling of her son were aspects of the same grand narrative of decline. And as soon as he had saved a bit of money Ivor left home, to move into a bedsit a few miles away, close to the mill. 'I wasn't sorry to see him go. It had become impossible, Ivor and Frank under the same roof. Frank had the patience of a saint and he was glad to see the back of him,' she says, but she seems to be seeing her son leaving home and is sorry to see him go, or sorry that she was not and cannot be sorry to see him go. 'In all the time he was there', she goes on, 'we never saw where he lived, and we hardly ever saw him either. Even after he'd bought his car, the trip was too far for him. Mind you, it was a wreck. Forever fixing it, he was. Or said he was. Too busy working on it to come and see us, anyway,' she says, with a movement of one eyebrow to signify that their estrangement had never been of much concern to either party. Then she stops talking and turns her attention to the afflicted hand, lifting it on to the arm of the chair.

We're waiting for her to continue, but when the hand, after numerous repositionings, has finally been made comfortable, she gives us a smile that tells us that the story of Ivor, for her, has been concluded, and suggests the possibility that she knows nothing about Katie Ellis. It's Ian who risks the question: 'This car. Is this the car in which he had the crash?'

But she answers immediately, equably: 'No. That was years after he left. Five or six years. Seven. He changed his car every year. Every one a wreck.'

'And how did the accident affect him? Did he seem different after it?'

'Well, it upset him, of course. Anyone would be upset. And he was worried that he was going to go to gaol. He was sure that he was going to be found guilty, it being a little girl who was killed. So he was relieved when it went the other way. Extremely relieved. Buoyant, almost. Unlike himself. We had a big Sunday lunch, all of us, when it was over. He managed to be civil to Frank. So yes, he was different for a while.'

'But in the longer term? Was there a change?'

'I really couldn't say. We didn't see him enough. Perhaps it affected him, but not that I noticed. He wasn't happy before and he wasn't happy after. That's all I can say.'

'He went to London how long after the accident?'

'To live, you mean?'

'Yes.'

'A couple of years. But he'd go down for weekends before that. He told us sometimes that he'd been to London and how good it was. We never knew what he did there, mind you. The nightlife wasn't really his kind of thing. He told us once about walking on Oxford Street at midnight in a crowd of people. That made a big impression on him, and the size of it as well, but night-clubs and that sort of thing – that wasn't really Ivor. And I don't think he was interested in the sights, the monuments and all that. History never interested him. Frank used to say that the main thing that London had in its favour was that it wasn't here, but thousands of places aren't here, so I don't know what it was. He turned up on a Sunday afternoon to say he was going and on the Monday he left. That was that.'

'But you did see him again? He didn't vanish completely?'

'As good as. We hardly ever saw him. The year after he went, he came home twice, three times at most. The year after, once or twice. Then nothing for nearly four years, except a card every now and then: Christmas, Easter, my birthday, not Frank's. He never rang and he never showed his face, until he turned up, out of the blue. He hadn't been looking after himself, you could see that straight away. Between jobs, he said he was, but when we asked what he'd been doing we got the usual stone-walling. "A bit of this and a bit of that." We didn't even know where he was living. There was no point giving us his address, because he had to leave next month. He'd send us the new address as soon as he was settled, but of course he never did. He stayed for a few days and in all that time I think we learned that he'd been working for some engineering firm, that was all. One evening he had a big argument with Frank and in the morning he'd gone, without a word. Then we had another three years of the same thing: a card occasionally, otherwise silence. Frank even went down to the steelworks to ask his old workmates if they knew where he was, but nobody had heard from him. They hadn't heard from him since the day he'd quit. He'd worked with some of those men for the best part of ten years, and not a friend among them. Ten years, and he just walks away. I don't understand how you can do that. I never understood him,' says Mrs Yarrow, as if the subject were not her son but someone in a film.

She was to see Ivor once more, in the summer of 1976, on a very warm Saturday afternoon. Dozing in a deckchair in the garden, she became aware that the sun had dimmed and when she opened her eyes, she saw Ivor standing over her, though for a few seconds she was not sure who it was, because the bushy beard was the first thing she noticed and he was also a lot thinner than the last time he'd been home. He had a large canvas bag slung over his shoulder. 'I've brought my washing,' he said, dumping the bag on the grass, and he laughed. Ivor wasn't kidding, either – the bag was full of dirty clothes, which he washed himself that night. For an hour or so they talked in the garden and Ivor was untypically chatty – cheerful, even. Frank had retired and was now very hard of hearing, after four decades on the printing press, and Ivor made a good show of caring about his health. He had questions about relatives and neighbours. As for himself, he was doing all right, he said. 'A bit of this, a bit of that.' But he wasn't doing all right, you could see that. The clothes that fell out of the bag were not much better than rags, and at the table that evening she could see that his hands weren't steady. He was all adrift and drinking too much, and she found herself, once or twice, despite it all, wishing that their lives had not gone the way they had, that she could help him in some way, that he could ask for her help. But Ivor was getting on for forty and she was worn out, and it was too late for anything to change. Just as she was getting ready to go up to bed, Ivor asked if he could see a photograph of his father. She brought down the picture of Isaac with two of his army pals, all of them shirtless, lying on the roof of a barn somewhere in France. 'This used to be in your room,' Ivor commented, seeming to accuse her of disrespect, though the photograph of Isaac and his comrades had been taken down a long time ago, after she remarried, and Ivor had never said anything about it before. Gripping it tightly, as if to prevent it from flying away, Ivor studied the photograph, staring at the face of his father, and then, with a sigh like that of someone at the end of an examination that has not gone well but was not as bad as it might have been, handed it back to his mother, saying: 'I don't remember him any more.' With that he went to bed, and the next morning he said goodbye. He shook Frank's hand, which in retrospect became a clue that this parting was final.

'That was, what, fifteen years ago?' says Mrs Yarrow. 'Doesn't seem possible, but yes. Fifteen years,' she repeats to herself, as though at a harmless and ingenious trick that someone has played on her. 'It feels like five. Most things I can remember seem to be five years past. It's all gone, but not far away. Everything's jumbled together in one box. But saying goodbye to Ivor, that was fifteen years ago, right enough. Once in a while we'd get a postcard, telling us next to nothing. They were never from the same place twice, but there was usually a picture of a beach on the front. In the end they stopped coming. I don't know when the last one was. It came from Cornwall, I think. It didn't say anything. We had no idea, really. All I had was a blank, until today,' she says, finishing, and she turns to us with an expression of deep weariness and apology, telling us that her mourning for Ivor has already been done. But then her gaze returns to the sky above the garden and she seems to be wondering what she should make of the story she's just related.

'Are you all right, Mrs Yarrow?' asks Ian, sensing a shadow falling.

'Oh yes, thank you,' she replies, with a frowning smile of perplexity at the offer of comfort. A further brief spell of reflection follows, and is ended decisively with: 'He wasn't a nice person, that's the problem. The world has a lot of not nice people and they all have mothers.'

There's no trail to be followed here, we know that, and Mrs Yarrow has no need of whatever comfort we might be able to offer. Less than five minutes later we're on our feet. Ian has his hand on the door when she calls out, from the chair: 'What did you say her name was? The girlfriend.'

'Gemma.'

'You met her?'

'We did.'

'A nice woman, was she?'

'We thought so,' says Ian, and he tells her a little more about Gemma, omitting almost everything, embellishing the rest.

'It's good he found a girlfriend,' says Mrs Yarrow. Before we're out of the room, she's picked up her book and opened it.

Now that we have a definitive identity and the next of kin has been located, the remains of Ivor Wesley Clifford can be buried. The interment takes place on a Tuesday afternoon in September. His mother sends a wreath of white flowers, which Hannah carries to the graveside. On the card Mrs Yarrow has written 'May his soul rest in peace', a sentiment that would have made Henry laugh, Hannah remarks. Hannah has not brought flowers. 'He can't see them, can he?' she asks, gesturing at the coffin. 'Who would be impressed?' The man in the cockpit of the cemetery digger, parked at a respectful distance, turns his face to the sun and lights a cigarette. It's a fine lukewarm afternoon, with a multitude of small white clouds and a low breeze to ruffle the long grass. 'Could you give me a minute?' says Hannah. 'It's stupid, I know. But just a minute.' Aggrieved more than grief-stricken, she stands beside the grave, Henry's solitary mourner. The cemetery worker, his cigarette finished, glances at her impatiently, but she stands her ground, looking towards the sea, down at the coffin, out to sea again. Her lips move, emphatically, and then she's walking quickly away from the grave. 'OK. Let's go,' she says, hooking arms as the digger's engine starts up.

30

'We came here one day, when I was a kid,' says Hannah, as we approach the wood. They had been walking for much of the afternoon and Conrad was carrying on as if they'd been on a forced march over the Andes. 'I want to go home,' he moaned to their mother. For a while he tried limping, but nobody was convinced. 'Nearly there, no complaints back there,' her father called over his shoulder as he strode towards the trees, with the rest of the family following at a distance in single file. He hadn't told them why they were taking this detour, but Hannah had trusted him: if he promised that a thing was worth seeing, it would be. On the edge of the wood he stopped, to scowl at the overcast sky. 'We need some co-operation from the Almighty,' he said, and he made them wait until a seam of the clouds began to split apart, then he led them on, with the beams of sunlight sloping over their shoulders and producing the effect he had brought them to see: the dark-grey soil sparkling with millions of tiny white points. Particles of mica, he explained. Micaceous iron oxide was mined here, for use in paint, for metal primer. The science was for Conrad's benefit, but he was having none of it. 'Twinkly mud. Worth an hour of anyone's time,' he grumbled, but to Hannah it was magical, even though – or because – the effect lasted at full intensity for less than a minute, until the clouds closed over again and they were left with just patches of dulled glitter, like a scattering of salt crystals rather than a constellation of minuscule lights.

And that's how it is on the afternoon we are there, when we arrive: an expanse of near-black earth, flecked with pale grains, but suddenly the sunlight pierces the wood and the low gleaming becomes a scintillation. 'Abracadabra,' Hannah laughs, snapping her fingers, and she laughs again with the joy of it, a joy that comes both from what we're seeing and from the revisiting of that remembered day.

Nothing was ever said, explicitly, about how we imagined this affair might develop. No declarations of love or commitment were ever made: the period with Hannah was, on the whole, an intermittent succession of more or less self-contained days and nights. 'See you tomorrow?' she'd say, and it seemed that the answer was not taken for granted. But the sharing of this scene from her past, in the very place to which it belonged, fleetingly felt like the sort of self-disclosure that is made at the start of a major relationship. And there were other occasions when it was possible to believe, sometimes for days beyond their duration, that what was happening would prove to be a stage in the establishment of a different life. From the walk to Bellever Tor, the evenings we spent working together on the basement flat, the thunderstorm at Seaton, the weekend at the Porthleven cottage – from these, too, arose an atmosphere of a significance that was greater than that of mere episodes of intimacy. On the other hand, it came to seem significant that whenever we spent the night together it was always at Hannah's flat, and that when she went out with friends she always went on her own. Once in a while she went up to London and it was a given fact that she would be going alone. So there was this sense of limitation, of occupying a strictly delineated segment of Hannah's world. There was never, however, any sense of the end approaching – until suddenly, one evening, there was.

'Dad would like to meet you,' she announced, having just spoken to him on the phone, and from her tone two things were apparent: that she would have preferred to avoid this breakdown of the categories into which her life was divided; and that her father's preference, as ever, would prevail. That weekend he was teaching a one-day course ('The human figure') in a converted church hall on the outskirts of town. We arrived in the last hour of the final session.

Easels are arrayed in concentric circles round a low stage, where a burly gentleman, aged about sixty, sits on a high wooden stool, with his arms folded on his belly and his chins squashed on to the upper slope of his chest. He's wearing a pair of collapsed white underpants which are more or less the colour of his skin. The students, most of them ladies of the same vintage as their model, are peering round the easels, squinting fiercely at the undressed gentleman. A younger woman, forty-ish, seated closest to the door, has painted the once substantial muscles of his torso in such a way as to make him look like a huge melting candle. Two easels to her left there's a cheery senior citizen with shoulder-length and curtain-straight dyed black hair and big circular silver-rimmed glasses; her outfit – distressed pink sweatshirt over a voluminous lizard-green skirt, plus black patent leather pumps – would seem to have been assembled in the dark, or in a very great hurry. Her work is receiving the appraisal of a tall and corpulent man in a blazingly white loose-fitting shirt, which is tucked haphazardly into a pair of capacious bottle-green corduroy trousers. This is Mr Rowe. Stooping to scrutinise a detail to which his notice has been drawn by the artist, he nods his head and strokes his cheeks, which are ruddy and extraordinarily smooth, like slices of bacon.

When his gaze slips over the top of the sheet of paper and lights upon Hannah, he seems to see only her, and his pleasure at her presence is so flamboyant you'd think she'd arrived unannounced from Tashkent. The eyes widen and the arms go out as he advances towards her, slowly, as though she's an apparition that may vanish if he rushes. Holding her hands, he looks her up and down, though no more than a month has gone by since he last saw her, then he gathers her to him for a sustained, eyes-shut hug. 'This is John,' Hannah says to him, upon being released. She thrusts her hands into the back pockets of her jeans, and at this moment, if you drew a line on the floor to connect our feet, you'd have a regular triangle, with a yard or more between the points.

A lot of effort goes into Philip Rowe's manly handshake, but the eye contact lasts a millisecond. 'John,' he says. That's all he says and he makes the name sound like a judgement. 'Five more minutes, ladies and gentlemen,' he announces to his artists, then he tells Hannah that Deborah Hardy is here. 'From the college? Deborah? Come and have a word.' Precisely who Deborah Hardy might be is never explained. 'I won't keep her long,' he says, already moving away.

The lady in the pink sweatshirt explains, as she had explained to Mr Rowe, that the creature sketched lightly in pencil at the feet of the model is going to become a lion when she gets home, and the thing in his hand, which looks like a bun, is a rock, because he's Saint Jerome, you see, and that's why the stool has been transformed into a boulder and the slack old underpants have, with minimal adjustment, been turned into a fur loincloth. She thinks Mr Rowe is not very pleased with her. He advised her to take more care with the articulation and to try to paint what's there in reality – and Mr Rowe had a good point here, because in their present state the legs of Saint Jerome are dwindling into unformed shapes that are more like carrots than feet. She likes to use her imagination, she says doughtily. If she'd wanted just to depict what's there she would have gone to photography classes, wouldn't she? On the other side of the hall, Hannah and her father are chatting to a woman whose shins and feet are the only parts not hidden; on Hannah's neck, her father's hand is moving as if massaging out a stiffness.

Four or five places to their right a woman in a pastel-lemon shirt has raised a hand and is doing a shy little wave with her fingers. It's Sophie Fazakerly, the party arranger, the blandly groomed and tightly buttoned Mrs Fazakerly from the spotless big house, but today she's let herself go a little: there's a spatter of watercolour on one cuff and on her lip there's a flake of black paint, bitten from the handle of a brush. 'Hello,' she says with a smile that's startling in its candour, and she is brightly surprised to find that her name and her house and husband should be remembered as clearly as she remembers the visit from the police. 'I must have been so annoying,' she says, shaking her head at the recollection of the state she had allowed herself to get into, but she's dismayed, too, at how quickly the shock of the murder wore off. 'But if it didn't wear off we'd find it hard to sleep at night, wouldn't we?' she suggests, at which point we're diverted by a loud laugh from Hannah's father. He's an excellent teacher, she says, with an acolyte's ardency. 'I'm always signing up for things like this. It's an addiction,' she confesses innocently. 'Evening classes. Weekend courses. Residential courses. I can't get enough of them. Phil is the best, for me. Some of them don't teach you. It's like a club where we all get together and do our own thing and that's OK, in its way, but I want to get better. I want some-one to teach me and that's what he does.' There's a modest wince when she moves her stool back to allow a better view of her work, but her reticence, though appealing, is hard to understand, because her painting is more than merely proficient. The figure is small, sitting in a wide white space of paper, but somehow, with hundreds of overlapping dabs of pale-coloured water, Sophie has caught all the mottlings of the ageing skin, every gradation of shadow, each bulge and fold. The swell of a calf is captured with a tiny tick of grey, an almost invisible stroke shows the crease below a shoulder blade. The skill of it is astounding, but it's pecu-liarly touching as well, in its painstaking attention to the facts of the decaying body, an attention that has a quality of sympathetic attendance. 'What do you think?' she asks, with no suggestion that praise is being sought. She's looking at the picture as though at the work of someone else.

'I like it.'

'You do? You're not just saying that?'

'No. I like it a lot.'

'Well, in that case, thank you,' she replies, disarmingly pleased by the response. Leaning forward, propping her head on her hands, she examines the painting for a minute more, as the old man, unfrozen by a word from Hannah's father, eases himself stiffly from the stool and, rubbing the sloppy flesh of his chest and ribs, pads off towards the toilet. 'It's not the worst I've done,' Sophie decides and she wonders if her husband will like it, because he really didn't like the last one – 'Too lardy, he said.' But her husband does seem to like it, very much. He's waiting in the Mercedes when we leave, and he takes the picture from her and rests it on the dashboard to give it his immediate attention. Sophie's fingers are messing up his hair at the back while he's talking, then they kiss like teenagers.

We're scanning the menus, at a restaurant chosen by Hannah's father. 'So you're a policeman,' he remarks, after checking the finger where the wedding ring should be. His statement of interest has almost nothing behind it and after a couple of minutes he's heard as much as he wants to hear about the career of his daughter's unsuitable boyfriend. 'I couldn't do it,' he concludes, and it doesn't sound like a criticism of himself. He muses over the wine list as if it's a page of Shakespeare, though in fact it's a very inadequate list, he decides. He orders for all of us, pronouncing the chosen wine with such a flourish that the waitress has to ask him to repeat it. In years to come, he informs us, there'll be as many scientists and computer technicians in our police stations as regular policemen. He read an article a month or two ago, about the forensic use of DNA science and how unsolved cases from decades back will be solved in the future. 'So the man you're after, he might think he's safe now, but one day, eh? A little scrap of something, just a couple of cells, and the biochemists will have him.'

Hannah, who has been very quiet so far, asks him about today's group. 'Some good ones' he says, 'and some not so good.'

The proposition that Sophie Fazakerly seems to be very talented is received with a shrug of a single eyebrow, as if he's deciding not to argue with someone who has declared a preference for cod over caviar. He applies himself to the spreading of his pâté, before stating that Hannah has talent, investing the word with a portentousness that distinguishes his employment of the word from common usage, and Hannah, taking the comment as a rebuke for what her father takes to be her lack of ambition, demands that the subject be changed. He touches her fingers and obliges her by recounting a conversation he had with Conrad last week, a proliferating anecdote that would mean nothing without Hannah's interruptions to give some background to each member of the cast, and means very little anyway.

Where other people make do with sentences, Philip Rowe cannot use anything less than a paragraph, and by the second bottle his paragraphs have become the length of pages. He talks about books he's read recently and not so recently, records he's bought and would recommend or not recommend, exhibitions he's seen, exhibitions he's planning to see. Only when he pauses to eat is there an opportunity to step in, and any intervention is likely to set him off on another monologue. Hannah mentions the client whose Polish au pair shut the kitten in the washing machine: he gives us five minutes on the Czech au pair who drove her employers' car through the window of a supermarket. She drops a spoon on the floor: he imparts his views on good cutlery design. A chair wobbles: cue a speech on the abject standards of British furniture manufacture. The subject does not exist on which Philip Rowe does not have an opinion – the management of the English countryside, town planning, civic architecture, the decline of standards in English schools, penal reform, road safety, trains, French trains, French film, French cuisine, French art – and he's more certain of his ideas on everything than most people are of anything. It's evident from her smile that Hannah has heard most of this stuff before. She knows too that his solos go on too long, but she's enjoying them nonetheless, the way you might enjoy the

ramblings of your favourite actor on a chat show, and the occasional signs of awkwardness from her – turning her glass in her
hands, a quick look across the table – betray not an impatience
with her father's ceaseless prattle, but an awareness that only two
people at the table are taking pleasure in his performance. We've
been in the restaurant for the best part of three hours when he
finally allows himself a rest, having accounted for two and half
hours of the evening himself. 'Don't mind, do you?' he asks, taking
an expensive cigar from his jacket. The unwrapping, the clipping
and the lighting of the cigar are performed with pedantic precision. He lets out a long breath, and Hannah looks at him as if
nobody else could possibly exhale smoke with such aplomb.

Back at her flat, the first thing Hannah says is: 'You didn't like
him, did you?' She does not react well to the proposition that the
reverse is equally true, if not more so. 'Not true. That's just his
manner,' she says. 'He loves an audience. He's always been a good
talker.' Turning off the light in the living room, she says: 'So don't
come along next time.' She closes the bathroom door behind her
firmly, on being told that this is an excellent idea, and as soon
as she comes out the argument blossoms. Within a minute she's
asking the room, but not with reference to her father: 'Why are
men so possessive? Why do they have to feel they own everything?' A minute later, and Henry – the man who owned and
wanted nothing – has made an appearance, which soon leads to
the revelation of the truth about the vagrant paragon: that he
behaved like a pig with Gemma, that he smacked her about from
time to time, that he was a lousy son and that, all in all, he was
not a person from whom anyone could profitably take lessons in
self-conduct. Standing in the doorway of the bedroom, with a
towel slung over a shoulder, Hannah listens, without interrupt-
ing, to the charges against Henry. 'Thank you for telling me,' she
says. She stands in the doorway for a few moments longer, her
eyes pensively downturned; she seems to be reappraising a judgement of character, but it's not certain that it's her affection for
the dead man that is being reappraised.

None of the facts makes much difference to Hannah's story of Henry. Some people get on with their parents and some don't. This is not news. Who knows what the old lady is missing out? Who knows what she may have done to make Henry the boy she says he was? To Hannah the essential shape of Henry's life could not be more clearly visible: it's a falling arc, curving downwards from the death of Katie Ellis, the disaster from which he never recovered. With Gemma, perhaps, he found some respite, but – for whatever reason – that relationship didn't work out, and then his life began quickly to unravel. His search for the Ellis family and his miserable attempt to return to Gemma are evidence of his ceaseless torment. He was never free of the memory of Katie's death, or so she concludes from Henry's distaste for society and his compulsive walking. In erasing his true name he was eradicating the name under which he committed the crime for which he could never absolve himself, and an unavoidable inference is to be made from the choice of the name Henry Ellis – and it's not that he just fancied a change from Baldwin or Wilson, and Ellis was the first name that came to mind on one particular day. Not once, in all their walks together, did Henry so much as hint that his life had been blighted by this terrible accident, and even this is proof of his suffering, of a wound too deep to be cured, a secret too painful to be spoken.

It's an offence to suggest that the life of Ivor Clifford might be less than heroic, that it's the story of a boorish young man who inadvertently caused a child's death and subsequently left his home town for an aimless new life in the capital, where a weakness for booze and an intractable fecklessness led to the breakdown of the only relationship he seems ever to have been able to sustain. Never securely on the right road to begin with, he later swerved irrecoverably off track, becoming a common-or-garden vagrant whose anchorless existence might or might not have been punctuated by one or two interludes of remorse, and nostalgia for his days with the girlfriend he abandoned. In the end, through alcohol or illness or both, there was not a great deal happening inside the head, and his past was available to him only on a random-access basis. On the other hand, years in the open air had given him a picturesque exterior, and the progressive disconnection and deterioration of his grey matter had created a haphazard manner of speech and thought, which some people found pleasing, or even profound.

Over the next morning's breakfast the diagnosis of Henry is resumed. 'You didn't know him,' Hannah retorts. 'There was nothing haphazard in the way he thought.'

'Let's just agree that we join the dots in different ways. But whichever way we join them, there's more blank space than anything else.'

'Sod that. I knew him, OK?' she says, slamming her palm on the table. 'I knew him and you didn't. He was not some brain-damaged piss-head.'

'Maybe not.'

'There's no "maybe" about it.'

'I don't agree.'

'There was something about him.'

'I'm sure there was.'

'I don't care if he was a nasty kid. It's irrelevant. I knew him thirty years later. Forty. People change.'

'They do.'

'And if you don't want a fork in the eye you'll stop patronising me,' she says, and she echoes 'They do', spicing the mimicked superiority with her own acerbity. We regard each other in a high-pressure silence, then she adds: 'I'm hearing something else as well.'

'And what might that be?'

'Clank, clank, clank. The chains are dragging.'

The reproach is made again, several times, in the weeks that follow. 'No clanking in my house, thank you,' she says one evening, administering a light kick to the shins, as if the perceived preoccupation were no worse than extremely ill-mannered. Another time she sings: 'Hello? Hello, can you hear me above the din? The chains are jangling,' and she clicks her fingers across the table, with a frown that says this may be the last chance before her patience expires. After that, with each repetition of the accusation it seems likely that a final crisis will crystallise some day soon. 'Look. I'm sorry your marriage went wrong, but it's not my fault. I didn't make it go wrong. It was wrong before. Don't carry on as if I'm to blame,' she says through tears, in a voice in which anger and pleading are mingled. 'I can't bear much more of this. I don't owe you anything. You made your own choice,' she says, also through tears, but anger by now is uppermost. 'I'm not going to waste my time with someone who's in mourning for himself,' she cries, and she's entirely in the right.

There have been hours, in the bachelor flat, of gazing at a dead television screen. Newspapers have been read and every word instantly forgotten. There have been moments – sitting at traffic lights, walking through town – where suddenly, as if on awakening, the location has become unrecognisable. Calls have been made to Alice at unreasonable hours, despite the certainty of achieving nothing. 'You're sorry for what? For ringing in the middle of the night?' Alice moans. She must be leaning on the bedside table, because the little ball on the end of the chain of the lamp can be heard ticking against the metal stem. 'It's four o'clock, John. This is ridiculous. I have nothing to say to you.' A skirt of brilliant grey cloud is spread around the moon and the walls of the bedroom are the white-blue of old milk. Frost is thickening on the grass. 'This is stupid and pointless,' says Alice. 'We'll see you on Saturday.' The phone dies, and the drone of the boiler in the flat upstairs is the only sound. The smell of gloss paint has still not faded from the room. Headlights are swivelling on a bend near the top of a hill on the far side of the estuary, miles away. In every life there are moments – not many – of such acuteness that it's known, as the moment is happening, that every detail of it will remain in the memory for ever, and this is one such moment. Alice is never going to weaken, that's certain.

Then, one Saturday afternoon, an hour or so after a visit that had ended with Luke in the garden, thrashing the grass with a length of washing line, and Alice going out to him, not hurrying, so that it would be understood that this sort of thing was now a regular aspect of her life, there's Michael Trethowen coming across the road and turning on to a collision course. The perfect image of the distracted boffin, he's wearing a light blue zippered jacket and too-tight trousers of a clashingly different light blue, and is frowning spectacularly at the pavement in an agony of thought, his eyes flicking this way and that, as though reading a gigantic blueprint beneath his feet. When he notices who's obstructing his path, a blush of instant fever stains his face. 'Oh,' he says. He has the look of a man who's been caught out, and this triggers a reaction, an overreaction that perhaps would not have happened had there not been, a day or two before, another row about Josh, who, emerging from a shop on the seafront, had called out, 'How's it going?', and had seemed, from his smothered grin, to know what was going on with Hannah. ('You're obsessed with him,' she said. 'What does it matter if I've fucked him? What does it matter if I like him still? You're not missing out on something because I like him.') So for a fraction of a second Michael Trethowen looks embarrassed and suddenly an explanation falls into place: the oddball prankster who had treated Tom Gaskin to his crazy knifeman routine, the self-proclaimed abominator of errant husbands, still smarting after his mistreatment at the hands of the police, nursing a grudge against all involved, somehow – snooping, perhaps – finds out about Hannah and, with a word to the betrayed and lovely Mrs Donohue, secures his revenge. 'Hi,' he says, as if he's being choked, and the next moment he is.

'It was you, wasn't it, you little bastard?'

'What?' he shrieks. The sound he makes is like a dog that's had its tail stepped on.

'You know.'

'What? It was me what? What was me?' His eyes are huge but he is not making any attempt to look away. It's not the fear of having been found out that's in his face: it's the terror of having been cornered by a lunatic.

'You know.'

'The old man?' he shouts, twisting free of the slackened grip. 'It wasn't me. You know it wasn't me. What are you talking about?' His lower lip is vibrating as if it has a current running through it. On the opposite side of the road a woman has appeared, pushing a buggy, and Michael ducks his head towards the wall, hiding his distress from her. 'It wasn't me. You know it wasn't me.'

'We don't know any such thing.'

'Yes, you do. I got a grilling from your boss. Ask him. He knows it wasn't me.' We're standing face to face, but only one of us, now, is trying to read the other. 'Why did you do that?' he whines, stroking the tendons of his neck.

'Do you miss me?'

'What?' He winces as though trying to make sense of something in a foreign language. 'Do I miss you? What are you talking about?'

'Beal's. You still go?'

'Yes.'

'I've cut him out.'

'I noticed.'

'Do you want to know why?'

'Not particularly,' he replies, locating a tenderness below of the angle of his jaw. 'Can I go now?'

'Sure. On your way.'

'Thank you,' he says, and he creeps away, working at his neck non-stop. At a safe distance he turns round, to say something that cannot be heard, but appears to be a threat.

When the encounter is reported to Alice, a small addition – a provocative glance from Michael, a questionable half-smile – is made to the facts, by way of partial mitigation. To Alice, the supposed taunt is of no relevance whatever. 'He gave you a look, so you hit him?' she responds, seeing her husband in a light that's

305

even more ghastly than the light that adultery alone had cast on to him.

'Not hit, exactly. Lightly throttled.'

'It's not funny, John. You get it into your head that Michael Trethowen has dropped you in it, so you try to strangle him.'

'Not strangle. Shake him about a bit.'

'You pin him to a wall, by the throat, in public, with a witness on hand for good measure.' Seated on the opposite side of the table, she's talking as if she were a lawyer, getting the facts straight on a hopeless case. The way she holds her mug, with her fingers meshed round it, making a shape like a prow with her arms, says everything

'Always a witness, isn't there? The spy in the sky.'

'It's not funny.'

'Who's laughing?'

'Ridiculous is what it is.'

'I tend to agree.'

Then Luke comes in, carrying a yellow plastic tractor that needs a new battery. Unsure which parent to go to, he hesitates before offering the toy to his father. Alice fetches the small screwdriver from the drawer and places it on the table. Attending to the operation, Luke does not say a word, but once or twice he glances up and there's a wariness in his eyes, as if he's looking at someone who might at any moment do something really stupid. Alice watches too, with an unwavering gaze that seems to be saying: 'Do you see what you've thrown away?' When it's fixed, Luke takes the tractor and stands there for a few seconds, holding it, looking down at the floor. 'Thanks,' he says, that's all. He closes the door behind him, which he never used to do.

We both look towards the door and neither of us speaks for a while. In every corner of the room there are things that belonged to us, objects that had become transparent over the years, but now seem to be reawakened, to be asserting themselves and their stories: the candlestick bought from the market stall in Normandy, on that amazingly hot day, when the boys were jumping into the river from the bridge; the tiny iron owl, found in the meadow at Zennor; the jade-green bowl that was sold to us from the back of an estate car, by the young Turkish man with the streak of pure silver hair; the little bear from Bern, sent to us by the Swiss girl we met on the mackerel-fishing boat. Everything in the room is meaningful and by the smallest distance estranged, like a museum of replicas.

'Will anything come of it?' asks Alice. 'Of your thumping Michael.'

'He's taking advice. That's what he's told Whittam. I doubt it, though. I hardly touched him.'

'But not a good career move.'

'Not very smart, no.'

Alice turns to check the clock. It's nearly four o'clock, the time that Kim Vanes and Terry will be arriving to take Luke swimming. 'I'd better get his stuff together,' she says.

'One last thing. Who was it? Who told you? If it wasn't Michael –'

'Of course it wasn't Michael.'

'Who then? Tell me. It's in the public interest. If you want to stop me beating up anyone whose manner doesn't please me.'

She lets out a sigh that eases all the air from her lungs. 'If you must know, it was a woman called Mary, a friend of Katharine Giles. You've met her a couple of times. She lives near a house where your friend was working. She saw you and waved, but you didn't notice. You said you were somewhere else. I can't remember,' she says, with a slack backward swat of her hand. 'We have to get ready,' she says as she pushes her chair back.

'You're never going to forgive me, are you?'

This delays her for a minute. Staying in her seat, she peers into her empty mug, as if trying to make out if there's water at the bottom of a well shaft. 'No,' she says at last. 'I don't know. Maybe I will, one day. But it's not forgiveness you want, is it?' she says.

'Isn't it?'

'No. It's me you want. Preferably me five or six years ago, I think. Failing that, me now. And the problem with that', she goes on, finger raised to forestall a response, 'is that I don't think I can love you again. Not now. I hope I'm wrong. I want to be wrong. But I can't force myself back into loving you. I'm sorry. I can't do it,' she says, with an intent gaze of warmthless pity.

A week later, at two o'clock on a Sunday morning, Clare Vigo, a nineteen-year-old shop assistant, is walking home from a party. It's not far to her flat, but it's a cold night and she wants to get home as quickly as possible, so she takes a short cut across the playing fields. Hurrying across the football pitches, all she can hear is the sound of her own breathing, then there's a hand over her mouth and a knife is in front of her. 'One sound and I'll cut you,' he says, in a tough London accent that doesn't sound real. His mouth is an inch from her ear. 'I ain't gonna hurt you, not if you're quiet,' he says. 'But you yell and I'll cut you. You look round and I'll cut you. You run and I'll cut you. Got that?' The hand peels off her mouth, and he tells her to take off her shoes and walk towards the pavilion on the far side of the field. After about ten yards he tells her to stop. 'Take the coat off,' he says. He makes her drop the coat and stand still for a minute, barefoot in the cold mud. When she tries to talk to him, he tells her to shut up. 'I'm not gonna hurt you,' he says, but he instructs her to take off her top and her jeans. 'Move,' he says. She walks another ten yards before he orders her to stop and strip completely. In a whisper she pleads with him. 'Shut it and move,' he says, touching the point of the knife to her shoulder. She starts walking again, and he seems to wait a moment before following. His shadow, which had been visible very faintly on the grass beside her, can't be seen now, and she can't hear his breathing either. 'Nice arse,' he says, forgetting to do the accent, and in that instant a match or lighter is struck on the edge of the field, beyond the pavilion, and Clare decides that this is her one chance to get away. She runs at the light and shouts as loudly as she can, which is not as loudly as she wants, because her throat is tight with fear, but it's enough to panic him into sprinting back to the road. The flame goes out and nobody comes to help her, but she keeps running until she's at the pavilion, where she risks a glance to check he's not following, and he's not. She can't see him anywhere. Terrified that he's watching in the darkness, waiting for her to fetch her clothes, Clare hides by the side of the building. For a quarter of an hour she hides, until she becomes so cold that she has no choice but to go out there. He's gone.

Though she never saw him and he barely spoke, Clare has a good idea who the attacker was. Around the wrist of the hand that was holding the knife there was a thin copper band, and at the party that night she'd been talking to a boy who had a copper band around his right wrist. Or rather, the boy had been talking to her. She'd spent most of the time trying to get away from him, because this lad seemed to think he was God's gift to women and he was a boring little prat as well, and he'd taken something that made his eyes look a bit mad. And the voice of the person who attacked her, when he dropped the phoney accent, sounded very much like the voice of the annoying bighead. Clare doesn't know his name, but she can describe his face and build, and – even more clearly – what he was wearing: black jeans, boots with big heels, and a black shirt with electric-blue spirals on the collar and breast pocket. Eight people who had been at the party give us the same name when supplied with Clare's description of the short, dark-haired boy in the embroidered black shirt. His name is Daniel Porton and three witnesses saw him leaving the house at around the same time as Clare: one has him leaving before her, the other two after. The hosts, moreover, when they were tidying up the flat in the morning, found that a knife had gone missing from the kitchen, a narrow-bladed six-inch knife that fits Clare's memory of the weapon that had been held to her face.

Strolling in for his interview, Daniel Porton surveys the room as though we're estate agents showing him round an apartment which, to be perfectly honest, is nowhere near as good as he'd been led to expect by the information sheet. He's quite a good-looking lad, if a few inches shy of optimum height, and he's kitted himself out in a well-pressed dark grey suit and pristine white shirt, accessorised with a turquoise silk tie that has a knot the size of a paperweight.

The tie is knotted slackly, but before the talking starts he keeps fiddling with it, as if it's too tight. As he raises his hand to the knot, his shirt-cuff slips down, exposing a thin copper band.

'So, Daniel, tell us about the party.'

He's sitting sideways to us, with his left arm lying on the table and his legs crossed, in the casual posture of a man chatting to new acquaintances in a bar. 'What do you want to know?' he asks, raising his arm from the elbow and turning a hand.

'What time did you leave? Let's start with that.'

'Half-one or thereabouts.'

'A lot of people said you were still there at two.'

'Like I said, half-one or thereabouts.'

'And where did you go?'

'Home. Where else are you going to go?'

'You went straight home?'

'That's right.'

'Walking?'

'I'd had a few. Not going to drive, am I? Responsible citizen.'

'Can you tell us the route you took?'

With a finger he traces the streets on the table top, reciting the street names like the answer to a too-easy quiz question.

'You talked to Clare Vigo at the party, didn't you?'

'Can't remember. I talked to a lot of girls. That's the point of a party, isn't it?'

'You tried to pick her up?'

'Like I said, I can't remember. Might have done.'

We show him our picture and he can't prevent his face from giving him away: the mouth is compressed and the brow furrowed in an imitation of conscientious scrutiny, but the eyes immediately quiver in recognition. 'Ring any bells?'

310

'Sort of familiar,' he concedes. 'Can't say for sure. The place was packed, you know? A lot of faces.'

'She says you did.'

'OK. If she says so.'

'Pretty girl, isn't she?'

'Seen worse. Seen better.'

'We've been told you spent a long time talking to her.'

'That what she says?'

'It's what a lot of people say.'

'Depends what you mean by long, doesn't it?'

'So you do remember talking to her?'

'No, I don't. I'm saying if I did talk to her it couldn't have been for long, because if it was I would have remembered her, wouldn't I?'

'Clare says she gave you the brush-off and you weren't too happy about it. She says you wouldn't take the hint and she had to tell you to leave her alone, and you were mightily pissed off about it.'

'Well, she's talking bollocks.'

'Other people have backed her up.'

'They're talking bollocks too. Her mates, are they?'

'We have witnesses who heard you calling Clare a stuck-up bitch.'

'No, you don't.'

'We do.'

'You don't, because I never called her that.'

'Two of them. Not friends of Clare. They both heard you clearly. "Stuck-up bitch" is what you said.'

'I might have said it, but it wasn't about this one,' he says, jabbing a finger on Clare's face. 'I know who I meant and it wasn't her. If you want, I'll tell you who. You want a name? I'll give you a name.'

'The man who attacked Clare had a copper bracelet on his right wrist.'

'So?'

'Identical to the one you're wearing.'

He makes a big show of inspecting the bracelet and being perplexed by the notion that there may be anything remarkable about it. 'See them all the time,' he says. 'Go out in the street and it'll take you five minutes to find one.'

'You left the party when Clare Vigo left. At the same time. To the minute.'

'Did I?'

'Yes, you did.'

'People were leaving all the time.'

'At two in the morning, people were leaving "all the time"? I don't think so.'

'You weren't there.'

'You followed her, didn't you?'

'Didn't even see her.'

'You followed her across the playing fields and you attacked her there.'

'Wasn't me,' he says, with a regretful shake of the head.

'A knife went missing from the flat where the party was.'

'Wow.'

'The same knife was used on Clare Vigo. The man who attacked her was at the party. He followed her.'

'Wasn't me. I told you.'

'He sounded like you.'

'Half the people round here sound like me.'

'It doesn't look good, does it, Daniel? We know you'd been pestering the victim –'

'I wasn't pestering her.'

'You leave the same time as the victim. The weapon goes missing from where you were.'

'Me and a hundred other people.'

'We have a motive.'

'You do. I don't.'

'And the guy was a short-arsed little fucker as well.'

For a few seconds, while he tries to come up with a reply,

312

Daniel gives us a glare of impotent resentment. 'Wasn't me,' he repeats.

'Stand up, please.'

'What?'

'You heard. Stand up.'

'What for?'

'Just stand up.'

Shaking his head at the pettiness of it, he rises from his seat. He straightens his collar and tugs at the cuffs of his jacket, as though preparing to have his picture taken.

'Walk to the door, please. Slowly. Now lift your right hand to shoulder height. Thank you. Hold it there. That'll do. Thank you. You can sit down.' This charade means nothing, but we exchange looks that are intended to let him know that in the mere act of walking five steps and raising his arm he has told us everything we need to know. We tell him to wait, then we leave the room and we go for a coffee. When we return, the photograph of Clare Vigo is no longer square to the sides of the table. We run through it all again: his leaving the party at the same time as Clare Vigo yet not seeing her; the route he took home; what was said at the party. This time round, we want the name of the stuck-up bitch.

'Vanessa Flitcroft,' he answers right away.

'She was there, was she?'

'She was.'

'We'll check it out.'

'Be my guest,' he says, then little smirk appears, and in that instant the hand comes up and cracks him on the cheek, sending him to the floor. Before he can get up he gets hit again. 'You'll regret that, you cunt,' he says, dabbing at his lip.

31

For several months things went Daniel Porton's way. On advice that a prosecution would be unlikely to succeed, the case against him was dropped and his complaint against the officer who punched him, in combination with the complaint from Michael Trethowen, contributed greatly to that officer's departure from the force. Within the year, however, Daniel himself was obliged to reassess his career options, having been released by the car dealership at which he worked, after a month in which three different women, after a test drive with young Mr Porton, reported to his manager that his conduct had fallen some way short of professional standards. With the first, Daniel allegedly proposed that they could make the exercise more enjoyable by driving out to a country pub for a drink, and became so persistent when his proposal was rejected that the woman threatened to get out of the car as they waited for the traffic to slacken on a busy roundabout. The second accused him of making similar advances and, upon being rebuffed, criticising her driving at every opportunity. The last one protested that Mr Porton, leaning over to demonstrate, needlessly, how to operate a switch, had let his hand slip on to her thigh and had done it again a few moments later, while showing her how to adjust the angle of the steering wheel. He'd also taken the opportunity to post his business card

– on which he'd written his home number – into the back pocket of her jeans as she stepped out of the car. Daniel, true to form, denied all charges (the woman had asked for his number; the drink wasn't his idea), but decided to call it quits when his manager informed him that his three accusers were all willing to come to the showroom, together, to confront him in person. Soon afterwards, one Friday night near closing time, he made the mistake of complimenting a girl, repeatedly, on the shapeliness of her rear end, a remark to which she took exception, as did her boyfriend, whose presence Daniel had unaccountably overlooked in the midst of the juiced-up throng, an oversight expeditiously corrected by the application, with no little force, of the boyfriend's fist to Daniel's nose. This, you could say, went some way to balancing the books. The broken nose seemed to teach him a lesson: a month or two after it had mended and the bruising faded away, he'd found work with a van-hire company, whose receptionist he ended up marrying. They both work there still.

The life of Michael Trethowen has described a somewhat steeper upward curve – or at least his life as technician and entrepreneur has, which perhaps in the case of Michael comes to the same thing. Operating out of a tiny factory in an industrial estate on the oustkirts of town, Michael and his employees – six equally devout acolytes of the cult of sonic purity – now hand-manufacture a small range of equipment for the uncompromising audiophile, the sort of person who needs to hear the drummer's breathing and the squeak of the guitarist's shoes. Michael's masterpiece, an amplification system that won an award at some prestigious German hi-fi fair last year, could be yours for only a little more than the price of an upmarket saloon car. Occasionally we pass each other in the street, and we acknowledge each other, but without ever stopping. He sometimes appears halfway maddened by the problems of higher electronics, but he has never, to give him his due, had the look of a man who's pleased by the downfall of an adversary: he seems simply content, rather, that things have settled down now and our lives can proceed on their separate tracks. The house in which he lived with his grandparents is now occupied by Michael alone. (Perhaps always alone: he's never been seen with anyone other than his sextet of fellow geeks.) His grandfather died five years ago, in his sleep, of heart failure. Two weeks later, as Michael related to Alice, he took his grandmother's breakfast up to her on a tray and found her lying in bed, with her eyes closed, so peacefully that it was not until he opened the curtains that he realised something was wrong. From the street, it appears that nothing much in the house has changed: the plum-coloured damask curtains still hang in the living room, with the rose-patterned wallpaper behind them, and the bowl of frosted white and blue glass in the centre of the ceiling; upstairs, the dressing table with the big oval mirror has not been moved.

Peggy Thurlow – Granny Thistle – died around the same time as the Trethowens. Her shop was taken over by an Indian couple, who promptly boosted the video-rental side of the business, after eradicating Peggy's adult selection. She's buried alongside her husband, two rows away from Tom Gaskin, who died last year while playing bowls, a sport he'd taken up only a couple of years previously, and for which he'd discovered a surprising aptitude. On a bench at the bowling club there's a small brass plaque with his name on it. From Tom's grave you could easily lob a ball on to the overgrown hummock that covers the remains of Ivor Clifford. The file on the murder of Ivor Clifford is still open; in the last decade next to nothing has been added to it.

Who else? Oliver Bywater eventually recovered from his accident and is just a fraction short of one hundred per cent: one eyelid has a tendency to droop, but otherwise he's fine. His parents diligently continue to attend the church, where the Reverend Beal has been succeeded by the Reverend Sawney, a younger and less smooth and rather hapless-looking man, who scurries rather than walks, and appears to be perpetually worried by something of pressing urgency and intractable difficulty. He

316

does not have quite the presence of Beal, Alice admits, and his voice lacks power, but he's an intelligent man, she says, and very popular.

The Kemps are still together too. On Saturday mornings, if the weather permits, Benjamin can be seen at work in the garden, pushing the lawnmower with all the *joie de vivre* of a man painting a white line down the middle of a fifty-mile straight road. His wife does the shopping one day at a time. Wherever she goes she lingers for a chat, even if she was in the same shop the day before. 'Mustn't tarry,' she has a habit of saying before she leaves, as if her chores are never-ending. Her daughter came to visit once, bringing a squad of children with her. Every afternoon for a fortnight Christine Kemp would march along the promenade at the centre of a line of grandchildren, all hand in hand, filling the whole width of the pavement, with Benjamin following, arm in arm with his daughter, in earnest conversation.

And every evening in summer, having finished his day at *SeaShed*, Josh McKee is on the beach or out on his windsurfer. He's maybe a stone heavier than he was when Hannah drew him, and he's cultivated a lush full-face beard that might be intended to put the girls – or any girls with some sense of history, anyway – in mind of Jim Morrison. When *SeaShed* closes for the off-season he reverts to being a barman, at a different place each winter. At any time of the year, in any weather, Miss Ryle, the creator of the *Heidi* house, might be observed on a Sunday morning, striding out of town and into the hills, usually alone but sometimes in the company of other doughty women on the downslope of middle age, and not far from the house of Miss Ryle you can still see an enamel advertisement for Old Spice on a windowsill. But Miss Leith, of the lurid make-up and controversial shoes, is no longer with us. Diagnosed with an unstoppably virulent cancer, she sat down in front of the TV one night and knocked back a bottle of pills and a half-bottle of whisky. She was found the next morning: her employers, an accountancy firm, sent someone to the house because she was not answering the phone and had not once, in more than thirty years at the office, failed to be at her desk by 8.30 a.m.

It was a Wednesday when Miss Leith died. The next week Ronnie Houghton received a small packet bearing a Spanish post-mark, and this was when George Whittam's steady ascent towards the highest echelons of the constabulary hit a patch of turbulence. The sender of the packet was Keith Guillory, who – along with Gary Quinton – had fallen off the radar for a while, and inside it was a cassette, on which Ronnie heard two voices, talking on the phone: one was the voice of Guillory himself and the other was a man named Geoff, who appeared to be remarkably well informed as to the current state of police investigations into the business activities of Quinton and his associates, and furthermore appeared to have received a quantity of cash in return for keeping Mr Guillory's chief associate apprised of the situation. And the situation was that George Whittam had been talking to someone called Kelvin Naismith, a gormless goon with a heroin habit, an epic roster of convictions and a brace of ongoing enquiries hanging over him, and had put pressure on him to testify that Quinton, through Guillory, had approached him to nobble Peter Jellico, who had been helping himself to some of Quinton's merchandise. A statement had been written for this sap, which would implicate Quinton and Guillory in a few other unsavoury incidents into the bargain, and in return for his co-operation the enquiries into his recent misdemeanours might be permitted to fade away, whereas a refusal to co-operate would hasten his prosecution, not just for those offences but for a selection of others, for all of which – Whittam assured him – the police had evidence that would satisfy any jury. From the tape a couple of things seemed clear: that Guillory had never had any dealings with this Naismith character; and that Gary Quinton hadn't guessed we'd been watching him at the harbour – he'd known we were watching him, because Geoff Salter had told him.

Presented with this material, Ronnie Houghton found himself in a dilemma. A chewy story had landed in his lap: should he grab what might be a chance to make a name for himself, or should he play safe, do nothing, and remain the policemen's friend? After a couple of days of dithering, Ronnie chickened out and sent the tape to a national paper, giving his name and CV (for future reference, should an opening arise) and some background to the tape, but asking that his anonymity be respected in this instance – a superfluous precaution, because Roland Ackerman, having been instructed by Guillory as soon as Guillory had heard that charges were imminent, had brought a copy of the tape into the station, and let it be known that the conversation between his client and Sergeant Salter was now known to Ronnie Houghton, who, when the story appeared in one of the London papers (two paragraphs on page five; slightly less space than a report on skulduggery among Yorkshire pigeon racers), was of course believed to be the source, even though the paper that ran the story was not the one that Ronnie had contacted and the journalist who wrote the story insisted that he had come upon the information by another route. So Ronnie was *persona non grata* and a few months later moved on, to edit an in-house magazine for some insurance company.

Roland Ackerman lost no time in offering his services to Kelvin Naismith, who of course went into reverse gear, claiming that not a word of the statement was true, that not a word of it was his and that he'd been threatened by several officers, among them George Whittam, who had boasted of convictions that had been secured on nothing more than the fabrications of his team. 'There's evidence and then there's evidence,' George supposedly had told him, lifting a detached hair from Naismith's shoulder. 'And this', said Ackerman, placing another cassette on George's desk, 'is what I would call evidence.'

The tapes were more than enough to finish Geoff Salter. Nowadays he works for a security firm in the Gloucester area and lives without Muriel, who had always been led to believe that Geoff's regular windfalls of cash, which had paid for fine wines and upmarket holidays and the most expensive home entertainment system on the street, were attributable to her incorrigible husband's good fortune in the betting shop. With the withdrawal of Naismith (now serving time for GBH) and the refusal of all other candidates to say anything that would incriminate Guillory and Quinton, the horrible duo were left to pursue their enterprises in Spain unhindered, and nobody has ever done time for the savaging of Peter Jellico, though everyone knows that if you want to find the man who gave the order all you have to do is hop on a flight to Malaga, hire a car, and an hour later you'll be there.

As for George Whittam, the allegations against him never amounted to anything, being based on the word of one drug-addled serial offender, but the smoke that came off them stained his reputation slightly and neither did his having been the boss of Geoff Salter do his standing much good. So for a while his career was in a holding pattern, but was soon on the rise again, albeit at a slightly lower velocity than the career of Ian Mowbray, who went on, after his flash of inspiration in the Henry/Ivor case, to distinguish himself in a couple of other investigations, demonstrating a keen eye for the crucial detail (the dog's hair found on the floor of the victim's car; the toothprint taken off an apple core discarded in a park), and to prove himself as brilliant an interviewer as George, but in one essential respect his opposite: whereas George is the master of silence, Ian prefers to talk and talk and talk, until the suspect, just for the relief of hearing a different voice, is provoked into talking as well. Not long after his first promotion he married Mary, whose anxiety about her husband's profession has steadily abated in tandem with his rise through the ranks, as more and more of his time is spent in the safety of his office, rather than confronting the lowlifes on the street. They have twin daughters, Rachel and Rosie, who attend a nursery at which Rachelle, still Mary's closest friend, is the manager.

Margaret Whittam's business is booming: for a well-equipped and well-made kitchen, featuring handcrafted cabinets and

Continental appliances of restaurant quality, Margaret's company is unquestionably the first place to go locally. She runs a very nice showroom, a double-fronted shop with big bay windows, just off the seafront. When it opened, the paper ran half a page on it, with a photo of the proprietor standing beside a gleaming steel fridge the size of a phone box. 'Rebecca's embarrassed by her mother's success, that's why she left town,' George joked, as Margaret, arching an eyebrow at him, came in from the garden. Nearly eighteen months had passed since the previous evening at the Whittams' and it was news that Rebecca had gone. She was in Bristol now, training to be an acupuncturist, and living with someone she'd met on the beach last summer. 'Another acupuncturist,' George explained, sipping his Scotch and looking straight ahead, towards the lantern that had been set up in the middle of the lawn. 'Her name's Rhona. Seems very nice, from what you can tell on the phone,' he went on, and then there was a pause, to absorb what this meant, and a sustained sidelong look to convey that the situation might not have been easy to accept, but was accepted now. Ruefully, as if thinking of an occasion when he had been outmanoeuvred in a manner that demanded admiration, he gazed at the ice in his glass. 'Makes sense, though,' he said. 'If I was a girl, I'd go for girls. I mean, wouldn't you? Men are a fucking catastrophe.' This was a sentiment with which Margaret, had she been involved in this exchange, would no doubt have concurred. Her smile when she opened the door, and the brief hesitation before she spoke, seemed to say that the invitation had not been her idea, and whenever, in the course of that evening, we found ourselves in close proximity, there were unambiguous signs – the evasive eyes, a stiffening of the neck, the fiddling with the earrings – that she was struggling to disguise her offence at the treachery committed against Alice. The strength of her disapproval may have dwindled over the years, but it is still perceptible and will never become extinct. Once a year, between Christmas and New Year, an invitation arrives, for the gathering of George's team, past and present, and Margaret will always enquire, with the air of at last getting round to asking the question she's been waiting to ask all evening: 'And how's Alice?'

A year after we fell out, maybe a little less, a van pulled up alongside at the traffic lights and it was Hannah at the wheel. Seeing the window being wound down, she wound down her window too. She looked at the driving school sign on the roof and smiled slightly at it, with an amusement that appeared to be without ill will. 'You OK?' she asked.

'I'm OK. And you?'

'I'm good,' she replied. Her right arm was bandaged between wrist and elbow. 'Scalded myself,' she explained. 'Handle came off the saucepan.'

'Looks bad.'

'Looks worse than it is. It's fine.'

'Nice to see you again.'

'Is it?'

'Yes. You look well.'

'Thank you. So do you.' Again her eye strayed upwards to the sign on the roof, before the driver behind gave the horn a couple of blasts. 'See you,' she called, and that was that for another year or so, then one afternoon her van was parked outside a house not far from Tom Gaskin's place, with the rear door open, and Hannah emerged from the garden. We talked for a while on the pavement. Her fingers were stained a storm-cloud grey-blue, the colour the client had selected for the woodwork of the dining room and hallway; he and his wife had taken weeks to decide on the paint, but now he was having second thoughts. 'He's saying it's not the colour I showed him when we talked about it, but it is. It's the same batch,' said Hannah, glaring at her hands. 'Time for coffee?' she asked. We sat on the front step of the house, drinking coffee from her flask. We talked about Conrad, and Sophie, and a picture that Hannah had sold for as much as she'd normally earn in two weeks; her father was not mentioned and neither was Alice, but a moment came when it felt as though the past – our past – was about to present itself for discussion, and at that point she stood up. We parted without touching, but we've come across each other in town many times since and sometimes we trade a kiss on the cheek. Our conversations never last long, but we say what we want to say and there's barely any undercurrent to the words. There's no tension and no regret – in fact, there's almost no feeling at all. It's as if the affair with Hannah and the separation from Alice happened at different times, in different places.

At the moment Alice is in Morocco with the new man, Doctor Simon Keston, an anaesthetist at the hospital. They met last year through a fund-raising fun run for orphanages in Romania, which Alice organised. That's what she does nowadays, with Katharine Giles: if you want to raise a lot of money for your good cause, you get in touch with Alice and Katharine and they take care of everything. They liaise with local authorities, get the T-shirts printed, hire the facilities, collect the money through their website. Deeply affected by the reports he once heard from a visiting surgeon, Doctor Keston now commits much of his spare time to the welfare of the Romanian kids. He and his wife were on the point of adopting a boy from Bucharest when his wife had a change of heart, about everything, and left him for a neurologist, a conceited high-flyer of whom Doctor Keston, as Luke reports, does an impression that makes Alice weep with laughter.

Luke says what he thinks. He doesn't modify his opinion out of respect for the susceptibilities of his audience. The previous boyfriend was not to his liking: too perky and yet too dull, and too weak. 'Mr I-Don't-Mind-Dear' was what Luke called him. But Doctor Keston, he says, is a thoroughly good thing, and Alice is happy. She always seems happy, but we don't talk about Doctor Keston very often. We rarely talk about anything, now that Luke can take care of himself. The last time we had anything substantial to say to each other would have been when she was selling the house.

It was shortly after she and Luke had moved that Alice met

Doctor Keston. They didn't need so big a place, she decided, and Luke might soon be going to university, so it would be a good idea to liberate some cash. The new house, at the end of a Victorian terrace, had been home to the same couple for more than fifty years and was in need of some major repairs. Alice had every room stripped out and repainted, and walls removed downstairs to lighten the space. It's all very cool and clean and serene now, and you could go through each of the rooms slowly, giving your attention to every object that's on show, and you would find not a single clue to indicate that Alice had been married, not until you came to Luke's bedroom, where, above the synthesiser keyboard, you'd see a photograph of a boy and his parents, all in swimming gear. The boy is leaning on the rail of a wooden terrace, with a dampened dog at his feet; the mother has a hand on her son's shoulder and the father has reached behind the boy to place a hand on the woman's bare hip; the boy is smiling at the camera, the woman is looking at the dog and laughing, and the man is smiling at her; a metallic white sea gleams behind them, backed by a huge outcrop of rock; a skim of sand covers part of the terrace. Since Luke was nine or ten this picture has been in his room, and for a long time it was not possible to look at it without a seizure of nostalgia. Now, though, the nostalgia is no longer a reflex, and usually there's not a trace of it, or nothing much more than a trace. More often there's simply curiosity as to what was going on in that person's brain.

Luke was invited on the Morocco trip – Doctor Keston was from the outset at ease with Luke (unlike 'Mr I-Don't-Mind', who often arrived bearing gifts for the boy, as if lobbing a bone in the direction of the guard dog, as Luke put it) – but decided to stay at home, with the intention of getting down to some intensive work on the songs he's writing with his gang of guitarist schoolmates (the drummer's chair is currently unoccupied, following a row), and thinking, at the time he declined the offer, that it would be nice to have the house to himself and his girlfriend, Caitlin. But in the interim Caitlin has opted to accompany her parents to their holiday apartment in Catalonia and Luke is finding it hard to concentrate on his songs.

We drive around for an hour. Luke is competent in virtually everything he attempts and he would probably pass his driving test tomorrow if he wanted to, but he wants to talk, and we tend to find it easier to talk, or to make a start, when we're staring through a windscreen. He had thought for a while that when he went to university he'd be studying music, but he's not sure he wants to spend three years poring over the work of dead men, and he's come to feel that his playing isn't as good as it would need to be. 'I think it would be a mistake,' he says, as if offering his analysis of some abstract problem. In this clear deliberation, this reasonable self-detachment, Luke as a child is discernible: taking care with his answers, pausing to consider consequences, at an age when other boys were all action. He's come round to thinking that it's a choice between politics or sociology. 'What do you think?' he asks. But this isn't what he wants to talk about.

It's not until we've parked the car and are walking over the High Land that he produces the card that came from Caitlin this morning. On the front there's a picture of a harbour, its ultramarine water almost wholly obscured by fishing boats. Caitlin's message, written in a tight, small and fluid script, begins as though in mid-paragraph, without so much as Luke's name at the top. 'What do you make of this?' he asks. Caitlin writes that she has been watching a small boat out on the sea, very close to the shore. She could see the people on board clearly: a man and woman, both middle-aged but good-looking nonetheless. She could hear their voices, but not what they were saying, and when the breeze carried the little boat away she suddenly felt terribly sad. Wincing at the sea, Luke says: 'Why can't she just come out and say it?' He knows she's leaving him. Last week she wrote about visiting a village that looked so magical from far away, but when they were in the village square, sitting in the shade of a plane tree that was as big as a parachute, the magic of the place started to seep away, as though her being there, looking at it, had spoiled it. She's pretentious, Luke knows that, but she has a brilliance as well, and he loves her. He's liked a few girls before, but Caitlin he's crazy about. We go down the wooden steps on to the beach. 'This is seriously getting me down,' he says, shaking his head at the predicament into which he's allowed himself to fall. He can't imagine he'll ever meet a girl lovelier than Caitlin, and he may be right.

At seven o'clock Natascha finishes teaching at the college, and we'll be picking her up and going out for a meal, the three of us. Alice thinks Natascha is too young and too pretty, says Luke, and she's afraid that the relationship with Natascha – unlike hers with Doctor Keston – will not last long, and there she may well be right, but that's beside the point. (And if she were to be told that her prediction, however well founded it may turn out to be, is thought to be beside the point, she'd take that as confirmation that her ex-husband still has much to learn.) Luke, on the other hand, thinks Natascha is cool, partly because she's youngish and pretty, and half-German, but mainly because she's serious, and he can discuss politics and other things with her. She's also a good thing because she has made his father think, a department in which, we acknowledge, there had previously been a degree of underachievement. We have a couple of hours to spare, so we walk all the way to Straight Point. We're on our way back, walking along the water's edge, when the sound of the small waves brings a memory of Hannah and Henry to mind. The whispering of the sea at night, she once said, made Henry think of the person who used to whisper in the emperor's ear as he rode in triumph through Rome: 'Remember you must die.' That is what Henry heard in the voice of the sea – 'You must die. You must die. You must die.' – and he thought it was a sound as soothing as any music, so Hannah said.

More of the cliff has peeled away in the last month or two. We inspect the fresh red rockface, then sit on adjacent boulders to watch a water-skier crash and crash again. Over the years the sea has remoulded the contours of the sand and the slope of the land, but the fallen stones to our right are still recognisable as the ones that surrounded the spot where the beach belched Henry's body up. Asked if he can recall the case of Henry, the man who turned out to be Ivor, Luke replies that he doesn't remember. It takes him a few seconds to relinquish his thoughts of Caitlin, then he asks: 'So what happened?'

P.S.

Ideas,
interviews
& features . . .

About the author

Read on

Narratives and Lives

Jonathan Buckley talks to
Louise Tucker

Your stories are often constructed like a jigsaw, with the whole picture revealed in stages: Alexander's life in *Ghost MacIndoe* is recollected through memories; Thomas Lang's life is pieced together from letters, interviews and other fragmentary evidence; Henry's life is understood through others' recollections of him. Amongst such intricate layers, where is the starting point of a story for you, and how do you then construct it?
I couldn't identify precisely a starting point for any of my novels. What tends to happen in the preliminary stage is that a large and chaotic flock of ideas is flying around for a prolonged period, and then something occurs, or a succession of events occurs, to suggest a way in which this scattered mass might be made to form a more coherent shape. Usually it's been a visual image that has prompted this coherence to emerge. A painting by Caspar David Friedrich was crucial in getting *Xerxes* under way, for example, and I started writing notes for *Ghost MacIndoe* after being startled by a photograph of the matador Antonio Ordoñez in a shop window in Ronda. With *So He Takes the Dog*, the subject of vagrancy had been put into my head by Ian Hacking's *Mad Travellers*, which is a study of what Hacking calls 'transient mental illnesses'. I think that the idea of making such a subject central to the story of a murder came to me on the last day of a holiday in Devon, when I was struck by the sight of a lone man striding across the beach.

Once the core characters – the victim and the investigating policeman – had materialised, it became apparent that some of the inchoate scenes and ideas that I'd had in my mind for a while could be developed to serve the stories of these two men, and that others were superfluous, for the time being at least.

I never begin the first chapter of a novel until I have amassed a substantial quantity of notes and a plan for the whole book. Or rather, I don't begin writing the book until I have a plan – in most cases I've not started at Chapter One, and with a couple of my novels the last page was the first to be written. Every day I write at least a couple of pages, and as the book grows the overall plan requires regular modification. Sometimes the modifications are minor, but frequently not: two separate characters might become one, for example, or the relationships between characters might be radically changed, or what had once seemed to be an important strand to the novel might be removed completely. I also go back and revise chapters as I go along, and as soon as a first draft is completed I begin to rework the whole text. There are always at least three drafts, and the redrafting generally entails the removal of a large amount of material. *So He Takes the Dog* more or less followed its initial plan, but the first draft was about thirty pages longer than the published text. *Invisible* was subjected to a particularly rigorous liposuction – it lost its first seven chapters. ▶

❝ I don't begin writing the book until I have a plan – in most cases I've not started at Chapter One, and with a couple of my novels the last page was the first to be written. ❞

Narratives and Lives *(continued)*

◄ **The sense of place in your novels, whether London, the Sussex coast or the English Riviera, is often as keenly described as the central characters. Is that because you are also a travel writer or is location as important as personalities in your writing?**
I don't think of location and character as being entirely discrete. Sense of place is important to any representation of our experience of being in the world. The ways in which we perceive and make sense of where we are, and the extent to which where we are makes us what we are – these are subjects that interest me, as is perhaps most obvious in *Invisible*.

The title *So He Takes the Dog* focuses on a random decision that leads to a murder hunt. Why did you choose this title: to emphasise that Henry's death could have been easily missed, to underline the haphazard nature of our lives and relationships, or simply because it was right?
Most of my books went through half a dozen titles before I settled on the final version, but as soon as I wrote the words 'So he takes the dog' I felt that this was the right title. I didn't quite intend to suggest that Henry's death might have been missed – had Benjamin not taken the dog, someone else would have found the body. But yes, the title hints at the unforeseeable consequences of a spontaneous and insignificant decision, while its unemphatic tone is indicative of the low-pitched voice of the whole book. I wanted it to imply that this isn't a book that shouts.

❢ The title's unemphatic tone is indicative of the low-pitched voice of the whole book. I wanted it to imply that this isn't a book that shouts. ❢

So He Takes the Dog is, in some senses, a detective story without a villain. What drew you to this genre?

In essence, the relationship of *So He Takes the Dog* to the detective genre is oppositional. Detective fiction typically requires a strong narrative line: crimes are perpetrated by clearly defined characters who generally turn out to have had clearly defined reasons for what they have done. The satisfactions of crime fiction (leaving aside the dubious pleasures of literary violence) tend to come from an involvement in the reconstruction of cause and effect, from a sense, at the end, that things have been explained. The detective story, in other words, could be seen as the supreme genre of linear narrative, and one reason that *So He Takes the Dog* turned out the way it did is that I find the idea of linear narrative very problematic, and have done so for a long time. *Thomas Lang* is overtly an anti-narrative; in *Ghost MacIndoe* the chapters proceed sequentially year by year but the central character does not perceive himself as a man with a story.

A few years ago the philosopher Galen Strawson published what I thought was a brilliant essay titled 'Against Narrativity', in which he takes issue with what he sees as a prevalent view in contemporary thought: that we experience our lives as a narrative, and that, to quote Oliver Sacks, 'this narrative is *us*, our identities'. Or, as Charles Taylor put it, that a 'basic condition of making sense of ourselves is that we grasp our lives in a narrative'. Strawson contends that, on the contrary, one can valuably live one's life ▶

6 To cast a life as a story, I think, is often to diminish its richness and complexity, even to falsify. 9

5

Narratives and Lives *(continued)*

◄ with absolutely no sense of oneself as a character in a narrative. I'm strongly in agreement with Strawson on this point. To cast a life as a story, I think, is often to diminish its richness and complexity, even to falsify. The question of how one arrives at and maintains a sense of oneself as a coherent being is of course profoundly difficult, and I can't pretend to have reached anything like an answer – possibly I wouldn't write novels if I thought I had arrived at a satisfactory explanation. One could describe *So He Takes the Dog* as a collision between narrative and non-narrative ways of understanding who we are. As a policeman, John Donohue is required to make the victim a coherent entity, a person with a comprehensible history; ten years later, as a narrator, he has come to understand that, in writing an account of things that happened a decade ago, the use of the word 'I' is impossible.

John, the narrator, makes a career switch from insurance to the police, to be 'in a different part of the process': would that be a good description of why you moved from travel publishing to fiction writing? And have you, like him, found your new career both satisfying and frustrating?
There hasn't really been a clear-cut move from one career to the other: I began writing fiction before I wrote my first guidebook; my first four published novels were written while I was still working in publishing; and I continue to write my guidebooks now. Writing, for me, has always been both satisfying and frustrating, intermittently. There's very great satisfaction

❝ One could describe *So He Takes the Dog* as a collision between narrative and non-narrative ways of understanding who we are. ❞

in getting a sentence or a phrase just right, and when the final page of the first draft is written, there's an exhilaration in seeing that the thing exists. This exhilaration is very brief, though. I remember Alex Ferguson being asked, after Manchester United had won the Champions League with two goals in the last couple of minutes of the final, how long the buzz of victory would last, and he answered, I think: 'about ninety seconds'. That's approximately how long the euphoria persists when the last full stop has been typed. Then comes the process of revision, during which I always become dissatisfied with the book – which I think is inevitable when reviewing a piece of work that has taken so much time: at the end of eighteen months of writing, I don't see things in quite the same way as I did at the outset. I find it extremely difficult to look at my books once they've been printed: every time I glance at a page, I see how it could – and should – be different.

And how difficult was it to make the shift in your writing practice, since travel writing is more social and physical, whereas novel writing is solitary and intellectual?
Well, the process of writing guidebooks isn't quite as sociable as one might think. Dashing around Italy is always hugely enjoyable, but when there are hundreds of pieces of information to verify and deadlines to meet, there's rarely a lot of time for conversation. Sometimes I get to the end of a day without having said much more than 'Does anyone know when the altarpiece will be back from the restorer's?', 'Any idea what's happened ▶

6 I find it extremely difficult to look at my books once they've been printed: every time I glance at a page, I see how it could – and should – be different. 9

Narratives and Lives *(continued)*

◄ to the bus to Fanzolo?' and 'I'll have the *bistecca*, thank you'. Of course, this is considerably more social interaction than one gets sitting at a desk all day, and sometimes I do look out from my window and think I'd rather be yomping across a meadow in the Apennines, but isolation from nine to five isn't arduous. On the contrary – I wouldn't be happy without regular doses of isolation.

Under the surface of *Invisible*'s Englishness is an undertow of other places, particularly Italy. What is it about this country that is so attractive to you, both personally and professionally, and how did your own love and knowledge of that country feed into Edward's?

It was necessary for Edward to be a translator, and so it was an obvious decision to make him familiar with a terrain and a culture with which I'm familiar. That said, Edward's experience of the country, as a blind man, is radically different from mine: the visual richness of Italy – the art, architecture, the amazingly varied landscapes – is for me, as for many people, a major part of its appeal. Edward's engagement with Italy is primarily verbal, and he's a far more proficient linguist than I am – Italian is his third language, after German. And Germany plays at least as large a part in *Invisible* as Italy does. In fact, although I've visited Italy more often than any other country, German culture is a more significant presence in my work overall. This presence is most overt in *Xerxes*, but the other novels are seeded with Germanic references – even *So He Takes the Dog*.

❝ Sometimes I do look out from my window and think I'd rather be yomping across a meadow in the Apennines, but isolation from nine to five isn't arduous. ❞

8

Each of your novels examines, in close detail, both the disappointments and pleasures of a life, and although there is no overarching moral, there is a sense that you are trying to capture an impression of how life is lived in close-up, rather than in broad brushstrokes. Is that my imagination, or your intention?

This connects back to the earlier point about narrative. *So He Takes the Dog* encompasses all of Henry's life from his boyhood to his murder; *Thomas Lang* similarly takes us from the pianist's childhood to death; *Ghost MacIndoe* covers half a century of Alexander MacIndoe's life. But it's true that these novels are episodic, that they don't create a long and continuous and evenly paced narrative span. Ten years might be covered in ten words, then ten pages devoted to ten minutes. The life of these characters is presented in fragmentary form, so the great trajectory of the years is implicit, as a sort of counterpoint to the specifics of their immediate experience, which – I agree – tends to be the primary object of attention.

Who or what inspires your writing?

I'm not very comfortable with the idea of inspiration. The word has connotations of exalted mental states, whereas for me the process of creating a novel is one of sustained accretion and constant reworking. That said, there are certainly moments when connections between various elements of the accumulated material suddenly become apparent, or when things seem to crystallise. Absolutely anything can be the occasion of these moments: a glimpse of a face, a ▶

6 I'm not very comfortable with the idea of inspiration. The word has connotations of exalted mental states, whereas for me the process of creating a novel is one of sustained accretion and constant reworking. 9

Narratives and Lives *(continued)*

◀ gesture, a street scene, an overheard conversation, a line in a book (and not necessarily one I'm enjoying). I have no idea where ideas come from – I don't mean just my own ideas, but anyone's. Does it even make sense for anyone to talk about 'my' ideas? This is a problem that's encapsulated in the dazzling aphorism by Georg Christoph Lichtenberg that was the epigraph to *So He Takes the Dog* until its final draft: '*Es denkt, sollte man sagen, so wie man sagt: es blitzt*' – which translates as 'One should say "it thinks", just as one says "it [i.e. lightning] flashes."'

What are you writing next?

The main character of the next novel is another in a long line of solitaries: a severely disfigured recluse, whose writings are juxtaposed with a commentary from the woman who cared for him. It's not quite as grim as it sounds, I hope. ■

Ten Great Novels

Don Quixote
Miguel de Cervantes

Tristram Shandy
Laurence Sterne

Moby-Dick
Herman Melville

War and Peace
Leo Tolstoy

Effi Briest
Theodor Fontane

The Golden Bowl
Henry James

Finnegans Wake
James Joyce

The Leopard
Giuseppe Tomasi di Lampedusa

Pedro Páramo
Juan Rulfo

JR
William Gaddis

Have You Read?

Other Novels by Jonathan Buckley

The Biography of Thomas Lang

Thomas Lang was an outstanding classical pianist, playing in concert halls around the world and making some remarkable recordings. But then, mysteriously and suddenly, he died. His would-be biographer enters into a correspondence with the pianist's brother Christopher, and starts to piece together the life of this elusive genius, but finds that the process is more tortuous than he had anticipated. In this, his first novel, Jonathan Buckley explores the nature of biography, questioning what a life means and what a life becomes after death.

Xerxes

In 1820s Munich, an aspiring young architect called August Ettlinger joins a salon of aristocrats and intellectuals, where he falls under the influence of Wolgast, a wealthy collector and scholar of sorts. But when Ettlinger falls in love with the enigmatic Helene, and passions intensify, the motives of Wolgast – who had at first appeared so generous – seem increasingly sinister.

Ghost MacIndoe

On a February morning in 1944, Alexander MacIndoe experiences what will become his first permanent memory: the aftermath of a German air raid. In the subsequent 55 chapters the life of Alexander is unfolded year by year, focusing above all on a succession of deep relationships, the most central of which

– with the orphaned Megan Beckwith –
endures for half a century.

....

Invisible

Edward Morton, a blind translator, arrives at
the Oak, a failing spa hotel in the west of
England, intending to stay for a few days to
visit his family and to work. The manager of
the hotel, Malcolm Caldecott, is preparing for
its closure, and for the visit of Stephanie, the
daughter he has not seen for eight years. Eloni
Dobra, one of the hotel's chambermaids, is
striving to establish a life in England, and to
free herself of a burden. As the nature of that
burden becomes clearer, each of these four
protagonists and the absent fifth – Morton's
lover – move towards a crisis and, like the Oak
itself, towards an uncertain future.

If You Loved This,
You Might Like . . .

Chosen by Jonathan Buckley

That Awful Mess on the Via Merulana
Carlo Emilio Gadda
In a middle-class apartment block in central
Rome, a robbery and a murder are committed
within three days of each other. The
consequent investigation reveals the
corruption of Mussolini's Italy and the
complexity of the 'field of forces' within which
any crime occurs. Published in 1957, Gadda's
prodigiously inventive masterpiece is
regarded in Italy with the same sort of
reverence as we give to *Ulysses*.

So Long, See You Tomorrow
William Maxwell
Fifty years after the event, the narrator of
Maxwell's fictional memoir reconstructs the
circumstances surrounding a murder in rural
Illinois – and the now-regretted ending of his
friendship with the murderer's troubled son.
The book is barely more than 100 pages long,
but Maxwell's lucid and subtle prose carries a
huge emotional charge.

Flight Without End
Joseph Roth
Franz Tunda, the wandering protagonist of
Flight Without End, is the quintessential Roth
hero – decent, intelligent and utterly lost. The
elegiac melancholy of this characteristically
economical little book is Roth's defining tone.

Revolutionary Road
Richard Yates
Charting the disintegration of a golden couple in a well-heeled Connecticut enclave in the 1950s, *Revolutionary Road* is a gruelling and magnificent novel. No other writer is quite as remorseless as Yates in depicting the quiet despair of suburbia, the slow corrosion of thwarted ambition and soured relationships.

Equal Danger
Leonardo Sciascia
Several judges are murdered in quick succession, and in trying to make sense of what has happened Inspector Rogas becomes ensnared in thickets of conspiracy. The Sicilian writer-politician Leonardo Sciascia has been described as the master of metaphysical detective fiction, and *Equal Danger* is a perfect example of his art. Its convolutions could be read as a parody of the genre, but it's also a gripping tale of political skulduggery and paranoia. As Sciascia himself wrote: 'I began to write it with amusement, and as I was finishing it I was no longer amused.'

That They May Face the Rising Sun
John McGahern
McGahern's last novel is a profound and beautifully understated portrait of a small community in rural County Leitrim: ▶

If You Loved This, You Might Like . . .
(continued)

◄ exquisitely nuanced in its presentation of character, and extraordinarily involving in its evocation of place. Modernity, advancing by degrees, is regarded warily, but this is no mere exercise in nostalgia – rather, McGahern has a clear-eyed appreciation of the values of life lived slowly. No finer novel has been written in English in recent years. ∎

A NEW BEGINNING

Rowena had only met her god-mother once, so why had Leonora Lawton left Cherry Cottage to her in her will? Should Rowena sell her bequest and continue to run her successful children's nursery, or make a new beginning in the chocolate box cottage two hundred miles away? The antagonism of Kavan Reagan, her attractive neighbour, who had hoped to inherit the cottage himself, only strengthens her resolve to make a new life for herself.

TONI ANDERS

A NEW
BEGINNING

Complete and Unabridged

LINFORD
Leicester

First published in Great Britain in 2008

First Linford Edition
published 2009

British Library CIP Data

Anders, Toni
A new beginning.—Large print ed.—
Linford romance library
1. Love stories
2. Large type books
I. Title
823.9'2 [F]

ISBN 978–1–84782–560–5

Published by
F. A. Thorpe (Publishing)
Anstey, Leicestershire

Set by Words & Graphics Ltd.
Anstey, Leicestershire
Printed and bound in Great Britain by
T. J. International Ltd., Padstow, Cornwall

This book is printed on acid-free paper

Cherry Cottage

'I understand that you never actually met Miss Lawton?' The elderly solicitor looked at Rowena over the top of his rimless glasses.

'I only ever met her on one occasion,' she told him, 'and I was only three years old at the time, so I don't remember anything about her.'

'I see.' The old man went back to studying Miss Lawton's will, which was spread out on his desk.

'She was a school friend of my mother's,' explained Rowena. 'Apparently they were inseparable when young, but something happened to drive them apart. I've no idea what caused the rift. I only know that a few years after my mother married, Miss Lawton came to see her — that was when I met her — and after that, they never spoke again.'

'Miss Lawton never tried to contact you at all?'

'No. I only knew of her because, before my father died, he gave me a box of photographs and letters belonging to my mother who had died two years before.'

She remembered the various small, faded, black and white photographs of two little girls, both blonde, showing off summer hats; proudly wearing school uniforms; nursing identical black kittens. Her eyes grew wistful as she thought of them.

A discreet cough from Mr Bevan recalled her to the present.

'I looked at the photographs and read some of the letters,' she continued. 'They were only girlish chatter. I did wonder whether to write to Miss Lawton to tell her that Mum had died, but I thought she probably wouldn't still be at the address on the letters, so I put the box away in a cupboard and forgot all about them — until I received the letter from you.'

'Asking you to call to see me here in

Allarton because I had information that was to your advantage.' He smiled.

'Yes.' Rowena smiled back.

The solicitor looked back down at the will on the desk and smoothed out a crease with a bony finger. 'Well, *you* may have forgotten *her* but Miss Lawton obviously remembered you,' he said. 'She appears to have had no relations and lived alone at Cherry Cottage for most of her life.'

'Cherry Cottage?' Rowena interrupted. 'That's the address on her old letters. So she *was* at the same address all this time. What can you tell me about her?'

'Well, she never married and she bred cats — Persian cats. She was a well-known judge at cat shows. She led a busy life, I believe.'

He picked up the will, glanced at Rowena over the top of it and began to read.

'This is the Last Will and Testament of Leonora Lawton.' He smiled apologetically at her. 'This is very dull but I have to read it all.'

She nodded, only half listening. *Leonora Lawton.* The letters to Rowena's mother had been signed *Lee.* She wondered why this woman she knew nothing about should mention her in her will.

She realised Mr Bevan was looking at her.

'This is the part that directly concerns you.' He read on, 'To Rowena Gage, the daughter of my dear childhood friend, Carrie, I leave my house, Cherry Cottage, in the hope that she will live there and be as happy in it as I have been.'

Rowena looked bewildered. 'You mean, she's left me her house?'

Mr Bevan nodded. 'There's very little money to go with it, most of that has gone in small bequests, but the cottage would fetch a comfortable sum if you cared to sell it.'

'She says in her will that she hopes I will live there.'

'But the idea might be quite impractical. She probably expected you would sell it.'

He busied himself folding papers and tucking them away in a file, tactfully giving Rowena time to think.

She turned to gaze through the small window of the office, not seeing or hearing the people and cars passing by.

Her own life was centred on a town two hundred miles away. She had a flat and a business there. She didn't need Cherry Cottage. Yet, for curiosity's sake, she wanted to see it. But what if she fell in love with it, what then? She turned back to Mr Bevan.

'I think perhaps I *shall* sell it. It was very kind of Miss Lawton, but I have my own life back in Melchester. I know nobody here. It would be a complete upheaval to move to the cottage.'

'I can understand that. You would have to uproot your family,' he said. 'That can be very difficult.'

'I have no family. My husband died five years ago and I have no children.' She stood up. 'Could you find an estate agent for me and arrange the sale, Mr Bevan?'

He held out a hand and she shook it.

'That will be very easy,' he said. 'Ed Tyler — the estate agent whose offices are next door to this building — was asking about Cherry Cottage on behalf of a client a day or two ago. I'll put it in his hands.'

He led her to the door and showed her out.

'I'm going away this afternoon for a few days so Mr Tyler will be in touch if he needs to contact you before my return. And I'll speak to you again in due course. Goodbye, Miss Gage.'

★ ★ ★

The solicitor's office was in a Victorian house in Allarton's village square. Next to it was a small garden and, further along, Rowena found the estate agent's office, its window filled with photographs and details of properties for sale. Between the cards she could see inside the office to where a fair-haired young man, presumably Ed Tyler, was talking to a dark-haired man who she took to be a customer.

The fair-haired young man looked up, caught her eye and gave her a cheeky grin.

Embarrassed at being caught staring, she pretended to be studying property details.

Suddenly, the door was flung open and the dark-haired man emerged, sweeping past Rowena in what appeared to be a state of extreme bad-temper, and his arm caught her handbag, knocking it to the ground.

She bent to retrieve it before he could do so, feeling very annoyed. He could hardly have avoided seeing her, for goodness' sake!

'I'm very sorry. Are you all right?' His voice was deep and attractive but its tone scarcely sounded apologetic.

'Perfectly.' Rowena turned away, but not before registering two bright blue eyes in a well-tanned face.

'I really am sorry. My mind was on something else. Could I . . . ?'

She turned back to face him. Blue eyes and curly black hair. What a combination! But she didn't like the air of short temper that went with it.

'Please don't trouble yourself, I'm quite all right,' she said coldly, and crossed the square before he could say any more.

In the Daisy Tearoom she ordered a cup of coffee and settled herself in a corner. The tearoom was a typical old-fashioned café; cream-washed walls, black beams, a fussy array of chintzy china and little pieces of brassware on every surface.

It was fairly empty, she was pleased to see.

She took out her mobile and tapped in a number.

'Molly? I've just come from the solicitor.'

'And?' Molly's voice sounded excited. 'Has she left you a fortune or a china figurine?'

'A cottage,' said Rowena.

'A cottage?' Molly squealed. 'What's it like?'

'I don't know. I haven't seen it.'

'When are you going to see it?'

'I'm not. I'm selling it.'

'You can't! Not without seeing it.'

'But if I see it, I might fall in love with it and then I won't want to sell it,' Rowena objected.

'And if you don't see it, you'll spend the rest of your life wondering what it was like.'

The coffee arrived. Rowena thanked the waitress and turned again to her mobile phone.

'Perhaps you're right. I'll think about it before I come home. See you in a day or two. Is everything all right at the nursery?'

'Yes, apart from Mrs Trent fussing over Richard's dinners. You know what she's like.'

'I'm sure you can handle her.'

'Mm. Well enjoy your little break. 'Bye.'

★ ★ ★

Rowena replaced her phone in her bag and began to drink her coffee. There was something in what Molly had said. How could she sell the cottage without even seeing it?

And Leonora Lawton was a mystery herself. Why had she chosen to leave her home to a stranger, the daughter of an old friend with whom she'd fallen out years ago and hadn't seen since.

If Rowena didn't see the cottage there would be another mystery in her life.

She stood up, slipped on her jacket, picked up her bag and left the café. She crossed the square to the estate agent's office and went in. The fair-haired man smiled his wide smile.

'So you decided to come in after all.'

'I'm sorry?'

'You were trying to make up your mind an hour ago. Have you picked out a property?'

'Oh, I see.' Rowena felt a little flustered. So he'd recognised her as the woman peering through his window.

'No, I don't want to buy. Let me explain.'

She told him about her visit to Mr Bevan that morning.

'So he said he would put the sale in your hands,' she finished.

'Ah! You're the mysterious lady who's inherited Cherry Cottage? I haven't all the details yet, but he mentioned the matter before he left. He'll be back in Allarton on Wednesday and we'll go into it then.'

'So you haven't got the key?' Rowena was disappointed.

'As a matter of fact, yes, I have. Mr Bevan thought I might want to go in and do a bit of measuring and photographing.'

'The thing is . . . ' Rowena felt embarrassed. 'I wonder now whether I was too hasty. I told Mr Bevan I didn't want to see the place but . . . '

'Now you're curious?'

'Yes. I'd just like a peep before I make a final decision.'

Ed glanced at his watch. 'I have an

appointment immediately after lunch, but I'll be free at three o'clock. Would that suit you?'

Rowena nodded eagerly.

'Be here at three and I'll take you to view it. I must say, I hope you decide to sell. I could get a good price for that cottage. I have someone interested already. It's a lovely old place and the garden's a picture.'

'Is it far away or in Allarton itself?'

'Half a mile outside; walking distance. Very convenient.'

She gave him a little nod. 'Thank you. I'll be back at three.'

★   ★   ★

Squinting into the bright morning sunlight, Rowena began to stroll round the square. The air was fresh and clear and Allarton was a picture book village. She passed a butcher's shop and a greengrocer; a tiny supermarket and a bakery.

Everything the inhabitants could

need, she mused . . .

A road turned off to the left and on the wall, she saw a sign that said, *To The River*. Might as well see everything, she thought, and began to walk in that direction.

The sound of children's voices drew her towards a fence that enclosed an expanse of grass fronting on to a wooden church hall. About twenty small children were running around on the grass, shouting and scrambling around on coloured plastic climbing toys and shrieking with laughter.

A sign looped over the gate said, *Lucy Locket Nursery*.

Rowena thought of the children in her own nursery back home in Melchester. They would be doing the same things as these children, under the watchful eye of Molly James, the co-owner.

Rowena smiled at the red-headed young woman who was looking after these children. 'Lovely morning,' she called.

'Beautiful. Such a change after the rain.'

'They look happy. Oh, to be that age again!'

They both laughed. Rowena watched their antics for a few moments more then strolled on.

* * *

The river was wide and swift flowing. It had rained heavily in the past few weeks and the level was high. A road bridge crossed it. She stood in the centre of the bridge and looked down the length of the river in both directions. Two swans glided past and a line of mallard ducks followed, the purple and green feathers of the males glinting in the sunshine. On the bank, a flock of Canada geese squabbled over chunks of bread which an elderly lady was throwing towards them.

The river flowed mostly through fields, but she noticed a cluster of small cottages dotted along the river bank to the left. She supposed that their long gardens protected them from flooding when the river was high.

She turned and made her way back to the square. Opposite the little nursery, she had noticed a black and white timbered inn with a garden overlooking the square. She would spend an hour there over a leisurely lunch.

The few occupants of the bar looked up and stared curiously as she entered. Perhaps strangers were few in Allarton, she thought. She gave them a cheery, 'Good day,' and they turned away guiltily and resumed their conversations.

She studied the menu on the blackboard behind the bar, ordered a ham sandwich and a fruit juice and, picking up a newspaper from a pile on a sideboard as she passed, settled herself at a corner table, The paper was the local free advertiser.

Won't be very interesting, she told herself, but it would give her a flavour of the area.

The landlord brought over her

sandwich and drink to her himself.

'Staying here or just passing through?' he asked, placing the plate before her.

'Staying a day or two.' Rowena didn't intend to satisfy his curiosity.

'Have you come from far off?' he persisted.

'About two hundred miles.'

He looked disappointed, realising he wouldn't get any more out of her.

She picked up her sandwich. Her plans were uncertain. She definitely wouldn't discuss them with a curious stranger, however friendly.

'Enjoy your food.' The landlord gave her a stiff smile and returned to his place behind the bar.

The sandwich was excellent. Rowena finished every crumb, realising how hungry she was. Then she settled to read the local paper.

Advertisements, photographs of local dignitaries, accounts of meetings — it was the same as any other free newspaper.

She flicked over the pages and

stopped at the job vacancies. A name jumped out at her. *Lucy Locket Nursery*. That was the place she'd passed on her way to the river.

Experienced nursery nurse required, she read. She wondered if the red-headed young woman was leaving.

What a coincidence that she'd spoken to her that morning!

She glanced at the wrought iron clock behind the bar. Time she was making her way to the estate agent's.

★　★　★

He was waiting for her when she reached his office. 'I wondered whether you would come back,' he said with a laugh. 'I thought you might have changed your mind again.'

'I'm really keen to see it now,' said Rowena. 'I can't believe I decided to sell without taking a look.'

Ed Tyler picked up his car keys from the desk. 'My car's outside. Come along.'

They crossed the bridge over the

river and reached Cherry Cottage in minutes. Rowena was surprised to find it was one of the cottages she'd seen from the bridge, the end one, which was set slightly apart from the others.

Ed drove past the cottage and parked in the gateway to a field.

'No drives or garages here,' he said cheerfully. 'This gateway isn't used so it's your parking space.'

Rowena climbed from the car and looked around. 'It's so peaceful,' she breathed. 'Not a sound but bird song and the munching of sheep. It's lovely.'

But as she spoke, engine noise roared its way towards them from further down the lane. Ed Tyler put a warning hand on her arm as a powerful red motorcycle hurtled past.

Rowena could make out nothing of the rider under his leathers and helmet but something told her she knew who it was.

'Kavan Reagan,' said Ed Tyler with annoyance. 'He thinks this lane belongs to him.'

Rowena looked at him questioningly.

'He lives up there.' Ed gestured along the lane. 'Smallholding. He's your nearest neighbour.'

'Was he in your office this morning?'

'Yes. As a matter of fact he was asking about Cherry Cottage.'

'He seemed rather cross when he came out. He bumped into me,' said Rowena.

'Yes. Well, he *was* cross. He wants to buy Cherry Cottage. I told him that I didn't know if it was for sale. The trouble with Kavan Reagan, he never wants to wait for anything.'

They crossed the lane and Ed opened the gate for her.

She paused and looked at the cottage, taking in its square windows with white wooden shutters folded back, the pale lemon walls and the stone porch smothered with soft blue wisteria.

'Oh, how pretty,' she breathed. 'I never dreamed . . . '

'Changing your mind?'

'I've only seen the outside. Let me take some photographs then we'll go inside.'

'It's eighteenth-century originally,' said Ed, 'but successive owners have altered it so that it's not remotely what it was when built. It hasn't been spoilt, but purists might object to some of the alterations.'

He unlocked the front door and pushed it open.

The deep stone porch gave a certain amount of privacy, but the entrance led straight into the living-room which extended the full width of the house, with a window at either end.

Dark oak furniture, polished to a soft glow, stood against clotted cream coloured walls. The floor was carpeted in soft green with rich red Axminster rugs here and there. Two deep arm-chairs, upholstered in pale green flowered chintz, stood each side of the fire and a narrow staircase wound upwards behind the fireplace.

'The floor would have been bare

flagstones originally,' said Ed. 'And certainly no carpet on the stairs. But Miss Lawton wanted warmth and comfort.'

'Who doesn't?' smiled Rowena. 'And the carpets could easily be removed if one wanted authenticity. I think it's charming. And what an interesting collection of china along the mantelpiece.'

'Staffordshire, I believe,' said Ed, gazing upwards at the row of jugs and mugs, shepherdesses and dogs. 'Quite valuable if they're genuine.'

He led the way to a door in the corner. 'Come and have a surprise.'

The door led into the kitchen. Any ideas Rowena might have had of stone sinks and ancient stoves were soon dispelled. The kitchen had been fitted out with the very latest units and a gleaming cooker, dishwasher and washing machine.

'I told you Miss Lawton liked her comfort.' Ed smiled at the surprised look on Rowena's face. 'There's another surprise over here.'

Ed opened a door to disclose a very small room furnished with just a desk, a chair and a bookcase. 'An earlier owner knocked through into the scullery and created this tiny study. That's all the ground floor. Let's go upstairs.'

In the bend of the stairs, a little staircase window perfectly displayed coloured glass bottles and goblets.

'Miss Lawton told me she dug up several of the bottles in the garden,' said Ed.

'So you knew her. What was she like?'

He looked at Rowena with interest. 'You didn't know her?'

'I only met her once, when I was three years old. So, no, I didn't know her at all.'

It was obvious that the estate agent was curious to know why — since she was virtually a stranger — Rowena had been left the cottage, but he was too polite to ask and she decided not to enlighten him. She didn't want any gossip spread around the town if she did decide to stay.

She carried on up the twisting stairs to the first bedroom.

Ed followed her in. 'Miss Lawton used this as her own bedroom. You ask what she was like. I didn't know her very well, but I always found her pleasant and friendly. Quite attractive, too, or rather, I should imagine she was as a girl. She still had very thick hair and soft skin. A handsome woman.'

Rowena tried to imagine Miss Lawton in this comfortable room with its brass bedstead and rose-sprigged wallpaper. Downstairs, the smell had been of rich wax polish, here she was aware of the subtle scent of pot pourri. She looked around, but Ed was already leading the way out of the room to the bedroom opposite.

'Guestroom, I suppose,' he said, 'though I don't know that she had many visitors. Too busy with her cats, I should think.'

'She bred them, didn't she?' asked Rowena.

'Not in the last few years. But she was a judge at cat shows all over the country. Here's the bathroom.'

It was small but comfortable and a glance was enough to take in all the features.

* * *

They made their way downstairs and out into the garden. It was very long; Rowena could barely see to the end of it.

'That's Kavan Reagan's land beyond,' Ed told her.

'It's a very large garden,' said Rowena doubtfully. 'And I'm not much of a gardener.'

'Plenty of people round here do gardening for payment in their spare time. You'd easily find someone to sort it out for you if you decided to keep the cottage.'

They returned to the living-room. Ed gestured to one armchair and took a seat in the other.

'Perhaps you'll let me know as soon as possible whether you want to sell or not,' he said.

Rowena looked around the sun-filled room. If she sold the cottage it would haunt her. It had been left to her and she suddenly *wanted* to live in it.

When one door opens . . . she told herself. What was so perfect about the life she led in Melchester? It was time for a change. She smiled at the estate agent.

'I can tell you now. I won't be selling it. I intend to live here.'

A Big Decision

They were both quiet on the short drive back to Ed's office. Rowena was considering the implications of her decision. Ed Tyler had lost a good sale, but covered his disappointment with a compliment.

'May I say you'll be a welcome addition to Allarton,' he said, as he opened the car door for her. 'I look forward to meeting you again.'

He locked the car and turned towards his office.

A sudden thought struck Rowena.

'Could you recommend a guest-house?' she asked. 'I don't want to stay at the inn. Perhaps you know of somewhere? I know I could stay at Cherry Cottage but it would be too much trouble to have to make the bed and buy groceries for one night.'

He thought for just a moment.

'There's a very nice little place in May Street,' he said, pointing to a small road which curved away to the left. 'It's called Briar House. Mrs King runs it. Tell her I sent you.'

Rowena made her way to the small public car park where she'd left her car. She slid behind the wheel, drove into the square and turned into May Street. She found Briar House easily and parked outside.

Mrs King, a neat, very elderly lady, welcomed her warmly when she heard that Ed Tyler had sent her.

'A lovely boy,' she said. 'Always bright and cheerful. Is he a friend of yours?'

'No. I had some business with him, that's how I know him.'

Really, the people round here did seem to want to know a lot, she thought.

'Well, come along in and I'll show you to your room. How many nights did you want to stay?'

'Only one at the moment.' Rowena

felt a little guilty. Perhaps guests who stayed for only one night were a nuisance.

Mrs King threw open a bedroom door.

'Why, it's charming.' Rowena took in the pink-striped wallpaper, pink flowered quilt and graceful white furniture. Mrs King smiled with pleasure.

'I'm sure you'll be comfortable. I'll give you a key to come and go this evening. I'm afraid I can't do dinners, but you'll get a good meal at the Black Boar. What time would you like breakfast?'

They settled a few details and Mrs King turned to go. 'If you'd like to come downstairs when you're ready, I'll make you a cup of tea,' she said, closing the door.

Left alone, Rowena unpacked the few clothes she had brought with her. She laid her nightdress on the bed and placed her make-up bag and sponge bag in the bathroom. Then she washed her hands, tidied her hair and prepared to go downstairs.

'In here,' called Mrs King. She was sitting, knitting, in a fireside chair with a tea-tray laid upon a little table in front of her.

She pointed to a large armchair. 'Make yourself comfortable.'

The knitting was returned to a bag which swung from the arm of her chair and she poured out two cups of tea.

'Cake?' She passed a plate and Rowena helped herself to a large slice of coffee cake.

'This is wonderful,' she said as she tasted it.

'My speciality,' said Mrs King with obvious pride.

She was a very elegant old lady, thought Rowena, with her beautifully styled hair and carefully matching clothes.

'Have you come far?'

'From Melchester. About two hundred miles.'

'I don't think I know it.' Mrs King looked puzzled. She took out her knitting again.

Rowena decided to tell the old lady

why she was in Allarton. After all, she might be able to tell her something about the mysterious Miss Lawton.

'I'm here about a cottage that I've inherited,' she explained.

Mrs King's head shot up. 'Not Cherry Cottage?'

Rowena nodded. 'You know it?'

'Of course. Miss Lawton was a friend of mine.'

'She and my mother had been friends when they were girls, but they drifted apart just after I was born. I only met her once, when I was three,' said Rowena. 'Can you tell me something about her?'

'You only met her once and yet she left you her cottage,' mused Mrs King.

She sat silently for a few moments before going on, 'Leonora always seemed to have a sadness inside her. She wasn't a miserable person, far from it — she could be great fun. But now and then she'd become very quiet and thoughtful as if she was brooding on a secret sadness.'

'And she never told you what it was?'

'No. We were friends, but we didn't discuss personal problems. And I would never pry.'

'I wonder why she never married?'

'She never mentioned a man,' said Mrs King, 'but I often wondered whether her sadness was to do with a long lost sweetheart. Perhaps she loved someone who died?' She smiled. 'I expect I'm being fanciful. Too many romantic novels.' She took a different coloured ball of wool from her bag. 'No point in speculating. She's gone now.'

'What are you knitting?' Rowena deliberately lightened the conversation.

'Teddies. *Teddies for Tragedies*, they're called. The church sends them to parts of the world that have suffered disasters, to cheer up and comfort the children.'

She handed a couple of brightly coloured woolly bears to Rowena.

'What a lovely idea. The children must be thrilled to get them.'

She handed them back and stood up.

'Thank you very much for the tea. I

have to phone a friend then I'll go out for a meal.'

Mrs King handed her a sheet of paper. 'You might like to watch this.'

'*Allarton Alight,*' Rowena read aloud. '*Come and join our lantern-lit procession at nine o'clock this evening.*'

There followed a description of the procession's route around the village, starting at a pub along the river bank called, appropriately enough, the Riverbank Inn.

'Sounds fun. Perhaps I will go along to watch.'

She went up to her room and took out her mobile phone. Opening the copy of the local free paper that she'd taken from a table at the bottom of the stairs, she checked the number of the Lucy Locket Nursery and dialled.

'Heather Robinson,' said a voice.

'Lucy Locket Nursery?' asked Rowena.

'Yes.'

'I wonder whether I could come and see you about the vacancy for an experienced nursery nurse that's advertised in the local paper?'

'Of course. Could you come now? Or would you rather see me at the nursery tomorrow?'

'Now would be perfect. Where will I find you?'

'Do you know May Street?'

'May Street?' Rowena laughed. 'That's where I am now. I'm at Briar House.'

'What a coincidence. Well, I'm about ten houses away, on the other side of the street. Number eighteen.'

* * *

Rowena decided not to change until she was ready to go for her meal. But she freshened her make-up and, five minutes later, was walking up May Street looking for number eighteen.

It was a small, whitewashed house in a terrace of four and the door was opened at Rowena's first knock by a girl who looked very familiar.

'Oh, it's you!' they said together, and both laughed.

It was the red-headed girl from the nursery. She'd recognised Rowena at once.

'Have you had experience of this kind of work?' she asked after introducing herself as Heather Robinson. They were seated in a tiny sitting-room. 'Well, you must have, mustn't you, or you wouldn't be here. What are your qualifications?'

'I'm a teacher,' said Rowena, 'and I have my own nursery school in Melchester, about two hundred miles away.'

'Then why . . . ?' Heather looked puzzled.

Once again, Rowena explained about the cottage. 'And when I saw it, I knew I had to live in it,' she finished.

'So you're looking for a job in Allarton?'

'I'll have to work. I'm afraid I can't be a lady of leisure.'

'And I want to expand,' explained Heather, 'but at the moment there's only myself and two assistants and, if I

34

want to take in more children, I need another qualified person.' She looked doubtful. 'But if you're a teacher and you've had your own nursery, perhaps it wouldn't suit you. Not enough responsibility?'

'It would suit me perfectly,' said Rowena. 'I want to concentrate on the cottage and the garden. And I want to explore the area round about. I don't know this part of the world. I'm very keen on history and there are many old houses and churches to explore. The last thing I want is the sort of responsibility I've had in the past few years.'

They talked for another half-hour, with Heather explaining her aims and ambitions for her business, and Rowena talking about the way she ran her own nursery.

'So you're intending to sell up in order to move down here?'

'Yes, and I think my friend and co-owner will buy me out,' said Rowena. 'I'm ringing her this evening.

And I shall sell my flat.'

'But how long will all that take?' asked Heather. 'I don't want to wait too long.'

'I could be ready to start work for you in one month, or as near to that as I can,' said Rowena, realising that she'd just made a firm decision. 'I'll leave the flat in the hands of an agent and just move straight into Cherry Cottage.' She felt a sense of lightness as she said this.

'In that case, I should like to offer you the job,' said Heather. 'Six months trial on either side.' She smiled.

She got up and went over to a sideboard, reached for a bottle of wine and poured out two glasses. She handed one to Rowena.

'To the future,' she toasted and Rowena echoed, 'To the future.'

They arranged that Rowena would visit the nursery as soon as she could organize a return visit to Allarton and then they parted, each convinced she'd made a new friend.

* * *

When Rowena returned to Briar House, Mrs King was nowhere in sight, but the sound of the radio from the back of the house suggested she was in the kitchen preparing her own evening meal.

Once she was back in her room, Rowena again picked up her mobile and called up a number.

'Molly? Are you busy?'

'Not too busy to hear your news.'

'There's a lot,' warned Rowena. 'I wondered whether to wait and tell you everything when I got back to Melchester, but I want you to think about something while I'm not there.'

'Very mysterious,' said Molly.

Rowena took a deep breath. 'How do you feel about buying out my share of the business?'

There was silence at the other end of the line. It went on for so long that Rowena asked anxiously, 'Molly?'

'I'm still here. Perhaps I shouldn't have encouraged you to see the cottage.'

'I'm sorry, I . . .'

'You've seen the cottage, you've

decided to stay and you want to cut your links with Melchester. Have I guessed right?'

'You have, but there's one thing you haven't guessed. I've had the offer of a new job. And — please don't be annoyed, Molly, I'm really excited — I've accepted. But wait till you see the cottage and you'll understand why I've made such a hasty decision to live in it.'

'Look — tell me all about it when you get back; this call will cost you a fortune.'

'But I want you to seriously think about taking over Tiny Tigers.'

'Let's wait till you get back, OK? Must go now. 'Bye.'

Rowena looked at her phone in dismay. She hadn't realised Molly would take her news so badly.

They'd been friends and colleagues for over three years and Molly hated change, so that was probably the reason. Tomorrow she'd talk to her friend face to face. Nothing to be done now.

She changed from her businesslike

grey suit into kingfisher-blue trousers and a white top, pushed the flyer about the Allarton Alight Procession into her bag and left the house.

Leaving her car in the parking space at the side of Briar House, she set off to walk to the Black Boar.

This time the lounge bar was busy. The landlord gave her a nod of recognition and indicated an empty table at the side of the bar.

★   ★   ★

'Rowena! We meet again.' A girl had stopped at her table. 'Are you eating here?'

It was Heather from the Lucy Locket Nursery.

'Yes.' Rowena smiled. 'I hope the food's good.'

'You're alone? That won't do. Come and join our group. It will be a change to have someone new to talk to.'

'But I'll be intruding,' Rowena protested, thinking that perhaps Heather was with a boyfriend.

'Nonsense. Come along.' Heather walked away from the table and Rowena was forced to follow.

They pushed their way across the crowded bar to a larger table in the window.

'Meet Rowena Gage, everyone,' said Heather, and Rowena found herself being greeted by about six men and women her own age or a little younger, all smiling and all willing to be friendly. Someone made room for her and she sat down, wondering whether she'd remember all their names.

'Rowena is coming to work for me at the nursery next month when she moves to Allarton,' Heather informed them.

'I'm moving into Cherry Cottage,' said Rowena. 'I'm very excited.'

'Cherry Cottage? Is that where Kavan . . . ?' began a girl, but someone hastily intervened.

'Where do you live now?'

Questions and answers were batted

to and fro until a waitress appeared to take their orders.

'Ah! Here he is at last,' said someone as a man carrying a tray of drinks appeared at the table. 'What kept you?'

'Come and sit next to me, Kavan,' called a girl sitting two seats away and Rowena found the vacant seat next to her being taken by Kavan Reagan.

Heather introduced them to each other and Kavan held out a hand.

'We have met,' he smiled, 'but we've not been introduced.'

What a lovely smile, thought Rowena. It's a pity his usual expression seems to be a scowl.

They began to chat to each other but something warned Rowena not to mention Cherry Cottage.

'So you've moved to Allarton,' said Kavan. 'That's why you were outside Ed Tyler's? To look for a house?'

Before she could answer, their food arrived and, in the confusion, his question was forgotten.

'Are you coming to watch the

procession?' asked a red-haired man seated opposite.

Because of his fiery hair, Rowena remembered he was Heather's brother, Peter.

'We usually walk up to the Riverbank Inn — the procession starts from there — and follow it through the village.'

'Sounds fun,' said Rowena. 'I'd love to come.'

'The children in the village make lanterns,' said Heather, 'and we have a couple of bands — one at the front, leading the procession and one at the back.'

'And they're usually playing different tunes,' said another girl with a laugh.

'The noise can be heard in the next village,' agreed Kavan. He looked at his watch. 'If everyone's finished, we should be making a start.'

And so, ten minutes later, Rowena found herself strolling through Allarton, laughing and talking with a group of people she hadn't even met the day before.

Kavan had begun talking to another man and Rowena was joined by Peter, Heather's brother. He was not attractive in any way, but he had an engaging smile and seemed determined to make her feel welcome.

'The village library is just down there.' He pointed to a small building behind a tiny car park. 'The school is just beyond.'

★   ★   ★

They walked through the village and out along a country lane. Kavan Reagan walked just in front of her and Rowena found herself watching him as he chatted to his friend, gesticulating with hands that seemed never still. She thought of Ed Tyler's remark, 'Kavan Reagan never wants to wait for anything.' Too much energy, she decided. He needs to calm down.

'When are you moving to Allarton?' Peter was claiming her attention again.

'In a month, if I can. I'm anxious to

make a start on my new life. Oh, are we here?'

They'd arrived at an inn, much smaller than the Black Boar, which they reached by a stone bridge that crossed a bubbling brook.

A motley crowd of children and adults, some in fancy dress and most carrying flickering lanterns, milled around in the inn's courtyard.

A samba band seemed to be in competition with a lively group of young people who were playing an array of small instruments, and the noise was deafening. The voices of the crowd grew ever louder as they tried to make themselves heard above the music.

Rowena decided to enjoy the evening and followed the group across the bridge, through the courtyard and to an empty table at the far side.

'The procession will be forming in a short time,' said Kavan. 'We'll join them as they move off.'

★ ★ ★

Rowena looked around. Across the lane was a row of tiny cottages and some ramshackle farm buildings.

The farmhouse, three storeys high, loomed over the outbuildings and she could hear the excited barking of dogs in the yard. Rich farmyard smells mingled with the garden scents of a spring evening.

The light was fading and though it was not cold, she was glad when everyone began to move and the procession formed up behind the samba band.

To loud cheers, and with lanterns gently swaying and flickering in the pale evening light, they made their straggling way towards the village.

This time, Rowena found herself walking next to Kavan.

'You didn't answer my question,' he said.

'I'm sorry, what question?'

He'd returned to the conversation that had begun in the Black Boar and the question she'd thought she'd avoided. She wasn't quite sure why she wanted to avoid it, but she was sure that her answer wouldn't be welcome to Kavan.

'I asked whether you were looking in Ed Tyler's window for a property to buy.'

She hesitated, then looked straight at him. 'I've inherited Cherry Cottage,' she said. 'I don't need to buy a property.'

Only the tightening of his lips betrayed his feelings. They walked on in silence. Then he said, 'Would you be interested in selling the cottage? I'd give you a good price for it.'

'And why would you want to buy it?'

'You know that it adjoins my land? I'm sure Ed Tyler must have told you. I think he probably also told you that I'm interested in buying it.'

'But why would you want to?' she repeated.

'D'you want a lantern, Kavan?' It was the girl who'd sat next to him in the Black Boar. 'There are some spares.'

She thrust a decorated jam jar on a stick into his hands and rushed off.

'Cherry Cottage has a very large garden. It would make a useful addition to my land. I want to develop my smallholding, so I'm desperate for extra ground.'

His gaily painted lantern bobbed and swayed on its stick, a foot from his face.

'This wretched thing!'

He turned and thrust it into the hands of the surprised-looking man who was walking behind him.

Temper, temper, thought Rowena, but she asked, 'And the cottage? Surely you can't want to demolish it?'

'It would be useful for my house-keeper, Mrs Morrow, and her son. To tell you the truth, I'm tired of having the pair of them living in my house. The cottage could be near enough and I'd have some privacy.'

What a pity for him that she'd ever seen the cottage, thought Rowena. If she'd returned to Melchester without seeing it, Kavan would now have his wish.

'I'm sorry, but I don't want to sell,'

47

she said. 'I intend to live in Cherry Cottage.'

She was conscious of the suppressed tension in the man. The face he turned to her was expressionless, but his blue eyes blazed.

'Excuse me,' he said, and stalked off to walk on his own.

'All alone?' Heather, a jam jar lantern bobbing in her hand, caught up with her.

'For the moment. I was talking to Kavan.'

'Did he tell you he wanted Cherry Cottage?'

'Forcefully,' said Rowena. 'He wasn't pleased when I said I wouldn't sell.'

Heather was silent for a few minutes as the procession turned a corner and began the final stage of the trek towards the Black Boar.

'Kavan is a friend,' Heather said at last. 'We all like him. But he is a bundle of energy. When he wants something, he wants it. He'll accept no alternative.'

Rowena gave her a rueful smile. 'Ed Tyler said something like that. But I'm afraid Kavan Reagan will have to accept my word. I've fallen in love with Cherry Cottage and I intend to live there.'

'Stick to your guns,' advised Heather. 'The cottage was left to you. The trouble is, Kavan thought Miss Lawton would leave it to him.'

'Leave it to him? Why would she do that?'

'They were quite friendly, despite the age difference. They used to play cards on winter evenings and he advised her on her gardening problems. She knew he wanted the land but perhaps she thought he'd demolish the cottage if she left it to him.'

Rowena thought about Heather's words. No wonder Kavan was furious. But before she could ask any more, they'd passed the Black Boar and were turning into the cricket club field next door.

'There are buns and pop for the

children.' Heather pointed to trestle tables covered with plates and bottles. 'We adults use the pavilion. It's a bit of a squash but we manage.'

Rowena followed her into the white-washed cricket pavilion. She was beginning to feel tired. It had been a long, eventful day. A yawn escaped her before she could stop it. Heather smiled sympathetically.

'Tired? Never mind. Just have one drink then you can escape.'

★ ★ ★

Heather's friends had commandeered a table and Peter made room for his sister and Rowena. 'What would you like to drink?'

He went off to fetch refreshments and someone slid into his empty seat.

'I just wanted to say that when I want something, I usually get it,' said Kavan in a low voice.

'Is that a threat?' Rowena asked surprised.

'Of course not. But I warn you, I

don't give up easily.'

What an insufferable man, she thought.

'You might as well accept it,' she said. 'In a month or so I shall come down to Allarton and move into Cherry Cottage.'

'Welcome To Your New Home . . .'

At home, Rowena seldom ate more than a piece of toast for her breakfast but when, next morning, Mrs King placed before her a plate of bacon rashers, glistening fried eggs and crispy hash browns, she made no protest.

The food was beautifully cooked and in no time the plate was empty.

She was sitting back, replete, enjoying a cup of coffee when Mrs King joined her and they chatted of Allarton and the surrounding area.

'I'm sure you'll be happy if you decide to come and live here,' said the old lady. 'I've had a good life in Allarton — and so did Leonora. We never wanted to live anywhere else. Mind you, Leonora liked her little holidays. She'd get all excited and disappear for a few days — never told me where she went, she said it was her little secret — but when she came back, she often seemed rather sad. It was very strange.'

Rowena wanted to say, 'Perhaps she had a secret lover,' but it sounded frivolous, so she didn't.

Mrs King stood up. 'I must let you get on,' she said, and began to clear the table.

★   ★   ★

Rowena wanted to take one more look around the cottage before she returned to Melchester. Her coffee finished, she went upstairs and packed her case and locked it safely in the boot of her car.

Mrs King was sorry to see her go, but with promises to return soon, Rowena made her way to the estate agent's office.

Ed Tyler produced the key to the cottage. 'By the way,' he said, 'I've had a call from Kavan Reagan this morning. He's still very keen to buy.'

'So he said last night.'

'He's increased his offer.'

'I'm not selling.' Rowena's voice was firm. 'I told him so last night.'

She turned towards the door.

'I'll bring the key back to you when I've finished.'

On her way to the cottage, she began to wonder whether it really was as beautiful as she remembered. She crossed the bridge and drove along the lane by the river. And there it was again, Cherry Cottage, looking just as perfect as when she had first seen it.

She parked in the gateway to the field and made her way up the path, under the cherry trees which edged it.

The living-room seemed suspended in time, waiting for someone to take up residence in it once more. A clock ticked languidly on the mantelshelf and a trapped fly buzzed around and around. Rowena opened the window to release it and to air the room, then she sank into an armchair and looked about her.

Her cottage.

She felt the pride of ownership. No one else should have it, especially Kavan Reagan, however much he sulked.

Taking a notebook and pen from her bag, she spent the next hour going from room to room, deciding what furniture she would keep and which pieces she would replace with something of her own.

There was no time to examine the garden but, from the window, she could see a collection of broken-down sheds along one side, probably the remains of the cattery. Those must go, she thought.

She took a final look round and left the cottage, carefully locking the door.

She'd reached the gate and was stretching out a hand to open it when, with a roar, a red motorbike raced past her and up the lane towards the smallholding at the end.

Kavan Reagan again! she thought, glaring after him.

★ ★ ★

'I'll return the key to Mr Bevan as soon as he gets back.' Ed Tyler locked the key to the cottage in the wall safe. 'Can I help you with anything else?'

'Would you ask Mr Bevan to get someone to clean up the garden. Remove those broken sheds and so on?'

'Of course.' The estate agent made a note on his pad. 'You're off home now?'

'Yes. Back to work tomorrow. End of my little holiday.'

'An eventful one, I think.' He escorted her to the door. 'I look forward to meeting you again soon.'

'In a few weeks.' Rowena smiled a farewell and climbed into her car.

★　★　★

Molly's face was set in a disapproving mask when she opened the door to Rowena that evening. Rowena decided just to jolly her friend along.

'You don't need me to run Tiny Tigers,' she said as they sat in Molly's comfortable sitting-room, both with a glass of Molly's favourite German wine in front of them. 'You do most of the organising anyway.'

'It won't be the same,' said Molly. 'We've run it together from the start.'

'One of us was bound to leave at some time,' Rowena pointed out.

'But you don't need to. It's just a whim. You might regret it.'

'I won't.' Rowena's voice was quiet but determined. 'I love Cherry Cottage. I've already made some friends and I have a new job.'

Molly looked into her glass. 'I wish I'd never told you to go and see it.'

'Well, I'm glad you did. Oh, Molly, wait till you see it. You'll be able to come and stay for weekends in the country.'

'But it's two hundred miles away. Won't you change your mind?'

Rowena didn't answer the question but asked one of her own. 'What did Graham say about my proposition?'

'He's away on a business trip. Germany this time.'

Molly's husband was a high-powered salesman and frequently had to work away. With no children, Molly needed her friends.

'So you haven't had a chance to talk about it?'

'He'll be back at the weekend. I'll mention it then.'

'Let me know when you want me to come round to discuss it. I'll not be greedy; you'll be able to afford what I'm asking. Now tell me what's happened while I've been away. Is Mrs Carpenter willing to take on the annual raffle? And what about little Kirstie? Is she over her fall?'

They chatted about nursery matters until it was time for Rowena to leave. Molly was in a better frame of mind by then and they parted cheerfully.

★ ★ ★

For the next few weeks, Rowena felt that she was never off the telephone and seemed to be forever writing letters.

How could so many people need to be informed of her new address? She made lists and crossed off items as she dealt with them — utilities, insurances, banks, friends, relations — the list was unending.

Mr Bevan phoned to confirm that he'd arranged to have the old sheds removed and to have the garden tidied. Rowena breathed a sigh of relief. Things seemed to be going well at that end.

She finished late at the nursery most days. There was so much to sort out and she reached home each evening exhausted, wishing for the day to arrive when she'd find herself settled in her new life.

One weekend, she decided to review her wardrobe, and was stuffing clothes into bags for the charity shop when Molly arrived.

'I won't be needing these dresses in the country,' she said defensively, as Molly eyed the pile on the bed.

'What if you get asked out by your

new friends? Won't you want to get dressed up then?'

'Life seems very casual in the country,' said Rowena. 'Trousers and shirts or jumpers seems to cover most occasions.'

'Well, I should keep a few dressy things,' Molly advised. 'I dropped in to invite you to dinner this evening,' she went on. 'Graham wants to discuss your offer to sell me your share of the nursery. Actually,' she turned to look out of the window. 'I'm coming round to the idea.'

'Oh, Molly, that's wonderful. I didn't want to sell it to a stranger.'

* * *

Molly wasn't a very good cook, but she always stuck to simple recipes and Rowena enjoyed the chicken casserole and supermarket cheesecake. In any case, the food wasn't really important. She was there to discuss selling her share of Tiny Tigers Nursery.

Graham, handsome but businesslike, placed a large writing pad on the coffee table in front of him.

'If Molly wants to do this, I'm in agreement,' he said, with a warm smile at his wife. 'I'm afraid I'll have to be abroad quite a lot over the next year or two and I'm sure she'll not miss me if she's extra busy.' He picked up a pen. 'Now, to business.'

For the next hour, Graham questioned Rowena and wrote copious notes and lists of figures while Molly sat anxiously watching them.

From being against Rowena's departure, she now seemed to welcome it as the chance to be sole proprietor of Tiny Tigers Nursery.

At last, Graham threw down his pen and sat back in his armchair with a sigh. 'I think that covers everything. I'll make an appointment for us to see Symons, our solicitor, next week. Will you be available?'

'Of course.' Rowena was relieved the session was over.

Molly stood up to make some coffee. 'Just a cup, then I'll be gone,' said Rowena. 'I have so much to do.'

★ ★ ★

Now that Molly and Graham were happy about buying her share of the nursery, a weight had been lifted from Rowena's shoulders. She decided to make a flying visit to Allarton in order to arrange for the removal of some of Miss Lawton's furniture to a saleroom.

She telephoned Mrs King to book two nights' accommodation at Briar House.

'I'm so pleased,' said the old lady. 'I was hoping you'd be back.'

Rowena was touched by how welcoming everyone in Allarton seemed to be. Then she corrected herself — almost everyone.

She engaged a relief teacher for three days and set off for the village early one Wednesday morning. This time, she made only the briefest of stops halfway and crossed the bridge at Allarton at midday.

She had prepared stickers for the furniture and ornaments she wanted to sell and the man from the saleroom had promised, in answer to her telephone call the day before, to be at the cottage at one o'clock.

He was on time, a small, plump man with a cheery smile and a brisk manner.

'Good afternoon, Miss Gage. Lovely day, isn't it? Now, if you'd like to show me the pieces, we'll get on with it.'

Rowena's stickers quickly identified the articles for sale and in less than an hour, the inspection was finished.

'When can you collect them?' she asked.

He took out a diary. 'Well . . . ' He flicked over the pages. 'What about next Tuesday morning?'

Rowena bit her lip. 'Oh dear, I was hoping you could come tomorrow.'

'In a hurry, are you?'

'I have to go back to Melchester on Friday. I won't be here next week.'

'Is there no-one who could help you out by being here while we take the things out? It won't take long.'

Rowena shook her head. 'I don't really know anyone in Allarton.'

The little man took pity on her. 'I'll tell you what we'll do. If you don't mind us coming in the evening, we'll do it tomorrow.'

'Oh, would you? Thank you so much. That's wonderful.'

He beamed, pleased to have found a solution to her problem, refused her offer of a drink and left, promising to see her the next day at six.

Remembering that the solicitor had written that the work on the garden was completed, Rowena opened the kitchen door and stepped outside to inspect the results.

The garden had been transformed! The old, broken down sheds along the wall had gone, the lawn had been cut, the hedges trimmed and paths swept.

Pleased, she locked the cottage and drove to Briar House where she renewed her acquaintance with Mrs King, but she decided not to contact Heather Robinson. The girl might have made plans for the evening which she would feel obliged to cancel in favour of Rowena.

I'll try the Riverbank Inn for my evening meal this time, she decided, remembering the little inn where the procession had gathered. They're bound to do food.

It was only when she was scanning the menu that she realised she hadn't eaten all day. She ordered macaroni cheese and sat back, looking around the tiny dining-room while she waited. It was early and there were few diners other than herself.

She was amused to see comic illustrations of *The Wind in the Willows* on the walls. Of course, the *Riverbank* Inn, she reminded herself. She was engrossed in studying the picture nearest to her table — of Mole decorating his house — when her meal arrived.

She enjoyed the food and then returned to Briar House for an early night.

★ ★ ★

The next morning, in the tiny supermarket in the square, she bumped into Heather Robinson.

'Rowena! Fancy seeing you! Why didn't you say you were coming down? We could have arranged to meet!'

Rowena felt embarrassed. 'I'm sorry, Heather, but it's just a flying visit. I didn't want to interfere with any arrangements you might have already made.'

'Don't be silly! It's lovely to see you. Let's meet for dinner tonight.'

Rowena held up a hand. 'I'm having some of Miss Lawton's furniture collected this evening so I'll be busy, I'm afraid.'

'OK. But we could have a quick coffee now, couldn't we?'

'I'd love to!'

As they left the supermarket, Heather said, 'Why don't you come back with me now and see the nursery? We'll have coffee there. After all, you've agreed to work with me and you haven't even seen inside the place.'

'I've met you, and seen how happy the children are,' said Rowena. 'I know it will suit me. But you're right, I should see where I shall be working. Everything has been decided in such a hurry!'

They were walking in the direction of the river. The sign, *Lucy Locket Nursery*, was still suspended from the gate of the church hall.

Heather unlocked the gate and led her visitor up the path to the small building. Inside, all was colour and noise. The hall was surprisingly large. Chairs screened off areas at either end where children sat with an adult and listened to stories or drew and coloured pictures. In the centre of the room, little boys and girls — at tables or on the floor — played with an assortment of toys.

'It would be lovely to have a purpose-built building,' said Heather, 'but we do the best we can.'

Rowena was taken round and introduced to the other members of staff and the volunteer helpers. Then Heather took her into the tiny room she used as an office — 'More a cupboard really,' she apologised with a smile — and over coffee they discussed the future.

'It will be very different from owning your own nursery school,' Heather warned.

Rowena smiled. 'Don't worry. I want a different sort of life.'

Heather poured some more coffee. 'How are your plans going? Will Molly buy your share of the nursery?'

'All settled. We saw the solicitor this week.'

'And your flat?'

'Lucky again. The teacher who's replacing me is going to buy it. Everything is going so well that I'm worried.' She laughed. 'No, I'm not. I'm really happy. I'll soon be here for good.'

* ★ ★

Back in the cottage, she made a picnic lunch and carried it outside. Shc'd decided against doing any gardening this visit; she wanted to plan everything slowly and carefully once she'd moved in for good. This was going to be the perfect cottage garden.

Instead, she stretched out on an old recliner she'd found in the utility room behind the kitchen.

The garden was incredibly peaceful. The only sound was a lazy buzzing from the bees and the soft lowing of a cow in a nearby field.

She put down her tray on the grass and lay back, soon falling into a doze until, suddenly, she was awakened by the rattle and clatter of a tractor and trailer passing by in the lane. It had come from the direction of Kavan's smallholding.

That wretched man, she thought to herself, he won't even let me rest in my own garden! She sat up, annoyed, then realised that he had to work.

She went to the gate but the tractor had disappeared.

Well, I certainly didn't want to speak to him, she told herself and — picking up the tray — strolled back to the cottage to make a pot of tea.

Despite herself, her thoughts were of Kavan as she bustled around the kitchen. He would be her nearest neighbour. Would she see much of him? And if she did, for how long would he resent the fact that she was now the owner of the cottage that he'd expected to inherit?

★   ★   ★

Despite the fact that the men were later in arriving to collect her surplus furniture than had been promised, they had taken it all away by eight o'clock that evening. She wandered around looking into all the rooms and thought how bare they now seemed. She couldn't wait to get her own belongings in place.

She made a salad and opened a tin of salmon, glad she'd had the foresight to get in groceries that morning, then set about vacuuming and polishing. Her furniture would come into a gleaming home.

At ten o'clock, she went back to Briar House, well satisfied with her evening's work. She would make an early start for Melchester in the morning, and perhaps be back there by mid-afternoon.

★ ★ ★

Rowena settled on a removal date. The furniture she didn't want to take with her would have gone to the local saleroom long before then. She booked a small removal firm and was promised two strapping young men to do the hard work. She telephoned Heather to let her know the date.

'I shall follow the van in my car,' she said, 'but they're setting off very early and will probably arrive before me. I don't suppose you know anyone who could be there to let them in and make them a cup of tea, do you?'

'Well, I'd do it myself, but I've got a meeting that day. But I'm sure my brother, Peter, will do it. He's got a soft spot for you.' She laughed. 'You'd better watch out.'

Rowena joined in the laughter but wasn't too pleased. She wasn't at all attracted to Peter Robinson and didn't want to have to fend him off. But that problem was for the future. For now, she would be grateful if he could help her on her moving day. She said so to Heather.

'Consider it done,' said Heather. 'And let me know if there's anything else you want. I'm really looking forward to you coming. I'm depending on you to bring lots of new ideas to the nursery.'

* * *

Rowena's last day at Tiny Tigers Nursery was an emotional one. She arrived early and took a slow stroll around the rooms that were filled with small-sized furniture, toys and bright wall decorations. She remembered the fun she and Molly had had choosing them in the early days.

Her office was bare of her belongings now. On Monday, it would be occupied by Claire Jenkins, the young teacher Molly had chosen to be her assistant. Claire had started work last week so that the changeover would be smooth, and Rowena liked her but couldn't help a tiny pang of jealousy when she saw how quickly she and Molly had become close.

There was little for Rowena to do on the last day. Friends and colleagues from other schools had been invited to coffee and later, there was to be a little party for the children.

She wasn't sure how she got through the day dry-eyed. The children had given her so many gifts and bunches of flowers and she received many compliments from parents who were sorry to see her go.

When Uncle Roy, the children's favourite entertainer arrived with his puppets, Rowena, Molly and Claire were able to leave their small charges in his care and relax at the back of the room with cups of coffee.

Rowena sighed. 'This has been a most traumatic day,' she said. 'I never dreamed I should feel like this. Everyone has been so kind.'

'They'll miss you,' said Molly. 'I hope we can cope.' The smile she gave Claire said that she was quite sure they would.

Rowena agreed. No-one was indispensable, as the old saying goes.

'I hear you've inherited a beautiful cottage in the country,' said Claire.

Rowena reached into her handbag and brought out a packet of photographs and, for the next ten minutes, gave the girl an enthusiastic description of Cherry Cottage and the village.

'Looks idyllic,' said the young teacher.

Rowena crossed her fingers. 'It is,' she agreed.

★ ★ ★

Three days later, she packed her last minute belongings into her car and locked the door of her flat for the final time. She drove the short distance to the estate agent's office to deliver the keys, then she set off for Allarton without a backward glance.

The furniture van had left very early and would be there long before her but, as she'd heard nothing to the contrary, she assumed that Peter Robinson would be there to direct operations on her behalf.

After driving for an hour, she swung her car into a busy service station. A drink and a chance to rest her eyes would be welcome.

Sipping her coffee, she thought back to the previous evening and the farewell party that Molly had arranged for her.

Rowena had worn her favourite kingfisher-blue dress and Molly had smiled approvingly.

'Well, at least you kept one good

dress,' she commented.

'I wouldn't throw this away; it's my favourite colour.'

'And suits you beautifully,' said a voice behind her. 'Oh, Rowena, do you have to go?'

Although the party had only just begun, Craig Benson had obviously helped himself liberally to the drinks laid out on the kitchen table. He took Rowena's hand and attempted to plant a beery kiss on her cheek.

She twisted out of his grasp.

'Yes, Craig, I do. I have a new house and a new job.'

He'd slumped against the wall. 'But how shall I manage without you?'

'The same way you managed before I moved into the flat above you,' said Rowena.

Craig, a brilliant computer programmer who was quite incapable of looking after himself, lived alone, and was always running out of milk or sugar or bread. He always seemed to take it as his due that Rowena would come to his aid. She wasn't sorry to be rid of him.

She wandered into the sitting-room and sat on the couch next to Graham.

'Molly is pleased with the way everything has turned out,' he said. 'Claire Jenkins seems very efficient. Hopefully, Molly won't miss you too much.'

Rowena smiled at him. 'I can't believe how much has happened, and so quickly. A few weeks ago, I couldn't have dreamed of such changes in my life — or Molly's.'

Graham squeezed her hand and leaned across to kiss her cheek. 'Very best wishes to you in your new life. Don't lose touch with us, will you?'

★　★　★

The following afternoon at two o'clock, she drove once more into the village of Allarton and looked around with pleasure. There was Mr Bevan's office and nearby, the friendly estate agent's.

She remembered her first coffee in

the Daisy Tearoom and her first lunch in the Black Boar.

Now, this could be the future pattern of her life.

She crossed the little bridge and drove along the lane. Parking in her space beside the old gate, she swung her legs out of the car and stood up thankfully, stretching her cramped limbs as she breathed in deeply. The air was sweet and fresh.

The blossom had disappeared from the cherry trees but, never mind, she thought, she would be there when they bloomed again next year.

Grateful as she was to him, she hoped Peter Robinson had gone. She wanted the cottage to herself. But as she took the key from her purse and reached up to put it in the lock, the door swung open.

'Welcome to your new home,' said Kavan Reagan.

Village Life

With her hand still stretching up towards the keyhole, she stared at him stupidly. Kavan Reagan! What was he doing here?

'Where's Peter?' she asked. 'Why are you . . . ?'

He stepped back so that she could enter, then closed the door behind them both.

'Emergency,' he said. 'Peter chipped a front tooth early this morning and had to go to the dentist, so I stepped in.'

They'd reached the kitchen. Rowena was aware that everything was very tidy and that the kettle was beginning to boil.

'I'll make you a cup of tea, then I'll go,' said Kavan.

'No.' She put out a hand. 'Stay and have a cup.' She gestured round the kitchen. 'It looks as if you've earned it.'

'It was nothing.' He smiled. 'I couldn't just stand around till you arrived. I don't suppose I've put everything in the right place, but you can soon reorganise it.'

'It looks very nice,' she said warmly.

He poured two cups of tea and they drank them standing at the window. Rowena had been sitting in the car for hours and Kavan looked as if he felt more at ease standing than sitting.

'Perhaps you'd like to see what I've done to the other rooms,' he said diffidently. 'I'm sure you'll want to make some changes. I can stay,' he said, glancing at the clock, 'for another fifteen minutes if you tell me what you'd like me to move.'

'The sitting-room looks fine,' said Rowena, 'I don't want any changes.'

'Come upstairs then.' Kavan led the way. 'I had to guess what pieces you wanted in each room.'

Rowena went into the main bedroom then the guestroom. 'Well, if you don't mind helping me, I'd like the little round table in here by the window,' she said, 'and the armchair in the main bedroom. Otherwise, I'm very happy with everything as it is.'

Kavan effected the changes. 'You're right, that does look better,' he said. 'Now if you'll excuse me, I have to go.'

'Thank you very much,' said Rowena. 'It was so kind of you to give up your time.' And you really wanted this house, she added to herself.

'We're neighbours,' he said. 'If there's anything else I can do, just ask. Oh!' He reached into his pocket and brought out a small card. 'My telephone number in case you need it. I have your number.'

She looked puzzled then remembered he used to play cards with Leonora. Probably he often telephoned her.

* * *

Rowena spent a happy evening unpacking boxes and arranging china in cupboards, books on shelves and clothes in wardrobes.

She was so busy that she realised with a shock that it was eight o'clock already and she'd had nothing yet to eat.

For today, enough is enough, she decided. She made toast, heated some soup and carried a tray into the sitting-room. There was an Agatha Christie play on television. She'd just watch that and then get off to bed. But it was hard to concentrate on the TV. She found herself gazing round the room with quiet satisfaction and sighing with happiness. Cherry Cottage was her new home. She intended to be very happy there.

Later, lying in bed in a strange room, she was aware of the silence of the countryside outside her window. Now and again, there was a soft squeak or a sharp cry. But no cars, no buses, no streetlights. She thought, shall I miss the familiar noises? Will it be too quiet to sleep?

Her mind floated gently between sleep and consciousness. Unbidden, the face of Kavan Reagan appeared before her eyes in the darkness.

Kavan! I wonder whether . . . but then she was asleep.

★ ★ ★

It was a short distance from her cottage to the nursery school, but Rowena decided to take her car on her first day working there because she wanted to call at the little supermarket on her way home.

When she arrived at the nursery, Heather and her two other assistants were busy putting out hand towels in the cloakroom and toys in the hall.

'What can I do?' she asked Heather.

'Do you just want to observe on your first day, or would you rather dive in straight away?'

'Dive in.' She laughed. 'I can observe as I go along.'

'Right. Can you set up a creative art

table? I'll show you where we keep the paper and paints. Luckily we have plenty of cupboard space in the corridor at the back. Come along. It's down here.'

Heather led the way to a passage at the back of the hall and unlocked a cupboard. For the next ten minutes, Rowena was busy laying out coloured paper, scissors, crayons, buttons and glue.

She had just finished this when squeals of chatter from the doorway announced the arrival of her new pupils.

It was so strange to be eyed curiously instead of greeted enthusiastically, as in her own nursery, but she knew that small children need time to get used to a new person.

She busied herself at the table and gradually, one by one, the children came to see what she was doing. A few, more adventurous than the others, grabbed aprons and came to her to have them tied about their waists. Then they sat down and reached for papers and crayons. Rowena sighed with satisfaction. She was accepted.

★ ★ ★

'I can't believe you've only been in Allarton for two months.' Heather poured out the wine and settled back comfortably in her seat opposite Rowena, who smiled and reached for her glass.

'Neither can I. I seem to have been here for ever.'

She looked around the Riverbank Inn.

It was Friday evening and, after a busy week, Heather had suggested that the two of them have a meal out. Rowena had readily agreed.

She'd worked hard since her arrival in Allarton, allowing herself only a week to settle in before starting at the nursery, so her evenings had been taken up with arranging her pictures and ornaments and the weekends, which luckily were mostly dry, had been spent working in the garden.

'Do you ever see anything of Kavan?' Heather asked now, a shade too casually.

Rowena grinned. 'Do we chat over the garden fence, do you mean?'

'Well, you do live next door to each other.'

'Next door, if you don't count several fields. No. I've seen very little of him. He waves if I'm in the garden when he rattles by on that wretched tractor, but he doesn't stop to chat.'

Their food arrived and there was a lull in the conversation as they passed each other rolls and butter and shook out their napkins. Heather picked up her knife and fork.

'We all wish Kavan could find a really nice girlfriend,' she said.

'Meaning me?' asked Rowena. 'I don't think so!'

'So you don't find him attractive? He's interested in you.'

Rowena flushed. 'I don't think so.'

They ate for a while in silence, then Heather said, 'He was married at one time, you know, but his wife was no good for him at all.'

'Did you know her?'

'Oh, yes. She was a local girl, but very unpopular. Always out, dressed-up and made-up and eyeing up other women's menfolk.'

'I should have thought Kavan could deal with her. He seems the domineering type.'

'He's not domineering at all,' Heather said quickly. 'He used to be really very sweet. But he changed after his wife went off with another man.'

Rowena smiled. 'You seem to have a soft spot for him yourself.'

Heather picked up the ice-cream menu. 'As a friend,' she said, 'nothing more.'

★   ★   ★

One sunny afternoon about a week later, Rowena had arrived home from work intending to spend the rest of the day working in the garden. At the weekend, she'd drained the pool, laid a new liner and filled with it with water. She'd also bought some water plants and was now looking forward to putting them in place. Gardening was a skill she hadn't realised she possessed, and the garden was rapidly becoming her pride and joy.

She went through to the kitchen to put on the kettle and make a quick cup of coffee before she set to work, but what she saw from the kitchen window made her freeze in disbelief.

A cow! A cow in her garden!

The cow strolled leisurely down the centre of the lawn followed by another and another. Then, as she watched, a young calf attempted to jump the hedge at the side of the garden and, getting stuck on the top, flailed around until it extricated itself, beating down the hedge as it did so.

Rowena slammed the kettle down on the sink, seized a broom and ran into the garden. Now there were eight cows — five adults and three calves — strolling to and fro, trampling the flowers, scraping up the borders and threatening to fall into both the pond and the little greenhouse.

'Go back, go back!' she shouted, attempting to herd them back towards the hedge, their obvious mode of entry. But the cows' reaction was simply to stare at her with their liquid brown eyes.

'Oh!' She threw down the broom and ran back into the house.

She picked up her book of telephone numbers and out fell the little card Kavan had given her.

They were his cows! He could come and get them back!

Furiously, she dialled the number.

'Hello?' It was a female voice. 'Kavan? I'm sorry, he's not here. He's out in the fields.' The woman sounded as if she didn't care.

'There are cows in my garden,' Rowena stormed. 'He must come and get them out now.'

'Cows? They won't hurt you.'

'Maybe not, but they are ruining my garden.' The woman's laid back attitude had wound up Rowena even more.

'I'll send someone over,' the woman said with a sigh.

'As soon as possible, please.'

Rowena slammed down the telephone and went to the kitchen door to watch the cows. The calves were small and rather sweet but she was in no mood to admire them. The animals stood in a group in the centre of the lawn — planning their next move, she thought.

But before they could do anything else, she heard the front gate slam and a large farm worker and a skinny teenager marched up her path.

Ignoring her, they went through to the back garden. She followed them and watched as with slaps on large, hairy rumps and cries of 'Hup,' the cows were persuaded back through her fence to the field beyond.

Thankful, she went back to her kitchen, picked up the kettle and made her cup of coffee. Now she really needed it.

Carrying her mug, she went back out to inspect the damage. It was not quite as bad as she'd thought, but bad enough. Large hooves had scraped at the grass and several flowers had been sampled and given a good chewing before being spat out. The hedge was a mess.

She sat on a bench and looked around. She'd worked so hard on her garden; now she'd have to repair the damage and all her hard work had been in vain.

She looked up to see Kavan staring down at her from the other side of the hedge.

'Err . . . How are you today? My housekeeper said you were furious.'

'Your housekeeper?'

'You spoke to her on the phone. She sent Seth and Jed round.'

So the female voice belonged to a housekeeper.

'Oh — yes. Thank you. They removed the cows but look what I'm left with.' She gestured round the garden.

'We'll soon have it straight.' He bobbed down out of sight.

Rowena moved towards the hedge. In the field beyond, she could see a trolley laden with tools, wire and wooden stakes. Kavan was straightening the bent wire of the old fence.

He stripped off his shirt and, despite herself, Rowena was impressed with his deeply tanned chest and firm shoulder muscles.

'Excuse me,' he said, 'but it's hot work.'

'Would you . . . would you like a cool drink?' she offered. 'I'm afraid I haven't any beer but I made some lemonade last night. It's in the fridge and very cold.'

'Sounds wonderful,' he said, not pausing in his work.

Rowena chuckled to herself as she headed into the kitchen. Goodness! A topless man in her garden! Hmm! She poured out a large tumbler of lemonade and took it out to him.

'My gran used to make lemonade,' he said. 'I haven't tasted this home-made stuff for years. It's very good.'

Rowena stood, holding the empty glass, watching him work.

Effortlessly, he hammered the stakes into place before donning thick gloves to attach the barbed wire.

'I'll have to come into your garden to do the last bit,' he said, 'then I'll look at the rest of the damage.' He was straightening the hedge and twisting the branches around the wire as he spoke. 'There! This will be as good as new in a few weeks once there's been some new growth to cover the gaps.'

He turned to look at her and she was conscious of his masculinity only feet away. She flushed, and he looked down at his naked chest.

'I'm sorry,' he said, and quickly shrugged his arms into his shirt and fastened a few buttons.

Her flush deepened. 'It's quite all right. Would you like more lemonade?'

'If it's no trouble. I'll see what I can do with this grass.'

Thankfully, she escaped to the kitchen where she stared at her still flushed face in the mirror.

Rowena Gage, you're a fool, she

admonished herself. At your age, blushing at a bronzed chest.

She looked out of the window to where Kavan, on his hands and knees, was restoring her plants to some semblance of what they'd been before. He certainly was attractive. Too attractive to be furious with, even if his cows had messed up her garden.

She tidied her hair and patted just a little powder on to her shining nose. Then she poured another glass of lemonade and went back into the garden. The look Kavan gave her was frankly admiring.

'You look very cool in that pale blue sundress,' he said.

She smiled and handed him the lemonade. 'Can you do anything with the flowers?'

'I'm afraid not. The grass will soon recover but flowers don't like to be chewed. Buy new plants and send me the bill.'

'No. You've done enough. I'll replace the flowers myself.'

They strolled back towards the

cottage, Kavan carrying his tumbler of lemonade. Rowena gestured to the white table and chairs in a shady corner of the terrace. 'Sit down and cool off,' she said, taking a seat herself.

'You've settled in, then,' he said. 'How's the nursery job coming on?'

'Very well. I'm really enjoying it.'

He drank his lemonade.

'Your housekeeper . . . ' she began.

'Mrs Morrow.'

'Yes. Does she still live in?'

He gave her a quizzical look. 'She does — more's the pity. She and her son, Jed. You met him just now, he came with Seth to get the cows.'

He sighed. 'I should never have taken on a live-in housekeeper. When my wife left — I'm sure Heather told you about that — I couldn't cope with both the land and the house. Someone recommended Mrs Morrow to me. She needed a home, she'd just had a messy divorce, so I engaged her.

'Isn't she a very good housekeeper?' Rowena asked.

He sighed again. 'It's not that, it's . . . well, it's Jed. I don't like having a noisy, untidy great youth galloping round my house. I don't like his loud music and his even louder friends. That's why . . . well, that's why I wanted Cherry Cottage. I could have used the extra land and Mrs Morrow and Jed could have lived in the cottage.'

Rowena felt guilty, then resented the feeling.

'Cherry Cottage is not for sale,' she said quietly.

'It might be — some time.' He spoke lightly but there was a steely tone to his voice. 'You might decide not to stay in Allarton.'

'I can assure you, I'm staying,' she said. 'This is my home now.'

He drained his glass, replaced it on the table and stood up. 'Thank you for the lemonade. I'll see you around.'

'Thank you for your help with the garden,' she replied formally.

She watched him walk down the path and disappear through the gate. What might have been a friendly encounter had turned sour, she thought. Would he never give up? The cottage was hers and she would never sell.

★ ★ ★

'Rowena, there's a rather gorgeous man at the door asking for you.' Molly came into the bedroom as Rowena was hanging some freshly ironed blouses in the wardrobe.

Molly had come for a flying visit, unable to wait for the holidays to visit Allarton.

Rowena turned. 'I didn't hear the doorbell.'

'I spotted him through the window and opened the door as he came up the path.'

'Black curly hair and blue eyes?'

'A fabulous tan and a beautiful smile?' Molly's eyes were sparkling. 'Who is he?'

'My next-door neighbour.' Rowena brushed past her and went downstairs.

Kavan stood on the doorstep looking frankly annoyed at being kept waiting. He gestured towards some plant trays at his feet.

'Replacements,' he said shortly, and turned away to leave.

Rowena was conscious of Molly prodding her in the back.

'Would you like to come in for a coffee?' she called after him.

Molly disappeared into the kitchen. 'I'll go and put the kettle on.'

'Sorry. Can't stop,' he called back. 'Lots to do.'

Rowena closed the door. 'Make that just two coffees,' she said.

Molly appeared in the doorway with a downcast expression on her face. 'You didn't try hard enough,' she accused. 'And I was dying to meet him. You didn't tell me you had a next door neighbour like that. No wonder you wanted to move here.'

'Don't get excited. He's . . . difficult.'

'Is he married?'

'Divorced.' Rowena carried the coffee

mugs into the sitting-room. 'But forget him. Come and tell me how you're getting on in the nursery without me.'

★ ★ ★

One morning, as she was settling the children at the art table, Rowena was surprised to see Ed Tyler standing in the doorway. They recognised each other at the same time.

'Mrs Gage, I didn't know you worked here. How have you settled into Allarton life?'

'Mr Tyler! How nice to see you again. I'm settling in well, thank you.'

'My mother-in-law usually brings the twins,' the estate agent explained, 'but she had an appointment this morning, so I was roped in.'

Rowena fastened an apron round his little girl, Sally, while he did the same for Jeremy. Then he lifted them on to their chairs and gave them some paper and crayons.

'Gosh, these tables are low!' He

straightened up with a groan.

Rowena laughed. 'You get used to it.'

'This is your usual line of business, is it?'

'Yes. I had my own nursery school in Melchester. But being Heather's assistant suits me now.'

'And you still like the cottage?'

'It's lovely. You must call and see what I've done to the garden.'

'I will. Thank you. Actually . . . my wife and I are having some friends in for drinks tomorrow evening. I don't suppose you'd care to join us, would you? You'd get to meet a few more local people.'

'That's very kind. Are you sure your wife won't mind a stranger at her party?'

'Gosh, no. Anita loves meeting new people. And it's quite informal. See you at about eight?'

Rowena told Heather about Ed Tyler's invitation as they were drinking their morning coffee.

'You'll like their house, it's very

picturesque,' said Heather, without enthusiasm. 'Well, it should be; he's an estate agent! If he can't find himself a nice house . . . ' She gave a mirthless laugh.

'Do you know his wife?'

'Anita. Yes, I know her.'

And, from the tone of your voice, you don't like her, thought Rowena.

Heather stood up abruptly. 'Excuse me, I must make some phone calls. We'll need the man to look at the boiler. The water temperature isn't right.'

Rowena finished her coffee. I hope I shall like Anita, she thought.

★   ★   ★

The girl who came forward with Ed to greet her at the party was small and plump, with a cap of shining black hair and a wide smile. Rowena was sure she would like her.

'Hello, Mrs Gage. Ed's told me all about you. How nice to meet you.'

'Rowena, please.'

'Well, Rowena, I'll take you round and introduce you once everyone is here. Meanwhile, Ed, get Rowena a drink.'

As Heather had said, the house was very picturesque; a chocolate box cottage with diamond-paned windows and a flower-filled front garden.

Ed took her into the beautifully fitted kitchen to choose a drink. She looked at the array of bottles on the gleaming granite work surface and selected a white wine.

'I'm not a great drinker,' she told him.

'I'm so glad you decided to come.' He handed her the glass. 'We're a friendly village. You'll soon make new friends.'

'What a lovely garden.' Rowena moved towards the window. 'And look at that enormous cedar tree!'

'It's been here for absolutely ages — long before the cottage was built. Go into the garden, if you like. But would you excuse me for one minute? I must just speak to someone.'

He left her to her own devices and Rowena wandered out through the open door. Chairs were placed around outside, but as yet the guests were all indoors.

'Rowena!' A masculine voice behind made her spin round.

'Peter! Hello.'

Peter Robinson hurried towards her and, taking her arm, led her to a nearby bench.

'What a piece of luck! I'd no idea you'd been invited.'

They sipped their drinks and smiled at each other like old friends.

'Heather isn't here then?' she inquired.

'No. Well it would be a bit awkward.' He looked down into his glass. 'I suppose you ought to know, it's general knowledge after all. Heather and Ed were almost engaged when Anita came along and snatched him from under Heather's nose. So there's no love lost between them.'

'But *you* are friendly with them.'

'Ed's one of my oldest friends. We don't see as much of each other as we did, but we're still close.'

So there was a good reason for Heather's antagonism.

Rowena, thoughtful, sipped her wine in silence.

She suddenly became aware that Peter was watching her.

'I'm sorry. I didn't mean to stare, it's just that you look so beautiful in this soft evening light,' he told her impulsively.

'Thank you!' She stood up to prevent any more compliments which might prove embarrassing. 'I think we should go back inside now.'

'Must we really?'

'Anita has promised to introduce me to the other guests.' Firmly, she led the way back to the house. She must show Peter that outbursts like that were not really welcome.

Anita was in the kitchen. 'There you are, Rowena. Come and meet a few people. I hope we'll have time for a chat later on.'

As Rowena was shepherded into a large room full of people, Peter stood in the doorway, but his eyes followed her as she made her way round the room.

A Picnic

'Shall I help you?' Rowena, kneeling in her garden, paused in the act of pulling a weed from a bed of French marigolds.

'Shall I help you?' asked the small voice again.

Rowena sat back on her heels and turned to find a little girl of about three or four steadily watching her.

'Hello! Where did you come from?'

The child, prettily dressed in pink and white striped trousers and a pink jacket, gestured behind her. 'Frew the gate,' she said, simply.

The child must have walked down the lane and wandered in. But where had she come from? She wasn't likely to have come from Kavan's house. She must have come from one of the other cottages in the lane.

'Where's your Mummy?' Rowena asked her.

'Wiv Sinclair.'

Rowena stood up and tried again. 'What about Daddy?'

'He's busy.'

Hmm . . . Perhaps she'd better phone the police.

She walked to the gate, locking it securely.

'Why are you doing that?' asked the child.

'Because I don't want you to wander out on to the road again. You'd better stay here until we can find your Mummy. Would you like a glass of milk?'

'Yes, please.'

Rowena handed her a trowel and indicated a bare patch of earth. 'You can dig there and then we'll plant a flower. That would help,' she told the child, then set off towards the house to fetch the milk and to telephone the police.

Halfway towards the door, she checked herself and went back to the little girl. 'Er — what is your name?'

'Pansy Mary.'

Rowena looked at her. No surname. Never mind. Pansy was unusual. It might be enough for identification. She turned away again.

'Pansy! Pansy! Where are you?' shouted a man's voice as frantic footsteps approached the cottage.

'My daddy,' said Pansy calmly, continuing to dig.

'Kavan!' Rowena ran to the gate.

'Have you seen a little girl?' His face was a mask of anxiety.

'She's here.' Rowena unfastened the gate.

'Daddy!' The child dropped her trowel and ran towards him.

Kavan gathered her up in his arms. 'How did you get out? Why didn't you stay with Mrs Morrow?'

The child shrugged. 'She was talking and talking on the telephone. She wouldn't play with me. So I came out. I'm helping.'

She wriggled out of his arms and returned to her digging.

Kavan smiled at Rowena's expression. 'Did no one tell you about Pansy? I'm surprised.'

Rowena made no comment. 'I'm getting her a glass of milk,' she said. 'Can I get you something? Tea? Coffee?'

'A cup of tea would be welcome.'

He followed her into the house and leaned against the table in the kitchen as she filled the kettle and put cups and saucers on a tray.

'She was born eight months after Denise, my ex-wife, left me for someone else. Her new relationship didn't last and afterwards she had a succession of other boyfriends. Her latest paramour often has to travel abroad on business and usually takes Denise with him. I recently discovered that, whenever she took off on on of these trips, she'd got into the habit of leaving Pansy with anyone who would take her.'

Rowena glanced at the set expression on his face. The pain was obvious. She said nothing, but added a glass of milk and a plate of biscuits to the tray.

'When I found out what was going on I was furious. I insisted that if

Denise was going away, she was to leave Pansy with me. Of course, I'm busy during the day so Mrs Morrow has to take care of her.'

'Does Mrs Morrow mind?'

'I think she probably does, although she's well paid for it. But, of course, a child that age needs so much attention.'

Rowena picked up the tray, but he took it from her and carried it into the garden. The little girl saw him and ran over.

'Are we having tea with the lady?'

'This is Rowena,' said Kavan. 'You'd better ask her if you can wash your hands if you want a biscuit.'

The child smiled shyly at Rowena who took her into the kitchen and lifted her on to a stool in front of the sink.

'How long is Pansy staying?' asked Rowena, when they joined Kavan.

He was busy pouring tea for them and placing the glass of milk in front of his daughter.

'For three weeks this time,' he said.

'I have a suggestion to make,' she ventured. 'I don't know whether you'll like it.'

He looked at her curiously.

'I could take her with me to the nursery each day. Would she like that?'

Kavan looked from the child to the woman opposite.

'Would you do that? It's a marvellous idea. She'd have children of her own age to play with and I wouldn't have to depend on Mrs Morrow.'

Pansy was consulted and seemed very pleased with the idea.

'Are there children there? Will there be boys?' she asked.

'Certainly. Boys *and* girls.'

'Good. But I like boys best,' said Pansy, taking another biscuit.

'Takes after her mother,' said Kavan dryly.

'Can you bring her down at a quarter past eight?' asked Rowena.

Arrangements were made and after a while, father and daughter left, pleased with the new plan.

* * *

It was a great success. Every morning, Kavan delivered his daughter to Rowena and every evening, she took her home and handed her over to Mrs Morrow. The woman greeted Pansy but ignored Rowena, apart from a brief word of thanks.

Rowena could see no reason for the resentful attitude, unless Mrs Morrow was now receiving less money since she cared for Pansy for a shorter time.

Pansy settled into her new school life, playing happily with boys and girls. She was a sunny little thing and popular with everyone.

Heather was amused by the new arrangement.

'Making yourself indispensable to Kavan?' she teased.

'The child was lonely,' Rowena said, defensively. 'That housekeeper didn't bother with her.'

* * *

One evening, the telephone rang as Rowena was preparing her meal. It was Peter, Heather's brother. Since the drinks party at the Tylers', Rowena had seen nothing of him.

'I was wondering,' he said, 'whether you'd come out to dinner with me one evening.'

'Well . . . I . . . '

'What about tomorrow? Do you like dancing? There's a place over at Tinley with a good restaurant and a small dance floor. Would you come?'

Rowena didn't like being put on the spot. On the other hand, apart from the Tylers' party and a pub meal with Heather, she hadn't been out much socially since she'd moved to Allarton.

'That would be very nice,' she said. 'I'd like that.'

'Right.' He sounded very pleased. 'I'll pick you up at eight.'

Rowena was glad she'd listened to Molly and had kept some of her 'good' clothes, and when Peter arrived at the cottage at eight, she was waiting for him dressed in a long russet skirt and a ruffled cream blouse. He gazed at her with frank admiration.

'You look quite lovely,' he said.

She was pleased with her appearance but couldn't help wishing she'd made the effort for someone else. Peter was a dear but could never be her romantic interest.

★ ★ ★

He drove a little too fast for her liking, but the restaurant was only eight miles away, so she bore the discomfort in silence. She hoped he wouldn't drink then return at that speed.

The restaurant décor could have been designed to compliment her outfit. Comfortable chairs upholstered in chocolate brown, and tables set with cream napery. Thick rich brown velvet curtains were drawn to give the room a cosy feel that was enhanced by deep yellow walls and cream candles in golden sconces.

At one end of the room, a grand piano was set at the edge of a tiny dance floor.

Rowena had eaten little throughout the day, so she was ready to be tempted by the menu for which the Towers was apparently well-known. She was not disappointed. She read it through quickly then went back to the beginning.

Peter was watching her. She looked up at him and smiled.

'I'm afraid I have an unfashionably healthy appetite,' she confessed.

'I'm glad to hear it. I like to see people enjoying their food. Can you see anything you'd like?'

She studied the menu again. 'Mille feuille of mushrooms sounds interesting. Then I should like roast breast of duck with buttered leeks and croquette potatoes. What have you chosen?'

'Oh, I shall have the duck too, but I can't decide between salmon and sole terrine or smoked haddock tartlet for starter.'

The waiter arrived. They gave their orders and Peter ordered wine.

Rowena regarded him warily.

He smiled at her as if reading her thoughts.

'I've ordered water for myself since I'm driving,' he said. 'I'll just have one glass of wine with the meal. Now, tell me, how are you enjoying working with my sister?'

They chatted about the nursery until their first courses arrived.

'And what is your work?' she asked him.

'Civil engineering.'

'Is that interesting?'

'Mm. But I can't find a project that grabs me at the moment. I'm looking around. Perhaps I'll emigrate.'

Rowena looked at him quickly. Was he joking? And if not, what would Heather do? They had no other relations in this country. She'd be left alone. But, before she could decide whether it would be prying to ask, the waiter arrived to collect their plates and

116

serve the main course.

'How are you settling down in Cherry Cottage?' asked Peter. 'Have you had to make any alterations to it?'

'Very little. It's perfect as it is.'

'And the garden? I'm sure it looks much better without those old cattery buildings.'

Mention of the garden reminded Rowena of the incident with the cows, and they spent a few minutes laughing about that.

'It wasn't funny at the time. I was furious. But Kavan was very good. The garden is back to normal now.'

'Useful fellow, Kavan,' said Peter.

Rowena wasn't sure if that was a sarcastic comment.

But Peter smiled. 'I mean it. He's a useful next-door neighbour.'

The piano, which had been tinkling gently in the background, now began a lively quickstep and a few couples made their way to the dance floor.

'If you've finished, would you like to dance?' asked Peter.

When he'd asked yesterday whether she liked dancing, she'd replied without thinking. Now she realised the implications of taking to the floor with him.

The dance floor was tiny. Each couple had to dance pressed closely together, and Peter took advantage of this. He wrapped his arms firmly around Rowena and rested his chin on her hair, so that she felt unable to breathe. After a few minutes, she pulled away.

'I'm sorry, but the dance floor's far too crowded for me.' And she led the way back to their table.

Peter sat down looking disappointed and a little annoyed. He poured them each another glass of wine.

Wine or dancing, thought Rowena, noticing that this time he ignored the water.

'I'm with the most attractive girl in the room and I can't dance with her,' he said with a tight smile.

'We'll try again in a moment,' said Rowena. 'There might be more room on the floor by then.'

But as the evening wore on, more and more couples wanted to dance and there was even less room.

'If we don't try now, we'll never get a dance.' Peter stood up and pulled her to her feet.

But she was adamant. 'I can't dance like this. It's claustrophobic,' she said as she sat down again.

She felt guilty as she looked at him. The prospect of holding her close as they danced had probably been the main attraction of the Towers.

Then she began to feel a little irritable. Peter was fine as a friend but she didn't want to be crushed in his arms. They were the wrong arms.

She had a sudden vision of tanned skin and muscled shoulders. She looked across at her companion. Why wasn't he Kavan? Shocked at her thoughts, she picked up her evening bag and pushed back her chair.

'I won't be a moment,' she excused herself, and moved quickly between the tables to the ladies' room. Luckily, the room was empty. A few dabs of powder failed to reduce the rosy flush on her cheeks. Perhaps Peter would think it was caused by the wine and not by guilty thoughts.

Why ever had she agreed to come out to dinner with him? He was obviously attracted to her and probably thought it would be the beginning of a relationship. What could she say to show him she wasn't interested?

Two girls, laughing loudly, came into the ladies' room and Rowena left. She made her way slowly back to the table.

'I'm sorry,' Peter apologised as soon as he saw her. 'You're right, it isn't pleasant on the dance floor squashed together like that.'

His apology made her feel worse. Now he was taking the blame on himself. And she still had her guilty thoughts.

'Perhaps we could go somewhere bigger next time,' he was saying. 'Somewhere with a proper dance floor.'

A voice inside her wanted to say, 'I don't think so,' but she smiled weakly and mumbled an indefinite reply.

'Would you like to go now?' he asked.

She stood up rather too quickly and they made their way to the car.

'It was a beautiful meal,' she said. She had to sound enthusiastic about something and it *had* been a delicious meal.

★ ★ ★

At the cottage he took her key and opened the door for her. She knew he was expecting her to invite him in but she couldn't do it.

'Thank you for a lovely evening,' she said, and turned to go into the house.

'Could I have just one kiss?'

She turned slowly.

He took her in his arms and pressed his lips to hers. She tried to respond just a little, but felt nothing. He released her and she could sense his disappointment as she went indoors, firmly closing the front door behind her.

She stood in the darkened sitting-room window, and watched as the tail lights of his car moved down the lane.

When the telephone rang, she almost jumped out of her skin.

Quickly she drew the curtains and crossing to pick up the phone.

'There you are,' complained a voice, 'I rang twice earlier in the evening but there was no reply.'

'Molly! How are you?'

'I'm fine. Where have you been?'

'I've been out to dinner.'

'A date!' Molly dropped her aggrieved tone and became animated. 'With your dishy next-door neighbour? Where did you go?'

'No. Not with Kavan.'

'You're not wasting much time, are you? Another man. Who is he?'

'Peter Robinson. His sister is Heather, the owner of the nursery.'

Molly was all interest. 'Is he good-looking?'

'No, not really.'

'Wealthy?'

'I've no idea. What is this, the third degree? We just went out for a meal.'

'Take my advice. Concentrate on the next-door neighbour.'

'Thank you very much. What if he isn't interested in me?'

'Make him interested.'

'Molly, did you ring for anything special? I'm rather tired.'

'Nothing special. My lord and master is away. I just felt like talking to you.'

'Well, I'll ring tomorrow and we'll have a long natter. Now go to bed.'

'Tomorrow then,' said Molly. 'Goodnight.'

Rowena replaced the receiver. Concentrate on Kavan?

'If he isn't interested in me I certainly won't chase him,' she muttered as she slowly made her way upstairs.

*   *   *

Kavan arrived with Pansy a little earlier than usual the next morning.

'I wanted to ask you something,' he explained. 'Are you busy on Saturday?'

'Er — no. Just gardening, probably.'

'Would you like to come out with Pansy and me? Seth's going to look after the farm.'

She blinked at him. 'Come out? Where?'

'I haven't thought,' he said vaguely. 'But as you and Pansy get on so well, I thought a day together would be fun.'

Rowena looked at Pansy's expectant face smiling up at her.

'I'd love to,' she said. 'I'll bring a picnic. You can decide where we'll go.'

They parted, each looking forward to Saturday and with Pansy in a state of great excitement.

★   ★   ★

'There's a country park a few miles away,' said Kavan, as he picked her up on Saturday morning. 'I thought we'd go there for coffee first. They have a small children's zoo. Pansy would like that. Then we'll go up to the hills for our picnic.'

They sang nursery rhymes as they bowled along through the leafy summer countryside.

'Twenty men went to mow,' they were singing as they turned into the car park, 'twenty men, nineteen men, eighteen men . . . '

Kavan switched off the engine. Their voices sounded so loud without it that they all burst into laughter.

'Can we sing that again on the way home?' asked Pansy. Kavan lifted her out of the car.

'We might be too tired,' he said. 'We'll see.'

With an excited Pansy holding their hands and bouncing between them, they headed for the little café in the zoo.

Pansy was thrilled to see that many of the zoo's birds were allowed to wander around.

Kavan chose a table near the door so that they could watch them.

A haughty, colourful peacock stalked past followed by two brown and white peahens and a brood of six babies.

'They walk the same way as their parents,' Rowena observed delightedly. 'I've never seen baby peacocks before.'

Three ducklings appeared and settled themselves on the doorstep in a warm spot in the sunshine.

Suddenly, a mother duck, followed by a stream of little ducklings rushed past. The three babies in the doorway scrambled to their feet and raced to catch up.

'What a crowd,' laughed Rowena. 'Poor mother duck.'

'Drink your coffee,' said Kavan. 'It will be cold.'

'I've finished my juice,' said Pansy. 'Can we go and see animals?'

★ ★ ★

Rowena was really enjoying herself as they went from pond to cage to pen, exclaiming at each new discovery. There were no exotic animals, but Pansy was quite satisfied with the rabbits and guinea pigs and their assorted babies.

Suddenly she flopped down on the grass with a determined look on her face. 'I'm hungry,' she declared. 'I want my picnic.'

'Come along, then,' said her father. 'We've seen all the animals now. We'll go and find a nice place to sit.'

Rowena was not really a picnic person, preferring to eat at a table, but the picnic with Kavan and Pansy was one she was to remember for a long time.

Kavan spread a rug on the grass and lifted Rowena's basket from the car. Soon they were all enjoying quiche, chicken legs and juicy tomatoes.

Pansy threw herself backwards on the rug with her legs in the air.

'I wish I could always eat picnics,' she said. 'It's much nicer than eating in the house.' She jumped to her feet. 'Can we go for a walk?'

'Later,' said Rowena. 'Your daddy

and I haven't finished eating yet.'

'Well, can *I* go for a walk?'

'Run up to that big tree and back,' said Kavan. 'We'll watch you.'

For ten minutes, the child ran back and forth until she eventually threw herself down on the rug and fell asleep.

'Thank goodness for that,' said Kavan. 'Peace at last.'

It was shady under the spreading tree. Rowena sat with her back against the trunk and gazed out over the rolling countryside. Everything was peaceful. A cool breeze blew beneath the branches of the tree. The air was scented with grass and wild flowers.

She looked across at Kavan. The picnic basket was between them. He lifted it to one side and moved to sit next to her.

'How long have you been on your own?' asked Rowena.

'Nearly four years.'

'Aren't you lonely?'

'Sometimes. But I wouldn't risk being let down again. Better to be on your own then you can't get hurt.'

Rowena was silent, then she said, 'Not everyone is like your wife.'

He sighed. 'Perhaps I'll change my mind some day. But for now . . . ' He turned and looked searchingly into her face. 'And what about you?' he asked softly. 'How long have you been alone?'

'My husband was killed in an accident five years ago. We'd only been married for a year.'

He put a hand on her arm.

'Five years is a long time,' she said.

'And you haven't found anyone else?'

She shook her head. 'Once or twice I thought I had,' she admitted. 'But I was wrong.'

He bent towards her and gently kissed her cheek.

'Why are you kissing Rowena?' asked a voice.

'To say thank you for my nice picnic,' said Kavan.

To hide her blushes, Rowena began to pack the basket.

'I'll give her a kiss too.'

Rowena hugged the small body as

two arms crept round her neck and a sticky mouth was pressed against her cheek. She looked up to see Kavan watching them with a wistful expression on his face.

★ ★ ★

'I'll drop you both here if you don't mind,' said Kavan, when they arrived at Cherry Cottage. 'I want to see Seth before he goes.'

'I'll bring Pansy home in a moment,' Rowena promised. She and the child carried the picnic basket into Cherry Cottage between them.

'I wish I could stay here with you,' said the little girl.

Rowena smiled at her. 'That would be very nice. But your mummy will be expecting you back soon.'

The child nodded but didn't look very happy at the prospect.

To distract her, Rowena produced a box of sweets.

'You can choose two chocolates,' she

said, 'then I must take you back to Mrs Morrow.'

The housekeeper was on the doorstep when they arrived. 'So you've brought her back at last,' she said. 'Her tea's been ready for ages. I was wondering where she was.'

'You knew perfectly well where she was,' said Rowena coolly.

'Oh, of course, she's been out with you and her Dad,' said Mrs Morrow in a spiteful tone. 'Fancy me forgetting that. Did you enjoy yourself? Of course, time was when Miss Robinson would have been the one going on picnics with him.'

Rowena stood still. 'Miss Robinson? You mean that Heather was . . . ?'

'She *was*, until you came along. Lovely girl she is, a local girl. Just right for him. You've only been in Allarton five minutes and already you're setting your cap at him and interfering . . . '

'Mrs Morrow,' said Rowena. 'I'm not setting my cap at him, as you call it. And if you'd been looking after Pansy properly, I wouldn't have become involved with her. Bye, bye, Pansy, I'll see you on Monday.'

Without another glance at the housekeeper, she turned on her heel.

Kavan and Heather? thought Rowena as she shut the door of Cherry Cottage behind her. But Heather had said they were only friends.

★ ★ ★

'Kavan and I!' Heather looked at Rowena in astonishment. 'Honestly, that woman! Kavan and I have been part of the same crowd of friends for years. We always go out in a group. Yes, I went out with him two or three times, but that was all. Anyway, he's about ten years older than me. I'd rather someone nearer my own age.'

'But why would she say that?'

'I told you before, she's an unpleasant woman. My advice to you is to avoid her when you can — and her dreadful son.'

Rowena smiled and picked up the wicker basket filled with percussion instruments that she needed for later in the morning.

'By the way,' Heather called after her as she left the room, 'did you enjoy your meal at the Towers? Lucky you. I wish someone would take me there.'

'It was lovely,' Rowena called back. She didn't want to get into a discussion with Heather about her evening out with Peter.

A Sad Parting

The crash was so loud that Rowena, on her way upstairs for an early night, almost dropped her mug of drinking chocolate. It sounded deliberate, as if someone in the lane outside was beating on a tin tray with a metal spoon.

Shakily, she went back downstairs and into the sitting-room. It was not yet fully dark outside and she could see figures moving back and forth in front of her gate. It was a crowd of youths, at least eight of them, shouting drunkenly.

She dashed upstairs. She'd get a better view from her bedroom window. The gate swung open under the weight of several bodies and they poured into her garden. She was right; one was carrying a tin tray and beating upon it as if it were a drum.

She looked towards the telephone. Would the police come if she phoned?

134

And what damage would the youths do to her property before the police arrived?

The tinkle of glass as a stone smashed one of her windows decided her. She went through the back door to the garden and picked up the hose pipe. It was already connected.

'This should be our cottage,' a voice was shouting at the front door.

'You tell 'er, Jed,' shouted another.

So it was the awful Jed, son of the equally awful Mrs Morrow.

'You've got no right to this place. It was promised to me and my mum. Go back where you came from.'

Another stone hit the front door.

Rowena turned on the tap and, dragging the hosepipe along behind her, crept down the side of the cottage. Raising the hose, she directed it full at the crowd of boys. She scored such a good hit that Jed staggered back and almost fell. His outraged yell pierced the night. Then all went quiet as the mob scurried away along the lane.

Rowena carried the hosepipe back to the garden and turned off the tap. Her hands shook and she was glad to get back inside the cottage and lock the doors.

This was no time for drinking chocolate. She poured herself a brandy and stood at the window, looking out into the garden where all was now still and quiet.

Kavan had said he usually got what he wanted and he wanted the cottage. But surely he could have had nothing to do with tonight's attack? They'd had a lovely picnic with Pansy and parted the best of friends.

No, she refused to believe he'd had anything to do with it. That scoundrel, Jed, influenced by his mother, must have decided, with his friends, to do something about what he saw as an injustice.

Satisfied that the youths had gone, she inspected the broken window. She'd have to phone a glazier tomorrow. There was also a scrape on the front door where a stone had made contact.

Still feeling shaky, she went upstairs to bed for the second time, trying to decide whether or not to speak to Kavan about the incident.

* * *

The glazier was able to come early the next morning. 'These yours?' he asked, handing her a metal tray and a large spoon. 'Just picked them up in the garden.'

'Some trouble last night,' she explained briefly. 'That's why I need the window replaced.'

He looked at her with understanding. 'Dratted kids?'

She nodded and took the tray and spoon into the kitchen. Useful evidence, she thought.

There was knock on the kitchen door. It opened and Kavan popped his head inside.

'May I come in?'

'Of course. Want a drink? I'm just

making one.' She held up a jar of coffee. 'Only instant, I'm afraid.'

'That will do. What happened to your window? Johnson said you had some trouble last night. I spotted him working as I went past.'

Briefly, Rowena told him what had happened.

'The young fiend. You're quite sure it was Jed?'

'I saw him clearly. And I have some evidence.'

She produced the tray and spoon.

'May I take these? I'll see whether his mother can identify them. I wonder what got into him.'

'He said the cottage had been promised to him and his mother.'

Kavan looked down at the floor. 'That was my fault. Jumping the gun, you could say. I'd planned to move them in here if I'd bought the land. I suppose they were both disappointed. I'm sorry it's caused you all this trouble. I hope you weren't too frightened.'

'While it was going on I didn't feel at

all scared, but after they'd gone, I began to shake. I realised what an awful lot of damage they might have done if I hadn't frightened them away.'

'I like your choice of weapon,' he said with a laugh. 'And it may amuse you to know that Jed is in bed with a cold today. I thought nothing of it, but now I see it's rough justice.'

'I don't want him to be ill,' she replied, 'but I hope it will deter him from similar behaviour.'

'*I* shall deter him,' Kavan said with feeling. 'Thanks for the coffee. Before I go — you wouldn't let me take you out to dinner, would you?'

Two dates in as many weeks, she thought, amused.

'Thank you. I should enjoy that.'

'Good.' He gave her a wide smile. 'How about Friday?'

'Friday it is. I'll look forward to it.'

The glazier came into the kitchen. 'All done.' He tutted at Kavan. 'Don't know what kids are coming to these days.'

Rowena paid him and thanked him and he left.

'I must hurry now,' she said to Kavan, 'I just took an hour off to see to the window.'

She collected Pansy from the sitting-room where she had been sitting quietly, colouring a picture in a book.

'I was in such a rush when I dropped her off, I didn't notice your window,' he said. 'Thank you for looking after her. We are causing you a lot of trouble.'

They all left the cottage together. At the gate, Kavan turned to Rowena with a serious face.

'Thank you for not informing the police. Jed is a pain but he hasn't had an easy childhood and his mother is very severe with him. I should hate him to have a police record before he's even started his adult life.'

He gave her a wave and strode purposefully up the lane towards his house, the tray under his arm.

★   ★   ★

Rowena surveyed her wardrobe. What a pity she'd so recently been out to dinner in the russet skirt and cream blouse.

Kavan hadn't mentioned where he was taking her. Would it be somewhere grand? Please don't let it be the Towers at Tinley again. She'd feel such a fool walking in with a different man.

She selected a long black skirt and a long-sleeved white lace blouse.

Elegant, but not too dressy.

'I hope this is suitable,' she said anxiously to Kavan when he arrived. 'You didn't say where we were going.'

'More than suitable for anywhere. You look lovely.'

'I wasn't fishing for compliments.'

'I'm not very good at compliments,' he said. 'I'm just a rough farmer.' His eyes twinkled. 'But I know when somebody is lovely.'

She blushed and turned away to pick up her bag and shawl.

★ ★ ★

They set off, driving down the lane, through the village and out the other side along a road strange to Rowena.

'Where are we going?' she asked.

He smiled mysteriously. 'Wait and see.'

'Is it far?'

'About twenty miles.'

She was obviously going to get no more information, so she settled back to enjoy the comfort of travelling in style in Kavan's sleek Jaguar.

She smiled to herself.

'What's so amusing?'

'I did wonder whether we'd be going — wherever it is we're going — on your motorbike. I'm so glad I was wrong.'

'I did think about the tractor,' he teased, 'but I changed my mind.'

They'd reached a high road above a small town whose buildings climbed the side of a steep hill. Kavan gestured to the hill rising above them. 'Look up there.'

Craning her neck, Rowena could see, set amongst trees, a large white building.

'Is that where we're going?'

'It is. My favourite hotel. The Eagle's Nest.'

'Eagles?'

'Poetic licence. They don't have any eagles round here. But it's very high.'

The car swept off the main road on to a lane which wound its way up the side of the hill above them and they came out in front of the white building, its windows now glowing from the lamps inside.

The receptionist greeted them and waved them towards a wide flight of stairs at the far end of the hall.

Kavan guided Rowena up the stairs and into the dining-room where they were shown to a table to the side of the room. Huge windows, stretching the length of the room, gave amazing views over the countryside.

The light was fading fast. 'This is magical,' said Rowena, gazing entranced at the softly blurring view in front of her.

Kavan smiled at her pleasure. 'I knew you would like it here. Can you tear yourself away from the view long enough to study the menu?'

'I really can't decide. Would you choose? If you come here often you must know what they do best.'

'Are you sure? Very well.' He looked down at his own menu. 'Do you like beef?'

'Very much.'

'Are you ready to order, sir?' asked a discreet voice.

Kavan, ordering for both of them, asked for Caesar salad with parmesan and to follow, Welsh black beef with wild mushrooms.

When the wine waiter appeared, Rowena gazed, fascinated, from the window, while a discussion went on in the background.

'I don't know your taste in wine, but I've been recommended a Chardonnay-Semillion from Australia to start and, of course, a Burgundy with the beef.'

'Sounds perfect,' she sighed. 'I'm surprised you're such a food and wine buff.'

'Why?'

'You said you were just a rough farmer.'

They both laughed.

'My father was a chef. I was brought up to know food and wine.'

'But you didn't want to go into that business yourself?'

'No. My brother took over the family restaurant. I loved being outdoors. I couldn't bear to be shut up in a hot kitchen every day.'

'Do you cook at all?'

'Whenever I have the time. I'll cooking something for you, sometime, if you like?'

'I'll look forward to that. This is fabulous.'

She gazed at the crisp Caesar salad which had been placed in front of her.

'How is Jed?' she asked, a few minutes later.

'Better. His cold didn't come to much. Just made him feel sorry for himself.'

'What did his mother have to say

about his antics at the cottage?'

'At first she tried to deny he'd been there, but when I produced the tray, Jed confessed. She was afraid she'd be dismissed. When I left, she was tearing into him. I almost felt sorry for the lad.'

Rowena turned to look out of the window again. It must be dreadful to have no home of your own, she thought.

She looked around the dining-room. No dance floor, she noted.

The main course was brought to the table. The beef, on a bed of creamy potatoes, was garnished with just a hint of truffles and was surrounded by wild mushrooms and wine gravy. Rowena gazed at it in awe, then she bent forward and breathed in the rich aroma. Her eyes shone as she looked at Kavan.

'Taste it,' he urged. 'It's out of this world.'

They ate in silence, paying tribute to the perfectly cooked food.

Rowena refused more Burgundy,

preferring another glass of the lighter Chardonnay.

'If you're not absolutely full,' said Kavan, 'I can recommend a lovely light dessert.'

Rowena looked interested.

'Blackcurrant mousse with lavender ice-cream. You've never tasted ice-cream like it.'

Their order given, Rowena returned to the subject which had concerned her earlier. 'I feel sorry for Jed,' she said, 'and Mrs Morrow. If I'd never seen the cottage they'd be living there now and I'd know nothing about it.'

Kavan was watching her with a thoughtful expression.

'And you'd have your extra land,' she went on. 'I seem to have messed up a lot of plans.'

'The cottage was left to you,' he said. 'You have every right to live in it. As for my extra land, I've solved that problem.'

She looked up. 'How?'

'I'm negotiating to buy those two

147

large fields opposite my house across the river. Everything's almost signed and sealed.'

'Across the river?'

'I've bought a rowing boat *and* a little motor boat, so getting across will be easy. And I'll have some extra exercise,' he said with a laugh.

'I'm pleased you've found some land, but it won't help Jed and his mother.'

'They were quite comfortable where they were until I mentioned the cottage,' he said. 'Don't worry about them.'

★　★　★

After their dessert, which was as light and delicious as Kavan had promised, he said, 'We'll take coffee in the conservatory if you like?'

They went downstairs into a huge glass room furnished with comfortable rattan armchairs and little tables. Doors stood open on to a garden filled with night-scented flowers. At a grand piano, a young man played softly and skilfully, enhancing the atmosphere, but not intruding into their conversation.

Leaning back into her cushions, Rowena sipped her coffee and sighed deeply. 'What a beautiful evening.'

Kavan took her hand where it rested on the arm of the chair. 'I'm so pleased you agreed to come. This has been a wonderful evening for me too. Would you come out with me again?'

She gave him a lazy smile. 'I should like that very much.'

He squeezed her hand, then carried it to his lips.

'A rough farmer,' she teased.

'You're smoothing my edges,' he murmured.

They were silent on the journey home. Rowena was contrasting her evening with Kavan with her dinner with Peter. Poor Peter. His only fault was that he wasn't Kavan. Secretly, she stole a look at her companion, at his profile which was illuminated by the lights of the dashboard.

'You're very quiet,' she said.

He didn't answer for a few minutes, then, 'I don't want to spoil a wonderful evening,' he began, 'but I have something sad to tell you.'

'Sad?'

'Pansy is returning to her mother tomorrow.'

'Oh, no. I shall miss her. When will you get her back?'

'Probably not until she's old enough to make up her own mind about the situation. Perhaps then she'll want to live with me.' He sighed. 'Her mother is moving permanently to Spain with her latest boyfriend. Pansy is to live there with them.'

Rowena could see his grip tighten on the steering wheel. She placed one hand gently on his.

'Will you bring her to see me before she goes?' she asked softly.

'Of course. She'll miss you. You've been very kind to her.'

'I shall miss her.'

There was nothing more to say. They

drove in silence for the remaining miles, engrossed in their own thoughts.

Kavan drew up outside her gate. 'I'll bring Pansy down at about twelve. Do you have your key?'

He escorted her to her front door and inserted the key. Then he kissed her, first on one cheek, then the other. 'Goodnight, Rowena. Thank you for being a lovely companion.'

She went quickly inside. Her feelings as he'd kissed had taken her by surprise. From disliking him to tolerating him to — what? She could hardly say loving him. But as she'd felt his lips on her cheek, she'd wanted to wrap her arms around him and hold him close. Was that love? Did she love Kavan Reagan?

★　★　★

At twelve noon the next day, a subdued father and daughter walked along the lane to Cherry Cottage.

Rowena had prepared a jug of

home-made lemonade and it stood waiting for them on the garden table together with a plate of the tiny iced cakes Pansy loved.

'Pansy has come to say goodbye to you,' said Kavan. 'Her mummy is coming to collect her this afternoon.'

Rowena looked down at Pansy, who was dressed in a white lace smock over white trousers. Her long fair hair was tied back in a ponytail. She looked as fresh as a garden flower. Rowena didn't want to upset the child, but she couldn't stop herself from kneeling down and taking the little girl in her arms.

'I shall miss you, Pansy,' she said. 'I hope you'll come back and see me one day.'

'I shall,' said Pansy cheerfully. 'May I have a little cake?' She climbed on to a chair and, selecting a pink one, began to nibble the icing off the top.

'She hasn't realised that she may not be back for years,' murmured Kavan. 'Thank goodness she's too small to be really upset.'

Rowena poured them all some lemonade and tied a napkin round Pansy's neck.

'Can't have you spoiling that beautiful smock,' she said.

'Mummy sent it for me. May I have another cake, please?'

'Just one,' said Kavan. 'You must eat some lunch before you go.'

Rowena offered him the plate of cakes, but he shook his head.

'I couldn't eat a thing. I just wish they'd hurry up and get it over with and yet I can't bear to part with her.'

Rowena put a hand on his arm but could think of nothing to say.

'It's so unfair,' he burst out. 'If they were going to live in this country she wouldn't be too far away — but Spain!'

'You could go and see her. Spain really isn't too far.'

He nodded without speaking. Rowena could feel his anguish. Pansy climbed down from her chair, wiping her mouth with her napkin.

'Come along, Daddy, we mustn't be

out when Mummy comes.'

She held up her face to Rowena for a kiss.

Rowena felt tears fill her eyes, for herself and for Kavan. They would both miss the child so much.

Hidden Secrets

'And where were you going with Kavan Reagan on Friday evening?' asked Heather. 'I saw you in his car. You passed me near the bridge.'

Rowena looked up from the books she was sorting.

'I didn't see you.'

'Obviously your attention was elsewhere.' Heather gave her a coy smile.

Rowena stood up and folded her arms. 'Is Allarton one of those villages where everyone knows what you're doing before you've done it?'

'Not at all. I just happened to see you as you drove past.'

Rowena sighed. 'Kavan took me out to dinner.'

'Not the Towers again?'

'The Eagle's Nest.'

'The Eagle's Nest! You do get taken

155

to some grand places.' Heather sounded really envious.

Rowena returned to sorting the books.

'You're getting very friendly with Kavan, aren't you?'

'I helped him with Pansy. He was grateful. Look, we're friends and neighbours, nothing more.'

Heather opened a file and seemed engrossed in her work but suddenly she said, 'I should hate you to get hurt.'

'Whatever do you mean?'

'Kavan will never commit to a relationship,' Heather said. 'After his experience with that wife of his, he'll never trust another woman. He's said so, often.'

'Well, that's all right then,' said Rowena. 'Because I'm not looking for a relationship either.'

'How long were you married?' asked Heather after a while.

'For only one year. Then my husband was killed in an accident.'

'And that was five years ago?'

'Just over five years.'

'Could you see yourself marrying again?' When Rowena didn't reply, Heather said quickly, 'I'm sorry. I didn't mean to pry.'

'No, it's all right. I suppose if the right person came along . . . But how can I know? I loved Simon very much, but we had such a short time together.'

She got up and put the piles of books on a shelf. Then she turned to Heather.

'Please don't keep thinking of Kavan and me as an item. I've told you, we're just friends. By the way, Pansy won't be here again. She's gone back to her mother.'

'That was sudden, wasn't it?'

'Denise is getting married again. She's going to live in Spain and is taking Pansy with her.'

'Poor little mite. Denise won't want her. As soon as the child gets in the way of her pleasures, she'll throw her out. She always does.'

'I hope you're wrong,' said Rowena, quietly. 'Pansy's a dear little thing. She deserves better.' She glanced at the clock. 'Look at the time. I'll go and open up.'

She hurried out. She was beginning to wonder whether Heather was as nice as she'd seemed at the beginning. There was a bitter side to her which Rowena didn't like.

★ ★ ★

'Come in, dear,' said Mrs King. 'It's such a long time since I've seen you. Have you finished school for the day? I've got the kettle on and there's a nice coffee cake I made this afternoon.'

Chattering away, she took Rowena through to her little sitting-room at the back of Briar House.

'Now you sit down and relax and I'll get the tea,' she said, brushing aside Rowena's offer of help.

Rowena settled herself in an armchair and looked around the bright little room with its flowery cushions and curtains. There were vases of flowers on every surface. Mrs King's knitting bag swung from the arm of her fireside chair. It all looked very cosy.

'Still making teddies?' she asked as the old lady came back into the room with the tray.

'No. I'm knitting squares for blankets now,' she replied. 'I got a bit tired of teddies, but I like to have something to do with my hands.'

'You must spend a lot of time in the garden,' said Rowena, looking at the flowers.

'Oh, I do.' Mrs King handed her a cup of tea. 'I'm out there all day when the weather is good. Help yourself to cake. Of course, I have the best possible advisor on gardening matters.' Her eyes twinkled.

Rowena looked at her questioningly.

'The vicar. He's such a keen gardener. He has a beautiful garden himself and is always willing to give advice to his parishioners.'

Rowena laughed. 'Well you can't do better than the vicar.'

'Now, tell me what you've been doing since I saw you last.' Mrs King settled herself for a chat. 'Have you done much to the cottage? And what about the garden?'

Exhausting the topic of Cherry Cottage, Rowena told her about her two dinner dates and her visit to Edward and Anita's house.

'They invited me to their party,' said Mrs King, 'but I didn't really want to go out in the evening. They also have a house with a lovely garden. Did you see their cedar tree?'

With very little urging, Rowena helped herself to another piece of coffee cake.

'This is so delicious.'

A sharp knock at the front door startled them both, then Mrs King smiled. 'I know that knock.'

She went to the door and came back followed by a tall grey-haired man with a startlingly white beard and bushy eyebrows. He wore a clerical collar.

'We were just talking about you,' she said. 'Rowena, this is the vicar, Philip

Newman. Philip, Rowena Gage, Leonora Lawton's goddaughter.'

'You inherited her cottage, I believe,' said the vicar in a surprising Welsh accent. 'Lucky woman. It's charming. And a lovely sized garden.'

'We've been talking about gardens,' said the old lady. 'I said you're my special advisor. Sit down, Philip, and have some cake. I'll fetch another cup.'

Rowena felt slightly guilty. She was not a regular churchgoer. But it didn't seem to bother the vicar.

'I expect we'll see you one day when you're not so busy,' he said, waving away her explanations. 'Probably at Christmas. Everyone turns up at Christmas.'

He grinned at her. There was no note of criticism in his voice.

'How are you getting on with your compost bin?' he asked his hostess.

'I want to make my own compost,' explained Mrs King to Rowena, 'but when you live alone, you don't have a great deal to put in the bin. However, I remembered to put my egg shells in it this morning.' She looked at the vicar for approval.

'I must go now,' said Rowena, standing up. 'I've quite a lot to do at home. I'll leave you to your compost chat.'

The vicar gave her a warm handclasp. 'Good to meet you,' he said, 'I'm sure we'll see each other around.'

★ ★ ★

The telephone was ringing as she entered Cherry Cottage. 'You're back,' said a voice. 'I've been trying to contact you.'

'Is anything wrong?'

'No,' said Kavan. 'I just wanted to talk to you. I feel so low.'

'Is it because of Pansy?'

'Yes. I miss her.'

'Come over. Have you had a meal?'

'Mrs Morrow is cooking it now. I'll come over at eight, if I may. I need company.'

162

'See you then.'

Rowena replaced the telephone. There goes my chance to do some decorating, she thought, but without rancour. The decorating could wait.

She was too full of coffee cake to eat anything else so she showered and changed and by the time Kavan arrived, she was sitting reading.

A bottle of red wine and some glasses waited on the coffee table.

She opened the door at his first knock.

'This is good of you,' he said as he came in. 'Are you sure I'm not messing up your evening?'

'You saved me from the dreaded decorating.'

She led him into the sitting-room and pointed to the armchair opposite hers. 'Pour some wine. You walked down, I presume?' He nodded.

He poured the wine and sat back in his chair.

'I've been thinking about Pansy all day. I miss her so much.'

She looked with sympathy at his

agonised face but remained silent.

Perhaps the best thing I can do is let him talk, she thought, picking up her own wine glass.

'*He* came with Denise,' said Kavan. 'Her new man. Sinclair Allen. I wasn't expecting that. Made it difficult to talk.'

'What's he like?'

'Seems pleasant enough. Rolling in money, which is all Denise would worry about. Years older than her.' He turned his face away. 'To think of him bringing up my little Pansy.'

'Oh, Kavan, I'm so sorry,' Rowena burst out, 'I wish there was something I could say.'

'No, *I'm* sorry,' he said, 'for bringing my miseries to you.'

'If it helps to talk, I'm a good listener.'

'I'll tell you the ironic aspect of all this,' he said, then was silent for a few minutes as if wondering whether to finish what he was going to say.

Rowena waited.

Kavan went on, 'Pansy might not be my child.'

He picked up his wine glass and took a deep drink.

Rowena looked at him, amazed. 'Might not be your child?'

'She doesn't look much like me, does she?'

'No. But I imagine she looks like your wife.'

'Oh, yes. They're both blondes. But I can see absolutely nothing of myself in Pansy.'

Rowena looked at him.

'Denise left me when she was one month pregnant. But how do I know it was my baby? She'd obviously been seeing the man she ran away with for a while. Perhaps Pansy is his. Denise says I'm the father, but how can she know?'

'There are DNA tests,' she ventured.

'Denise refused. Anyway, do I really want to know? What if the result is negative? I'd lose her altogether.'

'So you don't really mind if she's not your child?'

'I adore her. I don't want any tests.'

He put a hand across his eyes.

Rowena waited.

There was a shuddering sigh then Kavan stood up.

'It's a lovely evening. Would you like a walk?'

'Let me change my shoes and get a jacket.'

★ ★ ★

The evening was cool and still. Kavan took her arm and they walked in silence up the lane, past his house and further on into the countryside. Here the air was fresh and scented with evening plants.

'This is the first time I've been up here,' she said. 'Is this your land?'

'Yes. Just for the width of two more fields. Look, I'm sorry about what I said earlier on — about Pansy. I'd be glad if you didn't say anything to anyone.' His face twisted awkwardly. 'I don't want gossip.'

'Of course not.' Though as for gossip, she thought, there was probably plenty of that when Denise left home. She didn't seem well thought of in the village.

He stopped, 'Shall we go back now? We both have work tomorrow — we mustn't be too late.'

They strolled back. This time he put an arm around her waist. Rowena was sorry when his house came into view.

'I'll walk you home, but I won't come in,' he said. 'I've been thinking — you mentioned decorating?'

'Yes. The little study. I'm going to do it up. Shouldn't take long.'

'You were going to start tonight and I spoilt your plans. So, tomorrow evening I shall come down and help you.'

'There's no need, really.'

'I'll be there at seven o'clock. I'll ask Mrs Morrow to make me an early dinner.'

'Actually, I've a better idea. Why don't you come and eat with me.'

His face broke into a smile. 'Thank you.'

They'd reached her gate. He bent

and kissed her forehead, gave a little salute with his hand and went off up the lane.

Rowena closed the gate behind him, went slowly up the path and sat on one of her garden chairs. She was reluctant to go inside and leave her garden on such a beautiful scented evening.

★   ★   ★

Kavan arrived the next evening with two boxes of fruit juice under his arm. 'No wine tonight,' he said, in answer to her surprised expression. 'Must keep clear heads for decorating.'

'That's a good idea,' she said, 'but we're only sloshing a bit of paint on the walls.' She put the boxes on the kitchen table. 'Somehow you don't seem the fruit juice type to me.'

'That's because you don't know everything about me,' he teased. 'Now take me to the scene of the action. There'll be furniture to move.'

'Not much. There's only a desk, a

chair and a bookcase.'

They went through the kitchen and stood in the tiny study.

'I could decorate it myself in an hour,' he told her.

'Certainly not. You can help, but you're not doing it all.'

'What a lovely smell.' Kavan sniffed the delicious aroma wafting in from the kitchen.

'It's ready now. Would you like to move the desk while I take our meal out of the oven?'

★ ★ ★

Ten minutes later, they were tucking into lamb steaks coated with mint and rosemary, green beans and carrots and Lyonnaise potatoes.

'You're a wonderful cook,' he said.

He's looking much happier than last night, she thought with pleasure. Perhaps this evening was a good idea.

'Oh, and I have some news for you,' said Kavan. 'You won't be troubled by

Jed for much longer.'

She looked at him questioningly.

'He's going into the army. His mother is most unhappy about it, but he's determined. Thank goodness you didn't report him to the police for that stone-throwing episode. It would have counted against him.'

'I'm glad he's found something useful to do.'

Rowena collected the plates, took them through to the kitchen and came back with a bowl of raspberries and a jug of cream. 'We mustn't eat a heavy meal if we're to do all that bending and stretching,' she said.

They drank some coffee, loaded the dishwasher then carried the paint into the little office.

Kavan eased the lid off the tin.

'This is a lovely colour — lemon cream.'

'I thought it would look sunny,' she explained. 'This blue is so cold. I shall lay terracotta carpet and warm up the whole room.'

'You paint that small wall,' said Kavan. 'I'll do this big one.'

'When I moved in, this wall was covered with photographs of cats,' said Rowena. 'Probably her prize ones. I've put them away. I'm not really a cat person.'

They worked energetically for half an hour until Kavan reached a corner usually hidden by a small chair.

'There's something loose here,' he said, laying down his brush. 'Two loose bricks, but quite cunningly covered. They're not obvious until you do something like this.'

Rowena joined him and stared at the corner.

'I've not moved that chair before so I've never noticed them.'

'Shall I ease them out?' Kavan was already fumbling with the first brick.

'Of course. There may be something interesting behind them. We can't just leave them now we know they're there!'

'Mrs Lawton used this room as an office. This may have been her secret safe.' Kavan was pulling out the second brick. He bent down and peered into the cavity.

'There *is* something here. It's a box.'

'Well, get it out,' she said excitedly.

It was an ordinary, black Japanned box — and it was locked.

'How frustrating. Where's the key?'

'She wouldn't keep the key with the box,' he reasoned. 'It must be in the desk or perhaps her bedroom?'

'Oh, dear. I can't look now. We must finish this painting. Give me the box and I'll put it on the kitchen table.'

'Not much more to do,' said Kavan cheerfully, 'then we can make a search for the key. That's if you really want to know what's in the box?'

'Of course I want to know, though,' she looked doubtful, 'should we look at something that was so private that she hid it away in the wall?'

'Have you thought that it might not have been Miss Lawton's? The house is old. Perhaps it's been there for years?'

'Mm.'

Rowena dipped her brush into the paint. 'That's possible, but we'll never know unless we open it.'

'Perhaps it's stuffed with money!'

'Or jewels.' She painted furiously. 'We simply must get it open tonight. I won't sleep if we don't.'

★ ★ ★

At last the walls were finished. Kavan carried the paint through to the kitchen and washed the brushes.

'Leave that. I'll do it later. Let's look for the key.'

'A good workman looks after his tools,' he said virtuously. 'I'll do this, you go upstairs and search the bedroom.'

Rowena stood in the middle of her bedroom and looked around. She'd cleaned both bedrooms thoroughly when she'd moved in. She'd found no keys then, so where else could she look now?

She went back downstairs. 'I'm going

to go through the desk.'

She began to feel under the few papers Leonora had left behind. Nothing. She felt around the little cubby holes. Nothing.

'Perhaps there's a secret drawer,' called Kavan from the kitchen.

'If there is, I can't find it. Why don't you try?'

He joined her and together they pressed and prodded inside and outside the desk. At last they gave up.

'If the key is missing, then we can't open the box,' she declared, passing a hand wearily across her forehead.

'We can force it. Where are your tools?'

'No.' She was adamant. 'If we can't find the key, then we're not supposed to open it. We'll put the box back in the wall and forget it.'

They carried the desk and the other pieces of furniture back into the study, admiring its fresh new look. Rowena placed the penholder, the lamp and Leonora's other bits and pieces back on the desk. Some day, she would replace them with her own things.

Kavan picked up a small black fluffy cat ornament, about six inches high.

'I remember this. She never liked anyone to touch it; she usually had it by her when we played cards. I expect she thought it would bring her luck. She said she always took it upstairs when she went to bed.'

'It's not my sort of thing,' said Rowena, 'but it is a black cat. It might bring me luck.' She placed the cat on the corner of the desk. 'I'll make some coffee; we deserve a rest.'

She carried the mugs into the sitting-room where Kavan was already relaxing in an armchair, placed them on the table and took a seat opposite him.

'Thank you for coming tonight. A job is much easier if you have company.'

He smiled lazily. 'I've enjoyed it. I only wish we could have solved the mystery of the hidden tin. But perhaps the key will turn up.'

They sat in silence, thinking, when suddenly, Kavan jumped up. 'Of course,' he said. 'Wait. I've had an idea.'

He dashed into the office and returned with the black cat. In its back, almost invisible, was a slim zip fastener. He handed the cat to Rowena.

Silently, she unfastened the zip. A small washleather bag fell out. Inside was a key. Speechless, she stared at it, then at Kavan.

Kavan went into the kitchen and came back carrying the black box. He put it on the coffee table.

Rowena eyed it for a moment then, leaning forward, inserted the key, turned it and lifted the lid.

Inside she found a packet of letters tied with pink tape. She lifted them out. Underneath, was a small pile of black and white photographs.

Kavan came to look over her shoulder at the first one.

'That's Leonora,' he said. 'She was younger then, but it's definitely her.'

The next photograph showed a

smiling man in the garden of Cherry Tree cottage.

'I don't recognise *him*,' said Kavan.

'I do.' Rowena's voice was quiet. 'It's my father.'

A Misunderstanding

Kavan moved round the table and seated himself in front of her, holding out his hand for the photograph. He studied it, looking from the image of the man to Rowena, searching for a resemblance.

'Look on the back,' she said.

'Nineteen seventy-six,' he read. 'And there's a name. Shand. What was your father's name?'

'Murray,' she answered.

He started to say, 'Well there . . . '

'Murray Shand Henley,' she said tonelessly.

She placed the other photographs on the table. There was another of her father, taken in the garden of Cherry Cottage, holding a large fluffy cat. There were another two, both showing him and a woman, arms round each other, leaning against a stone wall with the sea behind them.

'That's definitely Leonora,' Kavan said.

Rowena spread out the photographs and looked at them.

'How could this have been going on and we didn't know?'

'Perhaps your mother did know,' he suggested gently. 'Do you think that was why she and Leonora had a row and never spoke again?'

'Perhaps. But if my mother knew, she never discussed it with me.'

'How did he manage to get away from home so often?'

Rowena took a deep breath. 'He was on the sales staff of a jewellery company. Quite a good position. We were never hard up. I suppose that was how he could afford to lead a double life without anyone suspecting. The Head Office of the company was at Strawbridge.'

'That's only twenty miles from here,' said Kavan.

'Once a month,' she went on, 'he had

to visit his Head Office and he usually stayed overnight, sometimes two nights.'

'So it would have been easy for him to visit here.'

'About twice a year, the company took a stand at a gift fair where they could show their products to prospective trade buyers. When that happened, he was always away for a week.'

'Where did these fairs take place?'

'Usually at big seaside places like Scarborough.'

'She could have joined him there for the week.' Kavan picked up the seaside pictures and studied them. 'I'm so sorry, Rowena. What a nasty thing for you to find out.'

Rowena picked up the letters. 'I don't want to read these,' she said, 'but they might give me an insight into their relationship and tell me why he did it when he seemed to have a good marriage. What do you think I should do?'

'It's your father, I can't really advise you.'

'Please,' she looked at him in appeal. 'Would it be wrong to read them?'

He thought for a few minutes. 'If you don't,' he said, slowly, 'you'll never have any answers. You'll always wonder about him.'

She nodded.

'I'll go now,' he said. 'You should read these in private. Call me if you want me.'

'Kavan.'

He turned in the doorway.

'You won't . . . you won't mention this to anyone, will you?'

'We hold each other's secrets now,' he said. 'Goodnight, Rowena.'

When he'd gone, Rowena sat gazing at the envelopes, reluctant to begin her task. She looked at the familiar handwriting and reached out to stroke one of the letters with her little finger.

'How could you?' she whispered to the photograph, 'How could you?'

★ ★ ★

The next day, Heather dropped her bombshell. 'I'm thinking of selling the nursery after Christmas,' she said.

Rowena's eyes widened. 'Selling the nursery?'

'Yes. I've been considering it for some time. My mother lives in Australia; I've almost decided to go and stay with her for a while and see whether I'd like to live there.'

'But why? You love the nursery. And all your friends are here. And Peter.'

Heather removed the lid of the biscuit tin and held the tin out to Rowena, who shook her head. Heather didn't want one either and Rowena waited impatiently while Heather replaced the lid and sat down.

'Peter's part of the problem,' she said. 'He's never had a serious girl-friend and I think it's because of me.'

Rowena gave her a puzzled look.

'He's quite a bit older than me. When my parents moved to the other side of the world, Peter decided he had to take care of me. If I'd married . . . ' Her mouth tightened and Rowena thought she was probably thinking of Ed Tyler. 'If I'd married, he could have passed on the responsibility and found someone for himself. I'm afraid he'll never do that while I'm still here and still single.'

'I'm sure he doesn't look at it like that,' said Rowena.

'If he found someone who really liked him and wanted to marry him, I might not need to go.'

Does she mean me? Rowena thought wildly.

'I'm sorry to do this to you,' said Heather, 'when you've only been here for two terms. But the new owner will want to keep you on, I'm sure.' She looked at her watch. 'Break over. Back to work.'

She rinsed her cup and left the room.

Rowena went over to the sink and slowly washed her own coffee cup. Change again, she thought. Just when she was getting settled.

* * *

The telephone rang as she was finishing her evening meal. It was Kavan. 'Would you like to come to the Riverbank Inn for a drink?'

'I'd love to; I have several things to tell you.'

'Me, too. I'll be down at eight.'

The Riverbank lounge was almost empty. They chose a corner seat and Rowena slipped off her jacket. The walk to the inn had been enjoyable but the nights were drawing in and she might be glad of its warmth on the way home.

Kavan put two glasses on the table and slid in beside her on the padded bench seat.

'Well? D'you want to tell me about the letters? Did you read them?'

'Eventually,' she said. 'It took me a while to make up my mind, but I did in the end.'

'You read them all?'

'There were only ten, spread over as many years. He must have written many more than that, but she kept only ten.'

He waited for her to go on but when she didn't he prompted, 'And?'

'The affair must have started when I was very small. The row between my mother and Leonora was undoubtedly about him, but the affair seems to have continued until he retired. I suppose it would have been impossible for him to stay away from home after that.'

'And did you discover why he didn't leave your mother?'

'Yes. It was because of me. I was always a daddy's girl. He said he couldn't hurt me.'

'Even when you'd grown up?'

'Even then. He explained to Leonora that he loved her but that he would never break up his family. It must have hurt her dreadfully but, of course, there were no letters from her, so we shall never know how she felt.'

'I'll get some more drinks,' said Kavan.

When he returned, she handed him a letter.

'I've brought this one to show you.

There, on the second page. Read it.'

'Your decision to leave Cherry Cottage to my beloved Rowena is more than kind. I hope she will be as happy there as we have been. I agree that you will never be able to tell her why; it is best she thinks it is because you and her mother were such friends years ago.'

Kavan scanned it quickly then went back to the beginning to read it again. Then he looked at Rowena.

'What do you think about that?'

Her face contorted for a moment. 'It makes me feel ill! He hopes I will be as happy as they were! I wish we'd never found that box. I wish I'd never discovered anything about them. The cottage cannot mean the same to me now. When I think of my mother . . . ' She finished her drink. 'Perhaps you'll get your wish. Perhaps I'll sell Cherry Cottage to you and move back to Melchester.'

He clasped her hand between both of his. 'I don't want to get the cottage because you are unhappy. And I certainly don't want you to leave. You're upset now; don't make any decisions until you've had time to think properly.'

They sat for a while, then he said, 'My reason for wanting the cottage no longer exists.'

'What do you mean?'

'I wanted it for Mrs Morrow and Jed. Jed has gone and Mrs Morrow can't settle on her own. She's given notice — she'll be gone in a month.'

'Where is she going?'

'To live with her sister in Ireland. Jed will stay with them when he has leave. The sister has a shop. Mrs Morrow will help her run it and assist in the house. She's very excited. So, you see, I have no need of the cottage.'

'But you'll get a new housekeeper?'

'Not a live-in one. I'll get someone from the village to come in daily.'

'I see.' She fiddled with the glass in front of her. 'Did you know Heather is selling up?'

'Heather? Selling her business?'

'Yes. She's thinking of going to

Australia to live with her mother.'

'But she's part of the fixtures in Allarton! I can't imagine the village without Heather.'

'I believe it's something to do with Peter. She thinks he won't find someone of his own and get married while he feels he has to look after her.'

Kavan thought for a while then he said, 'She's probably right. But we'll miss her. When's she going?'

'Oh, not till after Christmas.'

'Why don't you buy the nursery? You had your own place before?'

'That's why I don't want another,' she said with a laugh. 'I've had enough of that kind of responsibility.'

'What will you do?'

'I may stay on if the new owner and I like each other. But I'd really like to find something different to do. Something right away from teaching.'

'You could come and work for me. I need someone to take over the PYO now that Jed has gone.'

'PYO? Oh, pick your own! But I

188

don't know anything about fruit or selling. Anyway, that's seasonal, isn't it? What would I do in the winter?'

'I'm sure I could find you something to do,' he said.

'I'll think about it, but I've never worked outdoors. I'm not sure I'm the outdoor type.'

He studied her. 'Dressed like that, I don't think you look like the outdoor type,' he agreed, 'but we could work on it. Get you some boots and grubby jeans and an old sweater!'

She stood up. 'That really appeals to me! Thank you very much.'

He followed her out of the inn and together they made their way towards the village. She was glad of her warm jacket. There was a definite autumnal nip in the air. Kavan wrapped an arm round her.

'You don't really want to go back to Melchester, do you?' he asked.

'I really don't know,' she replied.

* * *

'We must begin our Christmas preparations,' said Heather a few weeks later.

'But it's not even the end of October,' protested one of the assistants. 'There's about eight weeks to Christmas.'

'It's easy to see this is your first job with young children,' chided Heather. 'You've no idea how long it takes them to learn the Christmas story and the carols. Then there are the costumes to make and the rehearsals.'

'Not to mention making the Christmas cards and decorations for the school and presents for Mummy,' said Rowena.

The assistant looked suitably awed.

'So the sooner we make a start, the better,' said Heather. 'We'll begin with the Christmas story tomorrow.'

They were so busy that Rowena had little time to think about her father's letters, which she'd replaced in the tin box along with the photographs. The tin and its contents were now back in the hole in the wall. Sometime, she would have to decide whether or not to destroy them. For now, they could stay in their hiding place.

★   ★   ★

Her main responsibility in the run-up to Christmas was to produce the costumes for the Nativity play. In addition to the work of the normal school day, she had to measure each child, then buy or beg material and cut and sew until her eyes felt crossed.

'I dream of angels and animals,' she said to Heather. 'Last night I dreamt that someone put twins in Baby Jesus's cot and no-one noticed until Mary lifted them out at the performance!'

'You'd better check before each show,' said Heather. 'It might be a warning.'

Rowena loved Christmas. The nursery tree had to be put up early because it would be taken down before Christmas when the children started their holidays. The school had a large collection of tree ornaments but Rowena couldn't help buying more as they began to appear in the shops.

One day, in a nearby town, she bumped into Peter Robinson as she wandered through the busy market.

'Rowena, how lovely to see you. What are you doing here?'

'Buying Christmas decorations,' she said, 'I like to see the school turned into a magical place for the children.'

'Have you had lunch?'

'No,' she admitted. 'I was going to have a sandwich at one o'clock.'

'It's nearly that now. Will you have one with me? The Market Tavern over there does decent sandwiches.'

★   ★   ★

It was crowded, but they found a window seat.

'We can look out at the market,' she said. 'I love the busyness of it at this time of year.'

Peter was right about the food, she thought as she bit into a thick ham sandwich.

'Tell me what you've been up to,' he invited.

There was no way she was going to tell him about the cache of letters, which was the most important recent event in her life.

'Nothing out of the ordinary,' she said. 'Most of my time is being taken up by Christmas preparations at school.'

'Tell me about it,' he groaned. 'Every time I look at Heather she's making lists or cutting out cardboard templates for angels or Christmas trees. Our dining-room table is never free. Last night I had to have my dinner on a tray on my lap because she refused to move her artistic endeavours.'

Rowena began to laugh. Then she looked up to see Kavan standing beside the table. He didn't look pleased.

'Kavan! Come and join us,' she invited.

'No, thank you. Two's company,' he said with tightened lips.

'Come on,' said Peter, moving up. 'There's plenty of room.'

'I'm not staying,' said Kavan. 'I only

came in to see if a friend was here. I'll see you both another time.' He gave a slight nod, then pushed his way through the crowd to the door.

Rowena finished her tomato juice. 'I'd better be going,' she said. 'I still have some shopping to do.'

'I hope Kavan hasn't upset you,' said Peter anxiously. 'He can be a bit sharp at times. I'm sure he doesn't mean it.'

'No, of course not.'

But Kavan *had* upset her.

She couldn't understand it. She didn't belong to him. Surely she could have lunch with a friend?

Later, in the car park, she caught up with Kavan again. They were both making their way back to their respective vehicles. He took her shopping bags and insisted on carrying them for her. She was still feeling annoyed and barely spoke to him.

She found her car, took her keys from her bag and he loaded her shopping into the boot.

'You're annoyed with me, aren't

194

you?' He sounded shamefaced.

'I just don't understand why you were so hostile earlier. I thought Peter was a friend of yours,' she answered. 'Why did you refuse to sit with us?'

'I'm sorry.' He leaned against the boot. 'He *is* a friend. But when I saw him with you, so relaxed and friendly, I saw red.'

'But why? We were only having a sandwich in a very public place.'

'You know that my wife had affairs with several other men,' he said. 'Well, Peter Robinson was one of her conquests. I didn't blame him, she was very persistent, but I couldn't bear it if it happened again.'

'I'm not your wife,' she reminded him gently.

He didn't reply at first but stood looking at the ground. Then he looked up and put his hands on her arms.

'But we're friends, aren't we? Special friends?'

His blue eyes stared deeply into hers. She felt almost afraid at the intensity in his eyes. She moved away from him.

'Friends, yes. Even special friends. But Peter's a friend, too. I have many friends, but at the moment, no particular friend.'

His shoulders slumped. 'Of course, I have no right ... ' He made a conscious effort to lighten his voice. 'I'll see you some time next week, Rowena. I have a box of red apples for the children. If they polish them, they'll make a lovely Christmas arrangement.'

He was gone, and Rowena got into her car. What a strange man he was. So gentle and yet so fiery. She started the car and headed for home.

* * *

'Do you know a good odd job man?' she asked Heather the next day. 'I want a kitchen cupboard moved to another wall.

'Peter's good at DIY,' Heather said. 'I'm sure he'd be happy to help you out.'

'I couldn't impose . . . '

'Nonsense. I'll ask him tonight.'

So, on Saturday morning, Peter arrived complete with tool box.

'Heather says you want a cupboard moved?'

He carried his box through to the kitchen, put it on the table and opened it.

'I have more tools in the car if we need them. Now then, which cupboard is it?'

Rowena showed him. 'It's probably been here for years,' she said, 'but I think it would be more useful on that wall, nearer the stove.'

'No problem.' Whistling cheerfully, he began to work.

'If you don't need me to help, I have a few jobs to do upstairs,' she told him.

Ten minutes later, as she was tidying her dressing-table, there was a loud crash and she ran back downstairs.

Peter was standing in the middle of the room, looking dazed and holding his head. There was blood on his face and across his shirt. The cupboard lay on the floor.

'You said it had been there for years,' he said. 'The batten was rotten. I pulled and everything came down about my ears.'

Rowena led him to a chair and examined the wound. He was bleeding badly, but it was superficial.

'Scalp wounds always bleed a lot,' she said. 'Come up to the bathroom. We'll get it cleaned up.'

Protesting that it was nothing, he followed her upstairs. In the bathroom, she examined the wound on his head. It was still bleeding profusely but as she cleaned away the blood, she could see that the cut wasn't serious.

'It must have just been a glancing blow,' she said. 'If I can stop the blood, I'll put on some butterfly plasters. They'll hold it together.'

'Yes, Nurse,' said Peter. 'Can I have a gold star to show how brave I've been when you've finished?'

They both laughed, then Rowena

noticed the blood on the shoulder of his shirt.

'You'd better slip your arm out of there and let me see the damage,' she said.

Neither of them heard the call from below or the footsteps as someone climbed the stairs.

Friends Again

Rowena was holding Peter's shirt away from his shoulder when they both noticed Kavan in the doorway.

'Enjoying your yourselves?' he asked, before they could speak. 'The back door was open so I didn't think you'd mind if I came in. I see I was mistaken. Next time, you should remember to lock it.'

Without waiting for a word from either of them, he flung himself down the stairs and out of the door, slamming it behind him.

Rowena looked at Peter, then carried on examining his shoulder. There was a large graze, but the bleeding had stopped. In silence, she bathed it and applied some cream.

'I'm sorry but I've nothing you can change into,' she said. 'We're not exactly the same size.'

'It doesn't matter,' he assured her. 'Look, about Kavan . . . '

'Forget Kavan,' she said. 'He had no right to march into my house. You are here at my invitation and to help me. How dare he imagine — well I don't know what he imagined. But we won't talk about it. And I won't speak to him until he apologises to both of us.'

Peter felt much better after her ministrations and they went downstairs; he to finish the job in the kitchen, she to make a cup of tea.

★   ★   ★

The cupboard looked much better in its new place as she'd known it would. Luckily it had not been badly damaged by the fall. Peter was pleased with his handiwork, but reluctantly refused her offer of a meal.

'I'd better get home and change,' he said. 'I feel a mess in this grubby shirt.'

'Tell Heather I'm sorry to return you battered and dirty,' she said, 'but I'm very grateful for your help.'

After he'd gone, she prepared herself a chicken salad and took a tray into the sitting-room. While she ate she intended to watch a travel programme on TV, then wrap a few Christmas presents.

But she found it hard to concentrate on white-gold sands and the beauty of the Pacific islands. Kavan's face kept intruding between herself and the screen. How dare he be so judgmental! He had no right to interfere in her personal life. If she wanted to entertain men in her bathroom then she would. Realising the silliness of that thought, she began to giggle.

But, after a while, she didn't want to laugh. She felt depressed. She had thought that she and Kavan were becoming really good friends. However, if he was going to react like that every time she spoke to someone else, she would do without his friendship.

Christmas was just a month away. The previous year, she'd spent it with Molly and her husband. They'd had a few house guests and Rowena had enjoyed herself.

What would she do this year? She could drive up to Melchester and spend the holiday with Molly again, but she didn't want to travel at such a cold time. And she didn't want to leave her cottage empty. If there was a freeze, she'd be worried about her pipes.

She washed-up her lunch dishes. A whole afternoon stretched before her. She'd wrap presents and perhaps make a start on Mary's blue cloak for the Nativity play.

★ ★ ★

She laid out festive wrapping paper and a pile of presents on the table. What else did she need? Scissors, gift tags, sticky tape. Sticky tape? Oh no! She'd forgotten to buy any. There'd be no wrapping without sticky tape.

Sighing, she pulled on a warm coat and her boots, swung her bag over her shoulder and let herself out of the cottage.

The walk will do me good, she thought, as she set off for the village shops. Stop me from brooding over Kavan. It was cold outside but dry. She was well wrapped up and the gaily decorated shops cheered her as she came in sight of them. Outside the Black Boar, a large Christmas tree twinkled in the soft afternoon light.

In the little supermarket, she bumped into Mrs King.

'Have you much shopping to do?' asked the old lady, plainly delighted to see her.

Rowena explained her errand.

'Well, you'll have time to have a cup of tea and a mince pie with me at the Daisy Tearoom.' She looked at Rowena hopefully.

'Of course. I'd like that.'

★ ★ ★

'How are your compost bins?' Rowena asked with a smile as she poured the tea.

Mrs King made a face. 'I'm still doing my best with them, but I think it's going to be a slow job.'

'These are delicious mince pies,' said Rowena, 'A real taste of Christmas.'

'Aren't they? They're made here on the premises, you know? Not bought in.'

'Talking of Christmas and mince pies, would you like to come along to watch the children's Nativity play at the nursery? We serve tea and mine pies first to get you in the mood. And you can bring a friend to keep you company if you wish.'

'How kind! I should love that. Let me make a note of the date. By the way, has the vicar spoken to you about Christmas yet?'

'Spoken to me about Christmas? No. What do you mean?'

'If he hadn't said anything yet, then I won't, either,' said Mrs King mysteriously. 'You'll have to wait. But he'll be round to see you, I'm sure.'

'Carol singing, I suppose,' said Rowena,

but Mrs King would not be drawn.

The cuckoo clock on the wall sang the half-hour. 'I'd better be getting back.' Rowena gathered up her bag and gloves. 'I'm supposed to be wrapping presents.'

★　★　★

The doorbell rang at eight o'clock. Rowena, who was enjoying an exciting play on the television, sighed and went to the door.

Kavan stood on the step, his hands behind his back. He looked at her, shamefaced.

She looked at him without speaking. He brought his hands from behind his back and handed her a beautiful bouquet of golden chrysanthemums.

'I'm very sorry,' he said.

She stood aside. 'As you've apologised, you may come in.'

They stood facing each other in front of the sitting-room fire, Rowena cradling the flowers in her arms.

'I really am very sorry,' he said. 'My temper gets the better of me. I should have realised . . . '

'Realised what?'

'That you were doing a Florence Nightingale act — blood and plasters and so on. I saw the cupboard on the floor but I didn't stop to think.'

'Sit down. I'll put these in water.' Rowena took the flowers into the kitchen. She came back and sat on the other side of the fire.

'I met Peter in the pub just now,' Kavan explained. 'He told me what had happened.'

Rowena gave a stiff little smile. She still felt cross with him. 'Peter came round to help me,' she said.

'So he explained. Why didn't you ask me to help you?' He looked aggrieved.

'You are busier than Peter. Heather offered his services.'

He nodded and looked into the fire.

'Excuse me a minute,' she said, and returned to the kitchen. She was back in a moment with two mugs of coffee.

She took a bottle of whisky from the sideboard and handed it to him. 'Help yourself. It will keep out the cold on your journey home.'

'Are you throwing me out?' He sounded startled.

'Of course not. Take off your coat. I'll let you stay a while.'

He stood up, removed his coat and laid it at the end of the couch. Then he bent over her with his hands on her shoulders.

'Say we're still friends,' he said. 'I couldn't bear it if we weren't.'

She looked up at him. His face was very close, his blue eyes gazed beseechingly into hers. She wanted to kiss him, but she said, 'Of course we're still friends. Now drink up your coffee.'

Kavan settled back into his armchair and sighed deeply. 'This is cosy,' he said. 'My place is beginning to show the lack of a woman's touch.'

'Perhaps you should get another live-in housekeeper,' she teased.

He shuddered. 'Not that. I'll put up

with my cheerless bachelor quarters.'

'I don't think you could call your lovely house cheerless bachelor quarters,' she said.

She selected two logs from the basket at the side of the hearth and carefully placed them on the fire. They hissed and then settled down. She returned to her chair. She had to agree with him, the scene was cosy but she wasn't going to tell him to come whenever he liked, however lonely he felt. He had to prove he was in control of his fiery temper first.

'Have you made any plans for Christmas?' he asked. 'Are you going to family or friends?'

'I was thinking about that this afternoon,' she said. 'Last year I stayed with my friend Molly in Melchester, but I don't want to travel far this Christmas. No, I shall stay here and indulge myself.'

He watched the sparks shooting up from the logs, finished his coffee and said casually, 'I don't suppose we could spend Christmas together?'

Rowena looked at him with surprise. 'You mean here, or at your place?'

'Either. I can't go away because of the animals, but when I've seen to them, I'm free. And Seth will help as usual, of course. What do you say? It would be better than spending it alone in separate houses.'

Rowena was silent, thinking. She couldn't imagine anything she'd like more, but should she agree? It might lead to a lot of gossip.

He misunderstood her silence. 'If you don't like the idea, please say.'

Rowena made up her mind. At their ages, they should be able to ignore gossip and do what they liked.

'I think it's a good idea,' she said, 'I wasn't really looking forward to being alone on Christmas Day.'

'Your place or mine?' he asked with a grin.

'Here, I think. You'll still have work to do whereas I'll be free. You can come down here when you're ready.'

He gave her a wide smile. Their former friendliness was back.

'By the way,' he said, after a moment, 'I had a letter from Denise yesterday. Pansy has settled down in Spain and attends a little nursery nearby. She also seems to be getting on well with Sinclair.'

Rowena looked at him.

Sensing her thoughts, he grimaced. 'I have to be glad of that for Pansy's sake, but I wish I could have her back,' he said quietly.

'I've bought her a doll for Christmas,' said Rowena. 'Could you let me have her address? I'll need to send it soon.'

Before he could answer, there was a loud knock at the door.

'I'll go,' he said, jumping up. 'It's rather late for callers.'

Rowena heard a subdued mumble of voices then Kavan opened the door wide.

'I'm sorry to call so late,' said the Reverend Newman. 'I was on my way to see Kavan, when I noticed his motorbike at your gate. I hope you don't mind?'

'Of course not. Come and sit by the fire while you talk to him. I'll make some more coffee.'

The large man rubbed his hands in front of the fire before taking a seat.

'Actually, I'm glad of the opportunity to speak to you both,' he said when she returned from the kitchen.

'Is it about Christmas?' she asked with a smile. 'I warn you, I've got no voice, though if there are plenty of other carol singers, perhaps I won't be noticed.'

'This isn't about carol singing. It's a new idea the church committee have had this year. Plenty of other parishes are doing it, so we thought we'd try it — if we can get enough volunteers.'

'Uh-uh,' said Kavan. 'I'm not sure I'm going to like this.'

'You'll enjoy it,' said the vicar quickly. 'You spend a lot of time on your own in your work, this will give you lots of company at Christmas.'

'We've decided to spend Christmas Day together,' said Kavan, 'so we'll have some company.'

'Shall we hear the idea first?' suggested Rowena, handing round a plate of shortbread.

'If we can get enough volunteers,' began the vicar, 'we want to offer all the people of the parish who would normally spend Christmas alone, a meal and some entertainment on Christmas Day.' He sipped his coffee and waited for their reaction.

Kavan and Rowena looked at each other. 'How many people would you expect?' asked Kavan.

'We don't know yet. We've sent out some leaflets and as soon as we get a response, we'll work out the numbers.'

'It could be a very big undertaking,' said Rowena.

'No problem,' said the vicar airily, 'many hands make light work. It just needs careful planning.'

'And where will the many hands come from?' Kavan was looking at him with an amused smile. 'I suppose we are to be two of them — or should I say four?'

'You'd be surprised how many people are interested in helping,' said Philip. 'Even young people. We already have a cook-in-charge, and the volunteers will be divided into those who want to help in the kitchen, those willing to be waiting staff, and others.'

'Others?' Rowena looked puzzled.

'We'll need drivers for a taxi service, and some entertainers.' The vicar's face was glowing with enthusiasm behind his white beard.

Kavan looked at Rowena and raised his eyebrows. She nodded.

'OK, Phil,' said Kavan. 'We'll be there.'

The vicar drained his cup and stood up. 'I knew you would,' he said. 'You'll enjoy it. I'll give you full details nearer the time. Goodnight to you and thank you both.'

'Our Christmas seems to be taken care of,' said Rowena, when he'd gone.

'And to think I expected to spend it all alone.'

* * *

The Nativity play at the nursery was a great success. Rowena was pleased to see Mrs King sitting with a friend near the front.

'Have you checked the manger?' whispered Heather, as the audience took their seats. 'Remember your dream?'

Rowena chuckled. 'Oh, I've checked it all right! It's completely empty. So long as the angel brings only one baby, we'll be all right.'

Heather was narrating the story. Rowena guided the small actors on and off the stage.

There was a wave of emotion from the audience as a procession of tiny angels with hands folded on their breasts and tinsel halos wobbling precariously, walked through the seated rows of expectant adults and up the steps to the stage.

The innkeeper made the right response; Mary cradled the Baby Jesus in her arms the right way up — there had been a problem with this in rehearsal — and the kings remembered to walk regally as they approached the crib with their presents.

Rowena was just breathing a sigh of relief when a small, airborne, woolly toy lamb flew across the stage.

'That was Ben again,' whispered Heather. 'I did warn him.'

'The audience enjoy that sort of thing,' Rowena whispered back.

* * *

The last carol had been sung and parents, full of praise and clutching tear-stained tissues, were leaving the hall when Mrs King hurried up.

'I won't hold you up, I know you're busy, but I had to say how much my friend and I have enjoyed the show. You've all worked so hard and the children were sweet.'

Rowena smiled. 'Thank you. By the way, the vicar mentioned Christmas the other night. Kavan and I are going to help.'

'Kavan and you,' said Mrs King with a wicked little smile. 'I see!'

'Don't put two and two together and make six,' said Rowena. 'We're just friends.'

'Don't you mean, just *good* friends,' said Mrs King with a laugh as she left the hall.

★   ★   ★

Molly rang that evening. 'Are you fixed up for Christmas? I should have rung before, but things have been hectic here, as I expect they have been for you.'

'Tell me about it,' groaned Rowena. 'Final performance of the nativity play tomorrow then we can all relax.'

'We've finished our nativities,' said Molly. 'Only the Christmas party left to

217

worry about. But what about your own Christmas?'

Rowena told her about the Christmas dinner in the church hall.

'Will you enjoy that?' asked Molly doubtfully.

'I don't know, but we're going to give it a try.'

'We?'

'I meant, *I* shall give it a try.'

'You said *we*,' Molly persisted. 'You wouldn't be talking about your attractive next-door neighbour, I suppose.'

'All right,' said Rowena. 'Yes, I meant Kavan. We'd arranged to spend Christmas Day together anyway.'

'How romantic.'

'Not at all. We're being practical. It would be silly to sit alone eating Christmas dinner next door to each other.'

'Of course it would,' said Molly soothingly. 'I quite understand.'

'It's a pity you're on the end of the telephone,' said Rowena, 'I should like to throw something at you.'

'Joking apart, how are you getting on with Kavan? It is a serious friendship?'

'What do you mean by serious? If you mean romantic — no, it's not. Neither of us are looking for romance.'

'Everyone one is looking for romance,' said Molly.

'Kavan had a dreadful marriage. He doesn't want to repeat that. My marriage ended sadly. I don't think I want to risk it again, either.'

'But why should another attempt turn out badly for either of you? It seems to me you should both be looking for romance. You both deserve a bit of happiness.'

Rowena sighed. 'Let's see what happens, shall we? But don't count on anything. What are you two doing for Christmas?'

'Graham has an aunt and cousin in Devon. We're going there. They live in a picturesque village near the sea. I hope to spend Christmas Day strolling on the beach. Do you envy me?'

'Not if the weather turns snowy.

Anyway, have a lovely holiday and give my love to Graham. See you in the New Year!'

She replaced the telephone and sat thinking.

'*Everyone is looking for romance,*' Molly had said.

'Am I? Perhaps with Kavan Reagan, I might be.'

★ ★ ★

'But everyone loves carol singing,' Heather objected. 'You must come. You know all the others in the group.'

'I've got an awful voice.'

'Nonsense. You sing with the children.'

'Children aren't critical.'

'Do you imagine the rest of the carol singers have beautiful voices? It's just an enjoyable evening. Do say you'll come. It's the start of Christmas.'

'Very well,' said Rowena, reluctantly. 'Where do we meet?'

'Outside the Black Boar at seven. Wrap up well and bring a torch.'

Most of the carol singers were people she'd met on her first visit to Allarton. They all greeted her warmly.

'I hope you're wearing thick socks,' said Peter. 'It can be cold on the feet.'

Kavan was not with the group. She supposed he was too busy. She didn't like to ask if he was coming.

They sang two carols outside the pub then set off down the road.

'We don't call at many houses,' Heather explained. 'Mostly we stop at intervals in the village and people come out to us.'

'What are we collecting for?' asked Rowena.

'The vicar's Christmas dinner,' said a girl, and everyone laughed. 'I don't mean *his* dinner.' The girl blushed and flapped her hands. 'I mean the one he's organising.'

Rowena discovered that several of the group were planning to help with the meal. She was pleased. At least she wouldn't be with strangers.

They made several stops around the village. The evening was cold but dry. Many people came out of their houses to put money in the bag Heather carried.

At Ed Tyler's house, Rowena was sent to knock on the door. Anita listened appreciatively to *Good King Wenceslas* and a ten pound note went into the bag.

Rowena looked up at the clear, star-speckled sky. She was enjoying herself. The group crossed the bridge over the river and began to walk down her lane. They sang at the cottages on the way, but when they reached hers, she expected them to turn back to the village. Instead, they carried on.

'Where are we going?' she asked.

'Mustn't miss the hot punch,' said someone.

'And the mince pies and sausage rolls.'

They walked on.

Of course, Kavan's house.

What a fool she was. She'd forgotten for a moment that the lane led to his farm.

Kavan opened the door when he heard them approach, but barred the way.

'I haven't had a carol yet,' he said. 'No refreshments till I've had my carol.'

Someone began to sing *O little town of Bethlehem* as a solo.

Gradually, they all joined in. In the golden light from the hallway, she caught Kavan's eye. He was singing, too — she could hear his strong baritone voice. The effect of the different voices singing the well-loved carol in the clear night air was so beautiful that her eyes filled with tears.

But soon they were taking off boots and scarves in the hallway and filing into Kavan's large sitting-room.

On a table in the centre of the room was a steaming bowl of punch, and on a hostess trolley, plates of sausage rolls and mince pies were warming.

'Help yourselves,' said Kavan. 'I'm not waiting on anyone. Except you,' he said softly to Rowena, handing her a glass of punch. 'Are you cold? This will warm you up.'

'I wondered why you weren't with the group,' she said.

'This is my job,' he said. 'I've done it for the five years the group has been carol singing. Let me get you a couple of sausage rolls.'

'Made by your own fair hands?' mocked Rowena, as he brought her a plate on which lay two golden, crispy sausage rolls.

'Actually, they were.'

'They're delicious! He's famous for his sausage rolls,' said Heather, joining them. 'I don't know how he finds the time.'

'I'd be in trouble if I didn't,' said Kavan with a laugh. 'Imagine a bunch of hungry carol singers turning up at the gate and me saying I'd been too busy to make them. Excuse me, I must make sure everyone has had enough.'

Heather wandered off and Kavan came back to Rowena. 'Do you have to leave with the others?' he asked. 'Can't you stay for a while?'

'I don't think I should. It would look odd if I didn't leave with the rest of the group.'

'Will you be busy tomorrow?'

'Yes. I know we'll be having Christmas dinner at the hall, but we'll be back at Cherry Cottage for supper. I must shop tomorrow and make preparations.'

'But you'll be free for the Midnight Service?'

'Of course. I couldn't miss that.'

'I'll pick you up half an hour before. Till then.' He squeezed her hand.

Rowena followed the others out into the cold. At her gate they all called goodnight.

She let herself into her cottage, glad she'd banked up the fire before she'd left.

She locked the doors and climbed sleepily up the stairs. It had been an enjoyable evening. She washed and undressed, fell into bed and in a few minutes was fast asleep.

Christmas Eve

It was Christmas Eve. Rowena awoke with the excited feeling of anticipation that she'd never lost since childhood.

She thought of the small pile of brightly-wrapped gifts waiting for her under the Christmas tree. When she was a child, the tantalising sight of presents tormented her so much that she thought she would never be able to wait until Christmas Day.

Now, as well as presents, she had the prospect of a day with Kavan to look forward to. And perhaps they'd open their presents together — it was more fun with another person.

Oh, no! Kavan! How could she have forgotten? She hadn't bought him a present!

She swung her legs out of bed and reached for her dressing-gown.

It hadn't occurred to her to buy

something for him when she'd been shopping earlier in the week, but then she'd had no idea she'd see him over the holiday.

What could she buy for him? Frowning, she went through to the bathroom. And what if he bought nothing for her? That would be awkward, but she'd feel worse if she had nothing for him.

She dressed and went down to the kitchen for a quick breakfast. She'd have to go into Tinley, that was the nearest town. She'd look around the shops and trust to inspiration.

★ ★ ★

The town, which had a good range of specialist outlets, was full of last-minute shoppers. But she had no idea of Kavan's interests or hobbies. Did he have any?

A book might be a good idea. She wandered around the crowded bookshop looking vaguely at the shelves. She was amused to see other women doing the same thing. Men were so hard to please unless you knew them very well. Abandoning that idea she set off up the street.

The noise was deafening. From every doorway poured the sound of a different carol or song. The windows sparkled and glittered with lights and decorations.

She entered a men's outfitter's and looking around at the vast array of jumpers, socks, ties, all carrying merry little stickers saying, *Christmas Gift*. But could she really buy Kavan something so personal? She went back out into the throng of shoppers.

Just off the main street was a large supermarket, and she knew what she needed there. Pushing a trolley, she quickly collected pies, bread, pickles and an assortment of bits and bobs for a special Christmas Day supper.

On her way to the checkout, she grabbed an old-fashioned iced Christmas cake. Most men liked those, she thought.

* * *

She carried the bags back to her car. At the edge of the car park, a Salvation Army band attacked carols with gusto. Their cheery smiles were infectious and she happily opened her purse to add to their collecting tin.

A small coffee shop across the road looked inviting, its windows so coated with mock snow that you couldn't see inside, but she opened the door and took a look in, hoping there might be a free table.

Just beyond the door, a familiar face looked up at her with dawning recognition. 'Rowena, come and join me.' Anita moved bags from the seat opposite her and Rowena sat down.

'Anita! How nice to see you. Where are Ed and the children?'

'Gone to Father Christmas's grotto. I said I needed a rest. Aren't I a coward? By the way, it's self-service here, you have to go to the counter.'

Rowena collected coffee and a warm

scone and rejoined Anita.

'Are you shopping or just soaking up some festive atmosphere?' asked Anita. 'Personally, if it wasn't for the children, I'd stay away from the town at this time of year. I hate the frantic crowds.'

'I have just one present to get and I'm really stuck for an idea,' answered Rowena. 'What would you buy for a man you don't know very well?' I hope she doesn't think I mean Peter, she thought, as Anita gave her a quizzical look.

'Does he have any hobbies? What about a book?'

'Tried that. No inspiration.'

'Does he drink?'

'Not a great deal. But he enjoys wine. Seems to know quite a lot about it.'

'There you are then.' Anita looked at her triumphantly. 'A really good bottle of wine.'

Rowena considered. 'It's an idea, but I wouldn't know what to choose.'

'Go along the main street to Pedlar's Passage on the right. Down there you'll come to a little courtyard where you'll find several shops, including the best wine shop for miles. They'll help you.'

'Thank you very much.' Rowena stood up. 'I'm glad I ran into you. Give my best wishes to Ed and a Happy Christmas to you all. See you in the New Year.'

She hurried out before Anita could ask about her plans for Christmas and work out the identity of the intended recipient of the bottle of wine.

★　★　★

The courtyard at the end of Pedlar's Passage must have been a remnant of the old town, thought Rowena. There was even a covered well in the centre. The ancient cottages grouped around the courtyard had been converted into tiny shops and two of the cottages, knocked into one, formed the wine shop Anita had mentioned.

The staff of three older men were busy, but not too busy to help her. She explained her dilemma, and one of them took her over to a corner where all the red wines were arranged in racks.

'May I ask how much you were prepared to pay?' he asked discreetly.

Rowena told him and he selected two bottles, then after a pause for thought, he indicated a third. 'I can recommend all of these,' he said. 'A discerning man who enjoys his red wine would be delighted to receive any one of them.'

Rowena looked at the bottles, then at him and smiled. 'How can I choose? I know nothing about good wine. I'd be as well to go *eeny-meeny-miny-mo*!' She looked at the bottles again. 'I like that label.' She pointed to one of the bottles. 'I'll have that one.'

He was polite enough not to show what he thought of a customer who chose her wine by the attractiveness of the label.

'A good choice,' he said gravely.

Rowena couldn't believe she'd spent so much on a bottle of wine. It lay, swaddled in bubble wrap and tissue paper for safety, at the bottom of her shopping basket.

'I'll be glad when you're safely home,' she told it, making her way back to the car.

A shop window of brightly-coloured clothes recalled another purchase she really needed to make. The vicar had asked all the ladies to wear Christmassy red and white if they could.

In the middle of the window was an ankle-length red skirt. The quality was indifferent but it was the right colour and cheap.

Rowena tried it on and bought it. With a white blouse, it would make a cheerful Christmas outfit.

Satisfied with her morning's work, she made her way home.

★ ★ ★

All the helpers at the Christmas lunch had been asked to take along a small decorated tree to brighten the church hall where the meal was to be served, and Rowena had offered to decorate Kavan's tree as well as her own.

She spent a happy hour tying scarlet ribbons and golden bells on to the little branches while she listened to the lessons and carols from King's College on the radio. The start of Christmas proper, her mother had always called the service.

She looked round her warm sitting-room with its cheerful fire burning in the grate. Fat candles intertwined with greenery decorated the mantelpiece. Her own Christmas tree, with the traditional baubles from her childhood, stood proudly in one corner. This was Christmas as it should be; she had no interest in metal trees and black decorations as displayed in one elegant shop in Tinley.

Happy with her achievements, she tied a gold star to the top of each little tree and stood back to survey the effect. Kavan would be pleased when he saw them.

He arrived at eleven, well wrapped up against the cold. 'It's never warm in the church,' he said, advising her to take a thick scarf and gloves.

He admired the little trees and put them carefully in the boot of his car. 'We'll drop them off at the hall before we go into the service.'

The night was cold and crisp. The sky was clear and the stars shone and twinkled in a way they never did in towns.

'It's because we have so few street lights in the country,' said Kavan. 'The sky is easier to see. But I think there'll be a frost tonight.'

'No snow,' said Rowena sadly. 'I'd love a white Christmas.'

'I wouldn't,' said her companion. 'It makes my job very difficult.'

They parked the car and carried their trees into the church hall, the same hall Heather and Rowena used for the nursery. It was strange to see it full of adult tables and chairs instead of toys.

The church itself was packed. 'Only time of the year it is,' growled Kavan, who was a regular churchgoer. He led the way to a pew near the front.

Several people greeted them quietly. Rowena was surprised to see Mrs King and her friend. It seemed very late for such elderly people to be out.

The choir was in place and Rowena, looking upwards at the church's towering Christmas tree, failed to notice the vicar appear until she realised everyone was getting to their feet.

The first rich notes of *Once In Royal David's City* burst forth from the organ. Kavan found the correct place in the hymn book and reached across to share it with Rowena.

She smiled up at him and he smiled back and squeezed her arm. He began to sing and she joined in happily; softly at first, then with confidence.

It was her first Christmas in Allarton and it was going to be a good one.

A Merry Christmas

'You look a Christmas cracker and no mistake,' exclaimed Kavan, when she opened the door to him on Christmas morning.

Her red skirt swirled about her ankles, her white blouse outlined her neat figure and she wore a small frilly white apron.

'I'm glad you're not wearing those awful jokey Christmas antlers,' he said. 'They're all right for reindeer but they don't do much for women.'

'What about this?' She produced a circlet of silver stars.

'That's better.'

He adjusted it in her hair and she felt a frisson at his touch.

He stood back and looked her up and down. 'Perfect.'

She blushed and went to collect her coat.

'We'd better be going. I've to help drive the people who want to go to the morning service and they'll have to be collected soon,' he told her.

He looked wistfully around the room. 'It would be nice just to stay in, wouldn't it?'

Rowena shooed him out and shut the front door. 'Work to do. We can relax later.'

He gave her a wicked smile. 'Good.'

A kaleidoscope of colour and noise greeted them as, once again, they opened the door to the church hall.

Most of the women wore something red, but others had decided that green was just as festive. Some had placed a glittering ornament in their hair.

'Plenty of jokey Christmas antlers over here,' called a woman digging into a large box.

Kavan shuddered. 'I'm not wearing any.'

'You'd look very sweet,' teased Rowena.

She was pleased to see a few people

she knew — an assistant from the village supermarket; Linda from the nursery; and her friendly postman who brought his wife over to be introduced. And of course, several friends from the carol singing group.

There was a constant movement of people around the room, causing the huge silver and gold stars suspended from the beams to sway slowly to and fro.

'Someone's been busy.' Kavan nodded towards the stars.

'And look at all the little Christmas trees,' exclaimed Rowena. 'Don't they look effective?'

Dozens of the small decorated fir trees brightened the window sills and the corners of the room.

Suddenly, a large handbell rang out and there was silence.

The vicar was in the church preparing for the Christmas service and in his absence, the organisation of the Christmas lunch was in the hands of Mrs Dee, the formidable president of the Women's Institute.

She placed the handbell on a nearby table.

'Taxi drivers, on your way,' she called. 'People will be waiting.'

Kavan and a small group of other helpers left the hall.

'See you later,' he whispered to Rowena.

'Waitresses, waiters, everything you need to lay your tables is set out over there for you.'

Mrs Dee pointed towards a table piled high with tablecloths, cutlery, glasses and decorations.

Nine or ten tables had been arranged around the room and the volunteer staff set to work.

★ ★ ★

Despite a lot of laughter and chat, in half an hour the tables were beautifully laid, complete with table centres of holly and baubles.

A decorative ribbon arrangement was

tied to the back of each chair.

Mrs Dee and two helpers, each carrying a large basket, circled the room placing a cracker and a small but beautifully wrapped present beside each table setting.

The volunteers surveyed their handiwork with pride.

'What do we do now?' someone asked.

As if in answer, Mrs Dee rang her bell again.

'If anyone would like a cup of tea or coffee, please make your way upstairs. The church service will be over at eleven-thirty and people will be arriving for their meal straight after that. They are to have a drink upstairs first, so we must be back down here from our coffee break in good time. Thank you for all you have done already.'

Rowena joined the throng as they made their way upstairs. As she turned from the refreshment table, a coffee cup in her hand, she saw Kavan making his way across the room towards her. She took another cup for him and they found a quiet corner.

'Finished your taxi duties?' she asked.

'Mm. Two ladies and then an elderly couple. Only two journeys. They're in the church and looking forward to the meal.'

'The room looks lovely,' Rowena enthused.

'What happens now?' he asked.

'When we've finished our coffee, we have to clear off back downstairs to make way for the guests so that they can have a drink up here before the meal.'

Mrs Dee's bell rang out again. 'No visitors are to be allowed into the main hall until half past twelve,' she announced. 'Everyone is to come upstairs for a drink. Those who can't climb stairs will be taken into the committee room to be served there.'

'It's well organised,' said Kavan, admiringly.

By the time the vicar made his first appearance in the hall, he'd changed into a Father Christmas outfit which earned him a round of applause.

'At least you don't need a false beard,' said Kavan with a laugh, as he greeted him.

* * *

Mrs Dee handed over authority to the vicar rather reluctantly, it seemed, and as he moved to take up position at the top of the room, everyone turned towards him.

'Happy Christmas, everyone,' he began, and there was a chorus of Happy Christmases in return.

'Thank you again for giving up your Christmas morning,' he went on. 'I know everyone's going to enjoy today. Now, I'm sure you remember the procedure we decided on at our strategy meeting.'

Nods from some, puzzled looks from others.

'OK, let me remind you. Everyone lines up at the serving hatch and receives two soup plates. You take them to the nearest table where people are waiting. We'll do one table at a time all round the room.

'When the visitors have finished their soup course, waiters collect empty soup plates, waitresses start serving main meals. It's just a case of using common-sense, really. The aim is to serve meals that are hot and to keep people waiting the minimum time.'

He sniffed in the direction of the kitchen.

'Judging by the appetising smells, dinner is nearly ready. Now, would everyone line up round the room because I can hear our guests coming downstairs.'

The doors were flung open and the waiters and waitresses burst into, '*We wish you a Merry Christmas.*' Their guests, faces wreathed in smiles, took their places at the tables. There was a little confusion at first, as friends jostled to sit together, but the banter was good-natured and soon everyone was settled.

'Don't they all look smart!' someone whispered to Rowena. 'Talk about best bib and tucker.'

Rowena nodded in agreement. Everyone had dressed up for the occasion. She spotted Mrs King, elegant as ever, and waved.

★ ★ ★

The next hour flew by.

Rowena carried plates to and from the kitchen, chatted and laughed with the guests, mopped up spills, poured drinks and hurried back for more plates. She was so busy, she failed to take notice of Kavan at all until suddenly there was a lull. Everyone had been served a main meal and was busy eating. Then Kavan was beside her, taking her arm.

'Our turn now,' he said. At the top of the room, empty tables were being filled by hungry and exhausted volunteers.

'The idea is to get ourselves a meal from the kitchen and eat it as quickly as possible,' said Kavan.

The food was delicious, but there was no time to relax and they were soon back on duty serving Christmas pudding and custard.

By now, the room had lost its pristine neatness and the guests, who had wined and dined well, were in a very merry state.

Paper rustled as presents were opened, crackers snapped as they were pulled. It was a happy atmosphere and Rowena found herself smiling, even when there was no one to smile at. She had never had such a satisfying Christmas.

★ ★ ★

The vicar took up position in the space in the middle of the tables and held up a hand for silence.

'Is everybody nice and full?' he asked.

There was a roar of assent.

'I hope not,' he said, 'because next we

have coffee and mince pies and chocolates!'

Several people held their stomachs and gave mock groans.

'A round of applause for Mrs Kaley and the helpers in the kitchen. And for our glamorous waiting staff.' When the applause had died down, he said, 'While you are eating your mince pies and drinking your coffee, our entertainers will get ready.'

'Here we go again,' said Kavan, and they headed for the kitchen to fetch trays of coffee and mince pies. Mrs Dee insisted on taking the chocolates round herself.

By the time all this was finished, two young men with guitars were making themselves ready in the centre of the room. Their recital was followed by a popular local entertainer with his Christmas monologues. After him, an elderly lady took her place at the piano and struck up with the opening bars of *I'm dreaming of a White Christmas.*

At this stage, shyness had been

forgotten and everyone joined in with the familiar Christmas song.

Rowena and Kavan, standing together at the side of the hall, sang as loudly as anyone. Kavan slipped a hand round her waist. She did her best to pretend she hadn't noticed, so he deliberately pulled her closer.

'Don't. People will see you,' she protested gently.

'It's Christmas,' he said, and kissed her ear.

★ ★ ★

At last it was all over, and eighty happy people began to make their way home.

Those who lived nearby walked in groups. Others waited as Kavan and his fellow drivers brought their cars to the front of the church hall to pick them up and take them home.

The vicar discarded his red gown and wielded a broom as tables were cleared, rubbish collected and dirty crockery carried into the kitchen. The drivers soon returned to the hall to lend a hand and in less time than it had taken to set out the room, everything had been swept away.

There was an air of warmth and quiet satisfaction amongst the volunteers.

By four-thirty, everyone was ready to leave.

Rowena collected her coat, said her goodbyes and made her way to the door where the vicar was waiting, ready again with his thanks and handshakes.

'You were right, Phil,' said Kavan, 'we did enjoy ourselves.'

'Can I put you down for next year?'

'Let's finish this one first.' Kavan slapped him on the shoulder and laughed. 'Now our own Christmas begins,' he said to Rowena as they they both climbed into his car and he started the engine.

Rowena didn't reply. Her head was back against the seat and her eyes were closed.

'Hey, don't go to sleep. We've got hours of Christmas Day left.'

★ ★ ★

At Cherry Cottage, the fire was nearly out although the room was warm. Kavan, kneeling on the hearth, coaxed it back to life with some very dry logs.

'Tea or wine?' asked Rowena.

'How about a cup of tea? And a piece of that rich-looking Christmas cake I noticed this morning? We'll open a bottle of wine later.'

While Kavan went to fetch more logs, Rowena busied herself in the kitchen, then carried in a laden tray and placed it on a little table in front of the now brightly burning fire.

They settled themselves into armchairs on either side of the fire, each with a cup of tea close at hand and a plate of cake on their laps.

Kavan gave a deep sigh. 'What more could one want?'

'That was a really worthwhile day,' said Rowena. 'The guests were all so appreciative.'

'I didn't hear one grumble,' he

agreed. 'Phil should be really proud of himself.'

'More cake?' she offered.

He shook his head. 'I couldn't manage another bite.'

'I hope you'll have room for supper later on.'

She collected the plates and took them through to the kitchen

'What would you like to do now?' she asked, when she returned.

'Do? Should we do anything? Haven't we done enough today? Let's just relax.'

'I don't want you to be bored.'

'I won't be bored. I shall sit here watching the firelight play across your face.'

'Please don't.' Rowena put up a hand and his behind it. 'You make me feel embarrassed.'

He kissed his hand and blew the kiss towards her. 'Very well, I won't watch you. But it's a shame. You look very pretty in the firelight.'

'Have you spoken to Pansy yet today?' she asked, to change the subject.

'This morning, early. She was very excited, of course. She listed everything in her stocking. Oh, she sends you thanks for the doll. She intends to call it Rowena.'

Rowena gave a little laugh. 'I wonder what her mother thinks about that?'

'Talking about presents,' said Kavan, 'shall we open ours now?'

Rowena looked at the tree. 'Goodness. There seem to be a lot more there now than there were before I went out this morning!' she said. 'Where on earth did those extra parcels appear from?'

She pointed to a small pile of gifts that were wrapped in an unusual and very pretty paper that looked handmade and expensive.

'I put them there when you were fetching your coat this morning. Aren't you going to open them?'

He gathered up his gifts to her and handed them over.

'There are gifts under the tree for you, too,' she said.

'Open yours first.'

252

She began to unwrap the largest parcel.

'This is obviously a book,' she said. 'Oh, what beautiful photographs!'

The book was a coffee table collection of photos of churches and castles and stately homes in the county.

'You said you were interested in that sort of thing,' he said. 'Next year, we'll visit them all; that is, if you'd like to.'

'I'll look forward to that. Thank you so much! It's a lovely book.'

'Open the others,' he urged.

The next present was a box of marzipan chocolates. Looking at them, Rowena began to laugh.

'What's the matter? You like marzipan, don't you? I remember you saying you did.'

'I love them. I'll tell you why I'm laughing in a minute.'

She began to unwrap her last present. Inside was a small box. She lifted the lid to reveal a heavy silver bangle studded with deep turquoise stones.

'That was as near as I could get to

your favourite colour.'

'It's beautiful.'

Unbidden, her eyes began to fill with tears.

In a second, he was beside her, taking her hands in his.

'Rowena, what's wrong? Have I upset you?'

'No.' She freed one hand and dabbed at her eyes. 'I'm being silly, but I haven't received such lovely presents for years, not since . . . well . . . Simon used to give me jewellery for Christmas. And, always, a lovely book.' She gave her eyes a final dab. 'There, I'm fine now.'

He stood up. 'Would you mind if I rearranged your furniture?'

She looked at him in surprise. 'Well, no. But why . . . ?'

He pulled his armchair across so that it was next to hers. 'There. The nearest we can get to a couch. Much more friendly than sitting so far apart. Now I should like to open my presents.'

He was delighted with the wine,

holding it to the light and reading the label carefully.

'I thought you didn't know anything about wine. This is a beauty. I shall save it for a special occasion.'

'I didn't choose it myself,' she confessed. 'Well, only the label. Is it really what you like?'

'It will be a real treat,' he assured her. 'Now what have we here?' He unwrapped a flat parcel.

Rowena began to laugh and he joined in. 'Well, you did say you liked marzipan chocolates too!' she said.

'I won't say, *great minds think alike*, but perhaps, *two minds with but a single thought*.' He reached across and kissed her on the lips. 'Thank you very much.'

Rowena sat up and moved away from him.

'Kavan. I know this is Christmas, good will to all men, and so on, but this is moving rather quickly.'

'What is?'

'I don't know how to put it. We're

friends, aren't we? Good friends, but . . . '

'You're worried because I kissed you?'

She looked into the fire. 'I know you're lonely, but I don't want to be a stopgap.'

He began to interrupt, but she put up a hand.

'Let me try to explain. I had a wonderful relationship with Simon. We were engaged for a year then we had only a year of marriage. But it was a good two years. A commitment. I can't settle for less.' She looked at him seriously. 'Can't we just be friends — platonic friends?'

He stared back for a moment, then he said, 'How do you know I don't want a commitment?'

'You'll never marry again. You won't trust a woman again . . . '

'That sounds like something you've been told.' He looked annoyed. 'Do I detect the voice of Heather Robinson in that remark?'

Rowena remained silent.

'Can I take your silence for a yes? Heather has reasons for thinking that way about me. We did go out together for a while. But she was, how can I say, keener than I was. I had to end our relationship before people thought we were serious. She wasn't very pleased.'

He took her hand.

'Rowena, I'll make up my own mind about whether or not I ever want to fall in love again. And let's face it, do any of us ever have a choice in such matters?'

His hand moved across to take hers and they sat together looking into the firelight as the room grew dark; the only light came from the flickering logs.

'How did you and Simon meet?' he asked at last.

'We taught at the same school. We certainly had no choice over whether or not we'd fall in love. We were head over heels. Then, one Easter break, he and some other teachers took a group of children on an adventure holiday. One boy wandered away from the group, climbed some rocks and fell into a fast flowing river. Simon jumped in to save him.'

Kavan was watching her closely. 'Was that when . . . ?'

'Yes. He drowned. He managed to push the boy across some overhanging branches, and the child was rescued. Simon was swept away.'

Kavan held her hand tightly. 'I'm so sorry. I shouldn't have brought it up.'

She shook her head. 'I don't mind talking about it now. I'm very proud of him.' She gave Kavan a tremulous smile. 'Your turn. How did you meet Denise?'

He gave a rueful smile. 'She was the girl next door. We grew up together. She was a flirt from an early age. My mother warned me about her as soon as it seemed our friendship was turning into something more serious. But when do teenage boys ever listen to their mothers? It made me more determined than ever to marry Denise. The rest, as they say, is history.'

He jumped up.

'Why are we being so serious on Christmas night? Let's get busy in the kitchen, woman. I'm hungry.'

Just after midnight, Rowena accompanied him to the door. 'I must go now,' he said, reluctantly. 'Seth's done valiant work today. He's having tomorrow off and I must be up very early.'

'So I won't see you. Never mind, I shall have a lie-in in the morning.' She opened the front door. 'Kavan! Look! A white Christmas.'

Tiny flakes of snow floated down gently in the light from the open door. The thinnest carpet of white flakes covered the garden.

'I think that's a bit of an exaggeration,' he said with a laugh. 'I don't think you could call it a white Christmas.'

'Use your imagination,' she said. 'It's Christmas and the garden is white. It's a white Christmas.'

'If it makes you happy. But I, for one, don't want snow. It makes my job very difficult. I hope it's gone by the morning.' He put his hands on her shoulders. 'I don't know when I ever had such an enjoyable Christmas as I've had this year. Thank you, Rowena. May I kiss you goodnight?'

He gave her a mischievous grin.

Flakes of snow settled on his black curls.

She brushed them off and raised her face for his kiss.

'Goodnight, Kavan. Thank you for giving me a lovely Christmas, too.'

She watched him walk away down the path, then with a deeply contented sigh, she closed the door on the dancing snowflakes.

Flood!

A loud crash penetrated Rowena's dream. She had been about to serve Christmas dinner to the Queen when the loud bang caused her to drop the plate.

Startled, she awoke and sat up as a bright light flashed round the room. A storm! What had happened to her lovely snowy night?

She swung her legs out of bed and went to the window just as there was another crack of thunder overhead. The curtains were slightly open and, as she looked out into the darkness, a flash of lightening illuminated the garden. Hastily, she closed the curtains to shut out the sight of the rain that was driving against the window.

I'm awake now, so I might as well get a warm drink, she thought, pushing her arms into her dressing-gown.

In the kitchen, she listened to the drumming of rain on the roof of the utility room as she warmed some milk and refilled her hot water bottle.

The sitting-room fire had sunk to a few glowing embers. She crouched over the meagre warmth as she drank the milk.

She looked around the room. How cosy it had seemed when she and Kavan had been there together. Now it had a cold, abandoned look; the Christmas tree looked dull and superfluous.

She shivered, switched off the light and clutching her hot water bottle, made her way upstairs, hoping her bed had not become too cold.

The storm will be over by the morning, she thought, snuggling down under the duvet, trying to ignore the drumming of the rain which seemed to be getting heavier.

*   *   *

But in the morning, the rain was sheeting down as heavily as it had been during the night. She gazed out at the water-sodden garden, wondering what Kavan was doing. If he was out in the fields he would be soaked.

She willed him to call in for breakfast, but he didn't come.

She felt strangely restless all that morning. She remembered feeling this way when she was young. The anticipation of Christmas was a wonderful feeling, warm and exciting, but once the day was over, everything fell flat. She needed company.

She decided to ring Molly, then remembered that she and Graham were away. Was Molly walking on the beach? Not if she had the same weather as Rowena.

She would ring Mrs King. She was on her own and might like a visit.

'Rowena, how lovely to hear from you. Didn't we have a wonderful day yesterday?'

'I wondered what you were doing today.'

'In this rain, not a lot. My friend,

Connie, is staying with me. You remember she came to the dinner? We're going to watch television and eat chocolates all afternoon.'

'What a good idea.' Rowena forced herself to sound bright and cheerful. 'Enjoy yourselves.' She rang off. Mrs King wasn't alone.

She sat by the fire and opened the book that Kavan had given her. The illustrations were enticing. She wanted to visit every single building.

She looked into the fire. I miss Kavan, she thought as, unable to concentrate, she put the book to one side.

Perhaps *I* should watch television and eat chocolates. She stood up and wandered to the window. Rain, rain go away . . .

The telephone rang. 'Rowena, it's Peter. Did you have a good Christmas Day?'

'Wonderful.' She gave him an edited version of her day.

'And what are you doing today?'

'Well . . . I . . . '

'Heather and I wondered whether you'd like to come over. It just occurred to us that you might be alone.'

'Peter, that's very kind of you, but . . . ' She felt a moment of panic. If Kavan called in and she was out and then he discovered she was with Peter Robinson! But he'd said he wouldn't see her today. Although he might change his mind. Different thoughts chased each other through her head. Peter was waiting for her reply. She had to say something.

'It's very kind of you both, but I'm expecting a visitor this afternoon.' It wasn't really a lie, she was expecting Kavan, well, she was hoping he'd call in to see her at some point.

'Right.' Peter sounded disappointed. 'As long as you won't be alone. We'll see you after the holiday.'

She replaced the receiver slowly. Perhaps she should have gone to Peter and Heather's. Kavan might not come. She went back to her seat by the fire.

* * *

Ten minutes later, she was startled by a rapid series of knocks on the back door. She ran to open it.

'Kavan! You're soaked! Come in and get out of those wet things.'

He bent and gave her a kiss. His face was wet and cold. 'I'll not come any further than the kitchen. I've just called in to beg a hot drink and to make sure you're all right.'

'I'm fine. I've nothing to do but sit by the fire.' She reached for the kettle and began to fill it. 'I'll make you a bacon sandwich. Food will warm you up.'

'Thanks. That sounds good.' He took the towel she'd handed him and began to rub his face and hair. His black curls stood on end all over his head.

Water dripped off him and began to form a puddle on the kitchen floor. She shook his coat and hung it over a chair.

'Do go in and have a seat by the fire,' she pleaded.

266

'No. I'm not getting too comfortable. I'll not want to go out again.'

Then stay, she replied silently. He smiled at her as if reading her thoughts.

'It was a good Christmas, wasn't it? We had a wonderful evening.'

'Wonderful,' she agreed.

She took bacon from the fridge and put it in the pan, then began to cut slices of bread. In no time he was tucking into thick bacon sandwiches.

'What have you been doing to get so wet?' she asked.

'Storm drains,' he answered briefly. 'Unblocking culverts so that if the rain gets heavier, it can get away. They become full of debris if they're not cleared.'

'Where's Seth?'

'He's been working with me since eight o'clock. I've sent him home to change and get some food.'

'Do you think the rain will last? It's been pouring for hours.'

'Hard to tell.' He finished the sandwich and took a drink of his coffee.

'We don't usually get such heavy rain at this time of the year but the weather has been odd for months. Who can tell what it will do?'

He stood up and reached for his coat.

'Can't you go home and get some dry clothes?' she asked. 'Those must be so uncomfortable.'

'I'm making my way back to the farmhouse now,' he said. 'I'll change as soon as I get there.'

She walked with him to the door. 'When shall I see you again?'

He shook his head. 'I've a feeling I'm going to be very busy for a few days. I'll come over as soon as I can. Is there anything you need?'

'No.' She opened the door. 'Don't worry about me, I'm fine.'

He took her hands. 'Rowena I . . . ' He looked into her eyes as if he wanted to say something important, but changed his mind, bent and kissed her and stepped out into the teaming rain.

She heard the clanking of the tractor as it moved off up the lane.

* * *

The rain fell without ceasing all day. Rowena settled down to watch the television news. Pictures from different parts of the country showed that the awful weather was widespread.

She went to bed that night glad that it was holiday time and she had no need to battle against the elements in order to get to school.

She woke in the morning to the realisation that there was silence outside the window. The rain had stopped. With lifted spirits, she ate her breakfast trying to decide what to do with her day.

But as she washed the dishes, the ominous sound began again. Raindrops, light at first, then rapidly becoming heavier, pattered against the window and soon the familiar drumming began again on the roof.

This could be serious, she thought as she looked towards the river. Normally placid, it had begun to roar alarmingly.

She pulled on Wellington boots and an oversized raincoat and, taking a man's umbrella from the stand, opened the kitchen door. It took an effort to step out into the deluge but she had to see what was happening.

Luckily, the wind wasn't too strong and the umbrella remained protectively over her.

Slithering on the muddy ground, she eventually reached the gate to the river bank, and looked over.

The river was higher than she'd ever seen it and it was beginning to surge on to the footpath. It seemed to get higher as she watched.

For a few moments, she stood transfixed, watching the slap and splash of the water, moving ever towards her.

Then she turned and hurriedly made her way back to the cottage.

★　★　★

In the kitchen, she removed her wet clothes and made herself a mug of drinking chocolate.

Wrapping her hands around the warmth of the mug, she stood looking out of the window. Surely the water wouldn't reach her garden? No one had mentioned that the river flooded, but this rain was exceptional. It had raised the river level so that it was now lapping over the edge of the bank. From there, it was a short distance to her garden.

She turned away from the window as the telephone rang. 'Rowena, how are you?'

'Kavan! How nice to hear from you. I'm fine, or I would be if this rain would stop and I could go for a walk.'

'No sign of it stopping yet. What are you doing?'

'I went to the end of the garden to look at the river. It was making rather a noise. It's reached the footpath.'

'I know. We're going to move the cattle from the field next to you. We want to put them in the old barn, but I'm afraid there's a big repair job to do there. It hasn't been used for years. We need to make the roof weathertight. Seth's up there now doing a survey.'

'So you'll be busy for a while.' Rowena tried not to sound too despondent.

''Fraid so. But as soon as we're back to normal, we'll do something nice together. A meal or the theatre.'

'That would be lovely.'

'Must go now. Seth has just climbed down and doesn't look too happy. Don't worry about the river, you've got a long garden. The rain must stop soon.'

But the television weather forecast that evening wasn't as optimistic as Kavan. There was no foreseeable end to the deluge.

★ ★ ★

Rowena woke next morning to the now familiar drumming of rain. 'Oh no,' she groaned out loud, and pulled the duvet over her head. She contemplated spending the day in that position but the desire for a cup of tea got her out of bed.

Yawning, she pulled back the curtains as she fastened her dressing-gown. She stared unbelieving from the window. There was water halfway up her garden! The river must have burst its banks!

Forgetting all about the tea, she scrambled into warm trousers and a thick jumper. She had some idea that she might need to leave the cottage in a hurry.

She gave her hair a perfunctory brush, hurtled downstairs and switched on the television.

In disbelief she watched as shot after shot showed different parts of the country under flood water. Cars in difficulties, helicopters carrying out rescues from rooftops with the wind whipping up the water and adding to the problems.

She went back to the kitchen window. The water seemed to have crept even closer to the house. She ran to one of the windows that look out at the front, but the hedge prevented her from seeing the lane so she hurried upstairs and into the front bedroom. From there she could look over the hedge.

She gasped. A wall of water was racing down the lane, joined by the water that was pouring off the banks and sloping fields opposite.

For the first time, Rowena felt a shiver of fear. If the flood at the front joined the river overflow at the back, the house would be surrounded. If there was no let-up in the rain, water would begin to seep into the house. What could she do?

From the window at the back she could see fingers of water advancing towards the patio beyond the back door.

Sandbags! That was what she needed. But she had none.

She raced to the airing cupboard and pulled out an armful of thick bathtowels and an old blanket. Downstairs, she pressed them under the outer doors.

What else could she do? She rolled up some rugs and carried them upstairs. In a panic, she collected small pieces of furniture, books and ornaments and took them upstairs also. She looked ruefully at the armchairs. They were too heavy to move.

Dashing into the kitchen she emptied cupboards, putting their contents on to high shelves. She worked hard but had the feeling that whatever she did it would be useless against the forces of nature. The water was advancing on the house and nothing would keep it out.

If only Kavan would come. She felt so lonely. But he had enough to do looking after his stock. There would be no time to think of her. She was on her own.

Hunger pangs reminded her that she'd had nothing to eat or drink and it was nearly midday. She went into the kitchen, filled the kettle and lit the grill. If she didn't eat, she'd have no strength for the problems ahead.

She was buttering toast and listening

to the flood report on the radio, when she glanced towards the back door. Despite the towels, water was beginning to seep underneath.

With a gasp of horror she jumped up from her seat. From the window she could see water covering the garden and beginning to rise halfway up the hedge.

'Oh no!' The cry was forced from her involuntarily. She was aware of a dank, muddy smell. Water was forcing itself up between the floorboards in the living-room. She retreated halfway up the stairs and sat huddled, waiting.

How high would it come? This was like a nightmare.

She went upstairs and looked out of each window in turn. Her worst fears were realised. The house was marooned in a sea of muddy water.

I must stay calm, she told herself. No use getting in a panic. How high is the water now?

From halfway down the staircase, she gauged the height of the water in her kitchen and sitting-room. About a foot deep and rising. And the rain was sheeting down as heavily as ever. There was no way she could open an outside door.

She sat down, slumped on the stairs. There were other cottages in the lane, nearer to the town. They would be in the same situation as herself. The television had shown rescues from windows and rooftops. She wasn't sure how she could get on to the roof but if she waited, someone would come to her aid. She stuck doggedly to that thought.

★   ★   ★

An hour later, she rose stiffly to her feet and went up to her bedroom. When she was rescued, she'd need a change of clothes to take with her. It might be as well to prepare for that. She dragged a holdall from the top of the wardrobe and filled it with underwear, a clean sweater and trousers and some make-up. But her coats were downstairs and she couldn't face splashing through the muddy slime to get one.

In a wardrobe she found her old woollen jacket. That would be warm. In the pocket was her red baker boy cap. She dragged it on and couldn't help grinning at her reflection. Molly had always found the cap highly amusing.

Perhaps it would make her rescuers smile too?

Her rescuers. Where were they? She listened. No sound. No boat engine, no whirring of helicopter blades, no shouts. Just the drumming of rain and the splash of water.

* * *

'Rowena!'

She jumped. She'd been sitting in the armchair in her bedroom trying to wait patiently and attempting to concentrate on a book. The book fell from her lap with a crash as she flew to the window and opened it wide.

'Just call me Romeo,' shouted a voice

from below. Kavan, in a sou'wester and big wading boots stood beneath her window.

'You look more like Peter Grimes,' she said, laughing with the relief of seeing him.

'Can you climb out on to the roof of the utility room?' he called up. 'I can reach you from there.'

She ducked back into the room, fastened the window and hurriedly put on the heavy wool jacket. The cap sat at a rakish angle over one eye.

She made her way through to the other bedroom then suddenly remembering her bag of spare clothes, dashed back for it.

She reached the window above the utility room just as Kavan appeared below her.

The windowsill was low and she had no problem climbing out. 'Let's hope this roof is strong,' she called to him. 'I'd hate to fall through.'

She handed down the bag and he placed it in the small boat that he was pushing in front of him.

'Sit on the edge of the roof. If you drop forward I can catch you.'

She felt a shiver of fear. What if she was too heavy? Then she remembered his strong shoulders and muscled arms. He would catch her.

She leaned forward and dropped confidently from the roof. In a second, she was held tightly in his arms, one foot dangling in the cold river water. His lips found hers for one brief moment. Then he swung her round and into the little boat that was rocking dangerously.

★   ★   ★

Much later, sitting by the fire in Kavan's kitchen with a bowl of hot beef stew on her knee, Rowena thought back over the journey to his house.

It had been growing dark. The countryside looked eerie, with trees and hedges seeming to float in the still rising water. Kavan had waded through the cold flood, pushing the little boat while she'd sat back like Cleopatra in her barge. She'd mentioned this to Kavan and between gasps he'd said, 'I don't think Cleopatra ever wore a cap like that.'

'Don't you like it?' she'd asked indignantly.

'It looks beautiful on you,' he'd gasped, 'but perhaps you could keep it to wear when you're gardening.'

The farmhouse was on a hill. They'd soon left the flood behind and climbed up to the house, slipping and slithering on the mud-covered drive. The kitchen was full of the fragrant scent of the beef stew which he'd left to cook slowly while he went on his rescue mission.

Rowena had hurried to take a hot bath and change into fresh clothes and while Kavan showered, she'd dried her wet hair by the fire. Then they'd settled down to supper.

'You've finished the barn?' she asked.

'Yes. The cows are all tucked up nice and warm. It was a long job. I couldn't come to you any earlier. But I knew you'd be safe in the cottage. Were you afraid?'

'Yes,' she admitted. 'Not at first, but when the water began to rise and came through the floorboards I was worried. But I knew you'd come,' she said in a quieter voice.

He gave her a slow smile, then he stood up and took her hand. 'Come on, let's go and sit in comfort. There's a good fire in the drawing-room.'

★ ★ ★

A long couch piled with soft cushions was placed in front of the fire.

Kavan led her to it.

'Make yourself comfortable and I'll get the coffee.'

A few minutes later, he was back with a tray which he placed on a low table. He handed her a cup of coffee and a small glass.

'Whisky. Just a tot. It will keep out the cold.'

'There's no cold in here,' she argued. 'I'm lovely and warm.'

'It's medicinal. You were cold in your barge, Cleopatra! Drink it up.'

Taking sips from the whisky and then the hot coffee, Rowena felt warmth fill her insides and travel to every limb. She sank back luxuriously against the cushions.

'Now I feel like Cleopatra again,' she said. 'This is so comfortable.'

Kavan smiled. 'I must say, you don't seem dreadfully concerned about your cottage. I don't want to worry you, but there'll be a major cleaning up job to be done before you can go back to live there.'

Rowena took another sip of her whisky and looked at him solemnly.

'D'you remember telling me that you always got what you wanted?'

He gave a short laugh and made a brushing away movement with his hand. 'That was in my angry days. I'm much calmer now.'

'You are,' she agreed. 'I wonder why.'

'Could it be your influence?'

'Mine?' She looked surprised. 'But I don't have any influence over you.'

'Don't you?' His eyes were enigmatic in the firelight.

Rowena hurried on. 'You wanted the cottage. Do you still want it?'

'I don't understand.'

She sighed. 'I've tried but I can't feel the same about the place since I discovered my father's letters. The cottage has come to mean deceit and lies. What seemed a generous bequest now seems to be payment for guilt.'

'I'm sure Leonora didn't mean it like that.'

'Maybe not, but I can't help thinking of them there — together — while my mother and I . . . ' She bit her lip. 'And now the flood. The place is desecrated, muddy, dirty, spoiled. I don't want it.'

'But . . . you can't just give up your home. What will you do?'

'If you still want it, I'll sell it to you and go back to Melchester — or somewhere else. I've made one new beginning, I can make another.'

'Rowena, you're not serious?'

'I am. I thought long and hard while I was waiting to be rescued. I want to leave the cottage.'

Kavan stood up. 'You're not leaving Allarton and you're not leaving me.'

He almost fell into the seat beside her and took her hands in his.

'Don't you realise how you've changed my life? I can't lose you now.'

Rowena turned her head away from him.

'Rowena, look at me,' he demanded.

Slowly, she turned back to him and he leaned forward and pressed his lips to hers.

'Rowena, I love you. Will you marry me?'

She sat back and looked at him. 'I thought you didn't want another relationship,' she said softly.

'That was before I met you. Now I know my life won't be complete without you.' He reached out and she fell into his arms.

'Rowena,' he murmured against her cheek. 'Say you'll marry me.'

'*I* said I didn't want another relationship,' she reminded him.

'You can change your mind. It's a woman's prerogative. We'll both make a new beginning.'

She looked up at him from the cradle of his arms. 'I will marry you, Kavan,' she said, and this time there was nothing soft or gentle in his kiss.

* * *

It was some time before he released her, but at last they sat back, hands linked and looked into the fire.

'What did you do with the letters and photographs?' he asked her

'I kept the photos but I returned the box of letters to the hole in the wall. Perhaps, one day, they'll be discovered again, but no one else will know the person who wrote them, or the woman they were written to.'

He nodded. 'A good decision. But

you wouldn't like me to pull down the cottage?'

She gave him a startled look. 'Oh no. It's so pretty! I shouldn't like it to be destroyed.'

They sat in silence for a while, then he suggested, 'What about cleaning it up and letting it out as a holiday cottage?'

'Kavan! Aren't you clever? What a good idea. Then you can use the extra land as you'd planned.'

She snuggled into his arms again. 'We'll have a good life. We'll work together. You can teach me about farming and I'll help you.'

She looked up at him.

'I'm afraid that at our age, we probably won't have a family. Do you mind?'

He was quiet for so long that she thought he was thinking over the implications of what she'd said, and was perhaps regretting his proposal.

'Kavan, do you mind?' she asked anxiously.

He didn't answer but took his arms from around her and stood up.

'I must show you something,' he said. 'I didn't want to show it to you before in case it influenced you either way.'

He went out of the room and came back carrying an envelope. He sat down with it and drew out a letter. 'This came yesterday. It's from Denise.'

Rowena looked anxiously at his solemn face. 'There's nothing wrong with Pansy?'

He didn't answer but asked a question of his own. 'You love Pansy?'

'You know I do. She's a darling. I only wish I could see her more often.'

He looked at her. 'You could. You could see her every day.'

He handed her the letter.

'Read it if you like. Denise writes to ask if I want Pansy to come and live with me permanently. She hasn't settled in Spain and it annoys Sinclair. Denise would like to have her for a few weeks every year for a holiday, but if I like, I can have her back and bring her up in

England. It's time the child had a settled home. What do you think, my darling?'

Rowena's face broke into a radiant smile.

'Think? I think it's a wonderful idea. You, me and Pansy. I'm so happy. We'll be a real family from the beginning.

THE END

We do hope that you have enjoyed reading this large print book.

Did you know that all of our titles are available for purchase?

We publish a wide range of high quality large print books including: **Romances, Mysteries, Classics General Fiction Non Fiction and Westerns**

Special interest titles available in large print are: **The Little Oxford Dictionary Music Book, Song Book Hymn Book, Service Book**

Also available from us courtesy of Oxford University Press: **Young Readers' Dictionary (large print edition) Young Readers' Thesaurus (large print edition)**

For further information or a free brochure, please contact us at: **Ulverscroft Large Print Books Ltd., The Green, Bradgate Road, Anstey, Leicester, LE7 7FU, England. Tel:** (00 44) **0116 236 4325 Fax:** (00 44) **0116 234 0205**